Joanna froze, meeting glinting eyes that narrowed. Her heart somersaulted under the impact of his touch, his closeness. Every cell in her body was suddenly charged with a fierce awareness of Luc's potent male charisma.

His grip tightened for a painful moment, then relaxed.

But instead of letting her go, he drew her toward him. His face was set and intent, his eyes molten silver.

Something feverish and demanding stopped her from jerking backward, from saying anything. Helpless in a kind of reckless, fascinated thralldom, she forced herself to meet that fiercely intent gaze. In it she read passion, a desire that matched the desperate impulse she had no way of fighting.

He dropped his hands and took a step backward.

"A bit too soon—and very crass—to be making a move like that, surely?" he said in a voice so level it took her a second or two to register the meaning of his words. "After all, Tom's barely cold in his grave. You could make *some* pretense of missing him."

The flick of scorn in his last sentence lashed her like a whip.

Dear Reader,

We know how much you love Harlequin® Presents®, so this month we wanted to treat you to something extra special—a second classic story by the same author for free!

Once you have finished reading *Island of Secrets,* just turn the page for another story from Robyn Donald in which relationships are jeopardized by the secrets of the past.

This month, indulge yourself with double the reading pleasure!

With love,

The Presents Editors

Robyn Donald

ISLAND OF SECRETS

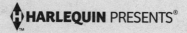

ISBN-13: 978-0-373-13134-1

ISLAND OF SECRETS

Copyright © 2013 by Harlequin Books S.A.

The publisher acknowledges the copyright holder of the individual works as follows:

ISLAND OF SECRETS
Copyright © 2013 by Robyn Donald

THE BILLIONAIRE'S PASSION
Copyright © 2004 by Robyn Donald

Recycling programs for this product may not exist in your area.

This edition published by arrangement with Harlequin Books S.A.

For questions and comments about the quality of this book, please contact us at CustomerService@Harlequin.com.

Printed in U.S.A.

www.Harlequin.com

CONTENTS

All about the author…
Robyn Donald

Greetings! I'm often asked what made me decide to be a writer of romances. Well, it wasn't so much a decision as an inevitable conclusion. Growing up in a family of readers helped; after anxious calls from neighbors driving our dusty country road, my mother tried to persuade me to wait until I got home before I started reading the current library book, but the lure of those pages was always too strong.

Shortly after I started school I started whispering stories in the dark to my two sisters. Although most of those tales bore a remarkable resemblance to whatever book I was immersed in, there were times when a new idea would pop into my brain—my first experience of the joy of creativity.

Growing up in New Zealand, in the subtropical north, gave me a taste for romantic landscapes and exotic gardens. But it wasn't until I was in my mid-twenties that I read a Harlequin romance novel and realized that the country I love came alive when populated by strong, tough men and spirited women.

By then I was married and a working mother, but into my busy life I crammed hours of writing; my family has always been hugely supportive, even the various dogs who have slept on my feet and demanded that I take them for walks at inconvenient times. I learned my craft in those busy years, and when I finally plucked up enough courage to send off a manuscript, it was accepted. The only thing I can compare that excitement to is the delight of bearing a child.

Since then it's been a roller-coaster ride of fun and hard work and wonderful letters from fans. I see my readers as intelligent women who insist on accurate backgrounds as well as an intriguing love story, so I spend time researching as well as writing.

Other titles by Robyn Donald available in ebook:

Harlequin Presents® Extra

ISLAND OF SECRETS

CHAPTER ONE

IN A VOICE that iced through the solicitor's office, Luc MacAllister said, 'Perhaps you can explain why my stepfather insisted on this final condition.'

Bruce Keller resisted the urge to move uncomfortably in his chair. He'd warned Tom Henderson of the possible repercussions of his outrageous will, but his old friend had said with some satisfaction, 'It's time Luc learned that life can mean dealing with situations you can't control.'

In his forty years of discussing wills with bereaved families Bruce had occasionally been shocked, but he'd never felt threatened before. The familiar sound of the traffic in the street of the small New Zealand town faded as he met the hard grey eyes of Tom's stepson.

He squared his shoulders, warning himself to cool it. MacAllister's formidable self-possession was a legend. 'Tom didn't confide in me,' he said steadily.

The man on the other side of the desk looked down at the copy of the will before him. 'So he refused to give any reason for stipulating that before I attain complete control of Henderson Holdings and the Foundation, I must spend six months in the company of his—of Joanna Forman.'

'He refused to discuss it at all.'

MacAllister quoted from the will. '"Joanna Forman, who has been my companion for the past two years."' His mouth twisted. 'It wasn't like Tom to be so mealy-mouthed. By *companion* he presumably meant mistress.'

The solicitor felt a momentary pang of pity for the woman. Thanking his stars he was able to be truthful, he said austerely, 'All I know about her is that her aunt was your stepfather's housekeeper on Rotumea Island until she died. Joanna Forman cared for her during the three months before her death.'

'And then stayed on.'

The contempt in Luc's voice angered the solicitor, but he refrained from saying anything more.

Whatever role Joanna Forman had played in Henderson's life, she'd been important to him—so important he'd made sure she'd never want for anything else again, even though he'd known it would infuriate his formidable stepson.

MacAllister's broad shoulders lifted in a shrug that reminded the older man of Luc's mother, an elegant, aristocratic Frenchwoman. Although Bruce had met her only once he'd never forgotten her polished composure and what had seemed like a complete lack of warmth. She couldn't have been more different from Tom, a brash piratical New Zealander who'd grabbed the world by the neck and shaken it, enjoying himself enormously while setting up a worldwide organization in various forms of construction.

Bruce had done his best to convince Tom that this unexpected legacy was going to cause ructions, possibly even cause his will to be contested in court, but his friend had been completely determined.

Anyway, MacAllister had no reason to be so scornful. The solicitor could recall at least two rather public liaisons in his life.

A just man, Bruce accepted that a relationship between a sixty-year-old and a woman almost forty years younger was, to use his youngest granddaughter's terminology, *icky*. Involuntarily his mouth curved, only to vanish under another cold grey stare.

Luc said crisply, 'I don't find the situation at all amusing.'

In his driest tone, Bruce said, 'I realise this has been a shock to you. I did warn your stepfather.'

'When did he finalise this will?'

'A year ago.'

MacAllister pushed the document away. 'Three years after he had that ischaemic stroke, and a year after this Forman woman moved in.'

'Yes. He took the precaution of having a thorough check—both physical and mental—before he signed it.'

In a clipped voice MacAllister said, 'Of course he did. On your recommendation, I assume.' Without waiting for an answer he went on, 'I won't be contesting the will—not even this final condition.'

The solicitor nodded. 'Sensible of you.'

MacAllister got to his feet, towering over the desk, his arctic gaze never leaving Bruce's face.

Bruce rose also, wondering why the man facing him

seemed considerably taller than his height of a few inches over six feet.

Presence...

Luc MacAllister had it in spades.

MacAllister's lip curled. 'Presumably this Forman woman will play along with Tom's condition.'

'She'd be extremely stupid not to,' Bruce felt compelled to point out. The other man's intimidating glance made him say bluntly, 'However difficult the situation, both you and she have a lot to gain by sticking to the terms Tom set out.'

In fact, Joanna Forman had the power to deprive Luc MacAllister of something he'd worked for all his adult life—complete control of Tom Henderson's vast empire.

Which was why the younger man's face looked as though it had been carved out of granite.

Once more MacAllister glanced down at the will. 'I assume you tried to persuade Tom not to do this.'

Bruce said crisply, 'He knew exactly what he wanted.'

'And like a good solicitor and an old friend, you've done your best to see that this is watertight.'

Luc didn't expect an answer. He'd get his legal team to go through the will with a fine-tooth comb, but Bruce Keller was a shrewd lawyer and a good one. He didn't expect to be able to challenge it.

He asked, 'Does Joanna Forman know of her good fortune yet?'

'Not yet. Tom insisted I tell her in person. I'm flying to Rotumea in three days.'

Luc reined in his temper. It was unfair to blame the solicitor for not preventing this outrageous condition. His stepfather was not a man to take advice, and once

Tom had made up his mind he couldn't be swayed. He'd been a freebooter, his recklessness paying off more often than not until that tiny temporary stroke had messed around with his brain.

Which was the reason, Luc thought grimly, he and Joanna Forman would be forced to live in close proximity for the next six months.

Not only that, at the end of the six months she'd make the decision that would either hand him the reins of Tom's empire, or deprive him of everything he'd fought for these past years.

One thing he had to know. 'Will you tell her that she'll decide who controls Henderson's?'

And watched closely as the solicitor expostulated, 'You know I can't reveal that.'

Luc hid a bleak satisfaction. When required, Bruce Keller could produce a poker face, but Luc was prepared to bet that Tom had stipulated Joanna Forman not be told until it was time for her to make her decision.

Which gave him room to manoeuvre. 'And if her decision is against me, what will happen?'

Keller hesitated, then said, 'That's another thing I can't divulge.'

Well, it had been worth a try. Tom would have organised someone he trusted to take over, and Luc knew who that would be—Tom's nephew.

He'd fought Luc for supremacy in various overt and covert ways, culminating a year previously in his elopement and subsequent marriage to Luc's fiancée. Who just happened to be Tom's goddaughter.

Damn you, Tom.

* * *

Jo stood up from the desk and stretched, easing the ache between her shoulder blades. After two years in the tropical Pacific she was accustomed to heat and humidity, but today had left her exhausted.

The last thing she wanted to do was play gooseberry to a pair of honeymooners, but her oldest friend had brought her new husband to stay one night at Rotumea's expensive resort so her two favourite people could meet…

And Lindy and she had been best friends since they'd bonded on their first day at school in New Zealand, and it would be lovely to see her again.

Also, she was eager to meet the man who'd generated Lindy's rave reviews during the past year. A non-existent bank balance had prevented Jo from accepting her friend's request to be maid of honour, and the current recession meant there wasn't much chance of things improving financially for her for a while.

Not that she was going to dim the couple's happiness with any mention of her business worries. But the sooner she got home and made herself ready, the better.

Several hours later she realised she was wishing she'd made an excuse. The evening had started well; Lindy was radiant, her new husband charming and very appropriately besotted, and they'd sipped a champagne toast to the future as the sun dived suddenly beneath the horizon and twilight enfolded the island in a purple cloak shot with the silver dazzle of stars.

'You're so lucky,' Lindy had sighed. 'Rotumea has to be the most beautiful place in the world.'

Before she'd had a chance to do more than set down

her glass, Jo heard a familiar smooth voice from behind, and the evening immediately lost its gloss.

'Hi, Jo-girl, how're things going?'

Jo froze. Of all the people on the island, Sean was the one she least wanted to see. Only a few days after Tom's death she'd refused his suggestion of an affair. His reaction had left her nauseated and furious.

However, she wasn't going to let his presence spoil the evening for her friends. She turned, wishing she'd chosen to wear something a little less revealing when Sean's gaze immediately dropped to her cleavage.

'Fine, thanks,' she said calmly, trying to convey that she didn't want him there without making it obvious to her companions.

Sean lifted his eyes to give the other two a practised smile. 'Hi. Let me guess—you're the honeymooners Jo's been looking forward to seeing, right? Enjoying your stay in the tropics?'

Seething, Jo wished she'd had the sense to realise what sort of man he was before she'd told him about Lindy.

Sure enough, her friend beamed at him. 'Loving everything about it.'

His smile broadened. 'I'm Sean Harvey.' Glancing at Jo, he drawled, 'A friend of Jo's.'

So of course Lindy invited him to sit down. Jo cast a harried look around the open-air restaurant, her gaze colliding with that of a man being seated at the next table.

Automatically she gave a brief smile. Not a muscle in his hard, handsome face moved and, feeling as though he'd slapped her, Jo looked away.

Fair men usually looked amiable and casual—surfer-style. Well, not always, she admitted, the most recent James Bond incarnation springing to mind. In spite of the sun-bleached streaks in his ash-brown hair, this stranger had the same dangerous aura.

Surfer-style he was not…

Tall and powerfully muscled, good-looking in an uncompromising, chiselled fashion, he had eyes like cold grey lasers and a jaw that gave no quarter. He also looked familiar, although she knew she'd never seen him before.

Perhaps he *was* a film star? He wasn't the sort of man anyone would forget.

As though that moment of eye contact somehow forged a tenuous link between them, Jo's pulses picked up speed and she rapidly switched her gaze to Lindy.

Don't be an idiot, she told herself, and concentrated on ignoring the stranger and enduring the evening.

Not that she could fault Sean's behaviour; he was gallant with Lindy, man-to-man with her husband, and managed so well to indicate his interest in Jo that when he eventually left Lindy challenged her.

'You haven't mentioned him at all—is he your latest?'

'No,' Jo said shortly.

Her friend had spoken in a rare moment of general silence, and the man at the next table looked across at her. Again, no emotion showed in the sculpted features, yet for some reason an uneasy shiver skated across her skin.

All evening she'd been aware of him—almost as though his presence indicated some form of threat.

Oh, don't over-dramatise, she scoffed. The stranger

didn't deserve it; she was still—unfairly—reacting to Sean's intrusions. Because of him she was totally off good-looking men.

For the rest of the evening she kept her gaze scrupulously away from the grey-eyed newcomer. But that sense of his presence stayed with her until she left the hotel and walked into the car park, stopping abruptly when a dark shadow detached itself from the side of her car.

'Hi, Jo.'

She froze, then forced herself to relax. On Rotumea the only danger came from nature—seasonal cyclones, drownings—or the very rare accident on the motor scooters that were everywhere on the roads. There had never been an assault that she was aware of.

Nevertheless, Sean's presence jolted her. She asked briskly, 'What do you want?'

This time he didn't bother smiling. 'I want to talk to you.'

Without changing her tone she answered, 'You said everything *I* needed to hear the last time we met.'

He shrugged. 'That's partly why we need to talk.' His voice altered. 'Jo, I'm sorry. If you hadn't turned me down so crudely, I wouldn't have lost it. I really thought I was in with a chance—after all, if old Tom had been able to keep you happy you wouldn't have made eyes at me.'

It wasn't the first time someone had assumed that Tom had been her lover, and each time it nauseated her. As for *making eyes*...

Jo reined in her indignation. Distastefully she said,

'As an apology that fails on all counts. Leave it, Sean. It doesn't matter.'

He took a step towards her. 'Was it worth it, Jo? No matter how much money he had, sleeping with an old man—he must have been at least forty years older than you—can't have been much fun. I hope he left you a decent amount in his will, although somehow I doubt it.' His voice thickened, and he took another step towards her. 'Did he? I believe billionaires are tight as hell when it comes to money—'

'That's enough!' she flashed, a little fear lending weight to her disgust. 'Stop right now.'

'Why should I? Everyone on Rotumea knows your mother was a call girl—'

'Don't you dare!' Her voice cut into his filthy insinuation. 'My mother was a model, and the two are not synonymous—if you understand what *that* means.'

Sean opened his mouth to speak, but swivelled around when another male voice entered the conversation, a crisp English accent investing the words with compelling authority.

'You heard her,' the man said. 'Calm down.'

Jo jerked around to face the man who'd sat at the next table as he finished brutally, 'Whatever you're offering, she doesn't want it. Get going.'

'Who the hell are you?' Sean demanded.

'A passing stranger.' His contempt strained Jo's nerves. 'I suggest you get into your vehicle and go.'

Sean started to bluster, stopping abruptly when the stranger said coolly, 'It's not the end of the world. Things have a habit of looking better a few weeks down the track, and no man's ever died just because a woman turned him down.'

'Thanks for nothing.' Sean's voice was surly. He swung to Jo. 'OK, I'll go, but don't come running to me when you find yourself kicked out of Henderson's house. I bet anything you like he left everything to his family. Women like you are two a penny—'

'Just go, Sean,' she said tensely, struggling to keep the lid on her embarrassment and anger.

He left then, and when his footsteps had died away she dragged in a breath and said reluctantly, 'Thanks.'

'I suggest you let the next one down a bit more tactfully.' A caustic note in the stranger's voice was overlaid with boredom.

Jo caught back a terse rejoinder. In spite of his tone she was grateful for his interference. For a few moments she'd almost been afraid of Sean.

'I'll try to keep your advice in mind,' she said with scrupulous politeness, and got into her car.

Once on the road she grimaced. The spat with Sean had unsettled her; she'd totally misread the situation with him.

Like her he was a New Zealander, in Rotumea to manage the local branch of a fishing operation. Although from the first he'd made it clear he found her attractive, he'd appeared to accept the limits she put on their contact with good grace. Several times she'd searched her memory in case something she'd said or done had given him the idea that she wanted to be more than friendly. She could recall nothing, ever.

Frustrated, she swerved to avoid a bird afflicted with either a death wish or an unshakeable sense of its immortality. Naturally, the bird was a masked booby…the clown of the Pacific.

Concentrate, she told herself fiercely.

After Tom's death, Sean's suggestion of an affair had come out of the blue, but she'd let him down as gently as she could, only to be shocked and totally unprepared for his sneering anger and contempt.

She didn't like that he'd lain in wait for her to deliver that insulting apology. His belief that she and Tom were lovers still made her feel sick. It seemed that Sean believed any relationship between a man and a woman had to have a sexual base.

Neanderthal! In a way Tom was like the father she'd never known.

That night she slept badly, the thick humidity causing her to wonder if a cyclone was on its way. However, when she checked the weather forecast the following morning she was relieved to see that although one was heading across the Pacific, it would almost certainly miss Rotumea.

Then her shop manager rang to apologise because a family crisis meant she wouldn't be in until after lunch, so Jo put aside the paperwork that had built up over the month since Tom's death, and went into the only town on the island to take Savisi's place.

And of course she had to deal with the worst customer she'd ever come across, an arrogant little snip of about twenty whose clothes proclaimed far too much money and whose manners reminded Jo of an unpleasant animal—a weasel, she decided sardonically, breathing a sigh of relief when the girl swayed, all hips and pout, out of the shop.

But at least Savisi arrived immediately after midday to relieve her. She drove back to the oasis of Tom's house, yet once she'd eaten lunch she paced about restlessly, unable to draw any comfort from its familiarity.

In the end, she decided a swim in the lagoon would make her feel more human.

It certainly refreshed her, but not enough. Wistfully eyeing the hammock slung from the branch of one of the big overhanging trees, she surrendered to temptation.

Her name, spoken in a deep male voice, woke her with a start. Yawning, she peered resentfully through her lashes at the figure of a tall man with the tropical sun behind him. She couldn't see his features, and although she recognised his voice she couldn't slot him into her life.

Groggy from sleep, she muttered, 'Go away.'

'I'm not going away. Wake up.'

The tone hit her like an icy shower. And the words were a direct order, with the implied suggestion of a threat. Indignant and irritated, she scrambled out of the hammock and pushed her mass of hair back to stare upwards, her dazed gaze slowly travelling over the stranger's features while she forced her brain into action.

Oh. The man from last night...

Feeling oddly vulnerable, she wished she'd chosen a bathing suit that covered more skin than this bikini.

Not that he was showing any interest in her body. That assessing stare was fixed on her face.

'What are you doing here?' she demanded. 'This is a private beach.'

'I know. I came to see you.'

Although Jo just managed to stop a dumbfounded

gape, nothing could prevent her jerky step backwards.
Shock, and a strange feverish thrill shot through her,
dissipating when she realised who he had to be. Hastily
she shoved on her sunglasses—a fragile shield against
his penetrating survey—and blurted, 'You're the solicitor, right?' Frowning, she added, 'I thought you weren't
coming until tomorrow.'

Not that he looked anything like a solicitor. Nothing
so tame! Pirates came to mind, or Vikings—lethal and
overwhelmingly male and almost barbaric. And very,
very vital. It was hard to imagine him sitting behind a
desk and drawing up wills…

'I am not the solicitor,' he said curtly.

Her eyes narrowed. 'Then who are you?'

'I'm Luc MacAllister.'

Like his face, the name was familiar, yet her groggy
mind couldn't place it. Warily, she asked, 'All right, Luc
MacAllister, what do you want?'

'I've told you—I came to see you.' Again he seemed
bored.

Before she could organise her thoughts he spoke
again, each word incisive and clear.

'My mother was Tom Henderson's wife.'

'Tom?' she said, everything suddenly clicking into
place with ominous clarity. Heat stained her face.

So this large, brutally handsome man was Tom's
stepson.

And he was angry.

OK, so after Sean's sneers last night Luc MacAllister probably believed she'd been Tom's lover. Even so,
there was no need for that scathing survey.

Humiliation burned through her. It took a few seconds for pride to come to her aid, stiffening her back-bone and lifting her chin sharply, and all the while, Luc MacAllister's gunmetal gaze drilled through her as though she were some repulsive insect.

An explanation could wait. This man was part of Tom's family. He'd taken over Tom's empire a few years previously, after Tom's slight illness. According to Tom, it hadn't been an amiable handing over of reins...

One glance at Luc MacAllister's arrogantly honed features made that entirely believable. Yet, although Tom had been manipulated away from the seat of power, he'd still seemed to trust and respect his stepson.

Fumbling for some control, Jo fell back on common courtesy and held out her hand. 'Of course. Tom spoke of you a lot. How do you do, Mr MacAllister.'

He looked at her as though she were mad, his grey gaze almost incredulous. At first she thought he was going to ignore her gesture, but after a moment that seemed to stretch out interminably, he took her hand.

Lightning ran up her arm as long steely fingers closed around hers, setting off a charge of electricity that exploded into heat in the pit of her stomach. Startled, she nearly jerked away. He gave her hand a brief, derisory shake before dropping it as though it had contaminated him.

All right, so possibly it hadn't been the most appropriate response on her part, but he was rude! And he couldn't have made it plainer that he'd swallowed Sean's vicious insinuation hook, line and sinker.

Disliking him intensely, she said crisply, 'I suppose you're here to talk about the house.'

Without waiting for an answer, she stooped to pick

up her towel and draped it sarong fashion around her as she turned her back.

'This way,' she said over her shoulder, and led him through the grove of coconut palms.

Luc watched her sway ahead of him, assessing long legs and slender curves and lines, gilded arms and shoulders that gleamed in the shafts of sunlight, toffee-coloured hair tumbling in warm profusion down her back. Unwillingly his body responded with heady, primitive appreciation. Tom had good taste, he thought cynically; no wonder he'd fallen for such young, vibrantly sensuous flesh. Even in her prime, long before her death, his mother would never have matched this woman.

That thought should have stopped the stirrings of desire but not even contempt—now redirected at himself—could do anything to dampen the urgent hunger knotting his gut. He'd never lost his head over a woman, but for a moment he got a glimmer of the angry frustration that had driven the man last night to bail her up in the car park. She must have trampled right over his emotions…

But what else could you expect from a woman who'd chosen to sleep with a man old enough to be her grandfather? Generosity of spirit?

No, the only sort of generosity she'd be interested in would be the size of a man's bank balance—and how much of it might end up in hers.

Bleak irony tightened his mouth as the house came into view through the tall, sinuous trunks of the palms. One of these trees had killed Tom, its loosened fruit as dangerous as a cannon ball. He'd known the risk, of course, but he'd gone out in a cyclone after hearing what he thought were calls for help.

It had taken only one falling coconut to kill him instantly.

Luc dragged his gaze from the woman in front to survey Tom's bolthole. It couldn't have been a greater contrast to the other homes and apartments his stepfather owned around the globe, all decorated with his wife's exquisite taste.

A pavilion in tropical style flanked by wide verandas, its thatched pandanus roof was supported by the polished trunks of coconut palms. With no visible exterior walls, privacy was ensured by lush, exuberant plantings.

The woman ahead of him turned and gave a perfunctory smile. 'Welcome,' she said without warmth. 'Have you been here before?'

'Not lately.' In spite of the fabled beauty of the Pacific Islands, his mother had found them too hot, too humid and too primitive, and the society unsophisticated and boring. As well, the climate made her asthma much worse.

And once he'd retired Tom had made it clear that his island home was a refuge. Visitors—certainly his stepson—weren't welcome.

For obvious reasons, Luc thought on a flick of contempt. With Joanna Forman in residence Tom had needed no one else.

His answering nod as brief as her smile, he followed her into the house and looked around, taking in the bamboo furniture and clam shells, the drifts of mosquito netting casually looped back from the openings. A black and white pottery vase on the bamboo table was filled with ginger flowers in gaudy yellows and oranges that would have made his mother blink in shock. Although the blooms clashed with an assortment of brilliant foliage, whoever arranged them had an instinctive eye for colour and form.

Luc found himself wondering whether perhaps the casually effective simplicity of the house suited Tom better than the sophisticated perfection of his other homes…

Dismissing the foolish supposition, he said coolly, 'Very Pacific.'

Jo clamped her lips over a sharp retort. Tom had loved this place; in spite of his huge success he'd had no pretensions. The house was built to suit the lazy, languorous climate, its open walls allowing free entry to every cooling breeze.

It would be a shame if Tom's stepson turned out to be a snide, condescending snob.

Why should she care? Luc MacAllister meant nothing to her. Presumably he'd come to warn her she had to vacate the house; well, she'd expected that and made plans to move into a small flat in Rotumea's only town.

But Luc had bothered enough to defuse that awkward scene with Sean. And at least he was staying at the resort.

Still, she counted to five before she said levelly, 'This *is* the Pacific, and the house works very well here.'

'I'm sure it does.' He looked around. 'Is there a spare room?'

His dismissive tone scraped her already taut nerves.

No, she thought furiously, you don't belong here! Go back to the resort where your sort stay...

Forcing her thoughts into some sort of order, she asked, 'Are you planning to stay *here*?'

He gave her a cynical smile. 'Of course. Why would I stay anywhere else?'

Sarcastic beast. Stiffly, she said, 'All right, I'll make up the bed for you.'

Dark brows lifted as he looked across the big central room to a white-painted lattice that made no attempt to hide the huge wrought-iron bedstead covered by the same brilliantly appliquéd quilting he'd noted on the cushions.

'Are there no walls at all in the place?' he asked abruptly.

Jo managed to stop herself from bristling. 'Houses here tend to be built without walls,' she told him. 'Privacy isn't an issue, of course—the local people wouldn't dream of coming without an invitation, and Tom never had guests.'

His black brows met. In a voice as cold as a shower of hail, he demanded, 'Where do you sleep?'

CHAPTER TWO

SOMETHING IN THE crystalline depths of Luc Mac-Allister's eyes sent uncomfortable prickles of sensation sizzling down Jo's spine. Trying to ignore them, she said shortly, 'My room's on the other side of the house.'

His frown indicated that he wasn't happy about that. Surely he didn't expect her to move out without notice? Well, it was his problem, not hers.

It would have been nice to be forewarned that he expected to stay, but this man didn't seem to do *nice*. So she said, 'I assume you won't mind sleeping in the bed Tom used?' And hoped he would mind. She wanted him to go back to the resort and stay there until he took his arrogant self off to whatever country he next honoured with his presence.

But he said, 'Of course not.' So much for hope.

She gave the conversation a sharp twist. 'I presume you flew in yesterday?'

'Yes.' Which meant he wouldn't be accustomed to the tropical humidity.

Good manners drove her to offer, 'Can I get you a drink? What would you like?'

Broad shoulders lifted slightly, sending another

shimmering, tantalising sensation through her. Darn it, she didn't want to be so aware of him… Possibly he'd noticed her sneaky unexpected response because his reply came in an even more abrupt tone. 'Coffee, thank you. I'll bring in my bag.'

Jo nodded and walked into the kitchen. Of course coffee would be his drink of choice. Black and strong, probably—to stress that uber-macho personality. He didn't need to bother. She knew exactly the sort of man Luc MacAllister was. Tom hadn't spoken much about his family, but he'd said enough. And although he'd fought hard to keep control of his empire, he had once admitted that he could think of no one other than Luc to take his place. A person had to be special to win Tom's trust. And tough.

With an odd little shiver, she decided Luc MacAllister certainly fitted the bill.

If he preferred something alcoholic she'd show him the drinks cupboard and the bottle of Tom's favourite whisky—still almost full, just as he'd left it.

A swift pang of grief stung through her. Damn it, but she *missed* Tom. Her hand shook slightly, just enough to shower ground coffee onto the bench. In the couple of years since her aunt's death Jo had grown close to him. A great storyteller, he'd enjoyed making her laugh— and occasionally shocking her.

Biting her lip, she wiped up the coffee grounds. He'd been a constant part of her life on and off since childhood. Sometimes she wondered if he thought of her as a kind of stepdaughter.

When she'd used up her mother's legacy setting up a skincare business on Rotumea, he'd advanced her money to keep it going—on strictly businesslike terms—but even more valuable had been his interest in her progress and his helpful suggestions as she'd struggled to expand the business through exports.

A voice from behind made her start. 'That smells good.' One dark brow lifted as Luc MacAllister looked at the single mug she'd pulled down. 'Aren't you joining me?'

A refusal hovered on her lips but hospitality dictated only one answer. 'If you want me to,' she said quietly.

Following a moment of silence she swivelled, to meet a hooded, intent survey. A humourless smile curved the corners of a hard male mouth that hinted at considerable experience in…in all things, she thought hastily, trying to ignore the sensuous little thrill agitating her nerves.

'Why not?' His voice was harsh, almost abrupt before he turned away. 'I'll unpack.'

Strangely shaken, she finished her preparations. He'd probably prefer the shaded deck, so she carried the tray there and had just finished settling it onto the table when Luc MacAllister walked out.

He examined it with interest. 'Looks good,' he said laconically. 'Is that your baking?'

'Yes.' Jo busied herself pouring the coffee. She'd been right; he liked it black and full-flavoured, but unlike Tom he didn't demand that it snarl as it seethed out of the pot.

Sipping her own coffee gave her something to do while he demolished a slice of coconut cake and asked incisively penetrating questions about Rotumea and its society.

She knew why he was here. He'd come to tell her he

was going to sell the house. Yet, in spite of his attitude, his arrival warmed her a little; she'd expected nothing more than a businesslike message ordering her to vacate the place. That he should come out of his way to tell her was as much a surprise as the letter from Tom's solicitor suggesting the meeting tomorrow.

Leaving the house would be saying goodbye to part of her heart. *Get on with it*, she mentally urged him as he set his cup down.

'That was excellent.' He leaned back into his chair and surveyed her, his grey gaze hooded.

It looked as though she'd have to broach the matter herself. Without preamble, she said, 'I can move out as soon as you like.'

His brows lifted. 'Why?'

Nonplussed, she answered, 'Well, I suppose you plan to sell this house.' He'd never shown any interest in the place, and his initial glance around had seemed to be tinged with snobbish contempt.

He paused before answering. 'No.' And paused again before adding, 'Not yet, anyway.'

'I wouldn't have thought—' She stopped.

He waited for her to finish, and when the silence had stretched too taut to be comfortable, he ordered with cool self-possession, 'Go on.'

She shrugged. 'This was *Tom's* dream.' Not Luc MacAllister's.

'So?'

The dismissive monosyllable sent her back a few years to the awkwardness of her teens. A spark of antagonism rallied her into giving him a smile that perhaps showed too many teeth before she parried smoothly, 'It doesn't seem like your sort of setting, but I do try not to make instant judgements of people I've only just met.'

'Eminently sensible of you,' he drawled, and abruptly changed the subject. 'How good is the Internet access here?'

'Surely you knew your father better than—'

'My stepfather,' he cut in, his voice flat and inflexible. 'My father was a Scotsman who died when I was three.'

In spite of the implied rejection of Tom's presence in his life, Jo felt a flash of kinship. Her father had died before she was born.

However, one glance at Luc's stony face expelled any sympathy. Quietly she said, 'There is access to broadband.' She indicated the screen that hid Tom's computer nook. 'Feel free.'

'Later. I noticed as I flew in that the island isn't huge, and there seems to be a road right around it. Why don't you show me the sights?'

Hoping she'd managed to hide her astonishment, she said, 'Yes, of course.' Her mouth twitched as she took in his long legs. 'Not on the scooter, though, I think.' Why on earth did he want to see Rotumea?

His angular face would never soften, but the smile he gave her radiated a charisma that almost sent her reeling. He was too astute not to understand its impact. No doubt it had charmed his way—backed by his keen intelligence and hard determination.

'Not on the scooter,' he agreed. 'I wouldn't enjoy riding with my knees hitting my chin at every bump in the road.'

Taken by surprise, she laughed. His brows rose and

his face set, and she felt as though she'd been jolted by an electric shock.

So what was that for? Didn't he like having his minor jokes appreciated?

Black lashes hid his eyes a moment before he permitted himself another smile, this one marked by more than a hint of cynicism.

Sobering rapidly, Jo said, 'We'll take the four-wheeler.'

'What's a four-wheeler?'

Shrugging, she said, 'It's the local term for a four-wheel drive—a Land Rover, to be exact.'

An old Land Rover, showing the effects of years in the unkind climate of the tropics, but well maintained. Jo expected Luc to want to drive, but when she held out the keys he said casually, 'You know the local rules, I don't.'

Surprised, she got in behind the wheel. Even more surprised, she heard the door close decisively on her, penning her in. Her gaze followed him as he strode around the front of the vehicle, unwillingly appreciating his athletic male grace.

Once more that provocative awareness shivered along her nerves.

He was too much…too much man, she thought as he settled himself beside her. All the air seemed sucked out of the cab and as she hastily switched on the engine she scolded herself for behaving like a schoolgirl with a crush.

'Basically the road rules here amount to *don't run over anything*,' she explained, so accustomed to the sticking clutch she set the vehicle on its way without a jerk. 'Collisions are accompanied by a lot of drama, but traffic is so slow people seldom get hurt. If you cause any damage or run over a chicken or a pig, you apologise profusely and pay for it. And you always give way to any vehicle with children, especially if it's a motor scooter with children up behind.'

'They look extremely dangerous,' he said.

His voice indicated that he'd turned his head to survey her. Tiny beads of sweat sprang out at her temples. Hoping he hadn't noticed, she stared ahead, steering to miss the worst of the ruts along the drive.

She had to deliberately steady her voice to say, 'The local children seem to be born with the ability to ride pillion without falling off.'

Her reaction to Luc meant nothing.

Or very little. Her mother had explained the dynamics of physical attraction to her when she'd suffered her first adolescent crush. And her own experience—limited but painful—had convinced Jo of her mother's accuracy.

She set her jaw. Sean's insinuations about her mother had hurt some deep inner part of her. Even in her forties, Ilona Forman's great beauty and style had made her a regular on the Parisian catwalks, and she'd been one great designer's inspiration for years.

To her surprise, the tour went off reasonably well. Jo was careful not to overstep the boundary of cool acquaintanceship, and Luc MacAllister matched her attitude. Nevertheless, tension wound her nerves tighter with each kilometre they travelled over Rotumea's fairly primitive road.

Luc's occasional comments indicated that the famous

romance of the South Seas made little impression on him. Although, to be fair, he'd probably seen far more picturesque tropical islands than Rotumea.

Nevertheless she bristled a little when he observed, 'Tom once told me that many of the Rotumean people live much as their ancestors did.'

'More or less, I suppose. They have schools, of course, and a medical clinic, and a small tourist industry set up by Tom in partnership with the local people.'

'The resort.'

'Yes. Tom advised the tribal council to market to a wealthy clientele who'd enjoy a lazy holiday without insisting on designer shops and nightclubs. It's worked surprisingly well.'

Again she felt the impact of his gaze on her, and her palms grew damp on the steering wheel. She hurried on, 'Some islanders work at the resort, but most of them work the land and fish. They're fantastic gardeners and very skilled and knowledgeable fishermen.'

'And they're quite content to spend their lives in this perfect Pacific paradise.'

His tone raised her hackles. 'It never was perfect,' she said evenly. 'No matter how beautiful a place is, mankind doesn't seem to be able to live peacefully. A couple of hundred years ago the islanders all lived in fortified villages up on the heights and fought incessantly, tribe against tribe. It's not perfect now, of course, but it seems to work pretty well for most of them.'

'What about those who want more than fish and coconuts?'

She glanced at him, caught sight of his incisive profile—all angles apart from the curve of his mouth—and hastily looked back at the road. So Tom hadn't taken him into his confidence—and that seemed to indicate something rather distant about their relationship.

'Tom set up scholarships with the help of the local chiefs for kids who want to go on to higher education.'

He nodded. 'Where do they go?'

'New Zealand mainly, although some have studied further afield.' With the skill of long practice she negotiated three hens that could see no reason for the vehicle to claim right of way.

'Do they return?'

'Some do, and those who don't keep their links, sending money back to their families.'

He said, 'So if you don't buy the tropical paradise thing, why are you here?'

'I came here because of my aunt,' she said distantly. 'She was Tom's housekeeper, and insisted on staying on even after she contracted cancer. Tom employed one of the island women to help her, but after my mother died she asked me to come up.'

He nodded. 'So you took her place after her death.'

An ambiguous note in his voice made her hesitate before she answered. 'I suppose you could say that.'

Tom hadn't employed her. He'd suggested she stay on at Rotumea for a few months to get over her aunt's death, and once she'd become interested in starting her business he'd seen no reason for her to move out. He liked her company, he told her.

Luc MacAllister asked, 'Now that Tom's not here, how do you keep busy?'

'I run a small business.'

'Dealing with tourists?'

It was a reasonable assumption, yet for some reason she felt a stab of irritation. 'Partly.' The hotel used her range.

'What is this small business?' he drawled.

Pride warred with an illogical desire not to tell him. 'I source ingredients from the native plants and turn them into skincare products.'

And felt an ignoble amusement at the flash of surprise in the hard, handsome face. It vanished quickly and his voice was faintly amused when he asked, 'What made you decide to go into that?'

'The islanders' fabulous skin,' she told him calmly. 'They spend all day in the sun, and hours in the sea, yet they never use anything but the lotions handed down by their ancestors.'

'Good genes,' he observed.

His cool comment thinned her lips. Was he being deliberately dismissive? She suspected Luc MacAllister didn't do anything without a purpose.

And that included passing comments.

Steadying her voice, she said, 'No doubt that helps, but they have the same skin problems people of European descent have—sunburn, eczema, rashes from allergies. They use particular plants to soothe them.'

'So you've copied their formulas.'

His tone was still neutral, but her skin tightened at the implication of exploitation, and she had to draw breath before saying, 'It's a joint venture.'

'Who provided the start-up money?'

It appeared to be nothing more than an idle question, yet swift antagonism forced her to bite back an astrin-

gent comment. Subduing it, she said politely, 'I don't
know that that's any of your business.'

And kept her eyes fixed on the road ahead. Tension—thick and throbbing—grated across her nerves.

Until he drawled, 'If it was Tom's money I'm interested.'

'Of course,' she retorted, before closing her mouth on
any more impetuous words. Silence filled the cab until
she elaborated reluctantly, 'It was my money.'

Let him take that how he wanted. If Luc MacAllister had any right to know, he'd find out about Tom's
subsequent loan to her from the solicitor—the man arriving tomorrow.

Was that why Luc had come to Rotumea? To be told
the contents of Tom's will?

Immediately she dismissed the idea. Luc was Tom's
heir, his chosen successor as well as his stepson, so he'd
already know.

Possibly Tom had mentioned her in his will; he
might even have cancelled her debt to him. That would
have been a kind gesture. And if he hadn't—if Luc
MacAllister inherited the debt—she'd pay it off as
quickly as she could.

A coolly decisive voice broke into her thoughts. 'And
are you making money on this project?'

For brief moments her fingers clenched around the
steering wheel. For a second she toyed with the idea of
telling him again to mind his own business, but it was
a logical question, and if he did inherit the debt he had
a right to know.

However, he might not have.

'Yes,' she said, and turned off the tarseal onto a narrow rutted road that led up into the jungle-clad mountains in the centre of the island.

A quick glance revealed Luc was examining a pawpaw plantation on his side. He didn't seem fazed by the state of the road, the precipice to one side or the large pig that only slowly got up and made room for them.

'This is the area we're taking the material from now,' she said. 'Each sub-tribe sells me the rights to harvest from the plants on their land for three months every year. It works well; the plants have time to recover and even seem to flourish under the pruning.'

'How many people do you employ to do the harvesting?'

'It depends. The chiefs organise that.'

She stopped on the level patch of land where the road ended. 'There's a great view of this side of the island from here,' she said, and got out.

Luc followed suit, and again she was acutely aware of his height, and that intangible, potent authority that seemed to come from some power inside him. The sunstreaks in his hair gleamed a dusky gold; his colouring must have come from that Scottish father. The only inheritance from his French mother was the olive sheen to his skin.

Did that cold grey gaze ever warm and soften? It didn't seem likely, although she could imagine his eyes kindling in passion...

Firmly squelching an odd sensation in the pit of her stomach, she decided that from what she knew of him and the very little she'd seen of him, softness wasn't—and never would be—part of his emotional repertoire. It was difficult to imagine him showing tenderness, and any compassion would probably be intellectual, not from the heart.

So, after an hour or so you're an expert on him? she jeered mentally, aware of another embarrassing internal flutter. *Remember you're totally off good-looking men!*

Although *good-looking* was far too weak a word for Luc MacAllister's strong features and formidable air of authority. Composing herself, she began to point out the sights, showing him the breach in the reef that sheltered the lagoon from the ever-present pounding of the ocean waves.

'The only river on the island reaches the coast below us, and the fresh water stops the coral from forming across its exit,' she said in her best guidebook manner. 'The gap in the reef and the lagoon make a sort of harbour, the first landing place of the original settlers.'

Luc's downward glance set her heart racing, yet his voice was almost casual. 'Where did they come from, and when was that?'

Doggedly, she switched her attention back to the view below. 'Almost certainly they arrived from what's now French Polynesia, and the general opinion seems to be it was about fifteen hundred years ago.'

'They were magnificent seamen,' he observed, looking out to sea. 'They had to be, to set off into the unknown with only the stars and the clouds to guide them.'

The comment surprised her. Like all New Zealanders, she'd grown up with tales of those ancient sailors and their remarkable feats, but she remembered that Luc had been educated in England and France. She wouldn't have thought he had a romantic bone in his big, lithe body, and it was unlikely he'd been taught about the great outrigger canoes that had island-hopped across the Pacific, even travelling the vast distance to South America to return with the sweet potato the Maori from her homeland called kumara.

'Tough too,' he said, his eyes still fixed on the lagoon beneath them—a symphony of turquoise and intense blue bordered by glittering white beaches and the robust barrier of the reef. Immense and dangerous, the Pacific Ocean stretched far beyond the horizon.

'Very tough,' she agreed. 'And probably with a good reason for moving on each time.'

'They must have had guts and stamina and tenacious determination, as well as the skill and knowledge to know where they were going.'

Yes, that sounded uncompromising and forceful— attributes as useful in the modern, high-powered world Luc moved in as they would have been for those ancient Polynesian voyagers.

'I'm sure they did,' she said. 'Over a period of about four thousand years they discovered almost every inhabitable island in the Pacific from Hawaii to New Zealand.'

She pointed out the coral *motu*—small white-ringed islets covered in coconut palms, green beads in the lacy fichu of foam that the breaking combers formed along the reef.

'When the first settlers landed there,' she told him, hoping her voice was more steady than her pulse, 'they didn't know whether there were any other people on Rotumea so they anchored the canoe in the lagoon, ready to take off if a hostile group approached.'

'But no one did.'

'No. It was uninhabited. Virgin territory.'

And for some humiliating reason her cheeks pinked. Hastily she kept her gaze out to sea and added, 'It must have been a huge relief. They'd have carried coconuts with them to plant, and kumara and taro, and the paper mulberry tree to make cloth. And of course they brought dogs and rats too.'

'You've obviously studied the history,' Luc said sardonically.

I don't like you, Jo thought sturdily. *Not one tiny bit. Not ever.*

Buoyed up by the thought, she turned and gave him a swift challenging smile. 'Of course,' she said in her sweetest tone. 'I find them fascinating, and it's only polite to know something of the history of the place, after all. And of the people. Don't you think so?'

'Oh, I agree entirely. Information is the lifeblood of modern business.'

Her heightened senses warned her that his words and the hard smile that accompanied them held something close to a threat.

Stop dramatising, she told herself decisively. He was just being sarcastic again.

Yet it was dangerously exhilarating to fence with him like this. Anyway, he'd soon leave Rotumea. After all, she thought irritably, there must be rulers all over the world desperate to speak to him about matters of national interest, earth-shattering decisions to be pondered, vast amounts of money to be made. Once he'd shaken the white sand and red volcanic soil of Rotumea from his elegantly shod feet, he'd never come back and she wouldn't have to deal with him again.

Cheered by this thought, she said, 'We'd better be going. I want to call in at the shop before it closes.'

And she hoped it bored the life out of him. She knew most men would rather chance their luck in shark-infested waters than walk into the softly scented, flower-filled shop that sold her products.

She turned to go back to the car, only to realise he'd done the same. Startled, she pulled away at the touch of his arm on hers, and to her chagrin her foot twisted on a stone, jerking her off balance.

Before she could draw breath strong hands clamped onto her shoulders and steadied her. Jo froze, meeting glinting eyes that narrowed. Her heart somersaulted under the impact of his touch, his closeness. Every cell in her body was suddenly charged with a fierce aware-ness of his potent male charisma.

His grip tightened for a painful moment, then re-laxed.

But, instead of letting her go, he drew her towards him. His face was set and intent, his eyes molten silver.

Something feverish and demanding stopped her from jerking backwards, from saying anything. Helpless in a kind of reckless, fascinated thraldom, she forced her-self to meet that fiercely intent gaze. In it she read pas-sion, and a desire that matched the desperate impulse she had no way of fighting.

No, something in her brain insisted desperately, but a more primal urge burnt away common sense, any innate protectiveness, and when his mouth came down on hers she went up in flames, the blood surging through her in response to the carnal craving summoned by his kiss.

Her lashes fluttered down, giving every other sense free rein to savour the moment his mouth took hers.

He tasted purely male, clean and slightly salty, with a flavour that stimulated far more than her taste buds. The arms that held her against his powerful body were iron-hard, yet somehow made her feel infinitely secure. And mingling with the tropical fecundity of the rainforest around them was his scent. It breathed of arousal and a need that equalled the heat inside her. She wanted to accept and unleash that need, allow it to overcome the faint intimations of common sense, surrender completely…

And could not—*must* not…

Before she could pull away, he lifted his head. Her lashes fluttered drowsily up, but when she saw his icily intimidating expression, all desire fled, overtaken by humiliation.

He dropped his hands and took a step backwards.

'A bit too soon—and very crass—to be making a move like that, surely?' he said in a voice so level it took her a second or two to register the meaning of his words. 'After all, Tom's barely cold in his grave. You could make *some* pretence of missing him.'

The flick of scorn in his last sentence lashed her like a whip.

Damn Sean's sleazy mind and foul mouth, she thought savagely.

But the brutal sarcasm effectively banished the desire that had roared up out of nowhere. Defiantly she angled her chin and forced herself to hold Luc's unsparing arctic gaze.

In a voice she struggled to hold steady, she said, 'Tom and I didn't have that sort of relationship.'

He shrugged. 'Spare me the details.'

'If you spare me your crass assumptions,' she flashed, green eyes glittering with some emotion.

After a charged pause, he nodded. 'I'm not interested in your relationship with Tom.'

He registered the slight easing of her tension. It seemed she was prepared to believe that.

Not that it was exactly the truth. For some reason the thought of her in Tom's bed sickened him.

But with a mother who'd made no secret of her affairs, Joanna Forman undoubtedly had an elastic attitude to morality.

As she'd just shown. Hell, she'd been more than willing. He could have laid her down on the grass and taken her.

Mentally cursing his unruly mind as it produced an image of her golden body beneath him, of losing herself in her carnal heat, he quenched his fierce hunger with the sardonic observation that possibly her response was faked.

Had she realised that giving away her lovely body might not be sensible at this time? Sex would mean she'd lose any bargaining power...

'For your information,' she said now, her tone crisp and clear, her eyes coldly green and very direct, 'when I was a child I spent quite a few of my holidays here, staying with Aunt Luisa. My mother travelled a lot, and Tom didn't mind me coming even when he was in residence.'

His brows lifted and she waited for some comment. None came, so she resumed, 'We always got on well.'

She stopped, then in an entirely different tone, the words a little thick as though fighting back a surge of grief, she finished, 'That's all there was to it.'

Cynically Luc applauded that final touch. She also made the whole scenario sound quite plausible; Tom had a history of mentoring promising talent.

However, he'd mentioned none of his other protégées in his will.

But her statement certainly fitted in with the information he had about her. She'd attended excellent private schools—paid for probably by the succession of rich lovers her mother had taken. However, she hadn't followed her mother's choice of career. At university, she'd taken a science degree and a lover, graduating from both just before Ilona Forman had developed the illness that eventually killed her.

Joanna had left a fairly menial job at a well-connected firm to care for her mother, and then found herself with an ill aunt who'd refused to leave Rotumea. Either she had a sense of responsibility for her family, such as it was, or she'd seen an opportunity to get closer to Tom and grabbed it.

No doubt it had seemed a good career move.

And it had paid off.

Luc let his gaze roam her face, unwillingly intrigued by the colour that tinged her beautiful skin. Perfect skin for a woman who made skincare products. Yet, in spite of that betraying blush, her black-lashed eyes were steady and completely unreadable.

Was she wondering if he accepted that her relationship with Tom involved nothing more than innocent pleasure in each other's company?

Tamping down a deep, unusual anger, he reminded himself that he had to live with her for the next six months. And that he needed her approval before he could assume full control of the Henderson organization.

You cunning old goat, Tom, he thought coldly, and held out his hand. 'Very well, we'll leave it at that.'

Surprised, Jo reluctantly put her hand in his. A rush of adrenalin coursed through her when long fingers closed around hers, a thrill that coalesced into a hot tug of sensation in the pit of her stomach. Her breath came faster through her lips, and she had to force herself not to jerk free of his touch.

OK, so he hadn't said he believed her. Why should she care?

Yet she did.

However, she wasn't going to waste time wondering about the reason.

But at the shop she was surprised. Tall and darkly dominant, Luc examined the fittings, and even took down and read the blurb on a package of her most expensive rehydrating cream.

She had to conquer a spasm of irritation at her manager's admiring glances. This was her domain, and he had no right to look so much in charge, she thought crossly, and immediately felt foolish for responding so unreasonably.

But something about Luc MacAllister made her unreasonable. Something more than his assumption about her and Tom. Something she didn't recognise, primal

and dangerous and…and idiotic, she told herself brac-
ingly.

*Face it and get over it. He has a bewildering effect
on you, but you can cope. He's not really interested in
either you or your product, and you don't want him
to be.*

Back in the Land Rover, he commented, 'You need
better packaging.'

She knew that. Though what made him an expert on
packaging skincare products? 'That's all I can afford
right now,' she said evenly, turning to take the track
that led to Tom's house.

'You haven't considered getting a partner?'

'No.'

He said nothing, but she sensed his examination of
her set profile as she negotiated the ruts. When she
pulled up at the house he asked, 'And your reason?'

'I want to retain control,' she told him, switching off
the engine and turning to meet his gaze with more than
a hint of defiance.

His dark brows lifted, but he said, 'Fair enough.
However, unless you're happy with your present turnover—' his tone indicated he considered that likely to
be peanuts '—you're going to have to bite that bullet
eventually.'

'Right now, I'm happy with the way things are
going,' she told him, a steely note beneath her words.

When Tom had suggested exactly the same thing
she'd refused his offer of a further loan without any of
the odd sensation of dread that assailed her now.

Luc's kiss had changed things in a fundamental way
she didn't want to face. His hooded eyes, the autocratic

features that revealed no emotion and the taut line of his sensuous mouth—all combined to lift the hairs on her skin in a primitive display of awareness. He looked at her as though she was prey.

And that was ridiculous! He'd taken over Tom's huge empire, and had built it up even further. He was accustomed to organising and managing world-spanning enterprises. He wasn't interested in her piddling little business.

Or her, she thought, feeling slightly sick. There had been something about that kiss—something assessing, as though he'd been testing her reactions...

And, like a weak idiot, she'd gone up in flames for him. So now, of course, he'd be completely convinced that Sean's insulting accusation was the truth.

Well, she didn't care. Neither Sean nor Luc meant anything to her, and anyway, Luc would be gone as soon as he'd organised the sale of the house.

She said, 'I have no illusions about how far I can go.'

Without moving, he said, 'It sounds as though you're planning to stay in Rotumea for the rest of your life.'

She shrugged. 'Why not? Can you think of a better place to live?'

'Dreaming your days away in paradise?' he asked contemptuously.

CHAPTER THREE

'I PRESUME YOU have no idea of how patronising you sound.'

It didn't need the subtle ironic uplift of Luc's dark brows to make Jo regret she'd voiced her irritation.

How did that slight movement give his handsome face such a saturnine aspect?

But he said levelly, 'I didn't intend to be. Rotumea is a very small dot in a very empty ocean, a long way from anywhere. If your stuff's any good, don't you want to take it to the world?'

Torn, she hesitated, and saw the corners of his mouth lift, as though in expectation of a smile—a triumphant one.

Goaded, she said explosively, 'Not if it means handing over any control to anyone else. I have an arrangement with the local people and I value the ones who work with me—I feel I've established a business that takes their ambitions and needs seriously. I don't believe I'd be any happier if I were making megabucks and living in some designer penthouse in a huge, noisy, polluted city.' She paused, before finishing more calmly, 'And my product is better than good—it's *superb*.'

'If your skin is any indication of its effect, then I believe you.'

Delivered in a voice so dispassionate it took her a second to realise what he'd said, the compliment disturbed her. Uncertainly, she said, 'Thank you,' and opened the door of the Land Rover, stopping when he began to speak again.

'Although if you were making real money you could choose wherever you want to live,' he said coolly. 'Modern communications being as sophisticated as they are, no one has to live over the shop any more.'

'Agreed, but apart from liking Rotumea, in Polynesia personal relationships are important in business.'

Another lift of those dark brows. 'No doubt.'

After an undecided moment she ignored the distinctly sardonic note to his words. Instead she said, 'I like to keep a close watch on everything.'

Luc's nod was accompanied by a measuring glance. 'How to delegate is one of the lessons all entrepreneurs have to learn.' He looked at his watch. 'When do you eat at night? I assume I'll have to reserve a table for us at the resort.'

Relieved, Jo permitted herself a wry smile. She'd been wondering whether he'd expect her to cook for him. 'It's sensible to do so.' But something forced her to add, 'We don't have to go there if you don't want to. I'm actually quite a good cook. Basic, but the food's edible, Tom used to say.'

'I'm sure he didn't employ you for your prowess in the kitchen,' Luc said smoothly.

Something about his tone set her teeth on edge. She

opened her mouth to tell him Tom hadn't employed her at all, then closed it again.

The arrangement she had with Tom was none of Luc's business, and anyway, he wouldn't believe her.

Taking her silence for agreement, he said, 'Then I'll reserve a table. Eight tonight?'

Jo hesitated, then nodded. 'Thank you,' she said and got out of the Land Rover.

Inside the house, she opened a wardrobe door and stared at its meagre contents. Her one good dinner dress had been aired the previous evening in honour of Lindy and her husband.

Of course it didn't matter what she chose. After all, she wasn't trying to impress anyone.

In the end she pulled on a cotton voile dress that floated to her ankles, its pale yellow-green background printed in the gentle swirls of colour that suited her colouring. In her hair she tucked a gardenia flower.

Once ready, she examined her reflection critically. Yes, it looked good, fresh and tropical and casual—and not, she hoped, as though she'd gone to any trouble... Deliberately she'd kept her make-up low-key and simply combed her hair back from her face.

When she emerged from her room he was standing on the terrace but he turned immediately and gave her a cool, speculative survey.

'If you say I'm looking very Pacific,' she said before she could stop herself, 'I might start to think you have a bias against Pacific style.'

His smile was brief. 'Not guilty,' he said. 'You look charming, as I'm sure you know.'

'I intend to take that as a compliment,' she said coolly.

'It was meant to be.'

A compliment with a sting, she thought with a mental grimace.

It set the tone for the evening. Not that he was overtly antagonistic; in fact he was an excellent host. Before long she was laughing, and his conversation both stimulated and challenged her. If Luc had been any other man she'd have enjoyed the occasion, yet she had to keep telling herself to relax. She was far too conscious of his hard-edged control and the coolly unreadable composure that set every nerve jangling.

Too aware of the man himself.

And made uncomfortable by the covert observation of others in the restaurant. Especially the women casting envious looks her way.

Of course the resort advertising hinted at the possibility of a romantic experience, enticing guests with the allure of the tropics—the seductive, languorous perfume of frangipani and gardenia floating on the breeze that played lazily across bare skin, the promised glamour of a lover's moon rising over the reef.

And in spite of its exclusive guest list, tonight Luc was definitely the dominant male in the open-air lanai, radiating that indefinable thing called presence.

However, vitally masculine though he was, she wasn't interested in Luc MacAllister.

In any way, she told herself trenchantly.

So her reaction to those appreciative feminine glances bewildered her. A spiky, territorial instinct, it was an emotion she'd never felt before, and her unusual susceptibility sharpened her voice with a brittle, almost aggressive note.

Luc's voice broke into her thoughts. She looked up, meeting his narrowed grey eyes with something close to defiance.

'Something wrong with the fish?' he drawled.

'Of course not,' she said swiftly, attacking it with what she hoped looked like relish. It seemed to lack flavour, as though by Luc's mere presence he overwhelmed any other sensory input.

And that was just plain ridiculous.

Thankfully the evening seemed to race by, but the unusually significant tension that twisted through her increased. By the time they returned to the house she was so tense she flinched when a blur of movement shot up from the sandy ground as they walked the few steps from the garage.

'It's only a bird,' Luc said, sounding surprised.

'I know.' She was being idiotic. Completely, foolishly, *childishly* over the top—behaving like an adolescent in the first throes of a crush.

She didn't even *like* Tom's stepson, she thought resentfully, invoking Tom's name as some sort of talisman while she showered in the tiny bathroom off her room.

And he certainly didn't like her. He'd listened to Sean's poison and chosen to believe it, convinced she was the sort of woman who'd sleep with a man for money.

When he didn't even know her...

It hurt. Snorting at her stupidity, she turned off the unrefreshing lukewarm water and resolutely switched her mind to other things.

And failed. In bed she lay open-eyed, wooing sleep.

For once the dull roar of the waves against the reef didn't work its usual soothing magic. Wild, baseless forebodings swirled through her head, playing havoc with her thoughts.

Eventually she slipped into a doze, waking to the sound of gulls squabbling on the beach and the gleam of the sun through the curtains. The angle of its rays told her it was well above the horizon.

Jerking upright, she glanced at her watch, gave a startled exclamation and leapt out of the bed.

In a couple of hours she had to be at the resort to meet the solicitor from New Zealand. The uneasy chill that tightened her skin was because the solicitor would probably tell her she had to pay back the loan Tom had made to her.

And that would be extremely difficult.

Actually, right now it would be impossible.

Every cent she possessed was invested in her business. She had already approached the small local branch of the bank, but after consulting his superiors on the main island the manager had indicated they weren't inclined to take over the loan.

Oh, Tom, she thought, aching with sudden grief, why did you have to die...?

She missed him so much. In his gruff, cynical way he'd taken the place of the father she'd never known.

Telling herself to toughen up, she raced through her morning rituals before walking into the kitchen. The house was as silent as it had been since Tom died, and even before she saw the note on the bench she knew Luc MacAllister wasn't in it.

She stood for a moment, looking down at the writing. Just as she'd have imagined it, she thought a little caustically. Bold and black and clear; a very incisive, businesslike—not to say forthright—hand.

It announced, *Back at eight a.m.* and was signed with his initials.

She crumpled it up and glanced at her watch again, then rummaged in the refrigerator. Most men his height and build probably ate a cooked breakfast, but this morning he could have the same as she did—cereals and a bowl of fruit—and if he needed more to fuel that big streamlined body, there were eggs in the fridge for him to cook.

She ate breakfast too fast, decided against coffee and glanced again at her watch. Half an hour to fill. It stretched before her like an eternity. The sea always calmed her—perhaps it would work its magic now.

But her stomach remained a refuge for butterflies even after she'd walked through the sighing palms and stopped in the heavy shade of the trees lining this part of the beach. A towel on the sand drew her gaze out over the lagoon.

Sunlight glittered across the water, bestowing heat to the sand and weaving radiance through the great rollers as they dashed themselves in a fury of foam against the obstinate reef. On the calm waters inside its shelter, a small canoe carrying two boys danced its way down the coastline.

Squinting against the brilliance, Jo spotted Luc swimming towards the shore, powerful arms and shoulders moving easily, soundlessly through the warm waters. An unexpected heat banished the dark cloud of worry; her breath locked in her lungs as he stood up, water streaming down to emphasise bronzed shoulders and chest and long, strongly muscled legs.

For such a sophisticated man he looked magnificently physical, like some ancient god of the sea—compelling and charismatic as he strode towards the shore.

Startled by a fierce stab of sensation in every nerve, her senses on full alert, Jo looked away and pretended to watch the little canoe darting across the water. It seemed intrusive to stare at Luc when he had no knowledge of her presence and she disliked feeling like a voyeur.

Her stomach clenched with a different sort of apprehension as he came closer. She stiffened her shoulders, turning to face a survey that held a cool enquiry. Every traitorous nerve in her body tightened in a brief, shocking acknowledgement of his compelling male magnetism.

Without smiling, Luc nodded and said briefly, 'Good morning.'

At least he hadn't noticed her wildfire reaction. She returned the greeting, her mouth drying when he stooped and picked up his towel. How on earth had he developed the muscles so lovingly highlighted by the sun?

Working out, she told herself prosaically, adding a wry addendum, *Lots and lots of it*. And weights. Very heavy weights…

After drying his face he said, 'Kind of you to come down, but I could have found my way back.'

'I hope so,' she said, hoping she sounded amused. 'But I always walk down to the beach in the morning.' And because it was important to make sure he realised she hadn't followed him, she added, 'I didn't know you were swimming.'

He draped the towel around his taut waist and came towards her, big and male and overwhelming. 'Do you swim?'

'Every day.' She turned to go back to the house.

He fell in beside her. 'Not afraid of sharks?'

'Tiger sharks—the ones to be scared of—don't come into the lagoon much, if at all,' she told him, glad to be able to change the subject. 'And they're usually night feeders, so daylight swimming is pretty safe. Besides, the islanders say they're protected from them.'

He was too close. She felt an odd suffocation as they walked along the white shell path beneath the palms, and increased her pace.

Shortening his long stride to match hers, he asked, 'How are the islanders protected?'

So she told him the ancient story of the son of the first chief of the island who saved a small tiger shark—son of the chief of the sharks in the ocean around Rotumea—from a fish trap. 'For his compassion, the chief of all the sharks gave the islanders the right to be free of attack for ever. But only in the waters around Rotumea.'

He said, 'A charming story.'

Mischief glimmering in her smile, Jo looked up and said demurely, 'In all recorded history there's no account of any Rotumean being attacked by a tiger shark.'

His answering smile set off alarm bells all through her. *Stop it this moment*, she told her unruly emotions, tearing her gaze away to frown at the path ahead.

But that smile was a killer…

Hastily she said, 'I've left the makings for breakfast

out, but if you want any more than cereal and fruit you'll have to get it for yourself. I have an appointment with Tom's solicitor at the resort at nine.'

And glanced up at his features for any hint that he knew of this.

Of course there was no alteration in the hard male contours of his face, and his eyes were hooded and unreadable. 'We'll talk when you've come back.'

Talk? About what?

The loan, she thought sickly.

Luc said, 'And I can get my own breakfast. I don't need looking after.'

An equivocal note in his voice kept her silent. She glanced at her watch. 'I don't imagine this meeting will last long. I assume it's to tell me what Tom wanted done with the house, so I'll go straight on to the shop afterwards.'

And spend the rest of the day trying yet again to work out how she could pay back that loan and still retain ownership of her fledgling business—an exercise she knew to be futile, as she'd already tried everything she could think of.

Think positively, she adjured herself robustly. Tom was too much of a realist not to know that his health was—well, not precarious, but the stroke had been a definite warning.

Surely if he felt anything at all for her beyond a mild affection for his housekeeper's niece he'd have made a fair provision for repaying the loan?

Bruce Keller looked up as Joanna Forman came into the room. Although he prided himself on his professional attitude, it took quite an effort to hide his curiosity.

He glanced at the documents on the table that served him as a desk. Joanna Forman, aged twenty-three, a New Zealand citizen, was not exactly how he'd imagined her. Tall, she had an excellent figure—she wasn't stick-thin like so many girls nowadays. And she had that intangible thing his daughters called style.

He wouldn't call her beautiful, yet as a man he could appreciate the subtle attraction of hair the colour of toffee and exquisite skin that seemed to radiate a softly golden glow. Not at all flamboyant—in fact, she should have looked out of place in the full-on exuberance of the tropics. That she didn't was probably due to her direct green gaze and softly sensuous mouth.

Yes, I see, he thought, and got to his feet, holding out his hand. 'Ms Forman?'

'Yes, I'm Jo Forman.' Her voice was steady, its slight huskiness adding to the impact of her mouth and her slender, curvy body.

He introduced himself, mentally approved the firmness of her handshake and said, 'Do sit down, Ms Forman. You do know why you're here?'

'You have something to tell me about Tom—Mr Henderson's—affairs. I presume it's that I need to vacate the house and pay back the loan he made me.'

Bruce blinked. She wasn't in the least what he'd imagined, and he needed to marshal his thoughts.

Tom Henderson had ignored his old friend's shocked cautions and flatly refused to discuss the arrangements he'd made for his mistress in his will, beyond making sure they were watertight.

The solicitor felt a twinge of professional pride at just how watertight they were.

No one would be able to break the terms of that will, not even Luc MacAllister—who'd almost certainly put a team of high-powered lawyers onto it once he'd learned what was in it.

After a slight cough Bruce said, 'No, there's nothing like that in his will.'

Surely she had some idea of the provision Tom had made for her?

She frowned, then seemed to relax a little. 'In that case, why am I here?'

Perhaps not...

Well, he'd soon see how that mouth looked when it smiled. He said, 'You're here because in his will Mr Henderson left you shares in his business enterprises worth several million New Zealand dollars.'

To his astonishment the soft colour fled her skin and she looked as though she might faint. No, he thought, wondering if he should offer a glass of water, modern young women didn't faint; that went out with the Victorians.

But after several moments of staring at him as though he'd grown horns, she regained her composure. *'What did you say?'* Her voice was low and intense, almost shaky.

Clearly she'd had no idea. The solicitor leaned forward and told her the amount of money Tom Henderson had left her, finishing with, 'However, there are conditions to be fulfilled before the inheritance becomes yours.'

The muscles in her throat moved as she swallowed. Huskily she asked, 'Why?'

He started to tell her why Tom had made the conditions, but before he'd got far she cut him short. 'Why did he leave me *anything*?'

Startled, he felt his skin heat. 'I…ah, it seems that he felt—' He stopped, cleared his throat and resumed, 'That is, his affection for you made him want to…to make sure you were cared for.'

She frowned. 'Why?'

Her response showed a brutal understanding of her position. Clearly she was no romantic, and under no illusions as to her place in Tom Henderson's life. It was true very few men left their mistresses a fortune—even though in Tom's eyes this had been only a small fortune—so she should be elated.

Instead, she seemed aggressively astonished, if those two emotions were compatible.

Feeling his way, he asked, 'Does his reason matter?'

'Yes,' she told him unevenly. 'I think it does matter. He never said anything about this to me.'

Once more he cleared his throat and tried to steer the meeting back on track. 'I don't know his reasons, I'm afraid. And as I said, there are conditions to this legacy.'

Breathless and dazed, Jo felt as though she'd been snatched from ordinary life and transported to an alternate universe. It took all of her energy to say, 'All right, tell me about them.'

And listened with mounting bewilderment and shock while he obeyed. He was careful to explain the legal jargon to her but, even so, it was too much to take in.

She took a ragged breath. 'Let me get this straight. You're saying that to inherit this…this money…I have to spend the next six months living with Luc MacAllister. Here, in Rotumea.'

And waited, almost holding her breath and hoping she'd got it terribly wrong.

The elderly solicitor nodded. 'That is so.'

Colour flooded her skin. Sitting upright, she said fiercely, 'Surely it must be illegal to make such conditions.'

'I thought I'd made it clear that Mr Henderson intended only that you occupy the same house,' the solicitor pointed out, not unsympathetically. He gave a little cough. 'Nothing more was intended than that.'

Fragments of thought chased each other fruitlessly through Jo's brain. She grabbed at one of them and blurted, 'I don't understand it. Why make such an imposition on me—on Mr MacAllister?'

'Mr Henderson didn't tell me, I'm afraid, but I imagine it was to safeguard you.' He paused, then added, 'It is a lot of money, Ms Forman, a lot of responsibility—' *more than you've been accustomed to*, his tone implied '—and there will be pitfalls. Mr MacAllister can help you manage this unexpected windfall and make sure you're aware of things that could go wrong.'

He'd sooner see me in hell, she thought trenchantly. Of course she'd need professional help to deal with so much money, but what had made Tom think his stepson would take on such a responsibility? Was this outrageous proviso some sort of revenge on Luc for ousting Tom from Henderson Holdings—and so successfully expanding it?

No, vengefulness didn't square with her knowledge of Tom. A sudden thought struck her. 'I don't have to accept this…the legacy, do I?'

After a shocked look, the solicitor said, 'Think about

it carefully, Ms Forman. Mr Henderson wanted you to
have this inheritance. His reasons for putting in such
a condition are unknown, but it was important to him.
He insisted on it being there, and he certainly felt it
would be best for you.'

'That might be so but it's a complete imposition on
L—Mr MacAllister.' Jo shivered, feeling the jaws of a
trap close around her. She resisted the urge to wring her
hands, and said bleakly, 'I can't believe Tom did this—
or that Luc will accept such a charge.'

'He has already accepted it.'

Confused, she asked, 'He *knows* of this?'

'Yes.'

Well, of course he did. No wonder he'd believed
Sean's assertion! He probably thought she'd weaselled
her way into Tom's life in the hope of getting money,
and now he was lumped with her for the next six months.

Her chin came up but, before she could speak, the
elderly man on the other side of the table said gently,
'If you refuse Mr Henderson's legacy, your debt to his
estate will have to be paid. And as he knew there will
be occasions when you need money for various things,
he set up an account for you with a monthly increment.
But it cannot be used to pay off the loan.'

Her stomach clamped in a twist of pain. 'I don't want
it,' she said automatically.

'Nevertheless, it is there.'

If Tom had wanted to help her from beyond the
grave, why hadn't he just forgiven her the debt?

What had been in his mind…?

Stop asking why, she ordered, because now she'd
never know. *Concentrate on the facts.*

If she turned Tom's legacy down she wouldn't be the only person to suffer. So would the people who grew the ingredients for her lotions and creams on their small plantations, who relied on her business to pay for their children's education and medical care.

She could sell the fledgling business and pay off the debt. There had been tentative offers from a couple of big skincare firms who'd wanted to get their hands on a reliable source of several of the plants she used...

Even as the thought came into her mind she rejected it. When she'd first started using the islanders' recipes and plants for her skin products she'd promised the chiefs that if it became a success the business would stay in her hands.

She couldn't sell out and turn her back on them.

Her deep breath hurt her lungs. When she could speak again she said harshly, 'All right, I accept.'

And felt a clutch of fear at the prospect of what lay ahead.

Bluntly she asked, 'But what if Mr MacAllister changes his mind and refuses?'

There was a moment's silence. 'Then he loses something that means more to him than money.' And when she opened her mouth to ask him what, he held up a hand. 'I can't reveal to you what that is. But be assured, he will not refuse.'

CHAPTER FOUR

SAFELY PARKED BEHIND the shop, Jo switched off the Land Rover engine and sat with her hands gripped together in her lap, trying to stop shaking.

It had taken all her powers of concentration to negotiate the road between the resort and the town. Now her eyes stung with sudden tears, and she had to fight off a catch in her chest that threatened to turn into sobs.

Why had Tom left her such an enormous amount of money and burdened her with this weird condition? Why force her to live with Luc MacAllister for six months?

Biting her lip, she scrabbled in her bag for her handkerchief and wiped her eyes, dragging in a long shuddering breath.

Stop feeling betrayed, she told herself trenchantly, and work things out sensibly.

Tom knew she was intelligent and a quick learner, but he had a practical man's contempt for her degree. And of course it would be no help in dealing with that sort of fortune. She'd learned a lot from him, but the solicitor was probably right on the mark when he'd suggested Tom saw her as too young and inexperienced to be able to cope, so he'd made sure she couldn't do anything foolish with the legacy.

But *why* insist she spend the next six months with Luc MacAllister? Even before they'd met, Tom's unexpected legacy must have made Luc very ready to believe the worst of her. Sean's malice had only cemented that conviction in place.

The prospect of living with a man who thought she was little better than a tramp sent chills down her backbone.

Oh, Tom, she thought wretchedly, what were you thinking?

The car door swung open, and Savisi Torrens, the shop manager, leaned down to demand, 'Jo, are you all right? What's the matter?'

'I'm fine,' she said automatically, grabbing her bag.

Savisi scanned her face. 'You look pale. Are you sick?'

'No, no, I'm all right. Sorry, I was just thinking about things.'

'Have you had lunch?'

Surprised, Jo glanced at her watch. 'Not yet. I didn't realise it was so late.' She'd spent well over two hours with the solicitor. 'I'll get something from the café over the road.'

'Let me order that, and you can sit down while it's coming.' Savisi urged her into the relative coolness of the shop.

After she'd eaten a sandwich and drunk some coffee Jo felt better, although her stomach was still churning. It was a relief to discuss the monthly returns.

'The recession's hit us quite hard,' Savisi said succinctly. 'Not so many tourists this year.'

Jo scanned the figures again. 'Actually, we're doing better than I thought we might. Well done.'

The older woman disclaimed the praise. 'A good product always sells well.'

Jo said, 'I've been thinking that we might be able to set up some sort of sales outlet at the resort. Or a spa…'

'A spa? Oh, yes!'

Jo said quickly, 'It would cost a lot, but we might be able to swing it.' Even though Tom's legacy wouldn't be hers for six months…

'Meru's sister works at the resort—she might be able to tell you if the management would consider it.'

'I'd planned to see what she thinks.' Jo glanced at her watch. 'I'm due at the factory in half an hour. But another thing I'm pondering is the packaging.' She mentally grimaced at the memory of Luc MacAllister's insultingly casual comment. 'Changing it would cost plenty too, but if we do go into the resort we'll need something more sophisticated.'

They discussed ideas over more coffee before Jo left to visit the small building where her range was manufactured.

Meru Manamai bustled out to greet her with her usual hug. Her reaction to Jo's idea was the same as Savisi's—and even more enthusiastic. 'I'll see what my sister thinks,' she said, 'but a spa sounds like a really good idea. I wonder why it wasn't part of the original plan?'

'Tom wasn't a spa person—he liked swimming in the sea.' Words wouldn't come until Jo pushed the sad memories away. 'Some of our skincare products would be useful there, but I'd need to develop others—massage oils, that sort of thing. I know mothers here massage their babies with coconut oil, so that would be a logical base.'

At Meru's nod she warmed to her theme. 'And if there's enough interest from the guests we could organise small tours of the factory. We could perhaps give free samples?' She grinned. 'Small ones, just enough to make a difference so they'd come back for more.'

Meru laughed, but said practically, 'It might work—people love to get something for free.' She gave Jo an anxious look. 'But a spa would cost a lot of money so perhaps now is not the time to consider it...'

But in six months' time Jo would have a lot of money... Everything seemed to be pushing her into accepting Tom's legacy.

'It would be really good for Rotumea,' she said thoughtfully. 'We'd probably have to import people who know different sorts of massage, but the Rotumean way of massaging would be a point of difference. Before we make any decisions I'll have to talk it over with the resort management.'

A spa would certainly get her product known internationally, and Luc's query about taking her line to the world tantalised her. Expansion would mean more jobs in Rotumea, the exhilaration of working to grow her business...

And huge risks, she reminded herself gloomily.

Later, driving home in the rapidly falling dusk, she braced herself to overcome her wary apprehension. Luc had every reason to profoundly dislike the position he'd been forced into.

At the house she switched off the engine and sat for a moment trying to ignore the tension knotting her stomach. She wouldn't—couldn't afford to—let herself get worked up about the situation, so when she discussed Tom's crazy scheme with Luc she'd be reasonable and tactful and practical. She would not, not, *not* allow her mind to be scrambled by the memory of the minutes she'd spent in Luc's arms, and the sensual impact of his kisses.

An impact she still felt, keen and precise like a dagger through armour, so that her blood throbbed thickly through her veins and she had to take several deep breaths before she could persuade herself to climb out of the vehicle and walk briskly into the house.

Only to realise that Luc wasn't there. Trying not to feel that she'd been given a reprieve, she set about preparing the dinner she'd bought at the market. Tom had always enjoyed the coconut and lime risotto cakes she made to go with fish, so fresh it still smelt of the sea, that she'd bought from a fisherman on her way home. It should please anyone but a certified carnivore who demanded red meat.

If that was Luc, tough.

She'd just put the mixture for the cakes into the fridge when instinct whipped her head around to meet a steel-grey gaze, hard as glacier ice and every bit as cold.

'Oh,' she said involuntarily. Her heart jerked violently, then seemed to skid to a stop for a second. She pulled herself together enough to say, 'I didn't hear you come in.'

'So I gather.' His tone was completely neutral, but she caught the darkness of contempt in his eyes, the same contempt she'd noticed when he'd held her and asked her what she wanted.

Still watching her, he leaned a hip against the counter that separated the kitchen from the rest of the house. Spooked by that unnerving survey, she said pleasantly, 'I usually have dinner in about half an hour's time. Is that all right for you?' And turned away.

'It's fine.' He glanced at his watch. 'Do you mind leaving the room? I need to talk to someone back home.'

'Of course. I'll go outside.' The telephone was an old handset, placed where any conversation could be heard right through the house.

Tom had rarely used it, so its position had caused no problems. Jo walked across the garden to pick a couple of Tahitian limes from the tree. Warned by the distant sound of Luc's voice that he was still talking, she stopped to haul out a seedling palm that had somehow managed to hide itself under a hibiscus bush. Tom had disdained tidy, formal gardens; this one was lush and thriving, its predominant greenness set off by brilliant blooms and exotic leaf forms.

She couldn't hear what Luc was saying, but the tone of his voice made it abundantly clear that he wasn't pleased. Not that he shouted; if anything his voice dropped, but the cold, unyielding menace in his tone raised bumps on her skin. He would, she thought with an inward shiver, make a very nasty enemy. So far he'd been reasonably polite to her; now she wondered why.

Silence from the house brought her upright. She picked up the limes, still warm from the sun, and walked inside, bracing herself for the discussion she knew they had to have.

Luc stood at the bar, his back to her as he poured drinks. Her steps faltering, she noted the strong lines of shoulders and back that tapered to lean hips above long, powerful legs. It didn't seem fair that one man should have so much—physical chemistry, a brilliant mind and that potent male charisma, as compelling as it was disturbing.

And extremely good hearing. Without turning, he said, 'I've finished. Come on in.'

She put the limes down on the table and stared at the tall-stemmed glasses with the faint lines of bubbles rising through the pale liquid.

'Champagne?' she said uncertainly. 'What's the celebration?'

Eyes hooded, he handed her a chilled glass. 'I thought it appropriate,' he said with smooth arrogance. 'After all, you've just become a rich woman. Congratulations on a game skilfully played.'

Jo's fingers tightened around the slender stem so fiercely she thought she might snap it. OK, he was furious. She'd expected that, and she would not allow him to get to her.

Remembering her decision on the drive back, she thought *sensible, reasonable, practical…*

Trying to keep her voice steady, she said, 'I had no idea what Tom was going to do. I'm just as bewildered as you, and just as upset. I don't like being manipulated.'

His lip curled. 'Presumably he wanted to recompense you for your services. I only hope they were worth the money.'

Jo realised her teeth were clenched. If he was trying to goad her into losing her temper he was making an excellent job of it. Deliberately relaxing every taut muscle, she said, 'I don't blame you for being angry—

Tom had no right to lumber you with my presence for the next six months. But if you think I'll be a whipping boy for your temper, think again. I'll walk out sooner than put up with insults.'

His face was unreadable, but his shrug conveyed much, and she had to stop herself from moving uncomfortably under his searching survey. 'I'm sure you won't,' he said, each word an exercise in contempt. 'Tom knew you'd stay.'

Goaded into indiscreet anger, she challenged, 'What about you? How did he make sure you'd fall in with his wishes?'

His smile was a taunt. 'Blackmail.'

Jo felt a momentary flare of sympathy, one that died when she met a gaze as harsh as a winter storm. Forcing a brisk, practical tone, she asked, 'So what happens now?'

'We leave for New Zealand tomorrow morning.'

Her jaw dropped. Recovering, she expostulated, 'I can't do that.'

'Why?'

'Because I'm needed here. I have responsibilities on the island—'

'Your little business?' he said, his negligent tone more galling than contempt would have been. 'You can keep an eye on it from New Zealand while we're away. But as you don't need it to pique Tom's interest any more it would be better to sell it.'

'I am *not* going to sell it,' she snapped, fighting back a rising tide of anger.

'Whatever. But you're coming to New Zealand tomorrow with me.' He examined her light, floating dress and drawled, 'You'll need warmer clothes, I imagine. I'll organise that.'

Her brows shot up. 'You're accustomed to buying clothes for women?'

With a smoothness that somehow grated, he said, 'My PA has excellent taste, and an encyclopaedic knowledge of the best places to hunt down the biggest bargains.'

His comment reminded her of the pathetic state of her bank balance. The small wage she took from her business barely covered her expenses in Rotumea. In New Zealand it would go nowhere. A hint of panic slowed her thoughts. No way could she afford new clothes. Second-hand shops?

She stifled a quiver of nervous amusement at the thought of Luc's PA seeking bargains for her in opportunity shops. Fortunately she had the perfect excuse. 'I can't afford any new clothes,' she said baldly.

In a voice that made her stiffen, Luc demanded, 'Use the money Tom left you.'

'I don't want it.' When he went to speak she added crisply, 'Living in Rotumea is cheap. I can manage on what I make.'

'You'll be spending some time travelling with me.'

Jo unclenched her teeth far enough to retort frigidly, 'Why? Tom knows—knew—how much the business means to me. I can't believe that he'd stipulate that I abandon it to jaunt around with you.'

Luc laughed, a cold, almost mocking sound. 'Welcome to the world of big money, Joanna Forman.' He raised his glass. 'The part of the will that dealt with my inheritance stated that when I go to any place that might help you, I am to take you with me.'

'Help me—in what way?'

'With your business, of course.' He sounded almost amused. 'Tom enjoyed power, and he probably relished the thought of forcing both of us to do his bidding from beyond the grave. So here's to his memory.' Luc drank some champagne, then set the flute down on the table with a sharp click.

Stung at this injustice, she said, 'Tom wasn't like that.'

'Then why did he do it?' he demanded, his tone derisory.

The same question she'd been asking herself since the solicitor had told her of the inheritance. The months ahead stretched out like a particularly testing purgatory.

Be reasonable, she told herself sternly, and forced herself to meet Luc's daunting gaze. 'I have no more idea than you do, but Tom would have had a reason. He wasn't an impulsive man. And we can't ask him, so it's useless speculating. I dislike the situation as much as you do, but the simplest way to deal with it is to take it one day at a time and try not to get in each other's way.'

'Indeed,' he said, a note of irony hardening the word. 'Unfortunately we have to share our lives for the next six months. That means there's no way of avoiding each other.' He paused, then added satirically, 'Unless you refuse the inheritance.'

And waited.

At that moment nothing—absolutely *nothing*—would have given Jo greater pleasure than to tell him fluently and with passion what he and that solicitor could do with Tom's bequest, and then turn and walk away.

Unfortunately she couldn't.

Before she was able to say anything Luc said with hateful sarcasm, 'But you're not going to do that, are you?'

She stiffened her spine and met his sardonic look with every bit of resolution she possessed. 'No,' she said shortly. 'I owe Tom's estate money and the only way I can be sure of paying it off is to obey the terms of his will.'

'Selling the business would probably clear the debt.'

Jo masked her rising panic with a fierce look. 'When I started, I promised the local people I'd never sell it to an outsider. It's their knowledge I'm using, and they have an emotional stake in the business.'

'That's very noble of you.'

'What about you?' Her tone changed from defiance to challenge. 'What have you done that Tom was able to blackmail you into agreeing to stay here?'

'That,' he returned, his tone warning her she'd over-stepped some invisible boundary, 'is none of your business.'

She shrugged. 'The reason I'm not walking away is none of your business either, but I told you anyway,' she said, then took a deep breath.

Remember—calm, reasonable, common sense, she reminded herself hastily.

Steadying her voice, she tried. 'Can't we just agree to disagree and leave it at that? I don't like quarrelling, and the prospect of spending the next six months at loggerheads is not a pleasant one.'

A thought of amazing simplicity flashed across her mind like lightning. Without giving herself time to think, she asked, 'Why don't you take over Tom's loan to the business? Then I could pay it back under the same terms as I was paying Tom, and we'd not be forced to live together for six months.'

He was silent for a few seconds, and when his answer came it was brief and completely decisive. 'No.'

'That way I don't get Tom's inheritance which is causing you so much angst, and we don't have to put up with each other,' she pressed.

His brows drew together. 'No,' he said again. 'Tom wanted you to have the money. I'm not going to take it from you.'

Startled, she asked, 'Then why not accept the situation and try to make it as painless as possible? Would that be so difficult?'

Her plea met with no answer. She surveyed his face, lean and arrogant and unreadable, steely eyes half-shielded by his thick lashes. An uncomfortable silence stretched between them, taut and somehow expectant, thickening until Jo was desperate to break it.

She said, 'OK, I tried,' and turned away, only to stop abruptly when he spoke.

'Are you suggesting taking a different tack?' he asked without expression.

She looked over her shoulder. Something about his stance—alert, like that of a hunter—summoned a stealthy excitement that pulsed through her, fogging her brain.

'Exactly,' she flashed, feeling like prey.

'I must be losing my grip.' His voice was thoughtful, his gaze level. 'I'm not usually so obtuse.'

They seemed to be conducting two different conversations. She said uncertainly, 'I don't understand you.'

'I think you do. You should have couched your proposition in less obscure terms,' he said, reaching out to touch the nape of her neck.

Too late, Jo realised what he meant. She opened her mouth to tell him she'd made no proposition at all, but his touch sent shock scudding down her spine, a secret craving that smoked through her like some addictive drug.

'No!' she said, her voice dragging.

'Why not?'

He didn't sound angry. In fact, if she could only trigger her brain into rational thought she'd guess his main emotion was amusement. The tips of his fingers were stroking softly, unexpectedly gentle, sending voluptuous, agitated shivers through her.

'Why not, Joanna?' he repeated, his voice cool, his gaze speculative.

She wasn't going to tell him that her experience was as limited as his kindness. Forcing herself to meet the intense blue flames that had banished all the grey from his eyes, she said hoarsely, 'Because, regardless of what you think, I'm not into casual sex.'

'One thing I can promise you,' he said, his tone suddenly raw, 'is that there would be nothing casual about it.'

And he pulled her into his arms.

Nothing—*nothing*—Jo had experienced had affected her like Luc's mouth on hers, the wildfire thunder of her pulse as his arms tightened to hold her against his lean body.

Before she had a chance to resist, sensation raced through her, his kiss detonating an involuntary response

hot as fire, sweet as honey, fierce as the pressure of
Luc's mouth on hers. When her knees buckled his arms
tightened around her and her heart rate surged; he too
was aroused.

Within Jo a pulse leapt into life, primal and dangerous, summoning a swift, mind-sapping hunger. As
though aware of her vulnerability, Luc deepened the
kiss, causing her body to flame into a passionate need
that built on her response to his first kiss.

And then he lifted his head, breathed something
short and brutal and let his arms fall, stepping back.
For a moment her only emotion was heated resentment
at his abrupt transition from passion to control. Fortunately common sense stiffened her spine and cleared
her brain. She grabbed the back of a chair and dragged
air into her lungs, her eyes wide and defiant as she
forced herself to meet his hooded gaze. Disconnected
fragments of thought tumbled through her brain. His
face was drawn and fierce—a warrior's face—and the
sensuous line of his mouth had tightened into hardness.

'I'm sorry,' he said curtly.

Jo's heart beat so loudly in her ears she couldn't hear
the dull roar of the waves on the reef. She shook her
head, finding that somehow her hair had escaped from
its confining ponytail.

Surely Luc hadn't run his fingers through it…? The
thought fanned an insidious tremor of something far
too close to pleasure, reawakening her nervous turmoil.

He broke into her thoughts with a harsh order. 'Say
something.'

'For once,' she retorted thinly, 'I'm speechless.'

Anger rode her, fuelled by shame. Once again she'd

been entirely under the spell of his kiss. She despised herself because the embers of that desperate sensuality still smouldered deep inside her.

But his kiss had been an arrogant act of power—one reinforced by her mindless response. He'd no right to assume she was proposing some sort of grubby liaison, then kiss her like that.

Why hadn't she remained quiescent—detached and unimpressed—instead of going up like dry tinder in his arms?

Because she'd had no defence against the hypnotic masculinity of it, the sheer male hunger that had summoned a similar sexual drive from some unawakened place in her.

'I find that difficult to believe,' he said ironically. 'And to refer to what I said before we kissed, there was nothing light or casual about it.'

He paused, and when she said nothing he added, 'But you knew there wouldn't be. We've been far too conscious of each other ever since your eyes clashed with mine at the resort. Are you going to deny that?'

Jo drew in another sharp breath and evaded the question. 'That has nothing to do with anything.'

His smile was tinged with cynicism. 'It has everything to do with it. I wanted you then.'

Another blazing pang of desire shot through her. She resisted it, obstinately folding her lips before any foolish remark could escape.

Luc's expression remained unreadable. 'And your kisses tell me that you want me. Like you, I dislike the idea of spending the next six months quarrelling, so I'm suggesting a much more pleasant way of passing the time.'

He almost made it sound reasonable.

In his world, it probably was. Luc had probably made love to any woman he wanted.

Humiliated, Jo fought a treacherous urge to give in to this potent desire and walk on the wild side, explore a world she'd never experienced.

Fortunately, another, much more protective instinct blared a warning. Allowing herself to be persuaded, surrendering to his terms and becoming Luc MacAllister's lover would be a risk too unnervingly dangerous to take.

She would never be the same again.

So, although she had to force the words through lips still throbbing from his kisses, she said stiffly, 'No. That's not what I want…'

His look—speculative and unsparing—shattered her already cracked composure, but she lifted her chin and continued, 'And when I suggested finding a way to spend the next six months other than quarrelling, I was *not* suggesting some sort of affair—if that's what you thought.'

Calmly he replied, 'In that case there's nothing more to be said. I apologise for misreading the situation. It won't happen again. Deal?' And he held out his hand.

Still dazed by her shocking need, she hesitated, then held out her own, shivering at the sensuous excitement that thrilled through her at his touch.

'Deal,' she said hoarsely, and forced herself not to snatch her hand away.

Six months…!

She winced, and broke into speech. 'Why do we have to leave tomorrow? It's going to make things difficult—not so much for me as for my manager.'

Luc frowned. 'I have to be in Auckland by tomorrow afternoon for a meeting.'

Something had obviously gone wrong, and Luc was going to deal with it.

But although he might be arrogantly accustomed to people accommodating themselves to his plans, she wasn't.

She said, 'That's impossible unless your meeting is very late in the afternoon. The next plane for New Zealand doesn't leave until two tomorrow afternoon.'

'A private jet will pick us up at eight tomorrow morning.' With an ironic smile he watched her eyes widen, and added, 'Also, I've just been informed that the following night Tom's favourite charity is holding a dinner in Auckland as a memorial to him.'

'So?'

'Apparently he wanted you to be there,' he said curtly. 'The charity is a children's hospital, and this is to raise funds for new equipment.'

Jo could think of nothing worse than going to such a dinner with him. One day at a time, she reminded herself with grim resignation, and surrendered.

'All right, but I can't just leave everything. I need to organise things—my shop and the factory, as well as someone to look after the house.'

'You've still got time,' he told her crisply. 'Time you're wasting in argument. Anyway, it's only going to be for a few days.'

Her lush mouth—its contours slightly enhanced by

his kiss—tightened. Luc's body alerted him in an involuntary and infuriating response, heat twisting his gut as raw hunger ricocheted through him.

She said coldly, 'You could have told me that at the beginning.'

'I don't remember getting a chance,' he said sardonically. But she had a point. He took another sip of champagne, and asked, 'Is it so impossible?'

She stared at him for a moment, her green eyes shadowed. 'No,' she admitted quietly. 'But it's not just me it's going to inconvenience. If this sort of thing happens again I'll need more time to organise.'

He said abruptly, 'It's extremely important for me to be there—I'd have told you before but it's just come up.'

'The phone call,' she said, recalling with a remembered chill the tone of his voice.

'Yes,' he said shortly.

Clearly he had a very good reason for getting back to New Zealand as quickly as he could. However, if they were to spend the next six months together—as flatmates, she thought with a shiver—he was going to have to understand she wasn't some kid to be ordered around...

He waited until eventually she said, 'Very well, I'll be ready.'

For some reason his frown deepened. 'I'll organise a set-up for you so you can video conference with your managers whenever you want to.'

'Thank you.' She tried not to be swayed by his unexpected thoughtfulness. After all, he'd probably just order some minion to see that she had video contact.

Later, safely alone in her room, Jo collapsed onto the bed and tried to whip up some remnant of common sense. So Luc had kissed her. And she—reluctantly she admitted she'd almost *exploded* with what had to be lust.

Nothing she'd ever experienced had come near the sheer primal intensity of his kisses. She wasn't a virgin; in fact, she'd hoped her one serious relationship would lead to marriage. She'd loved Kyle, and been hurt when he made it clear that he resented her preoccupation with her mother's health. Her discovery a few weeks later that he was being unfaithful had shattered her.

Their lovemaking had been good, but nothing— *nothing* like being kissed by Luc.

That was a miracle of sensation—unbidden, reckless and clamorous, a torrent of response that too easily had drowned every sensible thought in barbaric hunger.

And it felt so *right*…as though it was meant to be.

Stifling a shocked groan, she looked around the bedroom and fought a cowardly urge to hurl her clothes into a bag and flee from an intolerable temptation.

Think, she adjured herself fiercely. *Use your head.*

For some reason Tom had believed it was important she spend six months in close—make that *very* close— contact with his stepson. And he'd made it pretty near impossible for her to turn his legacy down.

So she'd just have to grit her teeth and cope—without surrendering to this wild, irresponsible appetite she'd suddenly developed for Luc's body.

An ironic smile turned swiftly into a grimace. 'Oh, it should be so easy!' she muttered, pushing back the drift of netting that kept insects at bay.

Her sleep was restless, punctuated by dreams that faded as soon as she woke, leaving her aching and unsatisfied. In the morning she showered and dressed with care, then forced herself into the kitchen. One thing she was not going to do was walk out to the beach...

She was eating breakfast on the terrace when Luc appeared. 'Good morning,' she said sedately, refusing to respond to the sight of him in swimming trunks, drops of water polishing his sleek, tanned torso, his hair ruffled as though he'd merely run the towel over it.

His assessing look sent little ripples of excitement from nerve to nerve. 'Good morning. I won't be long—no, stay there. I can get my own breakfast when I've changed.'

And he disappeared into the bedroom.

Her heartbeat soared uncomfortably when he reappeared, dressed in a casual pair of trousers and a short-sleeved shirt. Chosen for him by whom? His mother? No, she'd died several years ago. A lover?

Someone who knew him very well, because the colour matched his eyes.

Without preamble, he said, 'We need to talk.'

Jo tried to match his pragmatic unemotional tone. 'When you've had your breakfast. Would you like some coffee?'

He gave her another of those straight looks. 'If you're having some yourself. You don't need to wait on me. I'm capable of making my own coffee. And my own meals.'

'It's habit,' she said calmly. 'I acted as Tom's hostess, so I do it automatically.'

Actually, she needed something bracing—a cold shower would be good—but coffee was supposed to make one more alert. Besides, it meant she could get herself out of his way without looking stupid.

It was all very well to spend half the night telling

herself she could cope with the rush of sensual adrenalin that ambushed her every time she saw Luc, but when she actually laid eyes on him she had no defence against the hunger aching through her.

Getting to her feet, she said, 'Anyway, I need some and I might as well make some for you too.'

A false move, because he came with her into the kitchen and while she organised the coffee he assembled his breakfast.

She should have absented herself while he ate, she thought as she sat opposite him and drank her coffee. Sharing breakfast was altogether too intimate.

Mug in hand, she got to her feet and wandered across to the edge of the decking, keeping her gaze fixed on a bird with a yellow bandit's mask as it fossicked in the thick foliage of a hibiscus bush.

'What bird is that?' Luc's voice came from very close behind her.

She jumped, and whirled around. His hand shot out and gripped her shoulder for a moment, before releasing her.

Her breath locked in her throat as she stared mutely at him.

What could have been triumph gleamed for a moment in his hard eyes.

No! Gathering all her strength, Jo forced herself to turn away, to fix her gaze on the bird, now warily checking them out from the fragile shelter of the leaves.

In a distant voice she said, 'It's a native starling.'

The bird shot out from behind its leafy screen, flying straight and true, its alarm call alerting every other bird to a threat. Previously Jo had always been a little amused at the starlings' propensity for drama and flight.

Now she knew exactly how they felt. Threatened.

Quickly she said, 'They're an endangered species. Tom and the chiefs were working on a way to save them. Unfortunately, that means killing off the doves that were introduced a century or so ago. They compete with the starlings for food and nesting sites. And the locals like the cooing of the doves. They call them the lullaby birds. Sadly for the starlings, they can only produce that harsh screech.'

She was babbling and it was almost a relief when Luc said from behind her, 'I'm sure Tom would have overcome that prejudice. He didn't like being beaten—and, as we both know, he had a ruthless streak a mile wide.'

Indeed. And it would be useless to keep asking herself what on earth Tom had intended to bring about with his condition.

Only one thing was certain; he'd have had a motive.

Actually there was another certainty—neither she nor the man with her would ever learn what that motive was. Unless Luc MacAllister already knew...

But he'd said he didn't, and she was inclined to believe him. Quickly, before she could change her mind, she turned and asked, 'Do you really have no idea why Tom would have done this?'

His already tough face hardened. 'No idea apart from the one I suggested yesterday—a determination to force both of us to his will.'

CHAPTER FIVE

Jo SHOOK HER head. 'I can't believe that,' she said decisively and with some heat.

Luc recalled her objection of the previous day. *Tom wasn't like that.*

Not with her, perhaps.

But he didn't say it aloud. For some reason it irritated the hell out of him to accept she'd been Tom's lover. More infuriating was the fact that she wanted him to believe she'd felt something more for his stepfather than the mercenary greed of her sort of woman.

But what really made him angry was the fact that her kisses had almost convinced him she'd been feeling genuine desire.

With hard-won cynicism—based on being a target too many times to recall—he'd been sure he could tell the real thing from the fake. Clearly she was good...

Well, Tom only went for the best.

Abruptly he asked, 'Have you packed?'

Her answer was even more curt. 'Yes.'

She sat silently on the way to the airfield, watching Luc talk to the taxi driver from the back of the car. The tropical sun warmed the cool olive of his skin, outlined the breadth of his shoulders and limned his arrogant profile with gold when he glanced sideways at the resort as they drove past.

So, he turned her on. *Get over it—and fast*, she ordered, and dragged her gaze away to stare blindly at the pink and yellow flowers of the frangipani bushes along the road.

Oh, face the truth! He did much more than turn her on; he set her alight, stirring her blood so she had to fight stupidly erotic thoughts. And the memory of his kiss sent hot, secret shudders right down to her toes.

She had to make some rules—unbreakable ones. The first was obvious. No more kissing—it was too dangerous. She'd liked it far too much.

Actually, she accepted reluctantly, *liked* didn't come near it. She couldn't come up with words that described what Luc's kisses did to her.

And she wasn't going to try. Dwelling on her weakness was not only stupid, it was reckless and forbidden.

The private jet was a revelation, and provided some distraction. She tried not to stare like some hick, but the opulent, ostentatious décor was blatantly designed to impress. Which surprised her; Luc didn't seem a man to indulge in such crass showmanship.

'You don't like it,' he said as she looked around.

She gave him a suspicious glance. 'I don't have to, do I?' she asked sweetly.

He smiled. 'It's not mine. I chartered it because it's fast and safe, not for the interior decoration. Buckle up; we're ready to go.'

She watched Rotumea fall away beneath them, a

glowing green gem in a brilliant enamelled sea of darkest blue that faded swiftly to green. A mixture of emotions—part anticipation, part regret—ached through her heart.

Goodbye, Tom, she thought, before chiding herself for being overly dramatic.

'What's the matter?' Luc asked.

Startled, she looked up. 'Nothing,' she said quietly, wishing he weren't so perceptive.

After a disbelieving glance he handed her a magazine, a glossy filled with the latest in fashion. 'Is this all there is to read?' she enquired dulcetly.

'I believe it has excellent articles.' The amusement in his voice almost summoned a smile from her.

'Oh, that's all right, then.'

Whoever had told him that was right—it was both provocative and entertaining, as well as featuring the latest fashions.

Her incredulous gaze fell onto a photograph in the social pages. There stood Luc, elegantly dressed at some race meeting, and beside him a glamorous redhead.

His fiancée, according to the caption. Shocked into stillness, Jo blinked, forcing herself to keep her gaze on them, while something like cold rage squeezed her heart. How dare he kiss her when he was engaged?

A lean hand came over and flipped the magazine closed so she could see the publication date. A year and a half previously...

'Long out-of-date. Perhaps I could get a reduction in the charter fee,' Luc said. 'The week after that was taken she eloped with Tom's nephew. They're married now, with a baby on the way.'

'Oh,' Jo said inadequately, furious with herself because her first emotion was a violent relief, followed almost instantly by astonishment at the ironic amusement in his tone.

Clearly he hadn't grieved too long at the couple's betrayal.

She said, 'Tom's nephew? He didn't mention it.' Then wished she'd stayed silent.

'Possibly he didn't think you'd be interested,' he said negligently.

Or perhaps Tom hadn't considered it to be any of her business. He'd fleetingly referred once to a past relationship of Luc's with the daughter of an Italian billionaire, and she remembered a casual conversation about Luc's mother's hope he'd marry into the French aristocracy she'd come from.

Apart from that, nothing about Luc's personal life.

The seatbelt sign tinged off, and automatically she looked up. Luc met her gaze, his mouth curved into a satirical smile. 'I believe much the same thing happened to you,' he said coolly.

She went rigid. 'How did you know?'

'Don't look so startled.' He shrugged. 'When you moved in with Tom I had you checked out, of course.'

Outraged and a little afraid, she spluttered, 'You had a nerve!'

His gaze was keen and unreadable. 'As I said last night, welcome to the world of the rich and powerful. And your lover was a selfish pup to make you choose between your mother and him.'

'He didn't think—' She stopped again.

'Go on.'

It was her turn to shrug. Discovering that Kyle disliked her mother had been bad enough; what had shattered her was that he'd believed all the gossip about Ilona.

'He didn't like her,' she said stiffly.

'Why?'

Because he thought she'd been little better than a call girl. In their final argument before he'd left Jo he'd laughed in her face when she'd mentioned marriage, and told her brutally that no woman with a mother like Ilona Forman would be a suitable wife for him.

It still stung. Jo looked down at the magazine and turned the page, saying distantly, 'They just didn't get on.'

Luc nodded and bent to open a folder. After a few moments he realised that although he had a bitch of a meeting ahead of him, he couldn't concentrate.

Joanna's lover had probably realised her mother was being totally unreasonable to demand such devotion. She'd spent much of her daughter's childhood foisting her onto her sister while she flitted around the world on modelling shoots, walking the big catwalk events and being a muse to designers—whatever the hell a muse was.

At least she'd left her daughter enough money to start her business.

He had to admire Joanna for that. Even with Tom's help and advice, getting her skincare product out onto the marketplace, steering it into profit must have taken guts, creativity and hard work.

And loyalty to those who worked for her.

Not that he'd change his mind about her. And in six

months' time she'd be amply recompensed for her services to Tom.

Warily Jo sent a surreptitious glance his way. He was frowning as he read his documents, black brows drawing together over that uncompromising blade of a nose. Jo looked quickly back at the magazine, glad she wasn't the person or persons waiting for him to arrive in Auckland.

Shortly afterwards the steward came into the cabin with an offer of morning tea. Luc drank his the same way he drank coffee—black and to the point. Jo liked hers with milk, and after finishing it and one of the small muffins that accompanied it, she sat back on a wide sofa while Luc went back to his folder.

In Auckland it was raining, a soft autumn shower that stopped before the steward slid the door open. Shivering a little in the cool air, Jo hurried inside to be processed by customs and immigration officers.

Luc said abruptly, 'I'll organise an immediate advance of the money Tom left you.'

'Were there any conditions?' she asked with a snap.

'Bruce Keller wouldn't tell me if there were,' he returned indifferently. 'If he didn't say anything to you, then no, there were no conditions.'

She sighed. 'Thanks. And I'm sorry I bit—I'm already tired of this situation.'

And tired of being forced down a road she'd not planned to take. It hurt to think that Tom had done this to her—hurt more that her image of him was slowly crumbling.

'Think of the end result.' It was impossible to discern Luc's emotions from his voice. 'Give Bruce Keller the data and he'll make sure the money is in your bank account.'

Jo bit her lip. 'You have his contact details?'

Luc's brows lifted. 'I do.'

Well, of course. Clearly he thought he was dealing with an idiot. Heat warmed her face. If he hadn't whisked her so unceremoniously off the island she'd have been better prepared.

But she didn't care a bit what Luc MacAllister thought of her.

'Where are we going?' she asked, looking around as they left the building.

'To Tom's place on the North Shore.'

The house on the North Shore was about as different as anything could be from Tom's home in Rotumea, although it nestled into a garden of palms and luxuriant foliage beside a beach on Auckland's magnificent harbour. Jo examined the double-storeyed building of classic, clean architectural lines and much glass as the car eased up the drive.

'Very tropical in feel,' she observed when the car drew up outside a double-height door.

Luc sent her a narrow glance, clearly recognising the jibe. 'Tom's natural environment,' he said calmly, switching off the engine in front of a huge double door. 'Auckland has a pretty good climate for outdoor living. I'm sure you made the most of it while you lived here.'

'Of course,' she said automatically, then stiffened. She couldn't recollect having told him she'd spent her childhood in Auckland.

Of course, he'd had her investigated—hired some

sleazy private detective to poke around her life looking for dirt.

Distaste shivered through her, alleviated only by the cheering thought that it must have been a very boring investigation for whoever had done it.

Chin angled away from Luc, she got herself out of the car and went around to the boot where he'd stowed their cases. The soft sound of waves on the shore eased her tension a little, yet made her feel wrenchingly homesick for Rotumea.

One day at a time, she reiterated briskly, and reached in to get her pack from the boot.

Only to have Luc take it out. 'It's all right, I can manage,' she said stiffly.

'So can I.' After hauling his own suitcase free, he set off for the huge front door.

Baulked, she walked beside him, and was startled when the door was opened by a middle-aged man with an expressionless face.

He was Sanders, she was informed as Luc introduced them. Jo had never met a man with only one name before, and he seemed surprised when she held out her hand and said, 'How do you do.'

He shook it but dropped it as quickly as he could.

This was not at all like Rotumea, or the New Zealand she'd grown up in. Perhaps the two years she'd spent in the tropics had turned her into a yokel.

No, it was just that she'd become accustomed to the Rotumean way of doing things. In such an isolated society, almost everyone could find some blood relationship—however distant—so there was little social distinction. And Tom had fitted in really well—although, she conceded as she walked sedately into a high, light-filled entrance hall, he had been allotted the status of high rank in Rotumea…

As Luc would be. There was something about him that indicated strength—and not just of body. He moved with the lithe athleticism that spelt perfect health. One look at his hard countenance was all it took to appreciate the honed intellect and forceful personality behind his autocratic features.

'Is there something wrong with my face?'

His ironic voice brought her back to herself. Oh, hell, she'd been staring…!

'Not that I can see,' she said flippantly, hoping he wouldn't notice the heat burning across her skin. She looked around the high, spacious hall and breathed, 'This is lovely.'

'It was Tom's design.'

Surprised, she said, 'He didn't tell me he was an architect.'

'He wasn't, but he had definite ideas, and he worked closely with the architect, a chap called Philip Angove.'

'I've heard of him—I read an article not long ago that called him the only real successor to Frank Lloyd Wright.'

'I suspect he wouldn't exactly be pleased at the comparison, but he's brilliant.' Luc laughed. 'He and Tom had some magnificent differences of opinion, but Tom felt the result was worth the effort. I'll show you to your room while Sanders organises lunch.'

Her room was large, with its own wide balcony overlooking a pool—yet clearer evidence of Tom's profound love for the tropics. More palms and a wide terrace surrounded the pool, and the gardens featured the same hibiscuses that grew wild in Rotumea, but instead of the island's tropical abandon this garden had a lush, disciplined beauty.

'The en suite is through there,' Luc said, nodding at a door in the wall. He glanced at his watch. 'Lunch will be in half an hour—I'll collect you. If you like, Sanders can unpack for you.'

'No, thanks,' she said hurriedly. Sanders might be accustomed to doing such chores, but she wasn't accustomed to having them done for her.

Luc's smile was tinged with irony. 'There's nothing of that slapdash tropical informality in Sanders. He's British and has stern ideas about what is proper and what isn't. You'll get used to him,' he said. 'He, on the other hand, might find you bewildering.'

Childishly, she pulled a face at the door as it closed behind him, but quickly sobered, turning away to draw in a deep breath and set herself to unpacking. The wardrobe, she discovered, was a dressing room. She hung up the contents of her pack, smiling a little ruefully at the tiny amount of space her clothes took up.

But once showered and dressed in a shirt of clear blue over slender ivory trousers she walked across to the window and looked out beyond the pool. Beyond it, through the dark foliage of the pohutukawa trees that fringed all northern coastlines, she caught a glimpse of white sand and the sea.

Her main emotion, she realised with surprise, was a profound sense of homecoming.

Putting aside the fact that the man she was to share

her life with for six months thought she was little better than a prostitute, it was good to be back.

So she'd just keep out of Luc's way.

A knock on the door set her pulses haywire, forcing her to admit that she'd grossly oversimplified her emotions. The kisses they'd shared, backed up by Luc's admission that he wanted her, meant she'd never feel completely at ease with him.

With a silent heartfelt vow that she wasn't going to lose her head over him, she squared her jaw and opened the door, only to feel her foolish heart sing at the sight of male temptation in a business suit that moulded itself lovingly to his powerful frame.

'Ready?' he asked.

'Yes.' OK, so she was going to have to work on controlling her body's disconcerting response. She'd do it. Familiarity had to breed contempt. As her mother used to say occasionally, very few men were worth a single tear. Absolutely.

Lunch was set out on the wide roofed terrace leading to the pool. Without thinking, Jo picked three frilly, silken hibiscus flowers and arranged them in a scarlet dazzle at one end of the table.

Looking up, she caught Luc's eyes on her and realised what she'd done. 'Sorry,' she said, ignoring an odd quiver somewhere in the pit of her stomach. 'Habit dies hard.'

'Feel free.' He clearly couldn't have been less interested.

It wasn't the first time she'd eaten with him, yet the tension she always felt in his presence had become supercharged with a heady awareness that set her on edge.

Unlike Luc, who seemed fully in control. Trying to

match his cool reserve, she masked her inner turmoil, and they ate the meal like polite strangers.

She was relieved when he left for his very important meeting, but after a few irritating minutes spent wondering how he was dealing with whatever emergency he was involved in, she opened her elderly laptop and began to work on it.

The afternoon dragged. Sanders delivered her afternoon tea, followed by dinner without any sign of Luc.

Forget about him, she ordered, and applied herself even more rigidly to work.

A knock on her door near ten that night brought her head up from weary, frustrated contemplation of the screen. Heart jumping, she forced herself to walk sedately across the room and open the door.

'What's the matter?' Luc demanded after one penetrating glance.

'My computer's died,' she told him baldly.

He looked a little tired, his olive skin drawn more tightly over his autocratic features. Jo felt an odd impulse to tell him to go to bed and get a good night's sleep.

Fortunately it was derailed when he demanded, 'How much have you lost?'

'Nothing—it's all backed up—but it won't work, no matter what I do to it.' She would have liked to know how the important meeting had gone, but she didn't have the right to ask.

'Let me see it.'

Reluctantly she stood back to let him in. One grey glance took in the laptop set up on the makeshift desk, and he said, 'How old is that?'

'I don't know.'

'No wonder it died. It looks like a relic from the eighties.'

'Possibly it is,' she retorted with some asperity, 'but it's worked fine up until now.'

His stepfather wouldn't have been able to resist trying to find out the problem, but Luc said, 'You need a new one.'

'I know.' Jo didn't try to hide her frustration. Why did the wretched thing have to break down at the most inconvenient moment?

Luc gave her another of his penetrating looks. 'I'll lend you one of mine until you organise a new one.'

Surprised, she said, 'Won't you be needing it?'

'Not this one.' His incisive reply cut short her instinctive response to refuse.

Abruptly abandoning the computer, he went on, 'I forgot to tell you to let Sanders know about any food you're allergic to or dislike hugely, and he'll make sure it doesn't appear on the menu.'

'He's already asked, thank you, before he cooked dinner. But Luc, I can make my own meals—'

He gave her a brief smile. 'Not in his kitchen you won't.'

'Oh. OK.'

Clearly she needed to know the boundaries of Sanders' sphere of influence, but before she could ask tactfully, Luc said, 'Is there anything you need or want now?'

'No, thanks.'

He nodded. 'The computer will be here tomorrow morning—probably after I leave for another meeting, one that might last all day.' Grey eyes scanned her face. 'Go to bed,' he commanded. 'You look exhausted.'

'Fury with an inanimate object can do that to you,' she said wearily. 'Goodnight.'

She slept heavily, so soundly she didn't wake until after nine. Sanders appeared as she came down the stairs, and said, 'Mr MacAllister has left. He thought you might like to eat breakfast on the terrace.'

'That would be lovely,' she said, and smiled at him. His response was a mere movement of his lips, but he seemed a little less stiff than previously. 'I'm sorry if I've interrupted your routine. I don't normally sleep in.'

He unbent enough to say, 'Travelling has that effect on some people.'

It seemed a shame to waste such a glorious, beckoning day indoors, but once she'd finished work she could spend time in the pool.

The computer arrived around ten, with a desk and an office chair as well as a set of shelves and a filing cabinet. Under Sanders' supervision they were carried into her room and a temporary office was set up.

It worked well; the computer had been cleared and once she'd had a little more practice at dealing with its foibles she'd be fully confident with it. She ate lunch out on the terrace, and was on her way back to her room when the telephone on a hall table rang. Automatically she picked it up and said, 'Hello.'

'Who is this?' a woman demanded. 'Have I the wrong number? Is this Luc MacAllister's house?'

'Yes.' Answering had not been such a good idea, especially when she looked up and saw Sanders—more poker-faced than normal—advancing towards her, intent on taking over.

'Are you a cleaner?' the woman asked. 'Where is Sanders?'

Chagrined, she said, 'Sorry. He's on his way,' handed over the receiver to him and escaped.

But not fast enough to avoid hearing Sanders say, 'Certainly, Ms Kidd. I'll make sure Mr MacAllister gets your message.'

Whoever she was, Ms Kidd had no manners. And Jo had to endure a mortifying moment when Sanders told her that answering the telephone was his duty.

'Yes, I realised that,' she said ruefully. 'I'm afraid it was an automatic reaction.'

He relaxed infinitesimally. 'Mr MacAllister has all his calls screened except on his personal phone. You'd be surprised the sort of people who try to get in touch with him—reporters and such.' His tone indicated that reporters and poisonous snakes had a lot in common.

'I won't do it again,' she told him.

He nodded and said, 'Mr MacAllister's personal assistant has just rung. She'll be here in half an hour to take you shopping.'

'What?' she said, bewildered, before remembering the conversation about clothes she'd had with Luc.

'For tonight's dinner, I understand,' Sanders elaborated.

She'd pushed any thought about the dinner out of her mind, but had to admit to a secret relief that Luc had remembered.

CHAPTER SIX

LUC'S PERSONAL ASSISTANT turned out to be a superbly dressed woman in the prime of her life. At first Jo guessed her to be in her forties, but after half an hour or so in her company, she changed her mind. Sarah Greirson was probably the best-preserved sixty-year-old she'd ever come across. With a mind like a steel trap, an infectious sense of humour and an encyclopaedic knowledge of Auckland's best bargains, she made shopping for the dinner gown an amusing and fascinating experience.

In turn, she was intrigued by Jo's fledgling business. So much so that when they returned to the house Jo raced up to her room and returned with a jar of rehydrating cream.

'Thanks for being so helpful,' she said, and gave it to her.

Sarah looked taken aback. 'Are you sure?' she asked.

'Sure of what?' Luc said, appearing unexpectedly in the huge sliding doors that led out onto the terrace.

Jo jumped, colour beating up through her skin. Very aware of the older woman's perceptive gaze on her, she said swiftly, 'Of course I'm sure. I'll be interested to see how you like it.'

'I'm *very* interested in trying it out,' Sarah said cheerfully. 'Thanks so much.' She turned to Luc. 'And thank you for asking me to do this. Once I'd convinced her that hiring a dress would not be a good look we had a great time, and she'll be stunning.'

'Of course,' Luc said smoothly. 'She always is. I've got some papers for you before you leave, Sarah.'

Alone, Jo let out a ragged breath, and closed her eyes before walking out onto the terrace.

She always is... What was he up to? She waited until her heart rate levelled out, only for it to shoot up again when she turned to see Luc standing in the doorway, watching her with a quizzical amusement that brought another flush to her cheeks.

'Tired?' he asked, walking across to her.

'No—at least, yes, a bit.' She produced a smile. 'Sarah is a perfectionist in every sense of the word. Standing around has never been my thing, especially when people are inspecting me as though I'm a piece of meat, and discussing my measurements to the last centimetre.'

His brows lifted. 'You're pleased with the result?'

'It's a beautiful dress. And so are the shoes and the bag.'

Not to mention the new bra Sarah had insisted on, and the sheerest of tights.

She finished, 'Sarah has superb taste, and fortunately we agreed. I won't shame Tom. And I'll pay you for them when I get access to the money Tom left me.'

His expression didn't alter, yet a tenuous shiver snaked the length of her spine. 'You won't,' he said curtly.

She stopped herself from biting her lip, but ploughed on, 'That's why he left it, so I wouldn't be an expense on you. And, speaking of expenses—we need to talk about sharing them.'

Frowning, he said, 'We do not.'

Jo opened her mouth to expostulate, but the words died unsaid when he reached out and put a finger across her lips. Eyes widening, she froze, her heart thudding uncomfortably in her ears. Every nerve tightened; she could see a pulse beating in his throat.

He was too close—suffocatingly close. Her brain wouldn't work and she couldn't move.

Very quietly, in a tone that meant business, he said, 'I don't need any contributions to household expenses.'

'And I don't need charity—' she began, then stopped, stomach knotting because each word felt like a kiss against his finger. She could even taste him—a smoky male flavour that spun through her like a whirlwind.

He dropped his hand and stepped back. 'It's not charity. I want something from you.'

She'd just drawn a swift breath, but his final sentence drove it from her starving lungs. 'What?'

Her voice was too fast, too harsh, but she thought she knew what he wanted, and his proposition was going to hurt both her pride and her heart.

'Not what you think,' he said curtly, each word cutting like a whiplash. 'I don't need to buy or blackmail women into my bed.'

He paused. Jo waited, conscious of a vast feeling of relief alloyed by a sneaky and wholly treacherous regret.

When he resumed it was in that infuriatingly ironic tone. 'You're making heavy weather of this, Joanna. It's only for six months—in the grand scheme of your life barely long enough to consider.' He added on a cynical note, 'And think of the reward when it's over and you can thumb your nose at whoever you want to.'

Stung, she retorted, 'Thumbing my nose is not my style.' Her smile showed too many teeth. 'In fact, I don't believe I've ever seen anyone do it. Have you?'

'What a deprived life you've led,' he remarked idly. 'Children do it all the time.'

'Not me. Did you?'

He grinned. 'Only once. My mother caught me and after her scolding I never did it again. She said it was vulgar, and although I was too young to understand what that meant I understood it was bad.'

Intrigued, she said, 'So you were a good kid and obeyed her.'

He raised his brows. 'Of course,' he said. 'Didn't you obey your mother?'

'Most of the time,' she said wryly. Her indulgent mother had made up for the times she'd been away with treats and much love. A little raw at the memories, she asked, 'So what do you want from me?'

'A truce.'

Her brows shot up. 'I believe I suggested that not so long ago.'

'You did, and I agree—the least disagreeable way of coping with the next six months is to ignore the fact that we're forced to obey Tom's whim, and get on with our respective lives without getting too much in each other's way.'

Of course he was right. She should be glad he'd seen

reason—she *was* glad he'd seen reason and agreed with her. It was the sensible, practical, *safe* attitude.

Right now she needed safety very much.

So she nodded firmly. 'It's a deal,' she said and added rapidly, 'I've never been to a charity dinner. How do they run?'

'Drinks and mingling first, then excellent food, then a comedienne.' His smile held wry humour. 'I suspect the entertainer was chosen more for her looks than her wit.'

Some hours later, her hair coiled sedately at the back of her neck, Jo examined herself in the mirror. Wearing the clothes Luc had paid for, her make-up as perfect as she could get it, she thought dryly that she had one thing to thank heaven for—he hadn't held out his hand to seal the deal. She recalled only too vividly the way her intransigent body had responded to his touch.

As though champagne instead of blood coursed through her veins...

She was going to have to overcome this fascination, the way one look from those hard grey eyes sent chills—delicious, sparkly, *sexy* chills through every cell in her body.

'And you are just one out of a million or so women who probably suffer the same silly reaction whenever he looks at them,' she told her reflection, and turned—carefully—to pick up the evening bag Luc had also paid for.

She'd spent some time practising walking in the strappy shoes, but was still cautious. Two years spent in the tropics, where footwear was either sandals or thongs, hadn't prepared her for heels. She crossed her fingers against any chance of tripping.

Luc watched her come down the stairs, noting that Sarah had done a magnificent job. Critically he decided he preferred that sensual mass of amber hair loose, but the bun at the back of her neck certainly gave her an elegant, sophisticated air.

The ankle-length dress—a slim thing a shade darker than her hair—skimmed Joanna's curves. Too closely, he thought, his body tightening. He chided himself for being a fool; possessiveness had never been a problem in his previous relationships. He'd expected fidelity—

Where the hell had that thought come from? They were not in a relationship, and weren't going to be.

He resumed his survey, noting the swift burn of colour along her cheekbones. A piece of jewellery set off her slender wrist, a metal cuff the same colour as the dress.

And she walked like a queen, head held high, straight-backed and slender.

She looked exactly the way he wanted—like his lover, dressed by him, ready for him.

However, the glance she gave him when she reached the bottom of the staircase was narrowed, her smoky green eyes direct and challenging. 'I hope you think this was worth it,' she said with a lift of her square chin.

'Every cent,' he said coolly, enjoying the sparring.

'Which I'll pay back as soon as I get Tom's money,' she reiterated firmly. 'And you should give Sarah a nice bonus. She deserves it.'

He took her arm, feeling her tense against him as

he turned her towards the door. 'I don't discuss Sarah's salary.'

'I wasn't discussing her salary. I was subtly pointing out that I'm sure her job description doesn't include dressing your dinner partners.'

She smelt delicious, softly sensuous as a houri. To stop the swift clamorous surge from his body, he said, 'It includes whatever I want her to do. How are you getting on with the heels?'

'Warily. Ambling along the beach at Rotumea in bare feet is no training for heels this high.'

Her words summoned a vivid image—sleepy, golden and sleek as she rose from the hammock in her bikini, and again his body reacted with a fierce, primitive hunger. Controlling it was surprisingly difficult. 'Do you want me to walk you like this, or is it easier if you step out on your own?'

She relaxed a fraction. 'I hate to admit it,' she confessed, 'but it will probably be better for my confidence to lean on your arm.'

'In that case, use me as a prop whenever you want to.'

On the drive across the bridge he started to tell her about the charity, then broke off. 'I suppose you've already heard of this from Tom.'

'No,' she said. 'I knew he supported charities but he never spoke of them.'

'Possibly he thought you wouldn't be interested.'

'I'd say he realised I can't yet afford to support anything,' she said crisply. 'He wasn't the sort of man to boast about his generosity.'

He looked down at her, his teeth flashing white in a

humourless smile. 'I've never thought of Tom as being sensitive.'

'He did a lot of good for Rotumea and its people.'

'He could afford it, and he enjoyed his holidays there.'

Jo frowned at his dismissive tone. 'Didn't you like him?'

'He was a good stepfather,' he said evenly. 'Strict but very fair. He did his best for me, just as I'm sure he did his best for the islanders—for anyone who worked for him, in fact.'

He sounded as though he was discussing a schoolmaster, she thought and wondered again. Had the struggle for control after Tom's stroke soured their relationship too strongly for any repair?

At the venue they were ushered into a room filled with women in designer gowns and men in austere black and white. No one stared—or if they did, Jo thought, they made sure neither she nor Luc noticed. Yet she felt out of place and acutely self-conscious, especially when an exquisite woman swayed up to them, her smile a little set, her gaze softly shielded.

'Luc,' she breathed, and reached up to kiss him with all the aplomb of someone who knew she wouldn't be refused.

A fierce sense of denial ripped through Jo when Luc inclined his head so the woman's mouth grazed his cheek. She forced her stiff body to relax. Even that one syllable revealed who the woman was—the Ms Kidd of the phone call.

He straightened and said, 'Natasha, you haven't yet met Jo Forman, who's staying with me.'

He introduced them, adding, 'Natasha is the star of a very popular television show.' And with a smile at the other woman, he explained, 'Joanna has spent several years overseas, so she doesn't yet know anything about local television.'

What to say? Jo fell back on a platitude. 'Congratulations. I'll look forward to seeing it.'

In return, she got a practised smile and a look that was keenly suspicious. 'Thank you,' Natasha Kidd said sweetly. 'I hope you enjoy it.' She glanced up at Luc. 'I must go back to my friends, but I'd love to have a chance to chat later. So nice to meet you, Joanna.'

Her discomfort increased by a steely glance from Luc, Jo hoped her smile appeared genuine and unfeigned.

Everyone there seemed to know Luc; as waiters circulated with champagne and delicious nibbles a stream of people came up, and she was subjected to surveys that varied from veiled to avid. Like zookeepers viewing a rare animal for the first time, she thought, her sense of humour rescuing her.

Meticulously, Luc introduced them, mentioning that she owned her own skincare company.

Clever Luc. The topic interested everyone, and her feeling of dislocation began to ease.

Finally, some invisible signal indicated it was time to move. Luc took her arm, smiled down at her and said, 'Well done.'

'Thank you.' She hoped her smile showed no hint of challenge. 'What a lot of friends you have.'

His brows lifted. 'Not that many,' he told her. 'How many people do you call friends?'

And when she went to answer, he said coolly, 'Not acquaintances, or even people you like—but real friends? The sort you can ring at midnight and even if they're in bed with their latest lover they'll forgive you.'

Startled, Jo looked up, saw a glimmer of humour in the grey eyes and had to smile. 'None,' she said, dead-pan.

His smile set her heart singing. 'So what do you call a true friend?' he asked. 'Someone you can trust implicitly?'

'One who'll listen for an hour to me complaining when a new formula brings me out in a rash,' she said smartly.

His brows shot up. 'Has that happened?'

'Once. Turns out I'm allergic to one of the ingredients.' Jo totted up her friends, admitting, 'Actually, I can only think of three who'd listen for any more than twenty minutes. So I guess that gives me three good friends.'

'You're lucky,' he observed.

She stared at him. 'Yes, I suppose I am,' she said slowly. 'How about you?'

'One,' he said laconically.

Jo wasn't surprised. He didn't seem a man who'd give his trust easily, and a life spent in the cut-throat world of big business would have honed his formidable self-sufficiency.

Looking across the banqueting room, she caught Natasha Kidd's rapidly averted gaze and stifled an odd sense of foreboding. Was she Luc's lover?

Not yet, Jo thought, recollecting the hunger beneath

the other woman's lashes as she'd looked up at him. But possibly she had hopes, and saw Jo as an obstacle.

Jo wished she could tell her that any relationship she had with Luc was safe. But it was none of her business, and she had no right to interfere.

The evening was well run, the food magnificent, and in spite of Luc's reservations the beautiful comedienne proved both extremely funny and very clever. Their table companions were interesting and kept their curiosity within bearable limits. Again Luc mentioned her business, and to her delight one woman extolled the worth of her products.

And the amount donated to the charity exceeded expectations enough to cause excitement and applause.

A very glamorous evening, Jo thought when it was over. So why was she glad to be leaving?

She thrust the thought from her mind to concentrate on smiling and nodding as they moved through the crowd. Luc moderated his long strides and exchanged the odd word with various acquaintances, but made sure he didn't stop.

Natasha Kidd was nowhere in evidence, thank heavens.

Outside it was raining, harbinger of a tropical depression that had the north of New Zealand in its sights. Staring straight ahead as they drove across the Harbour Bridge, Jo thought how alarmingly intimate it was to be cocooned in warmth and dryness with Luc when outside the lights dazzled and flared in the rain.

'Tired?'

She shook her head. 'Not at all.'

'Did you enjoy yourself?' A note in his voice made her cautious.

After a moment's thought, she said, 'It was very interesting.'

His laugh startled her. 'I've seldom heard less enthusiastic praise.'

She shrugged. 'I didn't know anyone there except you, but everyone was pleasant, the dresses were stunning and the food was delicious. Didn't you enjoy yourself?'

'Mostly,' he said, almost as though startled by his admission.

Jo couldn't help wondering why.

But that thought went out of her head completely when she checked her email after she'd showered and got ready for bed. One from Meru in Rotumea made her heart jolt.

I'll contact you at ten tomorrow morning on the video—it's important.

CHAPTER SEVEN

JO STARED INTO the darkness, listening to rain that became heavier as the night wore on. Shards of confused dreams buzzed through her head—surely caused by Meru's ominous message, but somehow dominated by Luc's imposing presence. He'd just kissed her again…

No! She forced her wayward brain away from the memories. Worrying about Meru's message would play infinitely less havoc with her emotions than reliving those fevered moments. Even dreams of Luc's kisses had the power to set her pulse soaring.

Meru didn't flap easily, so whatever she had to discuss was not going to be good news.

The night seemed to drag on for ever, but eventually she fell asleep and dreamed again, waking to a dull light glimmering through the curtains. Rain beat against the windows, driven by a gale off the sea. Hastily she leapt out, but of course it was too early—Meru would still be in bed.

Still, there was work she could be doing. She opened the link on the computer, biting her lip as she waited for it to come through.

Nothing happened.

Angrily she stabbed at the keys, until a peal of thunder made her close down the computer and hastily switch off the power, grimacing in resignation. This tropical depression probably reached all the way from New Zealand to Rotumea, so it was more than likely there'd be no power on the island. So the communications system would be down.

Sighing, she accepted she'd have to possess her soul in patience, as her aunt would have said. Shower first, she decided, and then try again to see if Meru could get through.

But she'd only got halfway across the room when a noise erupted into the drumming of the rain—a violent crack that made Jo jump, and then a loud sighing crash.

'What—?' she gasped, swivelling towards the window.

She'd just pushed back the curtains when a knock on the door reminded her she was still in her nightgown, an elderly shift that finished at mid-thigh and was too transparent to be decent.

'Wait—I won't be a moment,' she called, and grabbed her dressing gown, also of faded cotton, though marginally less see-through than her gown.

She opened the door a fraction, her heart flipping when she saw Luc. 'What is it?' she asked.

Another bolt of lightning lit up Luc's unshaven face, followed by thunder rolling across the heavens.

'What happened?' she demanded.

'It sounds as though a tree's come down,' Luc said grimly, and strode into the room as the lights snapped off.

Together they peered out into the grey murk.

'Over there.' He pointed. 'On the beach front.'

Jo craned her head. Yesterday a large conifer had blocked the view of the outer harbour, but now she saw tossing, roiling waves as they pounded onto the shore.

'The Norfolk Island pine,' Luc said curtly. 'I'll collect Sanders and we'll make sure no one was walking past when it got struck.'

'I'll come with you.' She turned away, but Luc caught her arm.

As though on cue, lightning flashed again, and thunder rumbled like a distant cannon. Jo froze and for a moment the sound of the storm faded into nothingness against the reckless drumming of her heart.

Something kindled in Luc's hard eyes, but he dropped his hand and said harshly, 'You'd better get dressed.'

'All right.' Colour burned up from her breasts, and she took a step towards the wardrobe.

He went on, 'But stay inside. There's no need for you to get wet.' And you'd only be in the way, his tone implied.

Jo bristled, then managed to calm down. He knew this place; she didn't. More moderately she said, 'All right. But if I can help, let me know.'

'I will.'

He left then and she fled to the dressing room, closing the door behind her with a bang that echoed the drumming of her heart—only to have to open it again as she realised that without power she couldn't see.

How did Luc have that effect on her? Even with the door open the window provided hardly enough light to dress by, but she stripped off her night-clothes and

dressing gown and hauled on a T-shirt and trousers, re-
senting that now familiar, wilful excitement that ached
through her like an addictive drug.

The scream of a chainsaw cut through the keening of
the storm, bringing her back to the window. Red lights
were flashing from the road; someone had turned on a
car's hazard lights as a warning.

They were soon joined by other lights as emergency
services arrived, but the trees on the boundary prevented her from seeing what was happening, and the
persistent, inexorable rain kept her inside, pacing restlessly around her room and trying hard to think of anything other than Meru's email.

Half an hour after the power had been restored she
still couldn't contact Rotumea. She had to content herself with sending an email making another time for a
video conference with her manager, before going downstairs.

Sanders appeared silently and sketched a small smile.
'Good morning. Breakfast is ready if you are. Mr Mac-
Allister asked me to tell you not to wait for him.'

She was drinking coffee when Luc's voice brought
her to her feet. After a moment's hesitation Jo went out
of the room, stopping when she saw Sanders coming
along the hall.

'I thought I heard Luc,' she said.

He allowed himself a small smile. 'Mr MacAllister
is in the mudroom getting out of his wet-weather gear.'
He indicated a hallway. 'Second door on the right.'

Mudroom? After a second's hesitation, Jo headed for
the second door. Luc was shrugging out of a waterproof
jacket, his hair darkened and glossy against his head,

his features somehow made more pronounced by the shadow of his beard.

He looked up as she came in and his eyes narrowed. 'What's the matter?'

'Nothing,' she said automatically, wondering if her restlessness was painted in large letters on her face. She held out her hand and took the wet coat from him. 'I can't get through to Rotumea. How is it outside?'

'Give me that.' He whipped the coat from her and turned to hang it up, giving her an excellent view of broad shoulders dampened by rain.

The room suddenly seemed far too small and she wished she hadn't come. Why had she?

Because she wanted to make sure he was all right.

How stupid was that!

Hastily she said, 'I wondered if the tree had fallen near any houses.'

'It missed the nearest place by a few feet, although it gave everyone there a hell of a fright. They were lucky. We've cleared enough off the road for traffic to get through now.'

'That's good,' she said, hoping her expression was as cool as his.

He frowned. 'You look a bit wan. Did the rain keep you awake?'

'No,' she said too abruptly.

'Then what did?' He reached out to trace the skin beneath her eyes with a fingertip. 'These dark circles weren't caused by *nothing.*'

He hadn't moved any closer, but his touch set an exquisite anticipation singing through her. Her breath locked in her throat and she couldn't move, couldn't think of anything other than Luc's dark face, intent and purposeful as he scrutinised her.

She swallowed and managed to produce something she hoped sounded like her usual voice. 'I just had a restless night.'

'So did I,' he said, his voice suddenly harsh. 'I wonder if it's for the same reason.'

Jo squelched a nervous urge to lick her lips. 'Who knows?' she said, and managed to summon enough motivation to move back a step. 'You'd better have a shower before you start to get cold.'

His mouth quirked upwards. 'See you later, then.'

Stiff-shouldered, Jo walked away, hoping he didn't realise just how strongly his male charisma affected her.

But how could he not? Luc was experienced; Tom had told her once that he'd been a target for women ever since he'd arrived at puberty.

Everything about him proclaimed a man who accepted the elemental power of his masculinity, just as he accepted his brilliant brain and formidable character. He deserved more than to be a target—a horrible term. It made her feel ashamed of being a woman. He deserved a wife who'd love him.

Where had that thought come from?

Jo shook her head impatiently. She was being idiotic. Luc MacAllister would do exactly what he wanted when it came to choosing a woman to marry. She had her own pressing concerns to deal with right now. Crossing her fingers, she took refuge in her room.

And heaved a huge sigh of relief when at last Meru's face appeared on the screen before her—a relief that rapidly dissolved after one look told her to brace herself.

'What's wrong?' she blurted.

Without preamble Meru said, 'I heard something from my cousin yesterday that is…a problem. You know my cousin Para'iki?'

'Yes, of course.' He was a chief. Jo's stomach tightened in anticipation of a blow.

'Jo, the Council have received an offer for the plant essence—with much more money than we are paying.'

'Did he say how much—and who was it from?'

Frowning, Meru said, 'I don't know how much, but more—he said a lot more. As for who—' She gave the name of a worldwide cosmetic and skincare concern owned by a huge corporate entity.

'Why them?' Jo said shakily. 'They cater to the midstream market, not to ours. Why do they want the essence? It's scarce and it's expensive…'

'I don't know, but it seems to me that if they are now deciding to expand into the upper bracket of the market, this would be a good way to do it.'

'Yes, of course.' Jo let out a long breath. 'Does Para'iki have any idea how the other chiefs feel about this?'

Meru sighed. 'Nobody will know until they have finished discussing it, and that could—*will*—take weeks,' she said dolefully. 'It is not a thing to be decided without much thought and care—you know that.'

No, the decision wouldn't be made lightly. The chiefs had to take a lot more into consideration than their verbal agreement with her. They had to plan for the future of Rotumea and its people.

Meru said worriedly, 'My cousin said to tell only

you and to ask that you tell no one else until the decision is made.'

Jo swallowed. 'Of course I won't.'

The older woman said, 'He also said that Tom signed a paper with them when you were setting up the business; do you know what that was?'

Startled, Jo asked, 'A paper? Do you mean a legal document?'

'I think it must have been, or perhaps not—they would need nothing legal from Tom, his word was enough. But my cousin thought it would do no harm to remind the Council what Tom had promised...'

Tom had spoken for her during the negotiation process, but as far as Jo knew that was all he'd done. Her bewilderment growing, she said, 'I don't know anything—haven't heard anything—about a document. Tom certainly didn't mention it.'

'But perhaps you should look for one.' Meru sounded troubled. 'He was very respected, Jo. It is probably not important, but it might be.'

'I will.' Although it was foolish to hope that somehow there might be something that would save the day. Tom's papers had gone to the solicitor, who'd surely have let her know if anything concerned her, but she'd check. Just in case...

She produced a smile. 'Meru, thanks so much for letting me know. Please thank your cousin for me too. And remember—whatever happens, you and everyone on Rotumea will be fine.'

'Yes, but what about you?'

'I'll manage,' Jo said as confidently as she could. 'Don't worry about me.'

But when she'd closed the link she sat with her eyes closed while thoughts tumbled through her brain, each one heavier with foreboding than the last.

Only for a moment, however. After a ragged breath she stood, exhaled and took in a painful breath, then straightened her shoulders. Worrying wasn't going to help. First she needed to concentrate on keeping the business going. And then she should make plans in case the chiefs decided against her.

And once she got back to Rotumea she'd look for that document, if it existed, even though she couldn't see how anything Tom had signed or written could possibly make a difference.

Logically, a huge corporation could offer a much better deal than she had, even if she used all of Tom's legacy when it was finally hers. He'd warned her that relying on a verbal agreement was dangerous, although he'd acknowledged that on Rotumea it was common practice. Had that mysterious piece of paper been some sort of safeguard?

As soon as she got back to Rotumea she'd look for this document—if it existed.

But oh, it would be heartbreaking to give up the business she'd created and worked so hard for.

A sharp knock snapped her head around. Pinning a smile to her lips, she walked across and opened her door.

Luc's intent gaze searched her face. With an authority that sparked instant resistance in Jo, he demanded, 'What's worrying you?'

She lifted her chin. 'It's got nothing to do with you.'

His brows climbed. 'I'm taking that as a refusal to discuss the matter.'

And not liking it, judging by his tone. Had no one ever refused him before?

Jo clamped her lips on the smart answer that sprang to mind. It would be stupid—downright foolhardy— to add to the mixture of emotions and sensations he aroused in her.

As calmly as she could, she told him, 'It's just something I have to deal with.'

'Does it concern the young cub who made an idiot of himself over you on Rotumea?' His voice didn't alter, but his eyes were hooded.

For a moment she didn't realise who he was talking about. Sean had receded into a distant past. Memory jolted into action, she said shortly, 'No, it has absolutely nothing to do with him. It's not personal.'

And parried another piercing scrutiny until, apparently satisfied, Luc nodded. 'Your business, then.' And before she could answer, he finished, 'All right. There's obviously a problem, so if you want to talk it over, I'm available.'

'Thank you.' Luc's disconcerting way of swinging from autocratic command to something approaching support unsettled her.

And warmed her dangerously.

Possibly after six months she'd be used to it. An odd pang of regret hit her. If only they'd met as strangers, without his preconceptions of her relationship to Tom affecting his attitude...

Stupid, stupid, *stupid*! If it weren't for Tom they'd never have met at all—in normal life they moved in circles so distant they might as well live in different galaxies.

But she wished Tom had told her more about his stepson. Understanding Luc would have helped her, given her some guidelines on how to deal with the situation, instead of groping blindly, fighting against an attraction that was doomed to frustration.

Luc said, 'What are you thinking?'

How was he able to read her mind? Shaken, she said hastily, 'This whole business—you, me, enforced togetherness—is weird. Even though I know it's useless, I can't help wondering why Tom insisted on it.'

Luc bit back a short answer and said more temperately, 'It's quite simple. All his life Tom succeeded at doing exactly what he wanted, and I expect he couldn't resist extending his influence after his death.'

And watched with a sardonic amusement as her head came up and that firm chin angled in challenge.

'Whenever we talk about him we seem to be speaking of two different people,' she said, her gaze steady.

The way she idolised his stepfather was beginning to rub some unsuspected sensitivity in him to the edge of rawness. Luc resisted the urge to tell her to grow up, to accept that men behaved differently to the women who shared their bed.

Especially if they were young and lovely...

Into his mind there danced the image of her that morning, with her magnificent mane of hair tousled around her face above shabby night-clothes. He'd like to see her in satin, or something silken that clung lovingly to her breasts and revealed her long, elegant legs.

His breath quickened as he imagined running his hands through that hair, turning her face up to his…

Clamping down on a savagely primal response, he said, 'You're twenty-three, aren't you?'

She lifted startled eyes to meet his. 'Yes. What has that to do with anything?'

'It's old enough, I'd have thought, to realise that people present a different face to every person.'

Jo thought about that for a moment, before returning sweetly, 'That's a huge generalisation, and do you have the research to back it up?'

Taken by surprise, he laughed. 'Spoken like a true scientist. No, but if it's been done I'll find it. I'm giving you the benefit of my experience.'

'Very cynical experience,' she shot back, daring him with another swift tilt of her chin.

Luc could see why Tom had been intrigued by her—apart from the physical allure of young curves and burnished skin, of course. She'd have been a challenge, and Tom enjoyed challenges.

As did he.

'I don't consider myself a cynic,' he said coolly. 'I've learnt to be careful in relationships, but that happens to most of us, I imagine.'

Shrugging away the memory of a previous lover, paid to rave to a magazine about his prowess in bed, he said, 'Once most people get past adolescence they guard against flinging themselves into relationships without first making sure both parties understand the implications and expectations.'

She pulled a face. 'You make love sound like a business deal.'

'Love, no. It's marriage that's the business deal,' he said cynically.

She gave him a long, assessing stare. 'I bet you'd insist any future wife sign a pre-nuptial agreement.'

'Of course.' Too many promising entrepreneurs—including several mentored by Tom—had been burned by reckless marriages that ended in acrimony, forced to sell up to provide a former spouse with unearned income for the rest of her life.

He awaited her answer with anticipation.

'Actually, I think I probably would too.' She smiled. 'Although I've never considered it before, it does seem a sensible precaution.'

In any other woman in her situation he'd appreciate and understand such pragmatism. For some reason, in Jo it irritated him. For a moment he surprised himself by wondering what she'd be like in the throes of a heartfelt love, prepared to offer herself without thought of profit.

Cold, hard reality told him it would never happen. He doubted that such unconditional love existed. Even if it did, any woman who'd taken a man forty years older as a lover, bartering her body for the prospect of gain, was far too cold-blooded to allow herself to fall wildly in love. Joanna had made a very good show of shock when she'd discovered how much she'd inherited, but her chagrin at the condition in Tom's will revealed her true emotions. She'd expected the money to be hers immediately, to spend as she wished.

He owed it to Tom to make sure she learned how to take care of her inheritance, but once the six months was up she'd be able to do what she liked with it.

Yet somehow he couldn't see her squandering it.

Of course, plenty of courtesans had been excellent businesswomen…

He said coolly, 'Anyone who doesn't insist on a pre-nup is an idiot.'

With a look from beneath her lashes—a look she probably practised in front of her mirror—she said, 'I'll keep that in mind.'

No doubt of that, Luc thought caustically. He said, 'I'll be out for the rest of the day. What are your plans?'

'If this rain eases I'm going to spend the afternoon with a friend in Devonport,' she told him. 'You've seen her—I was with Lindy and her husband the night we… ah…met.'

He nodded. 'Do you have a current New Zealand driver's license?'

'Yes. But Lindy's coming to pick me up.'

He nodded. 'OK, then. I'll see you tonight.'

The rain did ease, although it didn't stop while Jo spent the day catching up with her friend in the small flat Lindy and her new husband were renting.

'Until we can save the deposit on a house,' Lindy said cheerfully. She grinned at Jo. 'Not everyone has your luck! Fancy living with a tycoon in a huge, flash mansion on the prettiest and most private beach on the North Shore. What's he like?'

Jo didn't need to think. 'Formidable.'

'Full of himself? Arrogant? Intimidating?'

'Not arrogant, and I haven't seen any signs of conceit.' She allowed herself a small smile before adding wryly, 'But very, *very* intimidating.'

'And gorgeous,' her friend supplied with a grin. 'Are you going to try your luck with him?'

'Do I look like an idiot?' Jo demanded, hoping her tone hid the embarrassment that heated her skin.

'No, but you're blushing.' Lindy laughed. 'Go on, admit you fancy him something rotten.'

'He's not my type,' Jo told her, picking up her teacup and hiding behind it.

'What's that got to do with anything?' Lindy asked. 'I never thought Kyle was your type either—he was too selfish—but you fell for him.'

'And look where that got me,' Jo said grimly.

Lindy knew of Kyle's betrayal. 'He was a louse,' she agreed. 'Charming and witty and great fun, and selfish to the core. I bet he wanted you to put your mother in a home.'

Jo bit her lip. 'Yes,' she said tonelessly.

'And when you wouldn't he slept with Faith Holden to punish you. I know you were shattered when he walked out, but I'm sure you realise now you're well out of it.'

'Of course I do.' Jo set her cup down. 'But Luc Mac-Allister is nothing like Kyle—and we don't have that sort of relationship anyway.'

'He was watching you that night at the resort on Rotumea,' Lindy persisted. 'And you were very conscious of him too.'

'He knew who I was, of course. I suppose he was checking me out.' She grinned. 'Though if he was watching anyone, it was you. You looked fantastic.'

'Honeymoons do that for you.' Lindy's infectious laugh rang out. 'You should try one some time. Seriously, you haven't let Kyle put you off men completely, have you?'

'Of course not,' Jo said firmly, ignoring the apprehension that contracted her stomach muscles. 'But right now I'm having too much fun with my business to spare the time for any sort of relationship, especially one as big as marriage.'

'Well, enjoy your stay with Mr Gorgeous Tycoon. And don't try to fool me into thinking you're not just the teeniest bit lusting after him, because I won't believe you.'

'I'm not into wasting my time,' Jo said a little shortly. 'He's had a couple of serious affairs—one with that stunningly beautiful model Annunciata Someone, and the other was with the almost as stunning Mary Heard, who writes those brilliant thrillers. Clearly he likes beauties in his bed, and I know my limitations.'

'You might not be model-beautiful, but you've got style,' Lindy said loyally. 'Anyway, I'm not suggesting you fall in love with the man—that would really be asking for trouble.'

Jo looked at her with affection. 'Exactly,' she said. 'Don't worry about me—I'm not planning to do anything at all for six months but cope with Luc MacAllister as best I can, and run my business.'

'OK, but you're selling yourself short. Even if you don't want to fall in love with the man, I bet he's fantastic in bed.' She fanned her cheek with one hand and laughed at Jo's startled face. 'Don't look so shocked— marriage hasn't stopped me appreciating an alpha male!'

What startled Jo was the jealousy that ripped through

her—a fierce, quite unwarranted possessiveness she'd never experienced before.

Lindy sighed. 'Funny how a woman just knows, isn't it? Some men just kind of reek of sex appeal, and they don't even have to be handsome—although it helps if they look as good as your tycoon. I wonder what clues us into it?'

'I don't know, and I'm not going there,' Jo said cheerfully. She glanced at her watch and said, 'I'd better go, Lindy.'

'Oh, stay for dinner. We can run you home afterwards, and it would be so nice to have dinner with you.'

Jo hesitated. 'I don't have a key,' she said, 'so I'd have to be back at a reasonable hour.'

'That's not a problem. We're early birds. My beloved gets up at some ungodly hour in the morning to run umpteen kilometres before breakfast. Should you let someone know?'

Sanders took the news with his usual taciturnity, and they organised for her to be home by ten. Smiling, she told Lindy, 'He sounded just like my mother used to.'

Lindy said with awe, 'Your Luc has a *manservant*?'

'He's not mine! And it's Tom's house—*was* Tom's house—so I guess Sanders was Tom's employee.'

'Good heavens… Is he a kind of valet?'

'I don't think so—more a general factotum and cook, which he does extremely well. The whole set-up is way out of our league, Lindy.'

Just before ten that night Sanders opened the door to her and said, 'Good evening.'

Jo acknowledged him and turned to wave Lindy and

her husband goodbye. 'Thank you, Sanders. I wonder when this rain is going to stop.'

'Not for another couple of days, according to the weather forecast.' Sanders ushered her inside. 'It's a very slow-moving tropical depression. They're forecasting floods in the upper North Island tomorrow.'

He paused, then said, 'Mr MacAllister isn't at home yet. He rang to say he'd be late. Is there anything I can get you?'

'No, thanks,' she said, stifling a suspicious regret.

Up in her room she showered and got into her nightclothes, then sat down at the computer. Nothing from Rotumea… Sighing with frustration, she closed the computer down.

Not that she expected any news so soon, but it irked her to be away at this delicate time. She had no doubt Meru and Savisi would be lobbying tactfully for her, but she really needed to be there herself.

Tom, you really made a mess of this, she thought dismally, getting up to wander across to the window. Of course he couldn't have foreseen this particular situation, but the offer to the chiefs had come at the very worst moment.

Conservative to a man, the members of the Council would be more likely to listen to their relatives who worked for her, but even so… She should be there, planning strategy.

The conversation with Meru echoed through her mind. Papers…

Some small door in her brain popped open. 'Of course!' she breathed, closing the curtains and turning back to the room.

If Tom had hidden papers she knew where they'd be—in the old Chinese chest where he kept his precious whisky.

He'd shown her the secret panel once, laughing when she'd expressed dismay that it was empty.

Perhaps there was now something in it...

She wasn't going to sleep tonight. The hours stretched ahead of her, filling her with tormenting fears that drove her downstairs to a bookcase in what Luc called the morning room.

It contained an eclectic selection of books ranging from bestsellers to local histories, one of which she chose. Clutching it, she tiptoed back up the stairs and had just opened her bedroom door when she heard a sound behind her.

Every sense springing into full alert, she stopped and swivelled around. Luc was a few paces behind her, saturnine in his black and white evening clothes. He looked...magnificent.

And vaguely menacing. Feeling oddly foolish, she swallowed and scanned his unreadable expression, heat flooding her skin. 'Oh. Hello. I went down for a book.'

'And have you found what you were looking for?' he enquired coolly.

CHAPTER EIGHT

LUC'S VOICE WAS deeper than normal, the words almost guttural. His gaze, narrowed and darkening in the semi-gloom of the hall, never left Jo's face. She saw heat in the depths of his eyes, and something else—a keenness her body reacted to with a sharp, frightening hunger.

Run! Every nerve and muscle tensed at the instinctive warning. Like a shield, she held up the book so that he could see it. 'Yes, thank you,' she said too rapidly, clumsily half-turning in an attempt to escape his penetrating scrutiny.

Her heart was hammering so loudly she was sure Luc could hear it, and a delicious, tempting weakness dazzled her mind.

Run—run while you can...

Yet her body resisted the command from her brain, refusing to obey even when Luc reached out to rest the tip of one long finger on the traitorous pulse at the base of her throat.

Eyes holding hers, he asked in that roughened voice, 'Are you afraid?'

Without volition, Jo shook her head. 'Of you?' Her voice was husky and low. 'No.'

'Good.'

If she'd heard nothing more than satisfaction in the single word she might have found the self-possession to pull away. But it seemed torn from his throat, raw with desire, as though he too had fought this since their gazes had clashed in the sultry, scented warmth of a tropical night.

It's too soon, the nagging voice of caution insisted. For once, Jo wasn't listening—didn't want to hear. Her whole being was concentrated on the subtle caress of Luc's finger while it slid from the pulse in her throat down to the first button of her loose shift.

Her breath came faster, keeping time with her heart, with her racing blood, with the emotions and sensations that surged through her, catapulting her into a place she'd never been before.

She craved Luc with a hunger powerful enough to wash away everything but that blazing need. And this time she didn't try to fool herself, as she had with Kyle. This wasn't love. She expected nothing more from Luc than fulfilment of desire, the unchaining of the passion—intoxicating, compelling and intense—that had been smouldering inside her.

He was experienced enough to discern the need flashing through her. In a rigidly controlled voice he asked, 'Joanna, is this what you want?'

For a second, a heartbeat, she wavered.

Until he bent his head and kissed the smooth skin his hand had revealed, his mouth a brand against her sensitive flesh, his subtle, fresh male scent overwhelming her feeble defences.

'Joanna?'

His lips against her skin were exquisite, shocking. Her breasts lifted when she dragged in a breath and muttered, 'Yes.'

He gave a smothered groan and lifted his head and kissed her mouth, and she surrendered. Luc kissed her as though he was dying for her, as though she had been lost to him and was now found again—as though he had longed for her during too many hopeless years...

And she kissed him back, glorying in his hunger, in the powerful force of his body, in the sensual magic they made together.

And then Luc lifted his head and demanded, 'Are you protected?'

Stunned, she stared at him, saw his eyes harden, and he said curtly, 'Tell me.'

Jo bit back a wild urge to lie. 'No. No, I'm not.'

He said something beneath his breath, something she heartily agreed with, and let her go.

'I don't have anything either,' he said.

Shivering, she stood still while the rain poured down outside, the sound of tears, of pain and loneliness. Her fierce physical frustration gave way to bleak humiliation.

It took every ounce of courage she possessed to mutter, 'I'll go, then,' and turn blindly towards the door.

'Joanna—'

She shook her head. 'No, leave it at that,' she said, fumbling for the handle. It wouldn't open and she flinched when his hand covered hers and twisted the opposite way.

For a few seconds his warmth enfolded her, his grip

tightening as though he didn't want to release her, and then the door gave way and he stepped back.

Shaking inwardly, she shot through the door and turned to close it, forcing herself to look up as she searched for words to say that might break the tension. None came.

In the darkness he seemed even taller, looming like some image from a dream.

'It's all right,' he said, each word level and cold. 'I can control my baser urges, if that's what you're afraid of.'

Her chin came up. 'I'm not.' She refused to admit even to herself that she wished—oh, for just a second— that Luc MacAllister wasn't always in control.

With a sting in her voice, she said, 'And I thought calling desire a base urge had departed with the Victorians. Goodnight, Luc.'

The door closed firmly, its small click barely audible above the renewed thudding of the rain.

Luc turned and headed for his own room, cursing his unruly body.

And his stupidity in not making sure he'd been prepared. He knew why; he'd been confident of his immunity. The fact that Jo had been his stepfather's mistress should have quenched his dangerous, unwelcome hunger.

But when he'd held her, kissed her, all he'd thought of was taking her, of making slow, deliberate love to her until she forgot every man she'd ever had before him, until she was lost in her own need.

For him.

Had she been faking it? He strode into his bedroom

and switched on the light, his expression set and hard.
He didn't think so—and in his youth he'd gained enough
experience of the wiles of women to judge whether their
passion was real or assumed.

Desire could be faked, but that delicate shudder he'd
felt beneath his hand, the heat of her exquisite skin on
his palm, the rapid throbbing of the pulse in her throat,
the widening of her eyes as she'd looked up at him—all
spoke of real hunger.

So, she wanted him.

Making love to her would have rid him of this itch,
because that was all it was—nothing personal, merely
a primitive heat in the blood. Calling it anything else
would be giving it an importance it didn't possess.

But they had to spend six months together. Making
love to Joanna would be stupid for so many reasons…

He walked across to the windows and looked out
at the rain. He'd like to be somewhere wild right now,
watching waves crash against cliffs.

The memory of Joanna's face as she'd closed the
door against him played across his mind. Seductive
lips, made a little more sensuous by his kiss, the smoky
depths of her eyes half-hidden by long lashes, the faint,
elusive fragrance of her warm satin skin…

His body hardened, his hunger so powerful he had
to lock every muscle to stop himself from swivelling
and walking back to her room. His hands folded into
fists at his sides.

Control of his life had been wrenched from him. The
months ahead loomed like a term of imprisonment or a
journey into forbidden territory.

Tom, you bastard, just why the hell did you set this up? What was going through your devious mind when you designed that will?

When Jo woke the rain had stopped. She blinked at the brilliance that glowed through the curtains, colour burning through her skin as memories swarmed back—of Luc holding her against his powerful, aroused body... and the erotic dreams her untrammelled mind had conjured during her sleep.

She wanted Luc with something like desperation. It was all very well to realise that going to bed with him would have been the most stupid, reckless, dangerous thing she could have done.

Her body didn't agree.

Driven by restlessness, she got up and pulled back the curtains, trying to be grateful for the iron control that had put an end to their lovemaking.

Respect wasn't something she'd expected from Luc, but it seemed he respected her decision that the game wasn't worth the candle.

And in turn she owed him respect for his instant acceptance.

With Kyle it had been different—he'd been eager for sex almost immediately, calling her an ice maiden when she'd refused. He'd insisted that he'd make sure nothing happened. She'd been steadfast, and later he'd laughed about it, telling her his words had been angry because he'd loved her so much, and her refusal had seemed cold and unfeeling...

Like an idiot she'd believed him. She should have guessed then that for Kyle his own needs came first.

She stared down at the glinting, dancing water in the big pool. Working with figures was her least favourite part of being a businesswoman, but she needed that discipline right now. Not only would it drive away the memories that fogged her brain with delicious thoughts of Luc's passion, it would force her to concentrate on what was really important.

But before she started on the accounts she'd ring Lindy, get the name of her doctor and see if she could wangle an appointment.

For a moment she wavered. Wouldn't getting protection make her more vulnerable to the hunger prowling through her?

What if somehow she found herself in Luc's arms again—surely it would be easier to keep her head if she was faced with the prospect of pregnancy?

Not going to happen, she thought stoutly as she pulled on her bikini and wrapped a sarong around her. Now that she knew how susceptible she was to Luc she'd be forewarned. Getting protection would simply be a sensible precaution—one both her mother and her aunt had insisted was the mark of a responsible woman.

Ignoring a treacherous flutter in the pit of her stomach, she picked up a towel and a change of clothes. Something told her that the silent Sanders would not approve of wet people wandering through the house, so there was bound to be a cabana or pool-room—whatever they called such an amenity.

There was. Sanders himself showed her how to get there. And very luxurious it was too—as immaculate as the rest of the house. Nothing like the house on Rotumea, she thought, aching with sudden grief. This place had been decorated by someone with exquisite taste. The house on Rotumea hadn't been decorated at all—Tom had just bought what he liked.

Dismay gripped her when she realised Luc had beaten her to the pool, tanned arms cutting incisively through the water, wet hair slicked into darkness. When he saw her he stood up.

Jo swallowed. He was too much—all sleek, burnished skin with the long, powerful muscles of an athlete. Hastily she said, 'Oh, hi. Great minds and all that…'

His expression was unreadable. 'I'll be out in a moment,' he said, almost as though conveying a favour.

'No need. I don't take up much room.'

He raised his brows but said nothing before diving back under.

Possibly exorcising the same demon she'd been wrestling with all night—a physical frustration so intense it burned. Jo dived in neatly and began to swim lengths too, determined to ignore the image of broad, water-slicked shoulders and chest—and the tormenting memories of how secure she'd felt in his arms…

She swam with steady strokes, forcing herself to focus on counting laps, hugely relieved when Luc hauled himself out.

The sun beat down with gathering heat, but she kept swimming until Luc called from the side, 'Breakfast.'

'Coming.' She finished the length before climbing out.

Even in a short-sleeved shirt and light trousers, he looked tall and powerful, very much in command.

Made uneasy by his unsmiling regard, she walked briskly towards him.

'It's all right,' he said curtly. 'I'm not going to leap on you.'

'I know that,' she retorted, embarrassed by a stupid blush.

'You're not acting as though you believe it.'

To which she had no answer. 'I'll get dressed and be out shortly,' she told him and forced herself to walk at a slightly slower pace past him.

Her shower was the swiftest on record, although her fingers were clumsy as she pulled on her pareu and combed her hair back from her face, wishing it didn't curl so obstinately. The pareu clung to her damp skin, revealing bare shoulders and every curve of her body. Under Luc's hooded scrutiny, clothes that were normal everyday wear on Rotumea—her bikini, the pareu— somehow seemed to constitute an overt attempt at seduction.

She bared her teeth at her reflection, braced herself and went out, her head held high. Luc was standing in the shade of the jasmine sprawling across the pergola, talking into a cellphone, his brows drawn together.

He looked up and something flashed into his eyes, a flaring recognition of what had passed between them the previous night. Her skin tightened.

This was not a good idea…

He said something sharp and conclusive into the phone, snapped it shut and strode towards her.

'You'll be cold,' he said. 'I keep forgetting you've spent years in the tropics.'

'Not that many. This is fine, but I'll sit in the sun instead of the shade.'

He nodded. 'I'll pull out the table.'

Before they sat down he asked, 'Are you wearing sunscreen?'

'Yes.' Skin like hers was very much at risk from New Zealand's unforgiving sunlight.

'So these freckles weren't caused by the sun?' He indicated her nose, where five pale gold dots lingered.

She stiffened, only relaxing when it was clear he wasn't going to touch her. 'They're relics from my childhood,' she told him. 'Even though my mother and aunt insisted I wear sunscreen all the time—and my aunt used to make me wear an island hat whenever I went outside in Rotumea—I still got freckles. These ones just don't want to go.'

'They're charming,' he said coolly. 'How do you manage to achieve that faint sheen, as though you're sprinkled with gold dust?'

Heat flamed in the pit of her stomach. Trying for a light rejoinder, she said, 'I've called my freckles lots of things, but never charming. As a kid I hated them. As for gold dust—it's a pretty allusion, but the colour's entirely natural.' Keeping her gaze steady with an effort of will, she returned his scrutiny. 'You're lucky. That built-in Mediterranean tan must be a huge help in resisting the sun.'

'It is,' he said casually. 'I don't rely on it entirely, however.'

All very civilised, she thought as she picked up a napkin, sedately unfolding it into her lap.

Watching them, hearing them no one would know that last night they'd kissed like famished lovers...

He said, 'I'm going to ask a favour of you.'

'What sort of favour?' she asked warily.

'An easy one for you to carry out, I hope. I'm asking for your discretion. I'd rather you didn't divulge anything of Tom's will or your relationship with him while we're staying together.'

Whatever she'd expected, it wasn't this. Frowning, she said, 'I'm not ashamed of anything I've done, if that's what you think. And I'm not going to lie about—'

'I'm not asking you to lie,' he interrupted austerely, 'but there's bound to be gossip.' He indicated the table with a sweep of his hand. 'Help yourself—or Sanders can cook breakfast for you if you want. And if you'd like coffee, I'll have some too.'

'No, thanks.' She helped herself to cereal and fruit and yoghurt, and poured the coffee.

Luc resumed, 'There's already been speculation about your place in his life. It will make things less stressful for everyone if you refuse to discuss your relationships with him or with me.'

He was clearly bent on damping down that speculation, but she felt obliged to point out, 'Usually a "No Comment" is taken as confirmation. If anyone is rude enough to ask, I'll tell them the truth—that my aunt was his housekeeper, and after she died I took over her position.'

His brows rose. Had he expected her to resist? She said, 'But how do we explain my presence with you?'

'We don't,' he said calmly. 'We fly back to Rotumea once I get this mess here cleaned up.' He looked at her narrowly. 'You did well the other night.'

'I'm not entirely sure in what way,' she said crisply, feeling sorry for whoever had created the mess he was dealing with.

He shrugged. 'It's called networking, and it's a necessary part of life when you're starting a business. Tom must have told you how important it can be.'

Sadly, she said, 'Yes. I wish he hadn't done this. It wasn't like him to leave things in such an ambiguous tangle.'

'He was always devious, but the stroke affected him.' Luc made no attempt to soften the blunt statement.

Reluctantly Jo nodded and drank a fortifying mouthful of coffee before saying, 'I need to be in Rotumea to run the business. It's very personal. Tom knows—*knew*—that. I'm sure he wouldn't have intended you to take me around like some...some extra piece of luggage!'

Luc leaned back in his chair and surveyed her. 'Tom was first and foremost an entrepreneur. He'd be thinking of the contacts you'd make.'

Exasperated, she demanded, 'And what contacts do *you* have in the world of skincare?'

'Very few, but I have a lot amongst those who use skincare. Witness those at the dinner that night.'

She looked up, and met a gaze that held cynical amusement. 'So that's why you mentioned my tiny business?'

'It's all part of the game,' Luc pointed out, not attempting to hide the cynical note in his voice. 'The demographic you're targeting has money. They frequent charity dinners, and by and large they're prepared to pay considerable sums for a good product.' His smile was brief, almost a taunt. 'I'm sure that anywhere I go you'll enjoy checking out spas and beauty shops and places like that.'

'If that was Tom's reasoning, he could have a point.'

And because her voice shook a little, she asked, 'When do we go back to Rotumea?'

'I have probably three days' work here.'

Good—so she'd have a chance to get that prescription. 'Fine. I'll check out the day spa here that stocks and uses our product.'

'Will you be trying for more business?'

'Not in Auckland,' she said. 'In the demographic I'm targeting exclusivity is a big asset.'

'While you're here, do you have any relatives you want to contact?'

She shook her head. 'Not a one. How about you?'

His brows lifted. 'Several in France and Scotland— none here now Tom's gone. How did you manage to end up with so few?'

She shrugged. 'My mother and my aunt grew up in care. My father came from a very religious family—they didn't approve of Mum, and they certainly wouldn't have approved of her having his child out of wedlock. He was killed in a motorbike accident going to see her, and they blamed her. They never contacted her. I don't even know who they are.'

Brows knotted, he said in a hard voice, 'If that's the sort of people they are you're better off not knowing them.'

Jo was oddly touched by his sympathy. 'I don't miss them. And while we're here I'll put flowers on his grave.' With a challenging glance she finished, 'What about these Scottish and French relatives?'

And held her breath, wondering if he was going to tell her to mind her own business.

Instead he said evenly, 'My mother grew up in Provence

in a half-ruined chateau. She had no siblings. She met and married my father—a Scottish gamekeeper—when she was visiting a school friend in the Highlands. It was a love match, but she couldn't cope with life there, and she returned to the chateau. I was born there. Five years later, after my father's death, she married Tom.'

He sounded like a policeman giving evidence, the colourless summary doing nothing to allay Jo's curiosity. What he left out was intriguing. Had his mother's family owned that half-ruined chateau?

For some reason she felt a pang of sympathy for him. Squelching it, she said, 'A half-ruined chateau—how very romantic.'

He reached for his coffee. 'It's not ruined any longer,' he said indifferently.

'Does it belong to your family?'

'It belongs to me.'

She recalled Tom's wry comment that Luc's mother had wanted her son to marry into the French aristocracy. Because she'd been an aristocrat herself? So what had her family thought of her marriage to a gamekeeper? And of Luc himself, product of what they possibly felt was a misalliance?

Or not. After all, she knew very little about French aristocrats down on their luck, or tumbledown chateaux.

And nothing about Luc, except that he kissed like a demon lover, and that just looking at him set every cell in her body on fire…

'That's an interesting expression,' he said mockingly.

Flushing, and hoping she didn't sound defensive, she said, 'I'm picturing a half-ruined chateau in Provence.'

'Once you get your hands on Tom's legacy you'll be

able to see as many as you like,' he told her. 'In fact, that amount of money will probably buy one for you. It might even be enough to turn the building into a live-able home instead of a wreck, but there wouldn't be any change.'

'I'll be quite content to view from a distance, like any other sightseer. And Tom's money will go to grow-ing the business.'

'How do you plan to conquer the cosmetics world if the base ingredient in your products is confined to only one small Pacific island?'

'As Pacific islands go, Rotumea is actually quite large,' she returned. 'And there are other, much more common ingredients we use too—coconut water from green coconuts, coconut oil, the essence from Rotu-mea's native gardenia.' She met his eyes squarely. 'I haven't yet worked out all the fine details of my plan to take over the world of skincare, but when I do, I won't be telling anyone about it.'

'Tom taught you well.' His smile was coolly ironic.

It always came back to Tom.

Deliberately Jo relaxed her stiff shoulders. What she and Tom had shared was precious to her. And she wasn't going to keep trying to convince Luc that his stepfa-ther had never so much as touched her, beyond the oc-casional—very occasional and very brief—hug.

Just keep in mind how very judgemental Luc is, and you'll be safe, she told that weak inner part of her that melted whenever Luc's gunmetal gaze met hers.

She drank more coffee and said cheerfully, 'He had a lot to teach. I'll bet he was a help to you when you started.'

Luc gave a short, derisive laugh. 'Not Tom,' he said. 'He told me I'd learn far more if I made my own mistakes.'

Again she felt that strange sympathy. 'And did you?'

'I learnt enough to take his life's work away from him.'

Jo blinked and ventured, 'You had a reason.'

His wide shoulders lifted in an infinitesimal shrug. 'I did.' After a pause, he added, 'I told you he changed after the very minor stroke he had. Not vastly, not obviously, but there were…incidents. He made decisions that could have—in one case definitely would have— led to disaster. The man who built Henderson's from scratch would never have made such decisions, but Tom wouldn't admit or accept that he could make a mistake. He had the failings of his virtues, and his determination got in the way.'

Which put a different slant on events. She'd known Tom before that stroke, but only as a child and during the holidays. While she'd lived in Rotumea he'd had the occasional spurt of what she'd thought was slightly irrational behaviour, but as her aunt had taken the incidents without comment she'd assumed this was normal for him.

But as head of a huge organisation, with thousands of people dependent on his health and managerial skills, one wrong decision could cause chaos. Perhaps Luc had been justified in ousting him.

Of course, Luc could be lying…

One glance at his strong features changed her mind. Lying didn't fit him. His behaviour last night had convinced her of his fundamental honesty as well as his formidable self-control.

Of course, he might have been trying her out, not really wanting her...

She had to stop second-guessing—something Tom had taught her to do, only he'd called it seeing situations clearly and from every conceivable angle. In business it worked well, but she was beginning to feel that in personal life it wasn't so efficient.

'You don't believe me,' Luc said without rancour.

Of course, he didn't care what she thought of him.

'Actually, I do,' she said, keeping her voice level. 'I can't see Tom ever admitting to a weakness. As you say, he had the faults of his virtues.'

'At least he didn't fail in the generosity stakes,' Luc observed.

That hurt, but she said calmly, 'No, he didn't. Although, being Tom, he still insisted on having the final word. You and I are caught in a trap of his making, with no way out.'

Luc laughed without humour. 'I'm sure that thought gave him great—and certainly as far as I'm concerned— rather malicious pleasure.'

'Whereas I think he meant some good for both of us by it.' Still smarting from his remark about Tom's generosity, she couldn't resist adding, 'Possibly you'd know him better if you'd seen more of him.'

And immediately wished she hadn't. Luc's expression didn't alter, but she received a strong impression of emotions reined back, of anger.

He finished his coffee, pushed his plate away and said calmly, 'We were estranged for the last years of his life. He wouldn't see me after I took over. When my mother sided with me—because she'd noticed and been worried by the change in him—he saw it as a betrayal, and although they kept up a pretence, they didn't live together as man and wife after that.'

Ashamed, she said, 'I'm sorry, I shouldn't have said that.'

'Especially as you were presumably the reason he settled in Rotumea and forbade either of us—or any of his friends—from visiting him.'

Stunned by his caustic tone, she said, 'I most certainly was not!'

He got to his feet and shrugged. 'You must have been. And I despise him for choosing to use such a weapon against my mother.'

The cold contempt in his voice shrivelled something vital inside Jo, made her feel sick and angry at the same time. 'I don't believe he thought of any such thing.'

And immediately cursed herself for saying anything at all. She tried to make it better. 'He always spoke of your mother with affection and respect. And we were *not* lovers.' Passion—a violent need to force him to believe her—made her voice harsh. She blurted, 'The very idea makes me feel sick.'

No emotion showed in his face, in those hard eyes, as he looked down at her. 'Your nausea obviously didn't worry Tom, or drive you away.' When she would have burst into speech again he held up his hand.

'Leave it, Joanna. Just leave it. He certainly wasn't the saint you seem to believe him to be.' His mouth twisted. 'And I can understand him. I've made it more than obvious I'm not immune to your not inconsiderable assets, so who am I to mock him? My mother was his age, and not well for the final years of her life. You must have been like a breath of fresh air to him, as well as a handy weapon.'

CHAPTER NINE

BACK IN ROTUMEA, Jo unpacked, then walked out onto the wide lanai. Sunlight streamed through the trees—so intense it looked like shimmering bars of gold in the salt-scented air. Her heart jolted when she realised Luc was gazing out to sea from the shade of a tangled thicket of palms.

It was all she could do to shield her hungry gaze. The past days in Auckland had been outwardly serene, but beneath it she'd been battling chaotic emotions. Luc's contempt hurt her more severely than Kyle's betrayal.

Facing that truth still terrified her.

Without preamble, she said, 'Would it be difficult for you to work with someone here? A housekeeper?'

Luc turned, brows drawing together. 'Not unless she talks.'

'She won't.' She expanded, 'The business is getting busy, and I'm going to be away most days.'

He nodded, although his gaze remained narrowed and keen. Colour warmed the skin over her cheekbones. Of course he knew why she was doing this.

He said, 'I'll pay her.' When she opened her mouth to protest he said curtly, 'At least you won't then feel obliged to offer me coffee or meals. And presumably you'll feel safer.'

Jo struggled to hide her chagrin. She'd hoped—uselessly—he wouldn't realise just how dangerously vulnerable she was. When Luc kissed her all self-control vanished, sweeping every vestige of common sense with it.

Heat burned up from her breasts, but before she could answer he went on, 'You obviously have someone in mind for the job.'

'My factory manager has a cousin who'll be perfect,' she told him.

Luc nodded. 'Organise her hours any way you want,' he said indifferently. 'I'll be away for the rest of the afternoon.'

Jo turned, relieved to be summoned to the house by the shrill call of the telephone.

Five minutes later she hung up, her gaze falling on the Chinese chest. Now was the perfect time to see if Tom had hidden something in the secret panel. Frowning, she pressed the centre of one of the mother-of-pearl flowers, letting out a sharp hiss of breath as the panel slid back.

'Yes!' she breathed triumphantly. It did hold something—not a thick wad, but definitely a couple of documents. One fell onto the floor; frowning, she picked it up.

A strange feeling of dislocation made her pause. 'Oh, don't be silly,' she said out loud. Fingers shaking a little, she unfolded it.

It was a copy of her birth certificate. Astonishment froze her into place as her gaze traced her father's name—so young to die, unknown to her except from a few faded photographs and her mother's loving recollections.

He'd been handsome, her mother had said, and kind. And funny. He was a mechanic; they'd been planning to marry when he'd been killed. Ilona hadn't known she was pregnant, and she'd been forbidden to attend his funeral by his parents, yet although her heart had been shattered she'd been so glad she carried his baby, so glad she had someone else to love, someone to take care of…

Why had Tom wanted a copy of her birth certificate?

Just another thing she'd never know, Jo thought drearily, and slid it underneath the small pile.

Looking at papers clearly never meant for her seemed too much like an intrusion. She sat down at the table, her fingers pleating and unpleating, until in the end she opened up the first sheet of paper.

It was the document Meru had told her about. A quick check revealed it was of no use to her—merely a note saying Tom guaranteed that her business would be conducted in a suitable manner.

She firmed her trembling lips. It was too much—the unexpected reference to her parents, the inevitable loss of her business—all of those she could cope with, but the constant tension of living with Luc had left her raw and fragile, as though she'd lost a layer of skin.

'Get over it,' she muttered and started to fold up the papers, saying something beneath her breath when one slipped out of the pile. She glanced at the heading as she picked it up and frowned again. It was from a medical laboratory in Sydney, Australia, and to her astonishment her name leapt out from it.

Stunned, she read it. Then, her hand shaking so much she dropped it, she picked up the document it had been folded with. Tom's handwriting leapt out at her. *Dear Jo*, it began…

She dragged in a painful breath and closed her eyes a moment before forcing them open and reading the letter he'd written to her some time before he'd been killed.

Three times she read it, before setting it back on the table and stumbling to her feet. She had to clutch the back of the chair to steady herself.

Luc walked in, took one look at her and crossed the room in long strides, demanding, 'What the hell's the matter?' as he grabbed her by the upper arms and supported her. 'It's all right,' he said roughly, pulling her stiff body into his arms. 'Whatever it is, we can deal with—'

'I know why Tom made it a condition that we live together,' Jo interrupted, her voice shaking.

Luc held her away from him, grey eyes searching her face. Struggling for control, she thrust out a hand towards the papers on the table. 'Look.'

His expression hardened. She waited for him to respond, but he said nothing until he'd put her back into the chair. Only then did he pick up the letter and began to read it.

Jo watched until he looked up, his narrowed eyes so dark they were almost black. 'He is—was—your *father*.'

'Yes.' Nausea and a great sorrow gripped her. 'My mother came to Rotumea twenty-three—no, twenty-four years ago. After my father—' she stopped abruptly, then resumed '—the man she thought was my father was killed.'

'How old was she?'

'Eighteen,' she said succinctly.

His frown deepened. 'Tom would have been thirty-five.' He paused, then said deliberately, 'It was just after my mother told him she could have no more children. I suppose it makes sense.'

Jo shivered. After another stark few moments he asked, 'Why didn't she realise she was pregnant with his child?'

She swallowed. In a voice so muted he could hardly hear her, she said, 'I th-think it must have been because she believed she was already pregnant with my father's...with Joseph Thompson's baby.' She hesitated and swallowed, but clearly couldn't go on.

A surge of compassion and another unfamiliar emotion overtook Luc. Mentally consigning both Tom and Joanna's mother to some cold, dark region of outer space, he said, 'It must have been that. Otherwise—'

He stopped abruptly. He'd already made one huge mistake about Joanna; he wasn't going to compound his cynical mistake by saying that her mother would no doubt have asked for financial support if she'd realised the child she carried was Tom's.

In that steady, expressionless tone she said, 'She was engaged to him—to Joseph Thompson. They were going to get married, only he was killed in a road accident. Every Sunday we used to visit his grave and leave flowers on it. She loved him and missed him until the end of her life. I was named after him.'

Luc frowned. 'How could she have made such a mistake?'

'I don't know.' She shook her head, then said, 'But it's not possible to know the exact moment of conception.' Bright patches of colour flaked her high cheekbones. 'And there was only a week…'

Her voice trailed away as Luc nodded. Her mother's lover had died a week before she came to Rotumea; shortly after that, according to Tom, an attempt by him to comfort her had ended in his bed. If she already had cause to believe she might be pregnant it had probably never occurred to her that she carried Tom's child.

Tom's only child.

He asked, 'Are you all right?'

And thought disgustedly that of all the stupid things to ask, that was probably the most stupid. All right? How could she be *all right*? Everything she'd ever thought or believed about her family—the foundations of her life—had been turned upside down. No dead young father, her conception an accident known to no one, not even her mother.

'I'm OK,' she said automatically.

He scanned her white face. 'You don't look at all OK. In fact, you look as though you're going to faint.'

Her head came up and some fugitive colour stole through her white face. In a much stronger voice she said, 'I've never fainted in my life.'

'Nobody would blame you for starting now,' he said curtly, and turned away to get her a glass of water and put on the electric jug. She needed some stimulant—coffee would probably be best. He'd put some whisky in it and make her drink it.

Actually, he admitted grimly, he could do with a stiff whisky himself...

He looked across the room. 'Where did you find these papers?'

Limply she told him.

His eyes on the electric jug, he said, 'It appears that when you were a child Tom had no suspicion you might be his.'

'So he says...said.'

'But when you arrived here to look after your aunt he realised you not only *looked* like his mother—you sounded like her, have hair the same colour and texture.'

'Yes,' she said again numbly.

'Hence the DNA sample.' He waited, and when she said nothing he elaborated, 'It would have been easy enough to get one with you living in the house.'

'I suppose so,' she said, still in that flat, stunned voice.

Luc paused. 'Did you notice any change in his attitude to you?'

'No.' She thought for a moment, then said slowly, 'Actually, yes. I suppose I did.'

'In what way?' Luc demanded.

She searched for words. 'He talked to me about his family, about how he'd got to be the man he was—all sorts of things. I just thought he was lonely.' She pressed a clenched fist to her heart, then forced it away, staring at her fingers with a look that summoned another unfamiliar emotion in Luc. 'He was really helpful when I thought of starting my business—made me do a proper business plan, discussed it with me. He invited friends of his who came to the resort to dinner—people he respected—introduced me to them…'

Her voice trailed away.

Recalling his own scathing refusal to believe anything she'd said about her relationship with Tom, Luc said bleakly, 'He did you few favours there—most of them are sure you were his mistress.'

She fired up. 'Then they must be totally lacking in any sort of empathy or understanding. He behaved like an uncle.' Again her voice thickened as she fought for composure. Taking a deep breath, she finished, 'Or a f-father.'

She dragged her gaze away from the letter to look back at him. 'But why keep it a secret? And why did Tom set up this whole situation?' She gestured wildly, encompassing the room and Luc.

'Tom trusted no one,' Luc told her uncompromisingly. 'Once he'd got this report, he wanted you to stay in Rotumea so he could find out what sort of person you are.'

She said numbly, 'It just seems…outrageous. Everything he's done. He was *testing* me?'

'Of course.' Luc paused, scanning her white face. That unusual compassion twisted his heart. She'd had enough.

But he owed her the truth—something Tom hadn't given her until too late.

He said, 'He was let down badly by his first wife. My mother married him because he was rich and was prepared to set up her family in the style they'd been accustomed to before they'd wasted their inheritance. After I was born she'd been told it was unlikely she'd have any more children, but she didn't tell Tom—she hoped the diagnosis was wrong. And I took Henderson's away from him. Why should he trust you?'

Jo was silent for a moment, then said quietly, 'I suppose I understand. At least we had that time together.'

Squaring her shoulders, she looked him in the eyes and said bluntly, 'I just thought he was lonely and bored. You'd taken over the enterprise he'd spent his life building, so it amused him to dabble in something as tiny as mine.' She paused, then decided to say it anyway. 'And it appeared you didn't care much about him.'

'I cared a lot,' he said curtly, adding in a level voice, 'but I also understood his desire to lick his wounds. Rotumea was his bolthole and his refuge. I'm sure he enjoyed helping you set up your business, and I'm equally sure he was pleased—and proud—to discover that his only child had something of his entrepreneurial spirit.'

'Just as he was proud of your ability,' she said, not quite knowing why.

Luc shrugged. 'I doubt that he ever thought of me as a son.'

Something about his tone caught her attention, although her swift glance found no regret in his expression. A sharp pang of probably unnecessary sympathy persuaded Jo into an impulsive reply. 'He always spoke of you with pride and affection.'

'You don't have to sugar-coat his attitude,' he said with crisp disbelief.

Her head came up. 'I'm not. I don't lie. He certainly didn't like being dumped, but he was quite proud at how efficiently it was done, without weakening the business or lowering its value in the marketplace.'

Luc gave an ironic smile. 'Yes, that would be Tom.'

She shivered. 'He knew for almost two years that he was my father. It seems such a waste. We could have been a…a family.'

It hurt that he hadn't wanted that. After all, families accepted each other as they were—without testing them.

Or was that a stupidly sentimental view?

Not without sympathy, Luc said, 'He wouldn't have been Tom if he hadn't checked you out thoroughly.'

'But he *knew* me,' she protested, trying to contain her pain. 'I used to come to Rotumea at least once a year for the holidays. Quite often he was here. In a way, he watched me grow up.'

'He knew you as a child.' He shrugged. 'A woman is an entirely different thing.'

'Why didn't he trust women?' she asked directly.

After a few taut moments Luc answered, a trace of reluctance colouring his voice. 'His first wife enjoyed the money he was making, but resented the time it took—time away from her. A few years into the marriage, when he'd overstretched himself and was skating very close to bankruptcy, she left him for his biggest competitor.'

Jo thought that over before saying, 'So he had one bad experience with a woman and that turned him sour on all our sex?'

Luc shrugged and poured water into the coffee pot before saying, 'There would have been other experiences, I imagine. Rich men are targets for a certain type of person. Which was possibly why he chose my mother—a practical, unsentimental Frenchwoman who married him for his money.'

This seemed to be Jo's day to ask questions. Why not an impertinent one? He could only give her that steely look and refuse to answer. 'And what did she bring to the marriage?'

Then immediately wished she'd kept quiet. It was too personal—something she had no right to know.

However, instead of the stinging riposte she expected, Luc said, 'This is guesswork—my mother wasn't one to talk about her emotions. She'd married once for love and that had been a disaster. I imagine she agreed with her family that her second marriage should be one of convenience. Tom was the ideal choice. And it was happy enough.' His mouth twisted. 'Much happier than many I've seen that began with high romance, only to disintegrate into chaos.'

Startled by this unexpected forthrightness, Jo realised she and Luc did have something in common, after all—mothers who'd used their beauty to secure a future for their children.

Luc went on, 'Their marriage was one of equals; as her husband, he was introduced into circles that boosted his career, and in return he supported her—and me—in the style she believed was her due. He practically rebuilt the chateau for her, and made sure she never wanted for anything again.'

And possibly she'd hoped Tom would be satisfied with Luc as a substitute son.

How had that affected Luc? A quick glance gleaned no information from his expression. From what he'd said, she suspected he had his mother's very practical attitude to marriage.

He said levelly, 'Tom would have been pleased when he found out you were his daughter. But even then, he'd have wanted to be sure he could trust you with that knowledge.'

At Jo's soft, angry sound, Luc shrugged. 'The prospect of acquiring large amounts of money often changes people, bringing out the worst in them.'

She nodded, accepting the coffee he handed her. She'd read enough to know that was true.

Luc went on, 'He'd have planned to tell you in his own good time, but that bloody coconut robbed him of the opportunity.'

Tears clogging her voice, she said, 'He was so fit, he looked after himself, he ate well—he thought he'd live for ever.'

'He was sure he had all bases covered,' Luc agreed. He was watching her, his brows drawn together. 'You really were fond of him, weren't you?'

'Yes.' She blinked ferociously and steadied her voice. 'It's odd, isn't it? He was a father to you, and a sort of father to me, but he never knew what it was like to be a real father.' She glanced up with a smile that trembled. 'I suppose that makes us sort of siblings.'

'Like hell it does!' Luc took a step towards her, then stopped.

Jo's breath blocked her throat, something dying inside her as she watched him reimpose control. He said between his teeth, 'We share an affection for a man, that's all. And now we have to work out what to do about this situation.'

His words killed the hope she'd kept locked in her heart—a weak and feeble hope she'd refused to face.

Because facing it meant she'd have to accept something else—that her feelings for Luc went far deeper than mere lust.

'I know,' she said huskily.

He looked down at his clenched fists as though he'd never seen them before. 'First,' he stated, his voice showing no emotion, 'we have to see out the six months Tom stipulated.'

She opened her mouth, then closed it again. He was right. They had to do that. But at what cost to her? Luc wanted her—he'd admitted that. But somehow, without realising it, she'd grown to crave more than the passionate sating of desire. And one glance at his stony expression told her that even without the barrier of his beliefs about her relationship with Tom, Luc was not going to surrender to what he probably saw as a temporary passion.

The months ahead stretched out like a prison sentence.

'I suppose so,' she said quietly.

Luc looked down at her. 'Drink your coffee. The next thing we need to do is contact Tom's solicitor and get some advice about his revelations.'

She gave him a blank look. 'Why? He left me enough to live on for the rest of my life.'

'As his daughter, you have a claim to his entire estate,' Luc said briefly.

The cup in her hand trembled so much she set it down on the saucer. 'I don't want it,' she said, snapping each word out. 'I do *not* want anything more than he left me.

I don't need it. If I end up with a fortune it will be one of my own making, not his. I will not contest the will.'

Luc looked at her, his mouth curving in a smile that held no hint of humour. 'Oh, yes,' he said levelly. 'You're his daughter, all right.'

And felt a coldly searing shame. Tom's silence and his own cynicism had made him angry and suspicious, even as he'd reluctantly come to admire her. *Admire?* He watched her get up, his gut tightening. There was a lot to admire about Joanna Forman, but that was too simple a word. His emotions were complex, warring with each other.

But he had time to assess them...

During the following weeks Jo sensed a subtle easing of Luc's aloofness. Slowly, carefully, without discussion, they negotiated a system of living together. She relished his dry sense of humour, and found herself eagerly driving home each afternoon to match wits with him. His keen intelligence intrigued her too much. And she enjoyed the rare moments when his spoken English revealed his French heritage.

However the tension was still there—ignored, controlled, but never entirely repressed. Luc had told her he felt nothing but lust for her, and she was too proud to be used.

So she warned herself to be satisfied that they were tentatively approaching something like acceptance of the situation.

The social life she instituted for them helped. The island chiefs and their wives were eager to meet Luc and, a little to her surprise, he seemed to enjoy being introduced to them.

'For a man who knows little of Pacific customs, you're proving very adaptable,' she said one evening, waving their last guests goodbye.

Luc gave her an ironic look. 'Protocol exists everywhere,' he observed negligently. 'Anyone with any common sense finds out what the prevailing customs and usages are before they travel. And these people are forgiving.'

And he made her laugh with a story of his naivety when he'd made his first trip to China, finishing by saying, 'They were charmingly polite about every mistake I made, and after that I vowed I wasn't going to be so stupid again.'

Perhaps it was the pleasant evening they'd had, or perhaps the eternal beauty of the stars overhead, jewelling the velvet sky with their ancient patterns, that persuaded Jo to ask something she'd often wondered about.

She said, 'Did you manage to deal satisfactorily with the mess you were handling while we were in Auckland?'

A certain grimness in his expression made her add hastily, 'If you can't talk about it, forget about it.'

His shoulders lifted briefly. 'I trust your discretion.'

Which startled her as well as gave her a suspicious frisson of pleasure.

Deliberately, Luc said, 'One of the executives there embezzled over a hundred thousand dollars.'

Shocked, she said, 'What was it—gambling?'

'That would have been easy to deal with. Her child— her oldest son—developed a rare form of cancer. She found that a highly experimental treatment was on offer in America. She didn't have the money to pay for it, and couldn't get it anywhere, so she took it.'

Jo frowned. 'What happened to the boy?'

'He died,' he said shortly.

'Oh, that's so sad.'

'Yes. No happy endings.'

Glancing up at the autocratic profile etched against that radiant sky, Jo decided not to ask how he'd dealt with the situation.

However, he said, 'We came to a decision that satisfied everyone.'

Including the poor woman who'd lost her son?

He went on, 'She's still working for us—under stringent supervision—and will pay back the money.'

And that did surprise her. When she remained silent he gave a swift, sardonic smile. 'You thought I'd sack her? Prosecute her?'

'Well, actually, yes,' she admitted.

'I do have the occasional moment of compassion,' he said smoothly. 'She is an excellent executive, and she's paid a heavy enough price—her marriage broke up over her actions and the strain of their son's illness.'

If she hadn't known that nothing cracked that granite façade he presented to the world, she thought a little wistfully, she might have thought her comment had struck a nerve.

Quite often they dined at the resort, occasionally with friends or business associates of Luc's who'd flown in. To Jo's surprise, she liked his friends. His easy companionship with them led to some wistful moments.

Slowly, guiltily, she realised she wanted more—much, much more—from Luc than friendship.

Each day his controlled courtesy grated more, pulling taut a set of nerves she hadn't known she possessed. Adding to her stress was the slow progress of the Council of chiefs on making any decision. They had accepted Tom's document, but Meru's cousin remained infuriatingly silent about any deliberations.

Between fear for the future of her business and her growing feelings for Luc, Jo endured long nights when she turned restlessly in her bed and wondered whether he too was awake—so close and yet so distant from her.

Almost certainly not...

It was a relief when, after a telephone call, Luc informed her he had to go to China for a meeting. 'We'll leave tomorrow and be away for five days.'

'I can't come.'

'Why not? I think you'd enjoy Shanghai, and contacts there should be valuable.'

'I can't leave Rotumea because any day now—I hope—I'll learn whether I still have a business,' she told him.

'What?' He frowned and asked curtly, 'What's going on?'

When she'd explained what was happening, his frown deepened. 'All right, obviously you have to be here for that.' He paused. 'Shall I stay?'

'No,' she said, touched by his thoughtfulness. 'It may not be decided yet. They hoped to have a consensus by now, but a couple of expatriate chiefs arrived from New Zealand yesterday, and they'll probably bring the wishes of the Rotumean community there to be considered.'

* * *

But there was no decision for several days. 'Something has happened,' Meru told her. 'I don't know what it is, but it means they cannot come to a decision yet.' She paused, then said quietly, 'I think you are going to lose, Jo. They will be very sorry, but of course they have to think of everyone, not just you. And this firm is promising big things—they have a very good eco-logical reputation, you know, and they are prepared to work with the Council to make sure the island is not changed in any way.'

'I know,' Jo said huskily. 'It's all right, don't worry.'

On the day Luc was due back, Jo woke late, slitting her eyes against the bright morning light. He'd been away less than a week, yet she'd missed him. How she'd missed him! His absence was an aching gap in her life, a silent emptiness that echoed through the days and haunted her sleep at night.

For the past two months she'd been continually tense, struggling to contain a need that grew ever stronger, engraving itself on her heart so deeply she'd never be able to erase it.

She gritted her teeth. She could cope; she had to cope. In a few months they'd have fulfilled the condi-tions of Tom's will, and could pick up their lives again. And she'd be spared the pain of seeing Luc ever again.

A gull called from outside, its shrill screech drowned out by the alarm siren of the blackbird in the garden. Taken by surprise, she hurled back the sheet and leapt out. That bird was a drama queen, but something or someone was out there, and today Luc was coming home—no, she corrected, he was coming *back*. Rotu-

mea wasn't his home, never would be. Just as it wasn't
hers. Yet excitement exploded through her, a starburst
of foolish anticipation doomed to be frustrated.

She grabbed the first thing to hand—a sarong slung
over the back of a chair—but had only wound it halfway
round her when she heard a car door slam. She snatched
up a hairbrush, dragging it through her tangled locks,
then took a deep breath and walked out onto the terrace, stopping after the first step. Her heart contracted.

Watching the blackbird as it peered nervously
through the screen of hibiscus blossoms, Luc stood
against a screen of bold magenta bougainvillea. A half-
smile curled his mouth. Her heart began to beat rapidly.
He was so…so *magnificent*, hair gleaming in the golden
light, his natural tan deepened by the tropical sun.

And she loved him.

CHAPTER TEN

THE REALISATION HIT Jo with the force of a blow, shocking her into immobility. Panicking, she heard herself drag in a jagged breath. It wasn't possible. She didn't know Luc well enough to take that final step. He'd shown himself to be judgemental and inflexible and autocratic and intolerant and…her mind ran out of adjectives.

But not recently, she thought despairingly. And then Luc turned, his face hardening when he saw her. Suddenly aware of her scanty sarong, she shot backwards into the shade of the terrace.

In a voice that sounded as though he'd been goaded beyond bearing, he demanded harshly, 'Damn you, Joanna, why can't you be dressed and ready to go to work?'

The words whirling around her mind, she blinked.

He headed purposefully towards her, stopping only a few inches away. Eyes widening, she stared up into his face. He looked as though it had been a hard sojourn in Shanghai. His arrogant bone structure was more prominent, but the grey eyes were hot and urgent, and when he made an odd sound deep in his throat and pulled her into his arms she didn't resist, melting into him with a shaky sigh of relief.

'What happened with the Council of chiefs?' he demanded.

She tried to pull away, but his arms tightened. 'They're still talking.'

His face hardened. 'How long do they need?'

He was holding her so close she could feel the stirring of his body, the hard shifting and flexion of muscles as though he clamped some tight control on them.

'Luc,' she said fiercely into his chest, 'let *go*.'

'You want this—don't lie to me, Joanna, I see it in your eyes every time you look at me.' His voice was rough and harsh, and the pressure of his arms around her didn't slacken.

'I didn't mean let *me* go,' she said indignantly, jerking her head upwards to glare at him. '*You*—I meant let yourself go.'

He stared at her as though she were mad, then startled her by emitting a short, unamused laugh. 'Very well, then—but only if it's mutual.'

Jo's heart missed a beat. 'You've just said you know it is.'

His eyes narrowed. 'The passion is mutual—how about the surrender?'

For a moment she hesitated, but only for a moment. 'Of course it is,' she said fiercely.

He bent his head. But instead of the fierce hunger she expected, his kiss was soft and tantalising, a slow sweet pressure that sent her pulse soaring. Enraptured, she returned it, letting instinct take over to openly reveal the love that had flowered within her so unexpectedly.

He lifted his head and surveyed her with an intent, almost silver scrutiny. 'Enough?' he asked.

'No.' A sudden thought struck her. 'Unless you're tired,' she added heroically, every cell in her body objecting to such restraint.

Something moved in his eyes. 'Not *too* tired,' he said in that thick, hard voice, and startled her by lifting her as though she were a child and shouldering through the doorway.

He carried her into her bedroom, standing for a few seconds to survey the tangled sheets on the bed before easing her onto her feet.

This time his kiss was different, much more carnal. Jo's blazing response shocked her—her reckless, overt need was both delicious and intoxicating, singing through her body like a siren's lure.

When he lifted his head and held her a half-step away her sarong fell to the floor, a puddle of coral and peach and blue-violet, leaving her only in her narrow bikini briefs.

Luc's hands tightened on her shoulders, then relaxed.

Eyes kindling, he said, 'You're beautiful. But you know that. And I want you—you've known that too, ever since we first set eyes on each other. And at the moment I don't give a damn for all the reasons we shouldn't be doing this.'

Jo had never felt so sensuous, so at home. The soft sea breeze caressed her skin, lifting the ends of her hair around her face, and Luc looked at her as though she was all he'd ever desired. She didn't know what to do, what to say.

So she let her expression tell him that a desperate need raced through her like some headstrong tide, carrying her further and further away from safety.

Nothing else but this moment, this sensation, made sense to her.

'Neither do I,' she said honestly, and reached out to touch his shoulder, tracing the hard swell of a muscle with a light, sensuous finger.

He tensed as though she'd hit him, then gave a low, triumphant laugh and yanked his shirt over his head, before stripping off the rest of his clothes.

Her low, feral murmur took her by surprise. It surprised him too, but he smiled and lifted a hand that shook slightly, reaching for her again, easing her against him as though she was precious to him.

Sighing with voluptuous pleasure, Jo relaxed against him, shamelessly letting him support her.

When his lips met hers rational thought fled, banishing all foreboding as she surrendered to the magic of her stimulated senses, the pressure of Luc's mouth as he explored hers, the erotic slide of heated skin against skin...

He lifted her again and set her down on the bed, sprawled across the sheets she'd left only a few minutes previously. He didn't join her; instead he stood like some pagan conqueror gazing down at one of the spoils of war.

In his face she read a fierce appetite that matched hers, roused it further and took her higher than she'd ever been. Without thinking, she held out her arms to him.

He didn't move.

Surely he wasn't going to call a halt now...

Quickly, before she could think better of it, she blurted, 'I'm taking the Pill.'

Luc's smile was taut and fierce. 'And I've got protection.'

Her heart soared as he came down beside her in a movement that lacked a little of his usual litheness, and slid his arms around her as though he too had been craving this moment, dreaming of it night and day, desired it like a man lost in the desert longed for water.

He bent his head, but didn't take her hungry mouth. Disappointment ached through her, only to disappear when he dropped a sinuous line of kisses from the corner of her mouth to the pulse in her throat.

'You taste like honey and cream,' he said against its frantic throbbing. 'Sweet and rich, with a tang.'

Shudders of exquisite pleasure shivered along her nerves, as he found the lobe of her ear and bit it gently.

With the pathetic remains of her willpower, Jo held back a gasp, sighing languorously when he transferred to the juncture of her neck and shoulder, biting again so gently she could barely feel it. More pleasure shimmered through her.

'I didn't know—' she breathed into his throat, her voice dying when he bit again, applying slightly more pressure.

'What didn't you know?' His voice was low and raw, as though he was holding himself in rigid restraint.

'That it—that anything could feel so good,' she whispered.

'Here?' Another sensuous nip sent more excitement seething through her.

'Yes,' she croaked, and turned her head to do the same to him, her hand over his heart.

She felt it leap beneath her palm, felt the swift tension in his muscles. A sense of power, of communion, of a subtle forging of bonds, surged through her when he slid a hand down to cup her breast, the lean fingers gentle yet assured as they stroked the tip into a taut little peak.

A groan ripped from her throat and her body tightened, driven by an urgency that brooked no disappointment.

'Ah, yes, you like that,' he breathed, and bent his head to kiss the spot, then took it into his mouth.

'Luc...' His name emerged as a long, shuddering sigh.

He lifted his head and watched her tremble with something so close to rapture it made her need even more keen, piercing her with a demand she couldn't articulate.

His hand slid further down, traced the narrow curve of her waist, moved past her hip and found the slick, heated folds at the juncture of her thighs.

'Yes,' he said, and came over her, testing her gently until she seized him by the shoulders and pulled him down and into her, drugged by a sensuous craving that insisted on satisfaction.

Her boldness cracked his iron control. A rough, feral noise erupted from deep in his throat and he thrust, deep and ever deeper, until at last the mounting wave of ecstasy broke over her, carrying her so far beyond rapture she thought her heart would break its bounds.

Even as the wave crested and ebbed he flung his head back, muscles coiled and flowing while he took his fill of her, finally easing down with her into a sated serenity punctuated only by the heavy beating of her heart against his.

Jo had never felt such sweet sorrow at the end of exhilaration, yet with it came a powerful contentment and peace, as though the experience had gone beyond the physical and was transformed into something spiritual.

For her, her mind told her drowsily. Not for Luc...

Right then, she didn't care. It was enough to hold him while their pulses synchronised to a steady regular beat, to savour his weight on her, his long muscles lax, his head on the pillow beside her.

But too soon he said, 'I'm far too heavy for you,' and before she could tighten her arms around him he turned onto his side and pulled her against him with her head on his shoulder.

No, you're not...I think I might have been born for this. Another thing she didn't dare say aloud.

So she made an indeterminate noise, and they lay together until he said, 'If I don't move soon I might go to sleep.'

Love and concern for him forced her to remember he'd flown in from China.

'Didn't you sleep on the plane?' she asked.

He paused, then gave a short laugh. 'Not much.' He released her and swung himself off the bed. For a moment he looked down at her, grey eyes narrowed and unreadable, before turning away and beginning to pull on his clothes.

Jo lay for a few seconds, wondering what to say, where to go from here. Before she'd made up her mind, he picked up her sarong and tossed it to her.

'Too tempting,' he said harshly.

Fumbling, she draped the cloth around her, feeling oddly empty, only to have to stand up and arrange it.

Fully dressed, Luc asked dryly, 'What happened to the businesswoman who raced off to work at the crack of dawn every day?'

Her whole world had changed, yet nothing had; they were back to fencing with each other. Perhaps the foils had been blunted a little, but they were still sharp.

Steadying her voice, she said, 'She got waylaid,' and then blushed. 'I'll head off in half an hour or so,' she said quickly. 'You'll be able to sleep then if you want to.'

'Jo,' he said quietly.

Desperately clinging to the remnants of her dignity, she faced him. 'What?'

He paused, scrutinising her face before saying, 'I thought I had enough strength of mind to resist you. I was wrong. Are you all right?'

Pride provided the answer. She even managed a smile. 'Of course,' she told him brightly. 'You don't have to be told you're a magnificent lover, surely?'

And was bemused by the tinge of colour along his autocratic cheekbones when he said, 'I'm glad you think so. It was…special for me too. And we need to talk once you get home again.' He turned and left the room.

His tone had been courteous enough, but an undernote to his words stayed with her. It hadn't been contempt, yet it left her feeling oddly disassociated and uneasy, and she spent too much time that morning at work wondering about it when she should have been marshalling her argument for continuing her contract with the Council of chiefs.

It was a relief when Meru knocked on her door, even

though the older woman looked worried. 'Jo, something's happened,' she said.

Jo's heart skipped a beat. She'd believed she was ready for what was probably going to be a refusal, but the worry that clawed at her was fierce and devastating. 'Do you think the decision will be made today? Has your cousin any idea which way the chiefs might be going?'

Meru sighed and sat down. 'Yes. But something unexpected has happened.'

'What?' The single word snapped out.

'There has been another offer.'

Whatever she'd expected, it wasn't this. 'From whom?' she asked blankly.

'I don't know, but it raises the first offer. I think we are going to lose, Jo.'

Jo reined in her shocked dismay. 'In that case, get your cousin to persuade the Council to sign a written contract—one made out by powerful lawyers who know the island. One that stipulates all of our employees' jobs will be safe.'

'Yes.' Meru looked anxiously at her. 'Jo, what will you do?'

Jo swallowed a lump in her throat. 'I'll set up another business—in New Zealand, probably.'

Meru's eyes filled with tears. 'We'll miss you,' she said, and came across and hugged her hard.

When she'd gone Jo sat for long moments, staring blindly at the computer screen.

Everything had been pushed off balance, all the foundations of her life revealed to be shaky. The knowledge that she was Tom's daughter had begun the process…

No, she thought, determined to face facts. Meeting Luc had started it. She'd started by disliking him as she fought that fierce physical attraction, then reluctantly learned to respect him. Falling in love had stolen up on her, ambushed her heart. *Making* love with him had set the seal on her change of emotions, and it had been— life-changing.

The end of all her dreams and plans for her business was life-changing too, she thought wearily, only in an entirely different way. Before she'd met Luc she'd have been completely devastated by the loss of her business, but that unexpected, newfound love had changed her.

What now?

Love battled with desire, fought caution, resisted everything that urged—begged, demanded, *insisted*— she yield to it.

She got to her feet and walked across to the window, staring out across the rustling feathery tops of the coconut palms. The faint evocative perfume of gardenia mingled with petrol fumes and the ever-present salty tang. Heat hit her like a blow. Closing her eyes, she wrestled her way to the hardest decision she'd ever made—much more difficult than choosing to care for her mother in the face of Kyle's threat to walk out on their relationship.

Did she have the courage to take the chance that Luc might learn to love her?

It didn't seem likely. All his lovers had been beautiful, yet the relationships had died. Did he even believe in love—the unconditional sort her mother had known, a love that lasted a lifetime? Because only that would satisfy her.

It didn't seem likely.

And she couldn't—wouldn't—cope with emotionless sex that meant nothing more than the satisfaction
of carnal needs. Loving Luc as she did, such a surrender would kill something vital, something honest and
basic in her.

So she'd tell Luc there would be no more rapturous
moments in his arms…

Her hands clenched on the windowsill.

Glimpsing paradise only to be forced to repudiate it
would be like enduring hell, but she had to do it.

At least Luc wasn't at home when she reached the
house. Shaking inwardly, Jo went inside and showered,
turning off the water to hear a car coming towards the
house. Luc, she thought, her heart going suddenly into
overdrive. She dragged on a long loose shift before forcing herself to walk sedately outside.

That foolish wild anticipation abruptly died when
she opened the door to Sean Harvey. He surveyed her
with the insolent half-smile that had become his usual
greeting for her.

'Hi, gorgeous,' he said, eyeing her up and down.
'How are things going?'

'Fine, thank you,' she said without warmth.

'I hear you've had some good luck.'

Uneasy under his stare, she asked, 'Really?'

Then remembered with relief that she'd been inter-
viewed by the local newspaper a few days previously,
and had mentioned that the latest range of skincare
creams had been accepted into one of New York's most
prestigious stores.

'Yep.' He never took his eyes off her. 'Word is that you're actually Tom Henderson's daughter.'

She felt the colour drain from her face. 'Really?' she said again, buying time. 'And where did you hear that?'

'Around,' he said casually. 'Is it true?'

She shrugged. 'My ancestry is no one's concern but mine.'

'So it is true,' he said, still watching her, his gaze as cold as a shark's. 'Why not admit it?'

'Why did you come here?'

He sneered, 'Could the secrecy have anything to do with your mother being a call girl? Was old Tom ashamed of you?'

'My mother was not a call girl,' she said sharply, despising him and so angry she had to stop and draw breath before she could say, 'Pity *your* mother didn't wash your mouth out with soap more often. I don't know why you're here, and you can leave right now.'

'What if I don't want to? After all, your lover's not here. You must be lonely, looking for a little warmth.'

She stepped back and slammed the door in his face, knowing it was flimsy protection. The house had few external walls.

At least the sound of a car engine meant Sean wasn't hanging around. Relief almost swamped her until she realised the vehicle was coming down the drive, not going away. The engine died, followed by a second's silence before she heard Luc's voice. His icy, ominous tone sent a shiver scudding down her spine.

Fingers shaking, she opened the door to see Sean trying to maintain his insolence in the face of Luc's anger. As she stepped out, Sean's hand clenched into a fist and he took a step towards Luc, lowering his head like a charging bull.

Shock ricocheted through her.

In a silky voice loaded with menace, Luc ordered, 'Don't try it.'

Intensely relieved, she saw Sean hesitate then drop his hands and step back.

'Sean's just going,' she said crisply.

Without looking at her, Luc ordered, 'On your way, then.'

Sean waited until he was in his car before he wound down the window and sneered, 'Not even you can put a stop to this, you know. Everyone on Rotumea knows.'

Gravel spurted from the wheels as the car surged forward, missing Luc by a foot, then shot down the drive.

Luc came to the door in a swift, noiseless rush, his expression controlled. 'What the hell was he doing here?' he demanded.

'He came to tell me he knows I'm Tom's daughter,' she told him shakily, furious with him. 'Luc, he tried to run you over! Why didn't you get out of the way?'

'I've outbluffed better players than him,' he said contemptuously. 'How did he find out?'

'I don't know, and I don't care.' She expelled pent-up air and steadied her voice. 'I don't know why he's being so...so *stupid*! We've never been anything more than friends—and not even that after the night he bailed me up at the resort.'

The night she'd met Luc. It seemed so long ago, as though she'd never lived before she met him...

He said now, 'I did tell you once that money has the power to change most people. Get used to it.'

'But *I* haven't changed!' She combated her fear and anger by banging a fist on the balustrade. 'I'm just the same person I was before!' And stopped, because of course she wasn't. She'd changed, but it had been love that did that, not money.

Luc took her elbow and steered her through the door. 'What did you tell him when he said he knew?'

'That my ancestry was no one's business but mine.' She took in a deep breath of warm, flower-scented air and tried to compose herself.

'And you've not told anyone?'

'No.' But then she felt colour drain from her face.

'You did.' He sounded bored, as though it was only to be expected.

Realising she was clutching his sleeve, she dropped her hand and took a deep breath while she strode across to the kitchen. Defiantly she said, 'Yes. Lindy.' And shook her head. 'But Lindy wouldn't tell anyone—I asked her not to.'

'Not her husband?'

She hesitated. 'I don't think she'd tell him. I don't know.'

'Marriage changes people too. She might think you didn't mean him.'

His cynical intonation made her angry. 'Surely it doesn't matter? I didn't tell her about the condition in Tom's will.'

'It matters,' Luc said curtly. 'Brace yourself, because the media is on the way. A gossip columnist got in touch with me an hour ago.' He demanded abruptly, 'Have you seen your lawyer yet?'

Hands shaking, she opened the fridge and got out the iced water. 'No. I told you, I don't need to.'

Luc said something under his breath, and she hurried on, 'It's nobody's business but mine who my parents were.'

'Agreed, except that as Tom's only child you have a moral claim to his estate.'

'I don't,' she said instantly, swinging around to fix him with a fierce glare. 'I don't want anything to do with it. I'll take what he left me, but no more. As for the press—well, they can say what they like. I'll stay here—they'll soon get bored in Rotumea.'

His gaze narrowed, then he shrugged. 'I'll get changed and then we'll talk.'

Ten minutes later, walking beside him along the beach, Jo tried to stifle a tenuous joy that could only be temporary.

Casually, Luc asked, 'Why don't you want anything more from Tom's estate?'

Jo stopped, watching a frigate bird soar and wheel in the sky. The sun dazzled her eyes and the familiar roar of the waves on the coral reef was no comfort.

She tried to organise her objection into words that made sense, finally saying, 'If he'd told me—if we'd been able to relate to each other, forge some sort of family feeling—I might feel differently.'

'I can understand that, but you told me that he treated you like an uncle—or a father.'

Surprised that he'd remembered, she said, 'He did, but…I never felt that we were family, the way it was with my mother and Aunt Luisa. If I'd known—if he'd told me—I might feel I have some further claim on his estate, even though he left me more than enough. But then, if he'd wanted me to have anything more than what he left me in his will he'd have seen to it. He didn't.'

He stopped and looked down at her, grey eyes hooded. 'He probably intended to before that damned hurricane.'

'In the Pacific they're called cyclones,' she said bleakly. 'And you don't know what he'd have done.'

She tried again to make him understand. 'Luc, I don't want anything more. I was shocked enough to get what I did. You deserve to head Henderson's. I think he knew that, even if he was angry with you for taking his place.'

Hoping she'd said enough to convince him, she met his piercing gaze staunchly. 'I don't know what lever Tom used to force you to obey his condition, but he had no right to do it.'

'His lever,' he told her deliberately, 'is that you have the power to make my life a hell of a lot harder.'

'What?' For a moment she thought her heart had stopped beating. She'd had too many shocks this morning. This was something she couldn't—didn't want to—deal with.

The cold, controlled anger hardening his expression cut her breath short. Pulse thundering in her ears, she waited.

He said, 'At the end of six months you'll be asked by the solicitor how you feel about me. Your opinion decides whether or not I take full control of Tom's estate.' His face more arrogant than she'd ever seen it, he went on, 'It won't be the end of the world if you say I'm the biggest bastard you've ever come across—I'll get what

I want eventually, but possibly not before considerable damage has been done to Henderson's. The shares will fall once shareholders hear you're his daughter.'

'Why?'

'They'll anticipate a legal battle for control.'

'So that's why…' Jo stopped, unable to continue. Now she knew why he'd relaxed his iron restraint enough to make love to her—because he wanted that power, that control over Tom's empire.

Sick to her soul with disillusion, she closed her eyes. Loving him was breaking her heart, but this—this was even worse.

'That's why I agreed to this farcical situation,' he said, each word clipped and cold and precise.

Whatever Tom had intended by his eccentric will, it couldn't be allowed to wreck Luc's career. But oh, how could he have used her with such calculated cynicism?

Pride forced her voice to remain steady. 'And after you'd vented your spleen for a few weeks by being as nasty as you could, did you decide that seducing me into some meaningless lovemaking would be the easiest route to my agreement?'

'Don't try to tell me that this morning meant nothing to you,' he said between his teeth. 'I was there, Joanna. I know how you look when we make love, and it wasn't *meaningless*.'

She stopped, and turned blindly back. *No*, she thought in anguish as his hand on her arm froze her into place. *No, don't try to persuade me with lies…*

He said, 'I made love to you because I couldn't stop myself. And because you wanted me as much as I wanted you. I wasn't capable of thinking beyond that—certainly not planning to seduce you.'

'Let me go,' she said thinly.

He paused, then let his hand fall. Jo set off towards the house, her thoughts in turmoil, her insides churning. He caught her up after a pace.

Dragging in a long silent breath, she said as calmly as she could, 'You don't need to worry. I'll stay. When the six months are up I'll tell Mr Keller that you're the ideal person to take over Henderson Holdings.'

Luc examined her silently. She was pale and her voice was shaky, but she met his gaze without wavering.

'Tom's played with our lives enough,' she said dispassionately. 'I don't want to live by his rules any longer. From now on, I suggest we don't mention his name. And I'll try not to get in your way.'

What the hell did she mean by that? Luc suspected he knew. She was closing the door firmly on any further lovemaking. After a silent, furious epithet, he tried to convince himself it was sensible.

Hell, you've made a total hash of this.

Surprising himself, he realised he believed she'd keep her word once this damned probation period was over. Probably because she'd fought so hard for her small business—not for herself so much as for the people who worked for her.

Yet every fibre of his body was taut and angry, as though something infinitely precious had been taken from him. Sensible or not, he wanted her in his bed. Their lovemaking had been a wondrous thing, satisfying a need he hadn't known existed in him.

If he believed in love, he might even think he was halfway there.

It was going to be sheer hell keeping his distance. But he'd misjudged her so badly he owed her that.

'Right, it's a deal,' he said, and held out his hand.

After a moment's hesitation she put hers in his. Her grip was warm but soon loosened, and images of her almost shy caresses, of the heat of her body and her ecstasy in his arms flashed into his mind.

His treacherous body reacted immediately. He dropped her hand and took a pace backwards. 'That's settled, then,' he said, controlling a primitive urge to take her in his arms and comfort her. 'No more dancing to Tom's tune. But you do need to talk to a lawyer about this. Do you have one?'

Long lashes shielded those slumbrous green eyes, hiding her emotions from him. 'I use the local one,' she said. 'And I don't see any reason to consult a solicitor; if you can cope with the next few months, so can I, and then it will be over.'

And we can go our separate ways, her tone told him.

Luc set his jaw. 'Nevertheless, see the lawyer.' He glanced at his watch. 'Right now, I suggest we go to the resort and have lunch.'

The more people around them the better; at the resort he'd be able to subdue his fierce desire to pull her into him and kiss her into submission, before making love to her all afternoon.

The effort showing, she shrugged. 'I'll just snatch a sandwich here—I have to meet the chiefs this afternoon to hear the result of their interminable deliberations.'

He nodded. 'Good luck.'

In spite of everything, she thought almost bitterly as she turned away, it hurt that he didn't offer to accompany her. Moral support would have been welcome.

Joanna arrived back at the house well after the swift tropical twilight had darkened into a velvet night. Luc heard the sound of her car and half-turned in the shelter of one of the big trees by the beach. Immediately he forced himself to stay. He'd been trying to make sense of the decision he'd come to—and was failing.

Infuriatingly, his desire still warred with his intellect. Why had he been crazy enough to reveal the power she'd been given in Tom's will? It had been a huge, reckless gamble—yet it had been the right thing to do.

What he really wanted to know was the reason she'd given him her loyalty. Because that was what she'd done when she'd told him she'd stay on so that he could keep his position at Henderson's without the infighting that would be inevitable if he'd been deprived of it.

As though she knew where to find him, she walked swiftly down the path beneath the coconut palms. He waited until she was within a pace before asking, 'What was the decision?'

With a little cry she swivelled. 'Oh,' she said, exhaustion flattening her voice. 'I didn't see you.'

'I realised that.' His voice was dry.

Abruptly she told him, 'The Council decided not to take up the other offer.'

Silence stretched between them, tense with unspoken words, hidden emotions. Luc broke it. 'Good,' he said roughly. 'Jo, marry me.'

Stunned, Jo stared at him, her involuntary flash of

incredulous joy evaporating as quickly as it had come. She drew a sharp breath and blurted, 'Don't be an idiot.'

But her voice broke. Desperately she hoped he hadn't caught that moment of sheer elation. What on earth was he doing now?

He shrugged, his expression unreadable in the darkness. 'This is the first proposal I've ever made, so I'm probably making a total hash of it, but I'd hoped that by now you'd have realised I'm no idiot.'

'Luc, this is ridiculous.' It took every ounce of self-possession to ignore the splintering of her heart. 'You don't have to marry me to make sure I'll keep our deal.'

'That's not why I asked you,' he said roughly.

'Then why did you?' A spark of humiliation persuaded her to ask, 'Because the sex was good? I'm sure you've had just as good before.'

'You have every right to be bitter, but I did not make love with you to win you onto my side.'

She drew in a deep breath. 'I'm not into expedient marriages, I'm afraid, like your—' and stopped precipitately because she'd just about been unforgivably rude.

Of course he guessed what she'd been going to say. 'Like my mother? Her first one wasn't expedient—it was all lust and parental defiance. The second was certainly financially practical.' He didn't wait for an answer. 'I'm not offering anything like the bargain she made with Tom.'

Jo had to boost her faltering courage to ask, 'So what *are* you offering?'

And *why*? Because there could only be one *good* reason—love.

He paused for at least three heartbeats. 'Ours would be a marriage of equals.'

Sorely torn, Jo hesitated, then took the biggest gamble of her life. 'I must be like *my* mother. She loved Joseph until she died—his name was the last word she said. I think that's possibly why she chose the life she did. She was no call girl,' she added, Sean's contempt vivid in her mind. 'She was a model and, in spite of the gossip, her relationships were long and faithful.'

'So *tell* me,' Luc said in a voice she'd never heard before. He stepped out of the shadows and looked down at her, starlight emphasising the strong bones of his face. 'Tell me what you want.'

'I've just told you.' She dragged in another jagged breath and met fierce grey eyes, narrowed and demanding. 'I want to marry someone I love—without limits, without fear, with total commitment and honesty.'

He said between his teeth, 'When we made love you gave me everything, without limits.'

'Desire isn't love,' she said sadly.

'I think that's what I've been trying to tell you.' He didn't move and his gaze never left her face. 'I've been attracted to women, lusted after some, made love to a few. Love is not a word I've ever used. Jo, do you feel anything more for me than passion?'

'I...I...' She struggled for words, then surrendered to the hard command of his expression. 'Of course I do. I love you. But that's not...'

When she stopped, he waited a few seconds before saying levelly, 'Go on.'

'That's not what you want to hear, is it?'

Incredulously, she saw his hands clench by his sides.

'I can't tell you I love you because I don't know what that is. I've had no experience of it. I *can* tell you that in spite of all I believed about you, I wanted you from the moment I saw you. It tore me apart. And as I got to know you I learned—with immense reluctance—to admire you. You're staunch and fearless and loyal, you work for what you believe in. You forced me to accept that you were not the woman I believed you to be.'

Eyes still holding hers, he shook his head. 'I'll admit I toyed with the idea of seducing you to make sure you gave me a good recommendation. I wanted to despise you for selling yourself to Tom, yet I couldn't reconcile my prejudice with the woman who spoke of him with such affection—a woman who'd cared for her sick mother and aunt, the woman whose main worry when her business was threatened was the welfare of her workers. Every day I saw some new instance of your spirit and your honesty, until I gave up looking for the wicked gold digger. If this is not love, trust me, it's a damned good substitute.'

'But will it last?' she asked quietly, unable to articulate the inchoate mass of doubts and fears that swirled through her.

'As long as I live.'

It sounded like a vow.

Jo looked at him and tried to speak but the words died in her throat and tears sprang to her eyes.

'Don't *do* that!' he ordered roughly. 'Joanna, marry me and I swear you'll never regret it.'

A wild response shuddered through her, insisting that she take this chance, and surrender without reservations.

But all she could say was, 'All right,' followed by a yelp of shock when he swooped and lifted her, and held her in a grip so tight she gasped for breath.

'Oh, *hell*,' he said remorsefully, and put her down and kissed her. After a while he looked around and said in a low, intense voice, 'Much as I'd like to make love to you here, there's a canoe with three fishermen in it not more than fifty metres out in the lagoon. Come back to the house with me.'

Laughing, tears still weirdly falling, she took the hand he held out and turned back to the house with him. 'It will be all over the island within two hours,' she gasped.

'Do you mind?'

'Not a bit.'

He lifted her hand and kissed the palm, then tucked it into the crook of his arm. 'There's nothing we can do about the media. And there will be innuendos—that I've married you only because you're Tom's daughter.'

She pulled a face. 'So, who cares?'

Luc grinned and hugged her. 'His will won't be accessible to the public until it's probated, which will give us some time to brace ourselves. Although, if I know Tom, that provision will never be available.'

'Do you think he had some idea of this? Of us?'

He looked down at her. 'I don't know, but I wouldn't be in the least surprised. Would you?'

Jo shook her head. 'No, not surprised at all,' she said slowly. 'Luc, do you mind if we get married here?'

'When?'

She laughed, feeling an enormous lightness and freedom and—yes, relief, as though everything had come

together for her and Luc. He hadn't said he loved her—
and she valued his honesty. One day, she thought with
complete trust, one day he'd say it and she'd value the
words even more because he'd wanted to be certain.

'In three weeks,' she said demurely. 'That's how long
it takes here in paradise.'

They were married on the beach in front of the house,
with friends around them. Jo wore a long floating sarong—cream silk appliquéd with pale gold hibiscus
flowers made by the local grandmothers during their
sewing meetings. Frangipani flowers the same colour
were tucked into her hair, and her sandals were jew-
elled with the glittering beads that adorned her bolero
jacket. She carried a spray of the precious gardenia
from the island, its scent floating clear and sensuous
in the sultry air.

The reception was a glorious mixture of Polynesian, European and French customs, as were the guests.
Lindy was maid of honour, still mortified that a work-
mate had overheard her tell her husband that her best
friend, Jo Forman, was Tom Henderson's—yes, *that*
Tom Henderson—*daughter*…

It was a noisy, touching ceremony, the church choir
adding their superb harmonies to the gentle hush of the
waves on the beach. Jo blinked back tears several times,
her hand firmly held by her new husband as they were
congratulated by Luc's friends—some with faces seen
often in the news—and hers, by her workers and several old school friends.

'Meru told me something today that made me realise
how very lucky I am,' she told her husband, when the

music and dancing had died away, and the guests had trooped off, leaving the beach empty once more. The sun had long set, and a golden lover's moon hung close to the tops of the coconut palms, casting its enchantment over the island and the sea.

Luc cocked a brow. 'What?'

'She told me that the reason the Council of chiefs didn't sell the rights to their plants was because they were made a better offer by someone else.'

He looked bored. 'Doesn't sound likely,' he said dismissively.

An upwelling of something close to pure delight tinged her smile with magic. 'It doesn't, does it? Would you like to know who made that offer?'

He shrugged. 'None of my business.'

'As it happens, I haven't been told,' she told him. 'Neither was Meru. It's a deep, dark secret, but she said she was pretty certain you know.'

He looked down at her, eyes silver in the moonlight, and laughed. 'I suppose you want me to tell you who it is?'

His body tightened when she sent him a glance that was both demure and mischievous. 'I don't think you should make it too easy for me to find out.'

Luc's grin widened. 'How good are your powers of persuasion?'

'I've never extended them before, but I bet they'll do the trick.'

'I like your style,' he said, and turned her into his arms and looked down at her. 'In fact, I like everything about you.' He paused. 'No, that's wrong. Joanna, I love everything about you.'

He said it calmly, his voice steady, yet she saw his love in his eyes, heard it in his voice, felt it in the gentleness of his arms around her.

It resonated through his words. 'I love you more than I ever expected to be able to feel. I wouldn't face it because it scares me. I don't *want* to love anyone as your mother loved—it makes me feel totally out of control—but I can't help it. And each day it gets stronger.'

Coming like that, unexpectedly, after the happiest day of her life so far, his confession was infinitely precious. Her eyes filled with tears, and she stepped into his embrace, holding him fiercely. 'I love you too,' she said simply. 'I'll always love you.'

Much later, lying locked in his arms after coming totally apart in them, Jo heard him say, 'Happy now that you know it was me who made the chiefs the offer they couldn't refuse?'

'I knew the moment Meru told me,' she said simply.

'Did you, indeed?' He tilted her chin and subjected her to one of his unrelenting surveys. 'So when did you know you loved me?'

'When you came back from Shanghai.' Smiling, she turned her head and kissed his shoulder. 'You were watching the blackbird doing her usual operatic show of suspicion, and you were smiling and…well, I realised that what I was feeling had to be love.'

'So you agreed to marry me before you knew about my dealings with the Council of chiefs?' He moved a little restlessly. 'I'm not usually such a coward. I don't even know when I fell in love with you—it was a process, not a moment.'

She hugged him, replete with pleasure yet still able

to thrill to the instant flexion of his muscles. 'I think that realisation is always part of a process, but I already knew before you told me,' she said demurely.

His chest rose and fell with silent laughter. 'How did you guess?'

'When we got married without any suggestion of signing a pre-nuptial agreement.'

'That's when I realised that you truly loved me too.' Luc laughed again before saying quietly, 'Thank you, Tom, wherever you are.'

'Amen,' Jo said.

And locked together, the soft sigh of the trade winds carrying the perfumes of the island to them, they slid into a sleep without cares or fears for the future.

* * * * *

THE BILLIONAIRE'S PASSION

CHAPTER ONE

ALLI PIERCE WOVE another frangipani blossom into the lei. After an appreciative sniff of the perfume from its shameless golden throat, she said, 'I'm completely determined to get to New Zealand, but I won't sell myself for the fare!'

'I know that,' her friend Sisilu said peaceably in the local variation of the language the Polynesians had carried across the immense reaches of the Pacific Ocean. 'Calm down. It was just a comment Fili made.'

'What's the matter with her lately? She's turned into a nasty little witch.'

Sisilu grinned. 'You're so naive! She's mad with you because she's got a serious crush on Tama, but he's got a serious crush on you. And she still reckons it's unfair that just because you've got a New Zealand passport Barry pays you New Zealand wages and not island ones. After all, you've been living on Valanu since you were a couple of months old.'

Alli anchored a lock of damp red-brown hair away from her hot face with a carved shell comb. 'Actually, I agree with her,' she said honestly. 'It makes me feel guilty, but Barry says it's company policy.'

'He'd know. Have you seen the new owner yet?'

'New owner?' She stared at her friend. 'Sea Winds's new owner? Here?'

Sisilu's dark eyes gleamed with sly amusement. 'Right here in throbbing, downtown Valanu.'

Alli laughed. 'Big deal.' But she sobered immediately. 'No, I haven't seen him—you know Monday's my day off. When did he get here?'

'Last night—arrived out of the blue on a private plane.'

A frown drew Alli's winged brows together. 'I thought Sea Winds was sold to a huge worldwide organisation. The head guy wouldn't come here—too busy being a tycoon. This man is probably just some suit from management. What's he like?'

'Big,' Sisilu told her, with a sensuous intonation that told Alli the new owner was tall, not fat. She sighed with purely feminine appreciation. 'And he's got presence—he's the owner all right. Not that I've seen much of him. He's been shut up with Barry all day, but he did a quick tour of the resort while we were rehearsing this morning.'

Alli's frown deepened. 'If he's the owner,' she said forthrightly, deft hands weaving more flowers into the lei, 'I'll bet that as well as being tall he's middle-aged, paunchy and going bald.'

Sisilu rolled bold dark eyes. 'I should take you up on that—it would be easy money! You couldn't be more wrong. He's got wide shoulders and long, strong legs—not a clumsy bone in his body and a stomach as flat as mine or yours. Flatter, probably.' Sisilu counted off his assets with frank relish. 'Slade Hawkings walks like a chief, looks like a chief, talks like a chief—he's already got the girls buzzing.'

Hawkings? Surprise scuttled on chilly feet down Alli's spine, but it was a common enough name in the English-speaking world.

Don't go imagining bogeymen, she warned herself. 'If he is the owner—or even an executive with power— he won't be interested in us islanders.' And to banish the cold needle of alarm she added briskly, 'So the girls might as well stop buzzing. Apart from the fact that he probably lives in America or England or Switzerland, men like him go for women who are sophisticated and knowledgeable.'

'If he's a day over twenty-eight I'll eat this lei,' Sisilu said cheerfully. Her tone altered when she said with a sideways look, 'As for that crack about middle-aged men—it just shows what a baby you are; the middle-aged ones are the ones to watch. Which is why you should be keeping an eye on Barry.'

'Barry?' Alli stared at her in astonishment. When her companion nodded, she went on with heavy sarcasm, 'You mean Barry Simcox? The hotel manager who was utterly broken-hearted when his wife ran back to Australia with their little boy because she couldn't stand living in this "godforsaken island in the middle of the Pacific Ocean"? I quote, of course. *That* Barry—who has never even looked sideways at me?'

'*That* very same Barry,' Sisilu said with a toss of her head. 'You might not have seen him looking at you, but others have.'

Alli snorted.

'Well, don't say I didn't warn you.' Her friend went

on. 'The new owner would be a much better lover. He looks like a film star, only tougher.' After an elaborate sigh she added, 'And you can tell by looking at him that he knows what he's doing when it comes to making love—he's got that aura, you know?'

'Well, no, I don't know.'

Sisilu eyed a hibiscus flower with a critical frown before discarding it. It fell with a soft plop onto the floor. 'Oh, yes, you do.' She added slyly, 'Tama has it too.'

Tama was the second son of the island chief, and Sisilu's cousin. Alli flushed. 'I wish he hadn't decided he is in love with me.'

'It's because you're not in love with him,' Sisilu said wisely, choosing another bloom. 'And because you're different—you don't want him when every other girl in Valanu would happily take him for a lover. As well, of course, virgins are special in our culture. Don't worry about him; he'll get over it once you leave.'

Both worked in silence for a few minutes before Sisilu ruthlessly dragged the conversation back to the topic foremost in her mind. 'And the new owner does not live in Switzerland or England or America—he lives in New Zealand.'

'So do about four million other people.'

'As for the sort of women he likes—when he saw you walk across the foyer five minutes ago he looked as though he'd been hit in the face with a dead shark. I know *that* look too,' Sisilu finished smugly.

In her driest voice Alli said, 'I'm sure you do—but are you certain it wasn't you he was watching? After all, you're the most beautiful girl in Valanu.'

Sisilu said prosaically, 'He didn't even see me.'

'Wait 'til he does.' Busy fingers pausing, Alli watched her friend thread several more hibiscus flowers into a head lei. Dark as blood, rich as passion, they glowed with silken light. 'Anyway, if he's that gorgeous he's probably gay.'

Sisilu's laugh demolished that idea. 'Far from it. When he looked at you he liked what he saw. He might be interested in helping a countrywoman, especially if you gave him an incentive.'

'Not that sort of incentive, thank you very much,' Alli returned with robust forthrightness, threading in several long pointed leaves to give the effect of a ruff. 'If he wants to help me he can keep the resort going.'

It was the only chance she had to save enough for her fare to New Zealand.

Her friend ignored her. 'Making love with him would not be difficult. He has the kind of sexuality that sets off fires. I wish he'd forget he's the boss and look my way.'

Alli closed her eyes against the shimmer of the sun on the lagoon. Beneath the high-pitched shriek of a gull she could hear the slow, deep roar of the Pacific combers smashing onto the coral reef.

The girls she'd grown up with on Valanu had a forthright, honest appreciation of their sexuality. Once married they'd stay faithful, but until then they enjoyed the pleasures of the flesh without shame.

Alli's father had seen to it that she didn't follow suit.

'Why are you so keen to leave Valanu?' Sisilu asked unexpectedly. 'It's your home.'

Alli shrugged, slender golden fingers still for a second before she picked up another flower from the fragrant heap beside her. Her generous mouth hardened.

'I want to know why my mother left us, and what drove my father to hide himself away here.'

'You know why. He went to school with the chief in Auckland. Naturally, when the tribal corporation wanted someone to run the system, they thought of him.'

Golden-brown eyes sombre, Alli nodded. 'But there are too many questions. Dad wouldn't say a word about any family. I don't even know who my grandparents were.'

Her friend made a clucking noise. To be deprived of family in Polynesia meant much the same as being an outcast. 'Your father was a good man,' she said quickly.

Two years previously, after Ian Pierce's death, Alli had gone through his papers and found the one thing she'd longed to know—the name of her mother. That find had encouraged her to save the money she needed to pay an investigator to find Marian Hawkings. Three months previously the dossier had arrived. Now she was saving desperately to meet the woman who'd borne her, only to abandon her.

She said steadily, 'My mother was an Englishwoman who married Dad in England and came to New Zealand with him. After they divorced she married another man, but she's a widow now, still living in Auckland. I don't want to intrude into her life—I just want to know a few things. Then I'll have some sort of closure.' She concentrated on weaving the final flower into the lei.

Her friend's shoulders lifted. 'But you'll come back, won't you? We are your family now.'

Alli smiled mistily, deft fingers flying as they tied off the lei with long strings of *tii* leaf. 'And I couldn't have a kinder one. It's just that the need to know gnaws at my heart.'

'I understand.' Sisilu grinned. 'Anyway, you'll hate New Zealand. It's big and cold and different—no place for someone who loves Valanu as much as you.'

She looked up as a woman strode towards them. 'Uh-oh, here's trouble,' she said beneath her breath. 'Look at her face!'

Without preamble the trainer of the dance troupe said, 'Alli, you'll be dancing tonight—Fili's sick. And we need to make a good impression because the owner of the hotel is deciding whether to keep Sea Winds open or close it down.'

Both girls stared at her. 'He can't do that,' Alli blurted.

'Of course he can, and from what I'm hearing he'd do it without thinking twice. When it was first built it paid its way, but the war in Sant'Rosa cut off the supply of tourists, and for the past five years it's been losing more and more each year,' the older woman said bluntly.

Alli frowned. 'If things are that bad, why did the new owner buy it?'

'Who knows?' She picked up one of the lei and examined it, then dropped it and turned away. 'Perhaps he was cheated. Although he doesn't look like a man who'd allow that to happen to him. It isn't any of our business, anyway, but make sure you dance well tonight.'

Aware that she was a widow, whose job at the resort paid for the schooling of her three sons, both girls watched her go.

Soberly Alli said, 'If the resort closes it will be a disaster for Valanu.'

Sisilu said with a wry smile, 'So perhaps if the owner likes what he sees when he looks at you it will help all of us if you are nice to him. You might be able to influence him into keeping the hotel open.'

As she dressed for the dancing that night, Alli remembered the hidden worry in her friend's voice. The man who'd caused this fear hadn't eaten in the restaurant, but he'd be there for the floorshow, watching from somewhere in the darkness of the wide terrace. The women getting ready in the staff cloakroom were more silent than usual; already everyone knew that the resort was threatened.

'He's there, so no giggling,' the organiser said sternly as excited yells and applause from the audience indicated that the men's posture dance had reached its climax. She cast an eye over Alli and her face softened. 'You look good—those cream frangipani suit your skin and your red hair.'

That was about the only thing she'd inherited from her mother. Shortly after her father's death Alli had found his wedding certificate, and with it a photograph—her father, looking so proud of himself she almost hadn't recognised him, and a laughing woman. Apart from hair colour, Alli didn't look at all like her mother, but the wedding certificate attached to the photograph implied that this woman had borne her.

And then left her. With the marriage certificate and the photograph had been a legal notification of divorce, and a newspaper clipping about her mother's marriage a couple of years later to another man.

The staccato rhythm of the drums settled into a sultry beat, and she and the other dancers took their places

in the line. Alli adjusted the uncomfortable bra and
began singing an old island love song. The dancers filed
out from behind the woven screen that shielded the door
from the audience, voices blending in harmony, mobile
hands eloquently conveying the story.

From the darkness behind the diners, Slade watched
them with a critical eye; amateurs they might be, but
they were good. Unfortunately the hokey bras made of
half-coconuts detracted from the effect. If he decided
to keep the place open they'd go.

Not that the audience cared. His mouth curved in
a cynical smile as he surveyed the enthusiastic group
of diners.

Give them erotically charged lyrics and lithe bod-
ies polished by the light of flares, dark eyes that beck-
oned from beneath garlands of perfumed flowers, white
teeth flashing in come-hither smiles, and they were
more than happy.

He examined the dancers again, realising with sardonic derision that his gaze kept drifting back to Alli
Pierce. His chief troubleshooter had come back with
photographs of her, but none had done her justice. In
them she'd looked young and enthusiastic, whereas in
the flesh the overwhelming impression was of glowing,
sensuous freshness emphasised by tilted lion-coloured
eyes, a laughing provocative mouth, and dramatic
cheekbones.

Although she danced with tantalising grace, and
managed to look both innocent and seductive festooned
with wreaths of flowers and green leaves, her hands

fluttering in stylised, exquisite movements, that sensual, enticing surface was a lie.

Beautiful, sexy and twenty years old, it seemed that Alli Pierce had decided on a career as a con artist.

Ignoring an unwelcome itch of desire, he focused on her with the keen brain and ferocious concentration that had propelled his father's thriving local organisation onto the world stage. The investigator he'd dispatched to the island had learned that her father had brought her there as a baby, and that the locals didn't believe she had Polynesian ancestry.

'Not,' the investigator had told him wearily, 'that they were at all forthcoming about her or her father.'

Slade's brows shot up. 'I thought places like Valanu were hotbeds of gossip.'

'But not to outsiders.' The middle-aged woman shrugged. 'They were extremely protective of her. I did manage to find out that the hotel manager's wife left him because of Ms Pierce, but the next person I talked to about it said that that was a lie.'

'What do you think?'

The older woman's expression turned cynical. 'The people there have a pretty liberated attitude to premarital sex, and she certainly seems like the other girls—flirtatious and light-hearted. I saw her several times with the manager and he's certainly hot for her. But so is one of the local boys—the chief's second son. She could be running them both, of course.'

Indeed she could, Slade thought as he watched the way the torches summoned mahogany flames from her long, flower-studded hair. Only slightly taller than the other women, she was built on more racy lines, and her skin gleamed gold rather than bronze.

And he shouldn't be eyeing her like some old lecher in an oriental slave market; he was supposed to be grading the show. Ruthlessly he bent his attention to the other dancers, the ambience, the effect of the whole package on the audience.

Song and dance finished on a sweetly melancholy note; after a moment's silence the audience erupted in exuberant applause, and the dancers, laughing, swung into a fast, upbeat Valanuan version of a hula.

Slade watched hips swinging suggestively, hands sinuously alluring and smiles that tempted every man in the audience—including him, he realised with disgust. Exasperated by the pagan appetite stirring into awareness, he sensed someone's arrival beside him.

'For amateurs, we think they're pretty good,' the manager said, his voice too easy and confident for a man who knew his job was on the line.

'Of their sort, excellent,' Slade said casually. 'Who are they?'

'Oh, just local girls—most of them are staff. The one on the far left teaches at the local school, and second from right is Alli Pierce, whose father was a New Zealander, like you. She's not a regular, but one of the girls is ill tonight so she's taken her place.'

'The girl who works in the souvenir shop?'

And possibly the mistress of the man beside him; there had been a far from fatherly intonation in the manager's voice when he spoke of her, and he certainly paid her three times the local wage. As she conveniently lived in a house next door to Simcox's, the accusation was probably correct.

Eyes fixed on the dancers, the man beside him nodded. 'Ian Pierce brought Alli to Vanalu when she was a baby; apparently her mother died in an accident when she was only a couple of weeks old.' His voice altered fractionally. 'She's a lovely girl, and she deserves more than Valanu can offer her.'

And you'd like to provide it, Slade thought grimly. His narrowed eyes followed Alli Pierce as the line of dancers swayed off into the darkness, his body tightening when she turned just before she stepped out of the light of the flares and looked directly at him.

Transfixed by a feral response to that swift glance, he barely noticed the three men who leapt out with a wild yell above a sudden clamour of drums.

Angrily he summoned the ragged remnants of his self-control; in his relationships he required much more than lust, the lowest common denominator. Hell, it had been years since his hormones had driven him along that bleak path.

Droning like a distant engine, the manager's voice intruded into his thoughts. Slade forced his mind away from an inviting, enticing face.

'Bright too,' the man was saying. 'But her father wouldn't hear of her going to a better high school in New Zealand. It's a shame she's stuck here—she'd do well if she had more opportunity.'

Slade thought cynically that she hoped to force that opportunity by extracting money from a total stranger.

Marian wasn't going to be her ticket to a newer, better life. Shocked and bewildered by the letter Alli

Pierce had sent her, his stepmother had done what she did whenever she was faced by something she couldn't handle—turned to Slade.

An image of the girl's face flashed with teasing seductiveness against his eyelids. He'd see her tomorrow and he'd scare the hell out of her—and enjoy doing it. Of all forms of crime, blackmail came close to being the most despicable.

And while he was doing it he'd find out why she'd targeted his stepmother.

In the small room where the dancers were getting out of their uncomfortable bras and the pareus swathed tightly around their hips, Sisilu said gleefully, 'He was staring at you. See, I told you he was interested! And so are you.'

'I am not!'

'Then why did you turn around to stare at him?' her friend demanded unanswerably.

Alli rubbed her palms over her cold upper arms and muttered, 'I just wanted to see what he looked like.'

'You felt him watching you.' Sisilu nodded wisely and quoted a local proverb about eyes being the arrows of love.

'Oh, rubbish,' Alli said, knotting her own pareu above her breasts.

In fact, she didn't know why she'd acted on that compelling impulse, but she could see him now as if he stood in front of her—a tall man, broad-shouldered and formidable, the starkly moulded framework of his face picked out by a spurt of flame from the torches.

He exuded authority and a compelling magnetism that still kept her pulse soaring.

'Well, what did you think of him?' Sisilu asked.

'He has presence,' Alli admitted grudgingly, pushing her hair back off her damp cheeks.

Sisilu laughed, but to Alli's relief left the subject alone.

An hour or so later, at home in the small house she'd shared with her father, she recalled the swift, hot contraction in the pit of her stomach when her gaze had clashed with that of the new owner. For a stretched moment the laughter and applause had faded into a thick, tense silence. Although it was sheer fantasy, she felt as though they'd duelled across the hot, crowded space, like old enemies—or old lovers.

'You're just imagining things,' she scoffed. 'You could barely see him.'

On an impulse she went to the safe and took out the folder containing all that she had of her family—the photograph of her father and mother, the legal certificates with their alien names, the newspaper cutting.

Why had her father changed his name when he came to Valanu? And hers too. It made her feel as though she'd been living a lie for twenty years.

Carefully she unfolded the newspaper clipping. Dated three years after her birth, a year after her parents' divorce, it told of the wedding between Marian Carter and David Hawkings.

If there'd been a photograph of the newlyweds she'd have been able to judge whether Slade Hawkings looked anything like David Hawkings.

'No, it's too far-fetched; coincidences like that don't

happen,' she reassured herself, and went to bed, where she lay awake for hours before sinking into a restless, dream-disturbed sleep.

Of course in the morning she woke too late to swim in the lagoon. As it was, she'd opened the doors of the shop only seconds before the first influx of customers arrived—a group of young men from America on a diving holiday.

They swarmed around her, teasing, laughing, flirting enthusiastically, but without any sign of seriousness. Because there was no harm in any of them, she laughed, teased and flirted back.

However, there was always one who pushed his luck; smiling, she eluded his hands, turning him off with a quip that made him yell with laughter.

He was saying with an overdone leer, 'Same time tonight, honey?' when Barry Simcox arrived.

Previously she'd have thought nothing of Barry's frown, and the way he watched the young man, but Sisilu's comment the previous day had put an uneasy dent in her easygoing friendship with the manager.

Once the divers left the shop, Barry came in. And with him came the new owner.

Alli's heart jumped so strongly she had to stop herself from pressing her hand over it to keep it in place. In the soft, bewitching clarity of morning Slade Hawkings looked even more forbidding than he had in the dramatic light of the flares.

Fussily, Barry performed the introductions. 'Mr Hawkings is here to check us over,' he said with a smile that just missed its mark. He turned to Slade and informed him, 'As you've seen from the figures, Alli has done well with the souvenir shop.'

Alli held out her hand and said quietly, 'How do you do?'

Green eyes, translucent and emotionless as glass, examined her—almost, she thought, as though she'd surprised him. His hand was warm, but not unpleasantly so, and dry, yet she sensed latent power in the lean fingers and brief grip. He didn't wring her fingers painfully together as many men did.

Colour heated her skin at the memory of Sisilu's summing up—this was definitely a man who knew women.

'How do you do?' Slade Hawkings returned in a deep, cool voice, dismissing her with his tone and the flick of a humourless smile.

Stung, Alli stiffened her spine. OK, so he was the boss, and the powerful angles and planes of his face were both compelling and daunting, but he had no reason to look at her as though she were rubbish underneath his shoes.

She turned to put out more stock, but Slade Hawkings said levelly, 'I'd like you to stay, please.'

So she waited in outwardly respectful silence while the two men discussed the shop at length.

Slade Hawkings commented, 'Stone carving isn't an art that Pacific Islanders are noted for. Why are you selling this stuff here?'

Barry opened his mouth to answer, but in a voice that stopped the other man's words before they could be uttered, Slade said, 'Alli.'

'We used to stock woven bags,' she told him, bristling, 'but the customs officers in New Zealand and Australia thought they might hide insects. Since fumigation doesn't do much for a bag, I looked around for something else.'

Slade nodded. 'And imported this cheap product to take their place?'

In a tone so courteous it skidded dangerously close to insolence, she said, 'They are not imported—there's always been carving on Valanu. Because there were no large trees on the atoll, the islanders worked coral instead. These are god figures—not the most sacred, of course, but they're carved with skill and all the correct ceremonies.' She indicated an eye-catching quilt on the wall. 'These are not imports, either. A woman whose mother was a Cook Islander showed the Valanuans how to make them. They're hugely popular, but I do make sure the buyers know they aren't a traditional craft on Valanu.'

She expected him to blench at the pattern of bold scarlet and white lilies, but he startled her by saying, 'I hope you're paying enough for them—they take years to finish.'

In answer she flicked the tag around so that he could see the price. He leaned over her shoulder to look, and she breathed in a hint of elusive scent.

Undiluted essence of male, she thought wildly—no hint of cologne or soap, just a faint whisper of fragrance, clean and salty and intensely personal. Astonished, she felt her mouth dry and her skin tighten unbearably. His closeness beat against her like a dark force of nature.

Appalled by her reaction, she dropped her hand and clenched it at her side, not daring to move in case she touched him. The only sound she could hear was the uneven thudding of her heart.

Then he stepped back, snapping the invisible bonds that had locked her into a trance.

Alli forced her face to register a bland lack of interest before turning to face him. Eyes as cold as polar ice and every bit as hard met hers.

'Do you sell many?' he asked laconically.

Alli's chin tilted. 'At least one a month. We'd sell more if we could get them. They're popular.'

'You look very young to be managing this shop,' he observed.

Barry jumped in. 'Since Alli's been here she's increased turnover considerably. She speaks the local language as well as English so she's an excellent liaison with the craftspeople on the island. And she has great taste, as you can see.'

Slade Hawkings's eyes turned colder, if that was possible. Ignoring the other man, he asked her about the turnover, about her ordering, relentlessly making her justify everything she'd done.

When he left half an hour later she felt as though he'd wrung every scrap of information from her. Shaking inside, she watched him stride beside the manager across the foyer, tall and lithe—a true chief, wearing his inborn authority with panache.

Or, considering him from another angle, a shark, right at the top of the food chain!

CHAPTER TWO

HER MOUTH PARCHED from Slade Hawkings's grilling, Alli poured herself a glass of pineapple juice, but had only swallowed a little when the after-breakfast customers arrived.

It turned out to be one of those days—hot, busy, with more than its fair share of irritating and irritated people. When she closed the doors at seven that night she was tired and hungry and badly in need of a swim. At least Fili had recovered enough to dance, so she didn't have to don the outrageously uncomfortable coconut bra!

The new owner of the resort had passed through the foyer a couple of times, cool and utterly sure of himself—the consummate predator. Beside him, Barry's fraying composure marked him as prey.

'Like the rest of us,' Sisilu said forthrightly when Alli hurried in to say hello before the show. 'Everyone's walking around as though they might tread on a stonefish.'

'Surely he wouldn't just close Sea Winds down and walk away from it— apart from anything else, the buildings are worth a lot of money.'

'He's a very rich man—someone said he's a billionaire now.' Sisilu shrugged as though that explained everything. 'You don't get where he is by not making hard decisions. And he's not here to lie on the beach and work on his tan; he came here to do something. It's like he's electrified the whole place.'

'With the sheer force of his personality?' Alli jeered. 'No matter what he was like everyone would be jumpy; people tend to get stressed when their jobs are at stake.'

'But this feels personal,' her friend said abruptly. 'He's got it in for someone. All right, you laugh—but he's a man who makes things happen, and something's going to happen now. I can feel it.'

Strolling towards the lagoon across sand still warm from the day's heat, Alli pondered Sisilu's words. In the distance she could hear the feverish drumming that heralded the fire dancers, and said a silent prayer for them all.

At the water's edge she dropped her pareu into a heap and walked out into the lukewarm water, sinking into it with a long sigh of relief.

Personal? No, how could it be? Sisilu was reacting morbidly to the situation.

But as Alli struck out parallel to the beach she wondered in selfish frustration why Slade Hawkings couldn't have waited another six months to buy the resort. By then she'd have saved enough to pay her passage to New Zealand—first the several days' trip to Fiji on a copra boat, then a flight to Auckland.

Her jaw tightened. She'd find a way to get there; no arrogant hotel owner was going to stop her. She had a mission, and she'd see it through.

Buoyed by the silken water, she floated on her back

and stared at the stars, huge and white and aloof, their lovely, liquid Polynesian names more real to her than the ones her father had given them. They'd be different in New Zealand. And she'd be leaving behind all her friends, a familiar, comfortable way of life...

She fought back a nascent shiver of homesickness. Much as she'd miss the island and her friends, she wanted more than Valanu could offer. And, judging by Slade Hawkings's attitude, even if he didn't close down Sea Winds she had no future there.

Diving as easily as the dolphins that sometimes visited the lagoon, she breathed out slowly and swam through a silvery wonderland towards the beach. Eventually her toes found the sand; frowning, she stood and wiped the water from her eyes, because someone waited for her beside the small pile of her pareu.

Tama.

Oh, not now, Alli thought wearily, and then felt mean. He didn't *want* to suffer from unrequited love!

She twisted her hair onto the top of her head and waded towards the beach. 'Good evening,' she said in English, deliberately using that language to distance herself from him.

He answered in the same tongue. 'Fili said you're going back to New Zealand with the new owner.'

'Where on earth did she get that idea?' Alli answered contemptuously, stooping to pick up her pareu.

'From Sisilu, I suppose.' His eyes were hot, but his voice revealed his pain. 'She said you'd talked about sleeping with him so he'd keep the resort open.'

Furious, Alli knotted her pareu over her scanty swimsuit. 'Slade Hawkings has the coldest eyes of anyone I've ever seen. I don't think he's open to negotiation.'

Tama gazed at her hungrily, his eyes sliding the length of the wet pareu. 'You want to go to New Zealand. He might take you.'

She drew a deep breath. 'Tama, be sensible.'

'Alli, marry me.' When she shook her head and started off up the beach he caught her up. 'I can change my father's mind. He knows you and loves you—he'll come around soon enough.'

The cluster of coconut palms beside the house was only a few metres away. Gently she said, 'Your father will never change his mind. The last thing he wants for you is marriage to a woman with no background, no family, no nothing. He is an aristocrat of the old school, and I'm a nobody. It simply won't happen.'

He grabbed her by the arm and swung her to face him. 'It could if you agreed.'

She said firmly, 'No. I'm going to New Zealand.'

'Why?'

She looked around at the glimmering expanse of the lagoon, the elegant statement of the coconut palms, the combination of soft sweetness and astringent salty scent that spelt Valanu to her—the sheer magical beauty of it all. Reverting to the local Polynesian tongue for emphasis, she said quietly, 'Because it's where I belong. Just as you belong here.'

He made a sound in his throat and pulled her against him. Startled, Alli stiffened, and when he began to press kisses over her face she mumbled, 'Let me go. Now!'

'Alli, you're driving me mad,' he said in a low, passionate voice. 'I need you—'

'No, you don't.' Instinctively repelled by his arousal, she had to remind herself that this was Tama, who'd teased her all through school, who'd laughed and picked her up when she'd fallen over, who'd been so like a brother that she hadn't even realised when he'd decided to fall in love with her.

He rested his cheek on her head. 'You don't know how I feel,' he muttered.

She freed her arms and cupped his face with both her hands, staring into his eyes and trying to convince him. He seemed older and harder, as though he'd made up his mind to do something.

'I know I don't feel the same way!' she said sadly.

'Because you won't let yourself—you think it's wrong because my parents are so old-fashioned. I can make you feel it.'

He pressed an urgent kiss on her mouth, and this time she pushed at his chest, her hand tightening over his solar plexus as she clenched her jaw. When she could speak she said, 'Tama, no!'

Something in her tone got to him, because he dragged in a deep breath and stepped back, dropping his arms. Tears stung her eyes as she watched him struggle for control.

Why on earth did this business between the sexes have to be so complicated?

He said thickly, 'I love you.'

'Tama, I think of you as my brother. Your mother is the only mother I've ever had,' she said gently. 'I love you too, but not like that.'

He looked away. 'We could make it impossible for

them to say no,' he said unevenly. 'If there was a child my mother wouldn't turn it away.'

Alli sucked in her breath, but said steadily, 'You'd have to rape me, and you wouldn't do that.'

'No,' he said, and the hungry, determined man disappeared, replaced by the beloved companion of her childhood.

'And we couldn't do that to your parents,' she said, aching for him. 'They trust you—and they trust me too.'

He gathered his dignity around him to kiss her forehead softly. 'Then there is nothing more to be said. I hope your voyage brings you happiness, little sister.'

And he turned and strode away down the beach, leaving Alli shaken and forlorn, wrenched by the loss of her last security as she watched him disappear into the darkness. Slowly she turned and walked towards the house she'd grown up in, no longer a sanctuary for her.

Two steps away from the clump of coconut palms her every sense suddenly woke to full alert, pulling her skin tight in primal fear. She stopped and stared into the shadows. Tall and dark and dominating, a broad shoulder propped against a sinuous trunk, someone waited for her there, silent and still as some sleekly dangerous night predator.

Foreboding knotted her stomach, and her pulse ricocheted. In her most matter-of-fact tone, she said, 'Good evening, Mr Hawkings.'

He straightened, but stayed where he was. Illuminated by the gathering radiance of a rising moon, she felt exposed and vulnerable.

'Good evening, Alli.' There was a subtle insult in his

use of her first name. 'I thought for a moment I might have to come to your rescue.'

'No,' she said curtly. 'Have you lost your way?'

'On the contrary. I came looking for you.'

A flash of fear hollowed out her stomach. Acutely aware of the way her pareu clung to her wet body, she asked huskily, 'Why?'

He paused. 'To see what a con artist looks like.'

The cold, implicit threat in his words silenced her until she produced enough composure to say, 'I don't know what you mean.'

'You wrote a letter to Marian Hawkings informing her you were her long-lost daughter and asking her why she abandoned you and your father.'

Sweat sheened her forehead and temples. Her heart skidded to a halt in her chest, then started up double time. She could only just discern the arrogant framework of his face, and what she saw there terrified her—icy distaste and a ruthless warning.

Alli swallowed to ease a throat suddenly dry. 'How—how did you know?'

'I'm glad you don't deny it. She told me.'

'Are you related to her?' she asked breathlessly.

'In a way.'

Frustration ate into her, but she rallied. 'I don't remember saying anything in my letter that could be construed as a con.'

'Perhaps blackmail would be a better word. I read your letter; it was aggressive, and there was a clear intimation that you were coming to New Zealand to meet her.' His voice was hard and uncompromising.

'I didn't intend it to be aggressive, but, yes, I said

that. She owes me one meeting, surely?' Alli fought back a bewildering mixture of emotions. 'So she's not going to meet me?'

'Why should she? She has no daughter called Alli—'

'Alison,' she said raggedly.

'Or Alison.'

'Actually, it's Alison Marian.'

'Is it?' He couldn't have made his disbelief more obvious. Without bothering to comment, he went on, 'On the date you gave for your birth she was in Thailand on holiday with friends. I don't know where you got your information, Alli—always providing it wasn't just a stab in the dark—but she rejects it entirely.'

Pain squeezed Alli's heart in a vice so ferocious she thought she might never be able to take a breath again. She fought it with every ounce of will. 'I see,' she said, each word deep and deliberate and steady. 'In that case there's nothing more to be said. Goodbye, Mr Hawkings.'

'Not so fast. Where did you hear about her?'

It couldn't hurt to tell him. Perhaps it might even rock his confident self-possession a little. She'd like that—it might ease the pain that gripped her.

'I saw her name on my father's marriage certificate.'

He moved so quickly she gasped and took a stumbling step backwards. In the moonlight his face was a mask, superbly carved to reveal no emotion, but she saw the glitter of his eyes and knew with a bitter satisfaction that she had startled him.

'You're lying,' he said, and covered the ground between them in two quick strides.

Head held high and eyes glittering, she stood her

ground. 'She was Marian Carter, born in Hampshire, England. She met my father there, married him a year later, and emigrated to New Zealand with him. I was born roughly two years afterwards. Not that it's any of your business.'

'I don't believe you,' he said icily.

'So?' Humiliated, she felt her wet hair tumble around her shoulders in a clammy mass. 'I'm not interested in what you believe. If Mrs Hawkings doesn't want to acknowledge me, I'm certainly not going to press the issue.' She gave him a brittle smile. 'Harassing one's own mother is not polite, after all.'

A lean, implacable hand clamped around the fine bones of her wrist. He didn't hurt her, but she felt like a bird caught in a trap.

'You're a cool one,' he said levelly.

It wasn't a compliment. Every cell in her body shrieked an alarm. 'Let me go.'

Moonlight gleamed on his face, lighting up a smile that chilled her with its cynicism. 'Who was the boy on the beach?' he enquired in a tone that combined both indolence and steel.

'An old friend.' She twisted away and stepped past him, aware that he chose to let her go. Although he hadn't marked her skin, his touch had scorched through her like lightning on a hilltop.

His smile narrowed. 'A pity your touching renunciation wasn't necessary.'

Alli looked up at him with apprehension tinged by fear. In spite of the fact that she disliked him intensely, he made her overwhelmingly conscious of the hard muscle under the superbly cut casual clothes, of the cutting edge of his intellect.

'Is eavesdropping a hobby of yours?' she asked, not trying to soften the scathing words.

She'd have said it was impossible, but the autocratic mask of his face hardened even further. 'Only when I can't avoid it. You should check that no one's around before you turn a man down,' he shot back, a raw note in his voice scuffing her nerves into shocking sensitivity.

They were quarrelling—yet she didn't know him enough to quarrel. 'I don't need to—the islanders are too courteous to intrude.'

'Or too accustomed to seeing you with a man to be interested?' he enquired pleasantly.

Her breathing became shallow; instinct warned her to get the hell out of there, but she couldn't move. Eyes widening, she stared up into his formidable face.

He lifted her chin with one forefinger and smiled as he examined her—feature by feature—with unsparing calculation.

Not a nice smile. Yet she couldn't move, couldn't do anything except suffer that inspection as though she was an object being examined with a view to purchase.

'It's no use casting your spells on me.' Each word was delivered with a flat lack of expression, although a contemptuous undertone sent wariness shivering down Alli's spine. 'Your mouth is slightly swollen from another man's kisses and I've always been foolishly fastidious. I'm also immune to the enchantment of a tropical moon and a pretty face.'

Ripples of feverish sensation threatening to carry her

away, Alli gritted her teeth until she could say evenly, 'Goodnight.'

She straightened her shoulders and strode up the shell path towards the house without a backward glance. Yet she knew the exact second Slade Hawkings turned away and headed back down the beach towards the resort.

Because it hurt too much to think of her mother's rejection, she spent the hours until she slept vengefully imagining what she should have done when Slade touched her. Unfortunately imagining him sprawled on the sand clasping his midriff and gasping for breath proved to be an unsatisfactory substitute for the real thing. Why hadn't she let him know bluntly that she resented strangers pawing her?

Instead of hitting him, she'd noticed the tiny pulse beating in his jaw, registered the elusive fragrance that was Slade Hawkings's alone, and felt the fierce demand of his will-power battering her defences.

She found some relief in punching her pillow before turning over to listen to the waves on the reef. Always before their pounding had soothed her, but tonight unwilling excitement still throbbed like a drug through her veins and, later, through her dreams.

Alli made sure she arrived at work ahead of time the next morning. After restocking the shelves she arranged a cluster of brazenly gold hibiscus on the counter, their elaborate frills reminding her of the frothy confections Edwardian society women had worn on their proudly poised heads.

'Good morning,' Barry Simcox said from behind her.

Pulse hammering, she straightened and whirled in one smooth movement.

He stared at her in bewilderment. 'Are you all right?'

Feeling an idiot, she muttered, 'I'm fine, thank you. You surprised me.'

'I didn't realise you were the nervous type.'

'I'm not!' she said truthfully, smiling to show him that she was completely in control of her erratic responses.

He nodded, and looked around the shop. 'You do have a knack with design,' he said absently. 'Hawkings mentioned it yesterday.'

'Did he?' She wanted to ask him what else the new owner had said, but of course she didn't. Instead she probed tentatively, 'Has he told you anything about his plans for Sea Winds?'

His pleasant mouth turned down at the corners. 'Nothing. He's playing his cards damned close to his chest.'

Like her and the rest of the staff, Barry stood to lose his job if the resort was abandoned. However, he could go back to Australia and resume his career.

She summoned a bright smile. 'A woman yesterday said we ought to mass-produce the quilts. She thought we should import some sewing machines and set up a little factory.' Her laughter blended with his startled guffaw. 'I didn't tell her that most of the islanders have sewing machines, or explain that the reason the quilts are so valuable is that they're handmade.'

A cold voice said, 'If you're ready, Simcox, I'll see you now.'

Poor Barry almost choked. 'Yes, sure, certainly,'

he said, turning away from Alli so quickly he had to grab the nearest thing, which happened to be her bare shoulder.

'Sorry,' he babbled, letting her go as though her skin had burnt his fingers.

Keeping her eyes away from Slade Hawkings, Alli retired behind the counter and opened the till.

'Good morning, Alli,' he said, the thread of mockery through his words telling her that he understood her reaction and found it amusing.

Her eyes glinted beneath her lashes. 'Good morning, Mr Hawkings,' she returned with every ounce of sweetness she could summon, ignoring Barry's alarmed stare.

'You're looking a little tired,' Slade said, adding, 'Perhaps you should try to get to bed earlier?'

Although she read the warning in the manager's expression, she showed her teeth anyway. 'You needn't worry. I won't let anything I do at night affect my work.'

She heard the hiss of Barry's breath whistling past his teeth. Far too heartily, he leapt in with, 'Slade, I've got those figures ready for you now.'

Slade Hawkings looked at him as though he was an irritating insect. 'Let's see them, then.'

Watching them walk back across the foyer in the direction of the one suite the resort boasted—which Slade had claimed—Alli wondered how two men, from the back rather similar in size and height, could look so different. Barry walked straight enough, and his clothes were good, yet beside the other man he looked...well, spectacularly insignificant.

Everything about Slade Hawkings proclaimed that he was completely in command of himself, his surroundings and his life. He looked, Alli thought with a sudden clutch of panic, exactly like a man who'd close down a poorly performing resort without a hint of compassion for the people who worked there.

So why did her body respond with swift, forbidden excitement whenever she saw him?

For the next two days rumours buzzed around the resort, growing wilder and more depressing each hour. Alli was kept busy with a new wave of tourists, most of whom wandered into the souvenir shop at some time to stock up on T-shirts, bright cotton pareus, or a hat for protection from the fierce sun. Excited children raced past the shop on their way to the lagoon, and each night the troupe danced and sang as though their lives depended on it.

'Barry's looking pretty sick, and the waiter who delivers the meals says the Big Man is getting grimmer and grimmer,' Sisilu said from the depths of an elderly cane chair on the second night.

She'd called in on her way home after the floorshow, joining Alli on the verandah.

'What's Hawkings doing?'

'Going over figures.' Sisilu could never be serious for long, and almost immediately she started to laugh. 'Hey, did anyone tell you about the girl who thought Mr Hawkings was part of the package that first night?'

Alli's brows shot up. 'No! What happened?'

'She saw him at the show and really came on to him.'

'What did he do?'

Sisilu grinned. 'He joined her group, and half an hour later he'd fixed her up with a good-looking American. Fili said she looked like a stunned fish, trying to

work out what had happened! He's clever, that man.'
She sent Alli a laughing sideways glance. 'So what's
with you and him?'

'Nothing,' Alli shot back.

'Fili said the Big Man saw you and Barry laughing
together in the shop and didn't like it.'

'Fili must spend all her time dodging round looking for scandal,' Alli said, resigned to the fact that on
an island the size of Valanu nothing was secret. 'And
when she doesn't find it she makes it up. If Slade Hawkings looked angry it's because he doesn't like me and
I don't like him.'

Sisilu chuckled. 'So why doesn't he like you?'

'Oh—we just rub each other up the wrong way.' Alli
wished she'd kept her mouth shut.

'Which usually means that there's something going
on underneath. I think he wants you, and men like that
are used to taking what they want.'

A hot little thrill ran through Alli, but she said,
'You've got an over-active imagination.'

'I saw him watch you walk across the beach yesterday.' Sisulu fanned herself and rolled her eyes. 'His face
didn't change, but I could feel his attention like laser
beams. I'm surprised you didn't.'

Alli moved uncomfortably and Sisilu started to
laugh. 'You did, didn't you? I can tell you did! You
going to do something about it?'

CHAPTER THREE

ALLI SHOOK HER head so swiftly the orchid behind her left ear went flying into the scented night. 'Even if he does, I don't know anything about…well, about anything. You know what my father was like.'

'He didn't do you any favours,' Sisilu said, wrinkling her forehead as she recalled Ian Pierce's strictness. 'Making love's nothing much—I mean, it's great, and I like doing it, but the world doesn't revolve around it. The longer you put it off the bigger and bigger it gets, I suppose. Are you scared?'

'Not exactly,' Alli said thoughtfully.

When Tama had kissed her she'd felt nothing beyond regret that she couldn't feel as he so obviously did. But Slade's touch had charged her with forbidden excitement. She could still feel it like fireworks inside, all flash and fire and heat.

Hastily she finished, 'But I feel that if my father thought it was so important then I shouldn't do it just for fun.'

Sisilu understood respect for one's elders. She shrugged, then cocked her head and got to her feet as laughter floated through the sultry air. 'Sounds like Fili and the others going home; I'll go with them.'

After she'd left Alli got ready for bed, but an unusual restlessness drove her outside again. She stood on the edge of the verandah and gazed around, wondering if she'd hate New Zealand, as Sisilu so confidently expected.

She'd certainly miss the moonlight glimmering on the still surface of the lagoon, and the breeze rustling the palm fronds, carrying the tang of salt and the tropical ripeness of flowers and fruit. And she'd miss her friends.

But she was going, whatever she missed.

She sat down on the old swing seat and rocked rhythmically. What exactly was Slade up to? Why had he bought the resort in the first place? It seemed an odd thing for a hard-nosed businessman to do. Surely he'd checked the figures before he'd paid a cent for it? He must have known that it was perilously close to failure.

Her mouth curved cynically. And he certainly didn't strike her as a philanthropist, ready to sink his own money into a dying enterprise just to help the islanders!

If he did close Sea Winds she didn't know what she'd do. She'd have nothing—no future, no present, no chance or choice. The island had a policy of jobs for native Valanuans, and she didn't want to take any work from them. In fact, she'd been training someone to take over in the souvenir shop.

Her father's income had died with him; even the house was hers only because the tribal council let her stay there as a mark of respect to her father.

Besides, there was Tama...

The crunch of shells beneath shoes brought her to her feet; heart beating feverishly, she peered into the darkness. Even before her eyes made out the man strolling up the shell path from the beach she knew who he was.

Fighting back a heady excitement that blasted out of nowhere, she blurted, 'What do you want?'

'To talk to you,' Slade Hawkings said coolly, taking the steps. He stopped at the edge of the verandah, his silhouette blocking out stars and the moonpath over the lagoon.

Dwarfed by his formidable presence, Alli asked abruptly, 'What about?' Oh, Lord, she sounded like a belligerent teenager.

'The resort.'

'Why?' she said warily, brain racing. 'I don't know anything about its financial affairs.'

'Simcox tells me that you're very well integrated into Valanuan life.'

She stiffened. Where was this going? 'I can't remember any other home.'

'But it's not your home,' he pointed out. 'You have a New Zealand passport.'

'What has that got to do with Sea Winds?'

He turned to examine the garden. 'I believe your father leased the house from his local tribal council.'

Chills chased each other across her skin. She said pleasantly, 'You've been doing some research. Why?'

'I make it my policy to learn as much as I can about my enemies,' he said calmly, turning back to look at her.

To cover her shocked gasp she rushed into speech. 'I suppose I should be terrified to be an enemy of the great Slade Hawkings? If I'd known that was a possibility I might not have written to my mother—'

'She isn't your mother,' he interrupted in a flat, uncompromising tone. 'And you're right. I make a bad enemy.' He paused to let that sink in. 'However, I can be a good friend.'

But not to me, she thought, suspicion snaking through her.

'Above all, I'm a businessman.' Another deliberate pause.

As a technique for unsettling people, Alli thought, trying to hide her growing unease with flippancy, it worked brilliantly. She didn't know whether he was trying to provoke her into speech, but common sense warned her that silence was by far the best option.

He said matter-of-factly, 'You know that Sea Winds is losing money hand over fist; I'd be a lousy businessman if I let such a bad investment drag my profits down year after year.'

This time Alli couldn't hold back her biting comment. 'I'm surprised a businessman of your reputation bought the place.'

'I had reasons,' he said shortly, a note of warning in the deep voice.

What reasons? The whisper of an implication smoked across her brain, only to be dismissed. Sinking though it was, Sea Winds would have cost him a lot of money— far more than he'd have needed to spend if he wanted to gain power over her.

Alli lifted her gaze to his dark silhouette. Against the radiance of the moon she saw a profile etched from steel, and shivered inwardly. Something Sisilu had said to her came back again—something like *be nice to him—for all of us…*

Her teeth worried her lip before she said neutrally, 'If you spent money on it—'

'Surprisingly enough, money isn't always the answer. It should never have been built here. There isn't room for a decent airport so everything has to come through Sant'Rosa, and the civil war there has made tourists extremely wary of this part of the world.'

Everything he said in that aloof, dispassionate voice was the truth, yet the conversation rang oddly false. Alli swallowed. 'Why are you telling me this?'

'I want your opinion on what closing the resort will do to the islanders.'

'Why me?' She didn't try to hide her incredulity.

He shrugged. 'I'm not stupid. You know these people, and I'm willing to accept that you want to do your best for your friends.'

'Even though I'm a blackmailer?' she flashed back.

'I assume that even blackmailers have friends.' His tone could have cut ice. 'You seem to.'

It had been stupid to let him see how his opinion of her stung. Compared to the welfare of the islanders, her hurt feelings were totally unimportant.

She drew in a deep breath and said frankly, 'Most of them will go back to working copra, planting and fishing and village life. The tribal council won't have as much money for schooling, because copra is not hugely profitable, so the secondary school will almost certainly close. Bright children won't be able to go to university. The health clinic will probably close too, except for tours by visiting doctors.' She couldn't see his expression, but he could see hers when she finished bluntly, 'Some people will certainly die.'

His silence lifted the hairs on the back of her neck. Should she have pleaded? Did he have any sort of social conscience at all, or was this a trick?

Eventually he said, 'So what would *you* do to keep the resort open?'

Panic kicked her in the stomach. 'I—what? What could I do?'

He walked across the verandah, stopping so close to her she could see the white flash of his narrow smile.

'Keeping Sea Winds going would be a sacrifice for me—I'm asking what you're prepared to sacrifice for your friends.'

Blood pumped through her, awakening her body to urgent life, but her brain seemed to have been overwhelmed by lethargy. She moistened her lips and croaked, 'If you mean what I think you're meaning...'

'That's exactly what I mean,' he said, that note of ironic amusement more pronounced. 'I want you, Alli. You must have guessed—it's not as though you're a sweet little innocent.'

Stunned, she licked her lips and swallowed. 'You're going to have to be clearer than that.'

Boredom descended like a mask over his face. 'Really?' he mocked, his mouth twisting. 'Then perhaps I should demonstrate.'

And he kissed her.

Alli had read books, she'd listened to friends discussing their love life—and she'd been kissed often enough to know what it was all about. But until Slade's mouth took hers she'd had no idea that a man's kiss could drive every sensible thought ahead of it like leaves in a hurricane, robbing her of breath and common sense until she was left witless and shaking in his arms.

His mouth was cool and masterful, and potent as lightning, she thought vaguely, before a rush of sensation blotted out everything but wildly primitive need.

When he broke the kiss her hands tightened on the fine cotton of his shirt and she pressed closer with an instinctively sinuous movement, afraid that he'd walk away and leave her.

'Sweet,' he said, his voice raw with sensual arousal. 'Open your mouth for me...'

Sighing, she said his name, and he laughed beneath his breath and kissed her again. And this time there was nothing cool about it at all.

Locked against his hardening body, she shuddered as her passionate response rocketed her into another universe. Desire merged inevitably into hunger, then blossomed into a desperate craving. This, she thought dimly as he explored the soft inner parts of her mouth, as she savoured the exotic taste of him, as she melted into surrender—this was what she had been waiting for...

Slade lifted his head, but only to kiss her eyelids. Strong arms tightened across her back, pulling her against him. Shudders of pleasure ran like rills through her. She moved languorously against him, and shivered at the fierce delight the heat and pressure of his taut body kindled in the pit of her stomach.

She felt his chest expand, and was filled with excitement because she was doing this to him.

No wonder her father had kept such a close watch on

her—this was dangerously addictive, a reckless abandonment to sensuous thrills.

And then Slade's arms dropped and he stepped back,
leaving her shivering in the warm night air, her body
filled with frustrated longing for something she'd never
experienced.

'Just so we don't get this wrong,' he said evenly, as
though nothing at all had happened, 'are you offering
me yourself in return for my keeping Sea Winds open?'

Humiliation doused every last bit of arousal. Cold
and furious, Alli clenched her hands by her sides to stop
herself from shaking. 'Is that what you want?'

'I'm always prepared to deal,' he said, watching her
with half-closed eyes.

'No,' she said when she could speak again. 'I'm no
prostitute.'

He wielded silence like a weapon, but two could play
at that game. Fighting back tears of shock, she refused
to let loose the bitter words that trembled on her tongue.

'I wasn't thinking of prostitution,' he said obliquely.
'More an exchange of benefits.'

'A business deal?' She didn't have to summon the
scorn in her voice—it came without warning. 'But that's
what prostitution is, surely? There's certainly no emotion in it.'

He smiled without humour and touched the corner of
her mouth with a knuckle. 'Really?' he drawled, tracing
its lush, tender contours. 'You could have fooled me.
Shall I kiss you again?'

Something unravelled deep inside her. Aching with
desolation, she stepped back, away from his knowl-

edgeable, tormenting caress, and said stonily, 'There's
a difference between sensation and emotion.'

'I think we could probably forget about semantics
while we made love.'

The best way to finish this would be to prove how utterly stupid she'd been. 'So let's deal. How often would
you expect me to sleep with you in return for the con-
tinuation of the resort? Just once? Or would you expect
me to be available whenever you came to Valanu? How
often would that be?'

'Whenever I wanted,' he said with a silky lack of emphasis. 'I don't think just once would slake either of us.'

'And how long would it last?'

'Until I got tired of you,' he said coolly. 'Of course
I'd expect you to be faithful in between visits.'

'And would you be faithful?' When he paused she
looked straight up into his face and said, in a voice that
shook with scorn, 'Nothing would persuade me to sleep
with you for money, or benefits, or any other reason. In
fact, I don't ever want to see you again.'

'That can certainly be arranged,' he said.

She was wincing at the sheer off-hand brutality of
his reply when he began again, and this time the sexual
edge was gone from his tone.

Brisk, businesslike, without inflection, he said, 'Get
down off your high horse, Alli—I don't want you in my
bed. However, I'll keep the resort going if you stay here
on the island and work in the souvenir shop.'

'What?' she whispered incredulously.

'You heard.' His voice hardened. 'If you agree, your
friends will keep their jobs, children will go on to university, and people will live.'

'Why?' But she knew why.

'It's a simple transaction. I don't want you contacting or trying to see Marian Hawkings ever again.'

Hearing it like that—a bald statement delivered in a tone that brooked no compromise—sent equal parts of anger and desolation surging through her.

'And you have the nerve to call me a blackmailer,' she said flatly.

'So we each use the weapons we have to hand,' he retorted with bland indifference.

Even as she admitted to herself that she had no choice, she looked for a way out. 'And do I have to stay here for the rest of my life—or Marian Hawkings's life?'

He paused, then said, 'You'll leave Valanu when I agree you can.'

Fear and frustration almost made her burst into a furious outburst, but if she lost control he might renege on the deal. She said wearily, 'Why are you doing this?'

He misunderstood her, perhaps deliberately. 'Because I want you kept well away from Marian.'

'If I promise not to contact her—'

He lifted a hand, but when she shrank back he dropped it again, saying incredulously, 'I wasn't going to hit you!'

'I know.' She'd realised that the second she'd jumped back.

'Did your father beat you?' he asked in a soft, lethal tone that scared her more than anything else.

'No—never!' Anger drove her to say, 'He was a gentleman—literally!' She let the word sizzle through the air before finishing woodenly, 'All right, I'll accept your offer—but I want it in writing first.'

She was shocked when he laughed, apparently with

real amusement. Mortified, she heard him say, 'You'll hear from my lawyers within a week.'

'If I don't, the deal's off,' she said rashly. 'And for your—and Marian Hawkings's—information, I had no intention of forcing myself onto the woman. I just wanted to ask her some questions.'

'Then learn to couch your letters in more diplomatic language,' he returned curtly, turning to go. 'As for your questions—she has no answers. If this whole business about looking for your mother is true, you've been searching up the wrong street.'

It took a real effort, but Alli kept her silence. She knew that Marian Hawkings was her mother, but the lies the woman must have told Slade fitted in with the profile she'd built in her mind—a woman who had never wanted anything to do with the daughter she'd borne.

She said, 'Before you go, tell me one thing.'

In a voice that conveyed both a warning and a threat, he said, 'I don't have to tell you anything.' But he stopped at the foot of the steps and turned to look at her.

Refusing to be denied, Alli ploughed on. 'This is going to cost you a huge amount of money, so what is Marian Hawkings to you? I know she's not your mother—unless you were the result of an affair before she married your father. I assume she's your stepmother.'

For a moment she thought he was going to refuse to answer, until he said, 'She is my stepmother. Now I want an answer from you—you said that you saw her name on your father's marriage certificate. She was married before she married my father, but her first husband's name was not Ian Pierce.'

'I know,' she said quietly. 'It was Hugo Greville. Hugo Ian Greville—Pierce was my father's mother's maiden name. He changed his name by deed poll when your stepmother left him. After he died, I found the papers with their marriage certificate, the divorce papers, and a clipping about her marriage to your father.'

Moonlight lovingly delineated his features, the silver flood dwelling on the strength and cold determination that stamped his face. 'So you knew who I was before I got here?'

'No,' she said acidly. 'You weren't mentioned in the newspaper clipping. And I had no idea the new owner of Sea Winds was another Hawkings.' She looked at him to see if he believed her, but his expression revealed nothing. 'Even when you got here I didn't make the connection. It is a reasonably common name.'

'I see.' He was silent for several seconds. 'I'm on my way out of Valanu in half an hour. Keep your nose clean and you might win some time off for good behaviour.'

Bewildered, furious and exhausted, Alli watched him stride towards the beach until the shadows swallowed him up.

CHAPTER FOUR

ALLI SWUNG A long leg over the horse's back and dropped gracefully from the saddle. 'Good girl,' she said, chirruping in a way the grey understood. It gave a soft whicker when she flipped the reins and stood looking along the beach, north, to where Valanu lay, thousands of kilometres away across the lonely Pacific.

Eighteen months after she'd made that bargain with Slade Hawkings she'd waved the island a tear-drenched farewell. Although she still missed her friends there, after six months in New Zealand she was becoming accustomed to its temperate climate, was enjoying the play of seasons and the new life she'd made for herself.

And, although today was chilly, the Maori celebration of Matariki had long passed, with the rising of the Pleiades in the northern sky. Spring was almost over and summer was on its way.

'Hey, Alli!'

She turned to wave to the middle-aged man loping across the short grass of the paddock, bald head gleaming.

'Hi, Joe! Trouble?'

'Might be. You've got a visitor.' He extended his hand

for the reins. 'I'll deal with Lady and you go on down to the Lodge; the guy doesn't look as though he's used to being kept waiting.'

Alli frowned, keeping hold of the reins. 'Who is it?'

'Come on, hand 'em over. He didn't say who he was, just that he wanted to see you.' He grinned. 'Perhaps he saw your photo in the paper when you helped rescue those yachties, and realised that under all that salt and sand there was a pretty face.'

'I hope not,' she said involuntarily.

She'd been desperate to keep out of the limelight, but a persistent journalist had managed to get one shot of her hauling on the line that had brought the crew of the yacht to safety through the huge surf.

At least her face had been barely recognisable. The other staff at the Lodge had joked that the only reason the shot had appeared in the paper was because she'd dumped her wet jeans when they'd dragged her down in the surf, and the tights beneath showed her legs to perfection

When she still hadn't moved, Joe jerked his head towards the backpackers' lodge and said, 'Go on. If he gets stroppy yell for Tui.'

She laughed. Joe's wife was built on sturdy lines, a woman with a tongue that could slice skin, yet sing tenderly haunting lullabies to her grandchildren. Sometimes she joked that she needed to do both with the backpackers who came to this stretch of coastline to surf the massive waves.

'Thanks,' Alli said, and set off along the narrow metalled race that led through the dunes to the Lodge.

Who on earth could her visitor be? The friends she'd

made all lived around the Lodge, yet if Joe didn't know who he was the man couldn't be a local.

Perhaps it was someone from Valanu?

She stepped through the door into the reception area and said, 'Sorry I took so long to get—'

Shock drove the breath from her lungs and the words froze on her tongue.

'I'm a patient man,' Slade Hawkings said calmly, turning around from his scrutiny of the scenic calendar on the wall.

Two years faded into nothingness and she felt as defenceless against his powerful male magnetism as she had when they'd first met. He was watching her with the aloof, unreadable expression she recalled so well.

She swallowed and asked thinly, 'What do you want?'

He cocked an arrogant black brow. 'Perhaps to see why you reneged on our deal.'

'I haven't contacted m—Marian Hawkings,' she shot back. 'Which is what the deal was really about.'

'That's a matter of opinion.' But he spoke without rancour and some of her apprehension faded.

'And the Valanu resort is no longer losing money,' she finished.

'Thanks, I believe, largely to you.' Lashes drooped over the hard green eyes, so startling in his tanned face. 'Who'd have thought that a little South Seas siren would turn into a hot publicist?'

'How did you know—?' She stopped abruptly. *'Siren?'*

'If it fits,' Slade drawled. 'When ideas for improving the hotel's publicity started to percolate through, the new manager had to admit they came from you. Targeting the upper end of the market and laying on a flying boat to get the guests in from Sant'Rosa was an inspired move. The nostalgia angle is working very well, and lunch on an uninhabited island seems to be appealing to plenty of would-be Robinson Crusoes out there.'

She shrugged. 'Well, those who are filthy rich, anyway. I was surprised your organisation ran with my ideas.'

'They were fresh,' he said indifferently, 'and it was clear that you had the backing of the chief.'

She had to stop herself from looking as uncomfortable as she felt. Tama's father had packed his son off to Auckland, ostensibly to take a degree but really to get him away from his unsuitable crush on Alli, who had, as the chief said, behaved properly. In return, he'd pragmatically thrown his considerable prestige and authority behind her plans for the resort.

And the new manager, who'd arrived two days after Slade left, and a week before Barry Simcox went back to Australia, had let her have her head.

Slade continued smoothly, 'Tell me, did Barry get back together with his wife once he landed in Australia?'

Something in his tone made her narrow her eyes, but he met her enquiring look with an opaque, unreadable gaze.

Alli shrugged. 'How would I know?'

He looked amused, but said easily, 'How did you get off Valanu? The manager said no one seemed to know where you were until they got a postcard from Fiji a week or so later.'

She said stiffly, 'If he'd thought to ask the chief he'd have found out. I worked my passage on a yacht.'

'I suspected so.' His smile showed a few too many teeth. 'The one with the group of young Australians?'

'The one with the middle-aged Alaskan couple,' she snapped.

His brows rose in a manner she found infuriating, but he said blandly, 'I suppose I should be grateful that before you left you trained someone to take your place in the souvenir shop.'

'I don't want your gratitude,' she returned. 'What are you doing here? And don't tell me you're going to force me back to Valanu. I didn't know how to deal with that sort of blackmail before—but I do now.'

'I'm pleased to hear it. No, I'm not ordering you back. I have no power to make you go, and I rarely repeat myself. And, as you said, the whole idea was to keep you away from Marian.' His demeanour changed from indolent assurance to one of decisiveness. 'But now she wants to see you.'

She said quietly, 'I don't want to see her.'

Slade waited for a long moment, his expression intimidating. When he spoke his voice was a lethal purr. 'A little revenge, Alli?'

'Alison,' she told him. 'I call myself Alison now—more adult, don't you think?' She still hadn't got used to it, though.

'Your employer called you Alli.'

She said curtly, 'He shortens everyone's name. And, no, it's not revenge.'

'Then what is it?'

Alli paused, trying to work out how she felt. Longing to see her mother vied with another instinct. 'Self-defence. I can only take so much rejection. And so far that's all she's done to me.'

In the intimidating, angular set of his face she saw the man who'd expanded the thriving firm he'd inherited from his father to a pre-eminent position on the world stage.

He said smoothly, 'I don't think rejection is what she has in mind.'

The desire to meet Marian Hawkings tempted Alli so strongly it almost overwhelmed her common sense. If she didn't take this opportunity she might never have another. And eventually she'd despise herself for sheltering behind the cowardly fear of being hurt. But caution drove her to probe, 'Then what *does* she have in mind?' Acceptance would be too much to hope for.

Slade wondered what was going on behind her guarded face. 'I don't know,' he said abruptly.

She looked at him with those exotic lion eyes. 'How did you find me?'

'The newspaper photograph.'

Her dark brows lifted in irony. 'That was a month or so ago.'

'Marian's been ill,' he said shortly.

Once he'd given Marian the dossier his investigator had put together she'd avoided the subject for several weeks. Then a bout of flu had laid her low, just after he'd seen the photograph of Alli in the newspaper.

It still irritated the hell out of him that, in spite of the grainy photograph, her face had leapt out at him from the page.

Not that she was classically beautiful, he thought critically, angered by the weakness that tested his self-control. But something about her challenging eyes and inviting, sensuous mouth stirred his sexuality into prowling appreciation, aided by the rare combination of dark, rich hair and glowing golden skin, and the body her lovers had woken to lush, svelte femininity.

When Marian had decided she wanted to find Alli he'd had to admit that he knew where she was, although he'd refused to contact her until the doctor had agreed that Marian was fit enough to cope.

He said abruptly, 'She wants to tell you something.'

Hope, so long repressed, flickered like a spark inside her. 'If it's just that she's not my mother she's already told me that, remember?'

His broad shoulders moved in a slight shrug. 'It's not that.'

'Then what?'

He walked across to the window and looked beyond the garden to the regenerating sand dunes, replanted with the native grass that had been the original vegetation. 'It isn't mine to tell,' he said curtly.

'I can't just leave the Lodge.' Her quiet tone hid a desperate hunger to see the woman who'd given her life.

'I've already talked to your boss.'

'Joe?'

He smiled. 'His wife. She's giving you the rest of the afternoon off, and I believe you're not working tomorrow. I'll drive you down and make sure you get back.'

Alli fought a brief, vicious battle with herself before yielding to temptation. 'All right, I'll get changed.'

'Take enough clothes for the night.'

Her incredulous glance met eyes as cool and unyielding as jade. 'I won't need them, surely?'

'Nevertheless, bring them.' When she looked mutinous he said matter-of-factly, 'I always believe in being prepared for any eventuality.'

Alli bit her lip, but when she came down twenty minutes later she carried a bag packed with a change of clothes.

She followed the sound of laughter to the kitchen, where Slade was drinking coffee and talking to Tui as she kneaded a batch of bread.

He seemed perfectly at home, and her employer was certainly enjoying his company, although that didn't stop her from saying firmly, 'Better give me your address and phone number in case I need to ring Alli up.'

Slade took out a slim black case and scribbled something on a business card. 'I've put my email address there as well,' he said, anchoring the card to the table with a sugar bowl. 'Sometimes it's the quickest way to get in touch with me.'

A look of sheer horror settled on Tui's face. 'I'm not touching any computer,' she said robustly, dividing the dough into loaves. 'Alli keeps trying to make me use it, but it's just like magic to me, and I've always been a bit wary of magic.'

'According to you the telephone is magic too,' Alli teased, 'and so is electricity.'

'I understand those,' her boss told her, 'because I learnt about them at school. You young things can deal with the latest technology—I'll stick to my generation's.'

Insensibly warmed by the older woman's cheerfulness, Alli dropped a kiss on her cheek and went out with Slade Hawkings into the unknown.

Once in the large car, she sat back in a divinely comfortable seat, with the scent of leather in her nostrils, and watched the green landscape sweep by until apprehension seeped in to replace the lingering warmth of Tui's presence.

If she turned her head a little she could see Slade's hands on the wheel; for some stupid reason the sight of his lean, competent fingers made her heart quiver, so she kept her eyes on the lush countryside.

As though he understood her wariness, he began to talk—at first about the rescue of the yacht. When they'd exhausted that subject, somehow they segued onto the subject of books. He had definite views, some of which she agreed with and some she didn't. Alli discovered that he was that rare thing, a person who didn't take disagreement personally, and halfway to Auckland she realised that she was in the middle of a vigorous debate about a film she had enjoyed.

'Weak in both plot and acting,' he condemned, 'and with a dubious moral base.'

'Moral base?' she spluttered.

He shrugged. 'I subscribe to the usual moral values.'

Astonished, she lost the thread of her rejoinder and stared at his profile, the strong framework of his face providing a potent authority that would last him a lifetime. Heat smouldered in the pit of her stomach. The two years since she'd seen him had only increased her susceptibility to his disturbing magnetism.

Her silence brought a slanting ice-green glance. 'Cat got your tongue?' he asked politely, before returning his gaze to the road ahead.

She plunged back into the argument, but tension more

complex than the merely sexual plucked at her nerves. She didn't want to like him; she certainly didn't want to feel this reluctant respect. It was far too dangerous.

The conversation lapsed as they approached Auckland and the traffic got heavier. Alli knew the route to the airport, and a few other necessary addresses, but once he left the motorway on one of the inner-city interchanges she lost all sense of where they were going.

It turned out to be one of Auckland's expensive eastern suburbs. Slade drove into the grounds of a modern block of apartments, parked in the visitors' car park and killed the engine, his face set in forbidding lines.

'She's expecting us,' he said.

Bewildering fear hollowed out Alli's stomach. Her mouth dry, she walked past camellia bushes and a graceful maple tree to the door, waiting while he pressed a button that activated a hidden microphone.

'Slade,' he said, adding, 'With a visitor.'

A woman—surely too young to be Marian Hawkings?—answered, 'Come on up.'

He opened the security door and said without expression, 'Marian's goddaughter is staying with her.'

Inside was discreetly luxurious—a bronze statue of vaguely Greek ancestry, a sea of carpet and marble, landscapes on the walls, a huge vase of flowers that only the closest observation revealed to be real.

'The lift is over here,' Slade said, his fingers resting for one searing moment on her elbow as he indicated the elevator.

It delivered them too swiftly to the fourth floor, and more carpet that clung to Alli's shoes, more statuary, more flowers.

Trying to inject some stiffness into her backbone, she told herself grimly that Marian had landed on her feet after she left the man who'd changed his name to Ian Pierce.

The woman who opened the door was a few years older than Alli, elegant and beautiful. And every black hair of her head, every inch of white skin, radiated disapproval when she looked at Alli.

'Caroline, this is Alison Pierce,' Slade said. 'Alli, Caroline Forsythe, who has given up her holidays to stay with Marian while she's convalescing.'

'How do you do?' Caroline Forsythe didn't offer her hand. Her blue eyes skimmed Alli's face with a kind of wonder. 'It's no hardship to stay with Marian. Come on in—she's expecting you both.' She directed a brief, conspiratorial smile at Slade that spoke volumes. 'She's in the sitting room.'

Masochist, Alli thought fiercely, letting her anger overcome a faint, cold whisper of danger.

In the sitting room Alli vaguely registered light streaming in through large windows, gleaming on polished furniture, on more pictures in sophisticated colours, on flowers that blended with the décor.

A woman in a chair stood up. Her eyes met Alli's and the colour vanished from her skin, leaving it paper-white.

Horrified, Alli saw her crumple. She cried out, barely aware of Slade's swift, silent rush to catch Marian Hawkings's fragile figure before she hit the floor.

As he lifted her in his arms Caroline hissed at Alli, 'Get out of here—*now*. Before she comes to, I want you out of this building.'

Blindly Alli turned away, but the whiplash of Slade's voice froze her. 'Caroline, get a glass of water with a splash of brandy in it,' he commanded, laying his burden down on the sofa, 'and make tea. Alli, stay where you are! She asked to meet you.'

Alli felt Caroline's dislike scorch through her. She didn't blame her; horrifying scenarios of her conception were blasting through her mind. The one thing she hadn't thought of was rape—but even now she simply couldn't conceive of her father doing that. After all, they'd been married…

'Sit down,' Slade went on, examining her with merciless eyes. 'I don't want you fainting too—you're as white as paper.'

She dropped into a chair, watching her mother's colourless face until Caroline came in with a glass and stood between them.

'It's all right, Marian,' Slade said gently. 'You fainted, that's all. You're fine now.'

'What—? Oh…' Marian Hawkings tried to struggle up.

'Lift your head a bit and drink this,' he said. 'I wouldn't have brought her if I'd known you were going to scare the hell out of us like that.'

'Let me see her.' But her voice was filled with dread.

'After you've had some of this.' He held the glass to her lips, only straightening when she'd taken several sips. He turned and with unyielding composure said to Alli, 'Come here.'

When Caroline started to object, Slade overrode her with one brief, intimidating glance.

'Alli?'

Slowly, skirting the furniture with extreme care, Alli made her way to the sofa, concern almost overriding her shock. The woman who lay there was still beautiful, with fine features and blue, blue eyes.

And after one swift, shaken glance Marian Hawkings went even whiter, and closed her eyes as though she'd seen something hideous.

With obvious effort she opened them again. 'Yes, I see. Caroline, my dear, do you mind leaving us? I'm sorry, but I need to speak to Alli and Slade alone.'

'Of course I don't mind,' the other woman said pleasantly, 'but do take care, Marian. You're not well yet.'

When she'd gone, Marian said weakly, 'Flu, that's all it was. Slade, would you help me up, please?'

He lifted her, propping her against the side and back of the sofa.

She looked at Alli, her eyes darkening. 'I wish I could say I was your mother, Alison, but I'm not.'

It was almost a relief. 'Then who is?' Alli asked in a cracked voice.

Marian swallowed, her face inexpressibly sad, and tried to speak. She whispered, 'I can't. Slade—please…'

Lying her back against the sofa, Slade said harshly, 'Your mother was Marian's sister.'

Nausea clutched Alli as the implication struck home. She sprang to her feet, saying contemptuously, 'I don't believe it.'

'It happens,' he said briefly. He lifted a photograph from the side table and handed it to her. 'Your mother. And a copy of your birth certificate.' He paused before adding, 'Which you must have seen, as you have a passport.'

'My father organised it when I was sixteen,' she said absently. Now that she was faced with the proof she'd sought with such angry tenacity she didn't dare open the envelope.

Slowly, her fingers trembling, she slid the photograph free. Yes, there was her father, his expression almost anguished as he looked into a face—oh, God—into a face so like hers it gave her gooseflesh.

The woman in her father's arms was shorter than she was, but she had the same features—the same tilted eyes, the same exotic cheekbones, the same full mouth. She was laughing and her confidence blazed forth like a beacon, defiantly provocative.

A piece of paper beneath the photograph rustled in Alli's hand. She looked at it and swallowed. For the first time she saw her birth certificate, and on it her mother's name: Alison Carter. She had been twenty-four when she'd borne her lover's child.

Cold ripples of shock ran across Alli's skin. Whatever sins Alison had committed, she must have loved Marian to give her child her sister's name.

But to betray her like that! Sickened, she stared at the betraying document. Oh, God, her demands for acknowledgement must have opened up bitter humiliation and pain in this woman who was her aunt.

'What happened to her?' she asked in a raw voice.

Marian Hawkings looked at Slade. He said levelly, 'When Marian discovered that her sister was pregnant she told Hugo to leave. He did so, and the guilty lovers disappeared to Australia. A month later Alison rang from Australia to tell Marian that she had aborted her child.'

Alli sucked in a ragged breath. 'Why?'

He shrugged. 'Apparently she was tired of Hugo and thought Marian might want him back. Then, a year or so after that, Marian was informed that she'd been killed in Bangkok. She'd flown into Thailand alone.'

Trying to sort this incredible story out, Alli looked down at her mother's photograph, then glanced at Slade's arrogant, unreadable face. 'So who am I?' she asked in a voice that shook.

'When Marian got your first letter I instigated a search. It's taken this long to find out that her sister lied about the abortion. You are the child she had. And, no, we have no idea why she lied, or why she left you with Hugo a few days after you were born and simply disappeared.'

Alli felt as though she'd taken the first step over a precipice—too late to go back.

As though he sensed her emotions, Slade poured a small amount of brandy into a glass and handed it to her. 'Drink some.'

She obeyed, shuddering as the liquid burned down her throat. It did help, though; when the alcohol hit her empty stomach, warmth eased the chill.

Leaning back against the cushions, Marian said weakly, 'Slade, finish it, please.'

'There's not much left. Hugo Greville changed his name and took you to Valanu because he'd been at school with the chief and could presume on their friendship to ask for sanctuary.'

Sick at heart, Alli got to her feet and addressed Marian Hawkings for the first time. 'I'm so sorry I brought all this back to you.'

The older woman leaned forward. 'This has been a shock for you too.'

'Not, perhaps, as much as you think. I've always known my mother abandoned me at birth, or very soon afterwards, so nothing much has altered.' She said steadily, 'Thank you for telling me. I'll go now.'

She'd got halfway across the room when Slade joined her. 'I'll take you home,' he said deliberately.

'It's all right—'

'Don't be an idiot.'

She paused, then nodded and went docilely with him, waiting in numb silence while he spoke to Caroline in the hall. Down by the car the sun still caressed the waxen glory of the last camellia flowers, and the harbour scintillated blue and silver, but inside Alli was cold, so cold she thought she'd never get warm again.

Slade said nothing as he drove away, and Alli stared unseeingly ahead, only focusing when the car slowed down outside a sturdy Victorian building.

'Where are we? Why aren't we going back to the Lodge?'

'I live here,' he said, manoeuvring the big vehicle into a parking spot in a basement car park.

She turned a belligerent face to him. 'So? I don't.'

He killed the engine. 'I don't think you should be alone tonight,' he said calmly. 'You're in shock, and I doubt very much whether you'd care to confide to anyone else what you've heard today, so you might as well stay here.'

'No,' she said dully, struggling to overcome the impact of the appalling story. She couldn't cope with the fact that the woman who'd wreaked such havoc had been her mother.

'Come on,' he said, and leaned over to open her door.

She caught a trace of the subtle scent that was his alone; that purely male scent, she thought confusedly, stamped him as definitely as a scar. 'I don't want to,' she said, a little more strongly.

He sat back and looked at her. 'You'll be perfectly safe,' he said pleasantly enough, although she registered the note of steel through the words.

'Aren't you afraid I might be like my mother?'

He lifted an ironic eyebrow. 'Promiscuous?'

She bit her lip and he said, 'It doesn't matter what you are. I'm not like Marian. I know how to deal with people who annoy me.'

She shivered. 'I need a cup of tea,' she said. 'After that I want to go home.'

'All right.' He hooked an arm into the back and brought out her case. 'You also need a shower to wash the slime off,' he said unexpectedly, and she looked at him in wonder, because that was exactly how she felt— unclean, as though her mother's actions had tainted her from the bones out.

Tiredness overcame her, sapping her courage and determination. She knew she should refuse to go with him, but it was so much easier to allow herself to be carried along on the force of his will.

Without speaking, she walked with Slade across the concrete floor and waited docilely while the lift whisked them upwards.

CHAPTER FIVE

LIKE THE MAN who owned it, Slade's apartment was large and compelling, so close to the harbour that reflected light played over the palette of stone and sand and clay. He showed Alli into a bathroom tiled in marble and left her there after explaining the shower controls.

Taking in its luxury, and the vast glossy leaves of a plant that belonged in some tropical jungle, Alli realised instantly that the room was a purely male domain. No toiletries marred the smooth perfection of the counter, and there was no faint, evocative perfume to hint at a woman's presence.

And she should *not* have felt a swift pang of relief. She stripped and turned on the shower; once in, she bewildered herself by sniffing gingerly at the soap in the shower.

Not even a touch of pine or citrus, so the faint fragrance she noticed whenever she was close to Slade was entirely natural.

'Pheromones,' she muttered. Years ago she'd read an article that suggested people unwittingly used subliminal scent to choose a genetically suitable mate.

If that were so, Slade would produce magnificent babies with her.

Tamping down the hot spurt of sensation somewhere deep in the base of her stomach, she thought stringently, and with Caroline.

Probably with every other woman on the planet too. Part of his magnetism was the impact of all that superb male physicality.

Oddly embarrassed, she got out her soap from its container and lathered up.

No wonder Marian Hawkings hadn't wanted to meet her! She must be a living reminder of humiliation and misery. Although logic told her it was ridiculous to take her parents' sins onto herself, she felt smirched. Her emotions were raw, and so painful she had to concentrate on the small things, like rinsing her hair until it squeaked, and wiping out the shower when at last she left it.

When she eventually emerged from the bathroom, every inch of skin scrubbed to just this side of pain, teeth newly cleaned and hair towel-dried, Slade met her at the door.

'I should have told you there's a hairdryer in the cupboard,' he said, examining her with formidable detachment.

Although she tried for polite gratitude, his nearness produced a stilted, ungracious tone. 'Thank you, but if you don't mind my hair wet, I'm fine.' She'd never used one before, and now was not the occasion to try something new.

'Why should I mind? The first time I saw it wet— when you walked out of the lagoon like Venus unveiled—I noticed that it looked like a river of fire,' he said silkily.

Alli's heart jumped. He'd changed too, into a cotton shirt the green of his eyes that moulded his shoulders. His trousers did the same to narrow hips and muscled thighs. Although she now wore her smartest jeans and a camel-coloured jersey that had cost her almost a week's wages, his effortless sophistication made Alli feel she should check for hay in her hair.

The sitting room overlooked the harbour and the long peninsula of the North Shore that ended in the rounded humps of two ancient, tiny volcanoes. Behind loomed the bush-clad triple cone of Rangitoto Island, thrust up from the seabed only a few hundred years ago.

Searching for a neutral topic, Alli commented, 'I'm always surprised when I'm reminded that Auckland is a volcanic field. I wonder when the next explosion will be.'

'I feel as though it happened this afternoon,' he said grimly. 'Come and pour the tea.'

Though he refused a cup.

'I need something a bit stronger,' He added dryly, 'Perhaps I should have asked if you'd like that too?'

'No, thanks.' So far she'd managed to behave with dignity; she wasn't going to jeopardise her control. It was, she thought desperately, about all she had left.

He splashed a small amount of whisky into a glass, half filled it with water, then came to sit opposite her on a huge sofa. She set the teapot down and picked up her cup.

'Put in some sugar,' he said abruptly.

'I don't like——'

'Think of it as medicine.' When she didn't move he leaned over and dropped in a couple of lumps before settling back to survey her through half-closed eyes. 'You're in shock.'

Shock? Oh, yes; when he looked at her like that, a smile curving his hard mouth, his eyes glimmering like jade lit by stars of gold, her throat closed and her heart sped up so much it hammered in her ears. Probably this was what had happened to Victorian maidens when they swooned.

Well, she wasn't going to be ridiculous. She'd seen the sort of woman he liked: sophisticated and elegant. Caroline Forsythe was about as different from her as anyone could be.

She sipped the tea tentatively, making a face at its sweetness, but its comforting heat persuaded her to drink it. Her father had considered coffee only suitable as a way to end dinner.

Glass in hand, Slade leaned back in the leather sofa and surveyed her. 'What do you plan to do now?'

'Do?'

'Do,' he repeated in a pleasant tone, adding with an edge, 'Beyond drinking two cups of tea.'

'Go back to the Lodge,' she said warily. 'Why?'

He was watching her with detached interest, as though she were a rare specimen of insect life. 'It seems strange that someone with a degree in English should be content with a job in the office of a backpackers' lodge frequented mainly by surfers.'

'How did you know—?' She stopped and glared at him. 'Why should I be surprised? You kept tabs on me, didn't you!'

'I always knew exactly what you were doing until you left Valanu,' he said calmly. 'I know you took an extra-mural degree from a New Zealand university and passed with A grades.'

'Was it part of the new manager's job to send you reports on me?' she asked, reining in her anger with an effort that almost chipped her teeth. 'I hope you paid him extra.'

When he spoke his voice was as careless as his shrug. 'I protect my own.'

'It makes my skin crawl to think you've been spying on me,' she retorted passionately.

'I don't take chances. As you can see, Marian is fragile. When I first went to Valanu the only thing I knew about you was that you were Simcox's lover and that you wrote an aggressive letter.'

Outraged, she stared at him. 'I was not his lover! Never!'

'My informant seemed sure of the facts.' He spoke with a calm assurance that made her want to throw the teapot at him. 'And he certainly felt more for you than the care an employer owes to an employee.'

'If you've got a dirty mind and listen to stupid gossip it might have seemed like that,' she returned with relish. 'That doesn't mean it was the truth.'

His ironic smile hid whatever he was thinking. 'It doesn't matter now.'

Alli wanted it to matter. She wanted, she discovered with something very close to horror, him to be furiously jealous. Alarmed, she steered the subject in a different direction. 'Given your opinion, what made you change your mind about contacting me?'

'Facts,' he said laconically.

When she directed a blank look at him he elaborated,

'Once I realised you looked like Marian's sister I got one of my information people to find the truth. It took her a while, for various reasons.'

'The name change?'

He nodded. 'Alison told everyone that she and Hugo were going back to Britain. Quite a lot of time was wasted trying to track them down there. The logical thing for them to have done was cross the Tasman Sea— in those days you didn't need passports to travel between Australia and New Zealand. It took a while for the researcher to find them.'

'Do you think my—Alison tried to put them off the scent?' She held her breath while he drank a little of the whisky.

'It seems a logical assumption. Then, of course, your father changed his name and yours when he went to Valanu, but eventually we pieced together a sequence of events, backed by legal documents. The records proved you were Marian's niece. But by then you'd left Valanu.'

'I'm surprised you bothered looking,' she snapped.

'Ah, there's a difference between an opportunist and a relative.' His mouth twisted in a smile that held equal amounts of wryness and mockery. 'Then the television news shortened the search by showing you hauling shipwrecked yachtsmen through the surf.'

'And you recognised me?' she said, before she could stop the words.

'I never forget a good pair of legs.' His smile was hard and cynical.

He was baiting her. Ignoring it, she said, 'Why did Marian decide to see me? Unless she wants to prove once and for all that I'm not her daughter. She doesn't have to—I won't insist on a DNA test. The photograph and my birth certificate are proof enough for me.'

When Slade didn't answer, she looked up and saw that he was swirling the liquid in his glass with an expression she couldn't interpret. Eyes enigmatic, he parried her enquiring gaze.

Something in her heart tightened unbearably. She said with stiff pride, 'If she wants to establish once and for all that I have no claim on her I'm perfectly willing to sign a disclaimer.'

His dark lashes came down to hide his eyes. In a level voice he said, 'It's not so easy. In certain cases signing a disclaimer might not be enough. New Zealand law can be tricky.'

Which meant that he, at least, had considered and researched the options. Alli swallowed more of the tea, shuddering at its cloying sweetness. 'So why did she want to see me?'

'I suspect that she felt you deserved to know your own parentage.'

'That's—kind of her,' she said reluctantly.

'And perhaps because you are her only living relative.'

Alli pointed out, 'She's got you.'

Slade watched her covertly as he drank some of the whisky and set his glass down on the table. 'But there's no blood relationship.'

Some years after his own mother had died Marian had come into his life like summer, bringing laughter and life and love into a silent, grieving house. That childhood adoration had matured into a protective love that still held.

'In Valanu,' Alli said quietly, 'a child can live with another family and he'll consider everyone in both his birth family and his adoptive family to be his kin.'

'In New Zealand the same thing happens amongst Maori families. But Marian grew up in England,' he said briefly, 'and things are different there.'

When she said brusquely, 'I know that,' he examined her tantalising face from beneath his lashes, wondering about her life on the island.

'Were you fostered by another family?'

'No.' She tempered her abrupt reply by adding more mildly, 'I did spend a lot of time with the family next door.'

'Ah, the home of the lovelorn Tama,' he observed blandly.

He was almost sorry when Alli ignored the taunt. 'I don't think you can be right about Marian; after all, she must have hated my—my mother. Why would she want anything to do with me?'

He shrugged. 'You know why—she now has the information she needs to convince her that you are her niece. You have a certain look of her father, apparently.'

This clearly didn't satisfy her, but it was all he was going to tell her. He watched her pick up her teacup again, her lovely face absorbed, the exquisite curve of her cheekbones stirring something feral into smouldering life inside him.

When he saw tears gather on her lashes he was astonished at the swift knot of tension in his groin. Even when she was distressed and unsure of herself, her glowing golden sensuousness reached out and grabbed him, angering him with an awareness of his vulnerability. He had to exert all his will not to pick her up and let her cry out her disillusionment and pain on his shoulder.

Any excuse to get her in your arms again, he thought savagely, despising himself. After two years he should have been able to kill this mindless, degrading lust. His lovers were chosen for more than their sexuality; it infuriated him that this woman's face and body had lodged in his brain for years, stripping away his prized control.

Deliberately, he sat back and decided to let her cry. She'd been unnaturally composed after listening to the real story of her life; weeping would help ease her shock.

'Sorry,' she muttered, getting to her feet and striding to the window with less than her usual grace.

Slade found himself following her. This, he thought grimly as he walked across to stand behind her, must have been how her father had felt—helpless in the face of an overwhelming hunger.

He, however, wouldn't allow himself to be dazzled by a face and a seductive body.

Or the unusual urge to protect her. His lovers were independent women, more than capable of looking after themselves. Nothing he'd seen or heard of Alli Pierce made him think she was any different, and too much hung on her character for him to lower his guard.

She was staring out of the window; when he came up behind her, her shoulders went rigid, but she didn't move. Gently he turned her around.

'It will probably leave you with a headache,' he said, gut-punched by the tears spilling from her great lion-gold eyes onto the tragic mask of her face, 'but I've read somewhere that crying is the best way to deal with stress.'

She gulped. 'Screaming and th-throwing a t-tantrum is a lot more positive,' she muttered, and suddenly her defences were breached and she began to cry, great silent sobs that tore through her slender body.

In a way she had been alone all her life, but she had never before been faced with her utter isolation; when her father had died she'd had friends, the time-honoured rituals of island life to console her.

Marian Hawkings might be her aunt, but she wanted nothing to do with her, and who could blame her? The mother she'd fantasised about and the father she'd never really known had taken the secrets of their guilty love to the grave.

But even as she shivered she was enfolded in warmth. Slade Hawkings pulled her against his big body and held her while she wept into his shoulder, his cheek on the top of her head, his heart thudding into hers.

He even thrust a handkerchief into her hand as though she were a lost child; the simple gesture made her cry even more.

Eventually the sobs subsided into hiccups, and she blew her nose and stepped back, wiping her eyes so that he couldn't see how embarrassed she was.

'Feeling better?' he asked, his deep voice so detached she knew he was wondering how to get rid of her.

'Not at the moment,' she mumbled. 'But at least I haven't got a full-blown headache.'

'Go and wash your face and I'll pour you a brandy,' he said.

'I don't need one, thanks.' She fled into the bathroom

and stared, horrified, at her face, puffy and mottled and tear-stained.

Cold water ruthlessly splashed on helped, and so did a brisk mental talking-to, and the swift application of lipstick.

But it took every shred of will-power she possessed to close the door behind her and walk into that elegant sitting room with her head held high and her chin angled just the right side of defiance.

'Brandy,' Slade said with an enigmatic smile, handing her a large glass with a minuscule amount of liquid in it. 'Drink it down and then I think we should go for a walk.'

She stared at him as though he was crazy. 'A walk? Here?'

'There are places.' When she didn't move he said more gently, 'I know you don't like it, but it does help.'

So he'd noticed her involuntary grimace at Marian's apartment. The taste hadn't improved, but it must have had some effect on her because after she'd drained it she said, 'All right, let's go for a walk.'

He parked the car at the foot of one of the little volcanic cones that dotted the isthmus. Silently they walked up the steep side, terraced by sheep tracks as well as trenches built centuries ago to defend the huge fort that had been the local Maoris refuge against enemies.

Although she considered herself fit, by halfway Alli was puffing, her mind fixed on one thing only—getting there. Pride forbade her to suggest a few moments' rest.

Slade's long, powerful legs covered the ground with ease, and when they reached the top he stood with the wind teasing his black hair and glanced at her search-ingly.

She knew what she looked like—red-faced and gasping. Yet one green look from him made adrenalin pump through her, banishing tiredness in a flash of acute awareness. When he smiled, she was mesmerised.

'Auckland,' he said, and gestured around them.

What's happening to me? she thought, unbearably stimulated. Instinct gave her the answer: you're at-tracted to him.

No, she thought feverishly. *Attracted* is not the way to describe this overwhelming response.

Struggling to reclaim some scraps of poise, she stared at the panorama below them—a leafy city be-tween two harbours, the dark lines of hills forming other boundaries, islands in a sea turned pink by the light of the setting sun.

It's quite simple and uncomplicated, she thought de-spairingly. You want Slade desperately and dangerously, on some hidden, primeval level you didn't even know existed until you met him.

It terrified her, this hot, sweet flood of desire, as lim-itless as the ocean, as fierce as a cyclone in the wide Pacific, as tempting as a mango on a hot day...

And hard on that discovery came another. Was this what had driven her parents to betray Marian?

'Alison—'

'Don't call me that,' she said, shuddering. 'Grown up or not, I've decided I prefer Alli.'

'I can't say I blame you,' he said unexpectedly.

'If it's the truth—'

'It is.' He spoke with such utter conviction that she believed him. 'I've never heard Marian tell a lie.'

'So my parents were sleazes of the highest degree. I don't want to be linked with them, not even by name.'

'Sometimes the truth has many facets. Your father was hugely respected in Valanu.'

Unsurprised that he knew this, she nodded. Ian Pierce had organised the accounts for the tribal corporation, helping them deal with trade and bureaucracy.

Slade resumed, 'You can't deny the link, no matter how much you disapprove of what they did. You set this process in motion. All right, so you've found out a few facts that you don't like, but they were your parents. I have no idea what your mother was like, but part of her is in you. And I presume you loved your father?'

Eyes filled with the glowing pink-mauve sky over a distant range of hills, Alli said, 'I don't know. I suppose I took him for granted. He didn't neglect me—he was firm and he made sure I ate properly and that I knew right from wrong.'

But he'd never cuddled her, or told her he loved her, or kissed her; although parcels of books had arrived several times a year he'd never read a bedtime story to her. When she'd been happy or sad or hurt she'd taken herself to Tama's family along the road. From them she'd learned about love and laughter and how to quarrel—all the subtle intricacies of relationships.

'He wouldn't be the first man to love not wisely but too well.' A cynical inflection coloured Slade's comment.

'If it *was* love.'

'If it wasn't, he certainly wouldn't be the first man

to lust unwisely and too much.' A note of derision ran through his voice.

But not you, she thought, humiliated afresh. Slade wouldn't think the world well lost for passion. He had too much self-control.

'Now that you know the circumstances of your birth,' he said, 'do you intend to take this further? Do you want to track down your father's family?'

She shuddered inwardly. 'Right now, no. I feel dreadful for bringing it all back to Marian—and I feel tainted.'

'An over-reaction. Of them all, you were the innocent one.'

'Marian and me,' she said, thinking that although his pragmatism was as sharply aggressive as a cold bucket of water in the face, it was also oddly comforting.

'As I pointed out before, you have only Marian's side of the story. Your mother might have had another one. If their behaviour disgusts you, make sure you don't follow their example.'

Was he referring to her supposed affair with Barry Simcox? She gave a sardonic smile. 'That's easy enough. As far as I know I have no sisters to betray.'

A car drove up to the parking area and disgorged a group of boisterous, laughing adolescents who swarmed up to the obelisk with much yelled banter. Someone produced a camera; Alli flinched at the flash, envying them their noisy, cheerful ease.

'You know what I mean.' Slade watched the young people with an alertness that reminded her of a warrior. 'If anything about your behaviour worries you, fight it. There is nothing will-power can't overcome.'

Probably the tenet he lived by! She blinked when the sun dipped behind the hills. 'It'll be dark soon—shouldn't we be heading back down?'

'We'll walk down the road.' He took her elbow and urged her onto the sealed surface. 'It's well lit.'

Keeping her eyes rigidly on the black bitumen ahead, she pulled away from him. He dropped her arm, but strode beside her.

Of all the shocks this day had brought, the knowledge that from tomorrow she'd never see him again was the one that hurt the most.

Surreptitiously she straightened her shoulders. When she'd first fought his disturbing, dangerous charisma, she'd been able to overwhelm it with constructive and vigorous resentment because he'd forced her to stay on Valanu.

Unfortunately, this time he'd been aloofly kind. Dislike and outrage weren't going to rescue her; she'd have to fall back on will-power.

So he was gorgeous? So he made her stomach quiver and her bones melt and turned her brain to soup? Get over it, she told herself with tough common sense. After all, she'd been totally unmoved by other gorgeous men.

But none of them had had Slade's combination of compelling physical appeal and inherent strength and authority.

And then there was Caroline Forsythe, who was probably in love with him.

Night fell softly around them, and the lights of the city shone out to combat the increasing depth of darkness.

Slade didn't give anything away, but his beloved

stepmother's goddaughter had to be a better partner for him than a woman who'd be a constant reminder to Marian Hawkings of shame and treachery.

A better partner? Listen to yourself, she thought with harsh scorn; what sort of fantasy are you spinning? Stop being so stupidly, wilfully, madly ridiculous.

Slade neither trusted nor liked her, and, although his potent sexuality made her too aware of her own femininity, she didn't know what she really thought of him.

Yells from behind and the sound of car doors slamming amidst gales of laughter swivelled her head around.

'Stay well on the side,' Slade commanded.

At the first squeal of brakes he swore beneath his breath and pushed her across the road onto the downward side, locking her against him as he dived over the edge into the darkness.

He twisted so that he landed beneath her, his hard body cushioning her fall. Gasping, she lay sprawled across him, wincing as a harsh, grating noise from the other side of the road was followed by a heavy thump and the sound of metal crumpling and tearing.

'Are you all right?' Slade demanded fiercely, his arms tightening around her.

'Yes,' she croaked. 'Are you?'

'I'm fine.' Apparently not convinced by her answer, he ran his hands over her arms and down her legs. Only then did he push her into a sitting position and say, 'Do you know anything about first aid?'

Alli scrambled to her feet, heart chilling as a scream sawed through the mild air. 'I've done a course,' she said, trying to remember one thing—anything—she'd learned. 'Check the breathing first,' she said aloud.

'OK.' He hauled her up the steep grassy bank and onto the road, where he thrust a mobile phone into her hands. 'Ring 111 and then SND. When they ask what service you want, tell them it's an accident on the Summit Road on One Tree Hill.'

'Be careful,' she blurted when he turned away. 'The car might explode.'

He gave her an odd glance and said ironically, 'And people might die. Don't worry—it's not on fire.'

He disappeared over the far edge of the road as Alli fumbled with the numbers before following him.

A few seconds later she told the woman who answered, 'At least five are hurt— one's on her feet, helping get the driver out, and one's sitting on the grass. She looks as though she's broken her arm. One's screaming, but she doesn't seem badly hurt.'

'And the others?'

'Two have been thrown out—they don't seem to be moving.'

'All right, we'll get ambulances there as soon as we can,' the woman said calmly. 'Check those on the ground—airways first, then breathing, then circulation. If they're a safe distance from the car don't move them.'

Alli went to each in turn, hugely relieved to discover that both men were breathing regularly. One had blood on his face, but when she touched his cheek he opened his eyes and frowned at her. The other didn't move.

She stood up, intending to head for the girl with the broken arm, when the one who'd been screaming came rushing across and tried to fling herself onto the unconscious man.

'No!'

Alli managed to stop her, but the girl turned on her, lashing out and sobbing, 'He's dead. I know he's dead!'

Slade grabbed her and pinned her arms, commanding harshly, 'Stop that, or I'll slap you.'

For a second she stared into his face, until his ruthless determination cut through her shock. Blinking, choking on her tears, she whimpered, 'He's dead.'

'He's not dead,' Slade told her.

The sound of a siren wailed up from below. 'OK, that's the ambulance,' Slade said. Releasing the girl, he said to the one who'd helped him assess the driver, 'Take her round the next corner and wave it down.'

'Come on, Lissa.' Her friend touched the girl's arm and together they walked down the road.

Slade asked, 'How are the others?'

'One is conscious; he's breathing freely.' She indicated the girl with the broken arm. 'I haven't had a chance to see how she is.'

She was white and in pain, but she said, 'I'm all right. They made us girls put the seat belts on. And Simon had one too, of course.' She bit her lip and looked across at the car. 'He's the driver. Is he all right?'

'He seems to be.'

'What about the others? H-how are they?'

Alli said quietly, 'They're breathing, and they look pretty good to me. I'm sorry, but I won't touch your arm—I think it's best to wait for the ambulance staff to deal with it.'

An hour later, after they'd both given their accounts

of the accident to an efficient young constable and been given a lift down the hill, Slade slid behind the wheel of his car and said briefly, 'Come on, let's go home.'

'Home?' Alli said on a slight quaver.

'I'm not taking you back to the Lodge now,' he said brusquely, backing the car out of the parking space. 'I've got a spare bedroom—you can spend the night there.'

When she opened her mouth to protest, he cut in, 'You'll be quite safe.'

'What about Caroline?'

Slade looked left and right, then eased out into the stream of traffic. 'What,' he said pleasantly, 'about her?'

The words like bricks in her mouth, Alli said, 'I thought she might have some reason to mind.'

'No reason,' he said.

Silently they drove beneath the streetlights until they reached his apartment.

CHAPTER SIX

SLADE'S SPARE BEDROOM intimidated Alli with its excellent taste.

He smiled ironically at her quick glance around, and said, 'Spare rooms do have a tendency to look like hotel rooms. A quilt from Valanu would make it more exciting.'

Dangerously cheered because he'd remembered such a minor thing, she said, 'But much less elegant. The decorator would have a fit. Anyway, I think it suits you.'

She flushed when he eyed her with an amused gleam in his green eyes. 'I'm not sure how to take that,' he observed. 'Cold and unwelcoming?'

'Restrained,' she said firmly.

The amusement vanished from his gaze, leaving it unreadable. 'The bathroom is through that door over there. Do you need anything?'

'No, thank you.' What had she said to be so completely rebuffed?

Up until then he'd been the perfect host; he'd persuaded her to eat, and been concerned when she'd only been able to manage two slices of toast. Because the edge of challenge in his tone had muted she'd let herself relax.

Now it was like standing next to a glacier.

Thick lashes veiling his gaze, Slade nodded. 'In that case, goodnight, Alli.'

After he'd left the room she showered, startled to discover blood on her skin and clothes. One of the men who'd been thrown from the car was in a dangerous coma; another, with the casual beneficence of fate, had suffered nothing more than mild concussion and a cut arm. The driver apparently would be all right too.

Once in bed, she felt her thoughts buzz around her mind in wild confusion; the adrenalin crash made sleep seem an unattainable nirvana. She listened to the alien sounds of the city, trying to block out the wail of a distant siren with the remembered roar of waves pounding the reef in Valanu.

Restlessly she turned on her back and stared at the ceiling, trying to push an unwelcome truth away. Valanu was her past; she couldn't go back. Besides, she wanted to be here—just through the wall from Slade...

When the dream began she recognised it, but as always, although she knew what was coming, she couldn't snap free from the prison of her mind.

She was cold, so cold the ice in her veins crackled when she moved. It stabbed her mercilessly with a thousand tiny knives, yet she had to keep going, had to find a warm place before the ice reached her heart. Panting, mindlessly terrified, she forced herself to run through the empty, echoing corridors of an immense house, hammering on every door she came to. Most of the rooms were empty, but occasionally she'd come to one and see light through the keyhole, hear laughing voices.

Then she'd call out, but entry was always refused, even after she begged to be allowed in. All she wanted was a few seconds in front of the fires she could hear crackling behind each obdurate door.

Eventually, all tears frozen, she found herself out in a bleak forest, with snow falling in soft drifts. She forced herself on until the drifts caught her feet and she fell. Shivering, she had to crawl…

But this time she didn't feel the terrifying ice creep through her veins. This time someone came and picked her up and carried her into the warmth. And when at last sleep claimed her she was in sheltering arms that melted the snow and kept the howling winds at bay…

She woke to heat, the gold of sunlight through her eyelids, and a subtle, teasing scent…

Lashes flying up, Alli jerked sideways, body pumping with adrenalin. Beside her Slade stirred, muscles flexing under far too much sleek bronze skin. He didn't appear to be wearing any clothes.

'Stop wriggling,' he murmured, his voice rich and slightly slurred.

When she gasped he woke instantly, without moving. Recognition narrowed his eyes into metallic green shards. Obeying instinct, Alli jack-knifed out of the bed.

Slade rolled over to link his hands behind his head and survey her with formidable self-possession. Alli suffered it a second before realising that while her T-shirt covered the essentials the briefs she wore beneath it revealed every inch of her long legs—inches he was now assessing with a heavy-lidded gaze and a hard smile.

She didn't have the self-assurance to walk away from

him looking like some good-time girl from a men's magazine, but neither was she going to reveal her embarrassment by scuttling across to her clothes.

Abruptly she sat down on the edge of the bed, as far away from him as she could, and hauled the sheet over her legs. His dark brows rose.

Alli swallowed, but her parched throat made the words gritty and indistinct. 'What the hell is going on?'

'Perhaps you could tell me that?' he suggested, subtle menace running through the words like silk.

She wanted desperately to lick her dry lips, but something stopped her. Instead she demanded childishly, 'What are you doing in my bed?'

'Before you start accusing me of rape—'

Her blood ran cold. 'Rape?' she croaked.

'Relax. Nothing happened.' The flinty speculation in his eyes belied his mocking tone. 'Unless crawling down the hall making pathetic whimpering noises could be called an event.'

Humiliation flooded through her. *'What?'*

He stretched and sat up, exposing far more skin than she could deal with. 'You appear to be a sleepwalker.'

Vague scraps of the dream swirled around her. She shut her eyes against both it and the effect his sleek bronze chest was having on her already strained nerves. 'Oh, God. What did I do?'

'You huddled dramatically on all fours outside my door, muttering that you were frozen, that you had to get close to the fire before the snow killed you.'

Rigid with mortification, she said, 'I—I haven't had that dream for years. And I haven't walked in my sleep since I was a kid. I'm sorry I inflicted it on you.'

'I imagine yesterday was traumatic enough to wake any number of old devils,' he said objectively.

Something struck her, and she opened her eyes to glare at him, trying to ignore the way the mellow light through the curtains burnished his broad shoulders and tangled in the male pattern of hair across his chest. He was utterly breathtaking in his potent male confidence. 'But—why are you here?'

'I carried you back, put you between the sheets and endeavoured to leave. You had other ideas,' he told her, the laconic irony in his tone lacerating her pride even more. 'Besides, your feet and hands were frozen. I planned to wait until you were warmed up and safely asleep, but every time I started to get out you woke crying and pleading, and in the end staying here seemed the easiest solution.'

Shamed colour swept across her face, then drained away. 'You could have woken me up,' she said lamely.

He shrugged, muscles coiled beneath his skin. Hastily Alli looked down at the floor, using every ounce of energy to resist the hot, untamed need that roared into life in the pit of her stomach.

Slade told her, 'I tried that too, but you didn't respond. Not even when I called your name.'

Desperately she said, 'I'm sorry.'

'Don't worry about it.'

There was no sophisticated way she could get out of this. Closing her eyes a second, she said, 'I—well, thank you.'

'At least we both got some sleep,' he said dryly. 'And now, if you don't mind, I'll leave you.' When she stared at him, he added in a tone that could have dried up a large river, 'I normally sleep naked, but I did have the sense to drag on a pair of briefs. If it doesn't embarrass you...' He started to fling back the covers.

Alli clamped her eyes shut and sat stiffly, longing for him to go and leave her to collapse into a puddle of raw chagrin.

He'd reached the door when she heard him drawl, 'I hope I don't have to tell you that if this was a ploy it didn't work.'

Her eyes flew open. Like some bronze god, from the arrogant carriage of his head to the set of his wide shoulders, he hadn't turned fully to face her, so the twist of his spine outlined the pattern and swell of muscles across his back.

Never before, she thought dazedly, had she appreciated the male triangle of wide shoulders and narrow hips, barely concealed by briefs. Sensation scorching through her, she dragged her gaze away from the long, powerful legs.

'A ploy?' she snarled. 'You must be joking.'

One black brow lifted. 'I've never been more serious. I don't let anyone blackmail me, and I don't fight fair.'

His level words sent a chill through her. Keeping her gaze level and composed, she retorted, 'So it's just as well I don't want to fight and I'm not a blackmailer.'

Her stomach churned when he gave her an edged smile and walked out, closing the door firmly behind him and leaving behind an impression of streamlined strength and ruthless, formidable power.

And a compelling male sexuality so potent Alli's pulse was still racing half an hour later, when she emerged from her bedroom, showered and dressed in the clothes she'd worn to see Marian Hawkings.

Following distant sounds, she arrived at the kitchen, where Slade was dealing efficiently with an impressive espresso machine.

'What do you want done with the sheets and towels?' she asked, hoping that the curtness of her voice concealed the jolt of arousal spiking through her.

'Leave them.'

'I've stripped the bed.'

He pushed a cup of black coffee towards her. 'Leave them, Alli. I have a housekeeper who'll deal with them.'

'Lucky you,' she said, and turned on her heel.

'Alli?'

She kept going.

'Don't put me to the bother of coming after you,' he said, his cool words underpinned by inflexible determination. 'You may not have had a mother, but from the little I've heard about your father he'd have made sure you were taught manners.'

'And I'm sure you know it's not polite to order around your guests—however unwelcome, seedy and suspect— as though they were your servants,' she returned.

His wry laugh shocked her.

'*Touché,*' he said. 'Except that I should point out that good servants are far too rare nowadays to treat badly. Come and have some breakfast. Tui told me you're pretty impossible in the morning until you've eaten.'

Alli turned slowly. 'Nonsense. I just don't like being accused—'

'I can't remember accusing you of anything,' he

stated grimly. 'Especially of being seedy and suspect.'
He paused, then added, 'Or unwelcome.'

Slade watched her glorious eyes darken into mystery. She said, 'I *know* I'm unwelcome, and you implied the rest when you told me you didn't blackmail easily.'

She was an enigma. Last night a weeping bundle of terror, this morning incandescent with indignation until he mentioned her sleepwalking—if that was what it was.

Courted since he'd grown into his shoulders in his mid-teens, experience had taught Slade that he could act like an ancient despot and some women would still pursue him.

Money, he thought cynically as Alli hovered in the doorway, talked very loudly.

'You are not unwelcome,' he said curtly. 'I'm sorry if I made you feel that you were. Do you want this coffee or not?'

'It certainly sounded as though you thought that—that I'd tried to set you up,' she said, but she came back warily into the kitchen.

She lifted the mug to her mouth, hiding behind it, but when she drank her lips moved in a slight, sensuous movement that made him glad he had a counter between them.

Last night had been endless. He'd lain in her bed in the darkness, so aroused by her soft curves and satiny skin that it had taken all his control to leash his hunger. It served him right for telling her so pompously that will-power could do anything!

Even now he desired her with a desperation that came too close to clouding his brain. In spite of the promptings of caution he wanted to believe it had been a nightmare that had driven her in search of some human warmth during the night. Although she'd clung to him she'd made no overt indication of wanting sex, seeming content to snuggle in his arms like a bird sheltering from a storm.

But he'd learned in a hard school not to take things at face value, and lust guaranteed poor decisions. He didn't know enough about Alli to risk trusting her.

Too much depended on not screwing up—and that, he thought, clamping down on memories of her body against him in bed, was not the most felicitous word to use!

'Tell me about the dream.' He poured himself a cup of coffee.

She hesitated, then shrugged. 'It's always the same— one of those self-repeating sagas. I'm looking for shelter, but no one will let me in.'

'Orphan in the storm? You kept muttering about being cold.' He watched as she took another mouthful of the hot liquid, noting the catspaws rippling its surface. Her hand was trembling.

'Yes—well, that's part of it. I know that if I don't get warm I'll die.'

She hadn't been shivering when he'd found her outside his door. In fact she'd been locked in stasis, her body rigid, not even moving when he'd searched for the pulse in her throat.

He could still feel the silken skin beneath his fingertips.

Ruthlessly he forced his mind back to the straighter path of logic. Her hands and feet, however, had been cold. 'No wonder you were terrified.'

Her shoulders lifted a fraction and she drank some more coffee, holding the mug as though she still needed to warm her hands. 'Children often have that sort of recurring dream, but mostly they grow out of it.'

'I'm surprised you dream of the cold when you couldn't have ever experienced it on Valanu.'

She stared at him for a time, golden-brown eyes thoughtful. 'Until now I've never thought of that. Interesting, isn't it?' she finally said. 'Although I had *Grimms' Fairy Tales*, so I knew there was such a thing.'

The peal of a doorbell made her jump; when she looked suspiciously at him he said, 'I'll be back in a minute.'

Alli watched him go, her taut nerves wound even more tightly. Who could this be—friends? A quick glance at her watch dispelled that idea; only very intimate friends would turn up before eight in the morning. Caroline Forsythe?

The opening of the kitchen door brought her upright, her armour tightly fastened around her.

'Breakfast,' Slade said, carrying a couple of takeaway packages. 'Bring your coffee and we'll eat it in the next room.'

She followed him into a combination dining and living room, less formal than the room she'd seen yesterday. Comfortable and expansive, it channelled the morning sun through a wall of glass doors. Outside, lounging furniture looked over the water from a wide, long terrace.

Slade unloaded the boxes onto a table and proceeded to set out the food. Noting her swift glance at the harbour, decorated with its colourful weekend bunting of sails, he said, 'It's still chilly outside—too cold to eat there in comfort.'

'I'm getting acclimatised to New Zealand's climate.' She gave a soft laugh. 'At first I thought I'd never get warm again.'

'Cereal?' he asked.

Another hungry growl from her stomach reminded her she'd had no dinner the previous night. 'Yes, please,' she said simply.

Incredibly, sharing the first meal of the day with him brought a wary happiness. As she ate her cereal, and the splendid Eggs Benedict that he'd unpacked, they discussed Valanu and the resort, and the people Slade had dealt with there.

'How is the chief?' he asked idly.

She swallowed the last of the delectable eggs and smiled. 'Very well. He's talking about a joint fishing venture with the Sant'Rosans.'

'And his son? Second son,' he amended blandly.

'Tama? He's fine,' she said stiffly. 'He's doing an administrative degree here in Auckland, and otherwise he spends a lot of his time, I'm told, nagging his father and the tribal council for more and more money for health issues.'

Slade's black brows quirked. 'Is he married?'

'Yes, to a charming Auckland girl.'

'Did you mind?'

'Not in the least.' She smiled with sunny nonchalance. 'His father has finally forgiven him, and the last photo Sisilu sent me was of the chief at a meeting with a small blonde girl perched on his knee.'

'And Barry Simcox?' When she looked blank he said lazily, 'I assumed you'd keep in touch?'

'No. Isn't he working for you now?'

'Not for a couple of years.' He offered her a bowl of fresh fruit. 'Try the cherimoya—it's like eating tangy custard. How about the dragon lady who ran the dancing troupe?'

Alli laughed. 'She's fine too. Still terrifying the manager into doing whatever she wants him to.'

He was, she thought after breakfast, when she went to get her bag, a good companion. His keen mind stimulated her, like his somewhat cynical sense of humour, and to her surprise she'd discovered that they shared some favourite writers and singers.

When he wanted to be he was utterly charming, but his charm masked a dangerously compelling strength. Skin tightening, she tried to banish the memory of waking up next to him. Had his hand been curved around her waist, or had that been another dream?

A nice one this time...

'He was asleep until you did your outraged virgin bit. He probably thought you were one of his girlfriends,' she said severely to her reflection, and carried her pack out into the hall.

He was waiting by the front door, but as she came towards him the telephone rang. 'Excuse me,' he said without hurry. 'I'll take it in the office.'

Alli lowered her pack to the floor and examined a magnificent, almost abstract landscape that was definitely New Zealand. It was a bush scene, sombre yet vibrant. With a myriad of greens and browns the artist had conveyed the sense of peril and hidden mystery she'd noticed in the New Zealand forest.

She thought nostalgically of the waters of the lagoon at Valanu—every shade of blue melding into glowing turquoise beneath a brilliant sky. Sometimes she dreamed of the soft hush of trade winds in the coconut palms, and the crunch of blazing white sand beneath her feet.

Safer than dreaming about snow, she thought sardonically.

Yet she was learning to love New Zealand. The parts of it she'd seen were beautiful in a wild, aloof way.

On a table beneath the bush picture a nude bronze art deco dancer postured with sinuous abandon. Absorbed in its mannered, erotic grace, Alli jumped when Slade spoke from behind her.

'That was Marian.'

Composing her face so that he wouldn't read the sudden wild hope there, she turned around slowly. 'Oh?'

'She wants to see you before I take you home,' he said briefly. 'It won't be much of a delay.'

Alli could read nothing in his face. 'Did she say why?'

'No.' He opened the front door, holding it to let her through in front of him.

They drove along Auckland's streets, busy with tourists and those who'd decided to eat brunch beside the harbour on this sunny Sunday morning.

Alli tried to rein in her seething thoughts, glad when Slade said abruptly, 'I rang the hospital this morning to find out how those kids were.'

'I meant to ask you at breakfast,' she said remorsefully. It had fled her mind because she'd been enjoying herself so much.

'They've all been discharged except the boy in the coma and the girl with the broken arm. She'll be discharged this morning, and the boy is critical but stable.'

'I do hope he recovers without any damage. The boys insisted that the girls wear the seat belts,' she said. 'They were so boisterous I wondered if they'd been drinking, but it didn't seem as though they had.'

'High on youth,' he commented dispassionately.

Alli glanced at him, her stomach tightening at the arrogant symmetry of line and angle that was his profile. How did he do it? she thought desperately. Being with him sharpened all her senses; today the sky was brighter, the perfume of jasmine through the window more musky and evocative, the texture of her clothes against her skin supple and fine and erotically charged.

Once more they took the silent lift up to the fourth floor. This time it was Marian who opened the door— a Marian much more composed than on the previous day. She accepted Slade's kiss, and then asked Alli, 'My dear, how did you sleep?'

'Fine, thank you,' Alli said mundanely, relaxing only when their hostess waved them into the room where she'd received them the previous day.

'Do sit down,' she said, and settled into her chair, examining Alli with a small frown between her exquisitely plucked brows. 'I was shocked when Caroline told me that Slade had rung to say you'd had to deal with an accident—what a ghastly thing! I'd have nightmares for a week!'

Without looking at Slade, Alli replied, 'At least only one person was badly hurt.'

'Do you know how he is?'

Concisely Slade explained what he'd learned.

Marian sighed. 'I feel for his poor parents.'

A slight pause stretched Alli's nerves to breaking point. She felt completely alien in this luxurious room—and that was odd, because she hadn't felt like that in Slade's apartment.

Marian picked up an envelope from the table beside her chair and held it out. 'I asked you here this morning because I want to give you something.'

Alli tensed. If she's offering me money, she thought disjointedly, I'll—I'll throw it at her!

Fingers trembling, she opened it. But there was no money. Intensely relieved, she took out a photograph and examined it, her heart contracting; this time the woman was in full face, eyeing the camera with a half-smile. In colouring and features she was almost identical to the face Alli saw in her mirror every morning.

She looked across at the older woman.

'Yes,' Marian said, 'it's your mother.'

Blindly, Alli turned it over. Her mother's handwriting was a bold scrawl. *To my sister Marian,* she'd written. *So you don't forget me.*

Well, running away with her sister's husband had made sure of that!

'Thank you.' Then she suddenly remembered something, and scrabbled in her bag until she found an envelope. 'I don't know whether you want this, but it's a—it's yours, anyway.'

She held it out. Automatically Marian accepted it, but she didn't open it. 'What is it?'

'It's a wedding photograph I found in my father's things,' Alli said uncomfortably.

Another awkward pause followed, broken by Marian's quick reply. 'No, I don't want it, I'm afraid.' She handed it back. 'Do you know anything about your mother at all?'

Alli tucked the photograph of her mother into the envelope and put it in her bag. 'Nothing. My father never spoke of her.'

For a moment the older woman looked inexpressibly sad, but the fleeting expression vanished under the mask of a good hostess. 'Were you happy as a child?'

Alli gave her a brilliant smile and stood up, Slade following suit. 'In lots of ways I had a super childhood. Children are very resilient, you know. They accept things.'

Marian's glance tangled with Slade's. 'Yes, I know. I'm glad you were happy.' She got to her feet and led the way to the door.

But before they reached it she stopped and turned to Alli. 'Thank you for coming to see me,' she said unexpectedly. 'You must have felt like telling me to go to hell when I rejected your approach so comprehensively two years ago. But your existence came as a...' she hesitated, as though discarding the word that came naturally to her tongue and substituting another '...a huge shock. I thought you'd   never been born, you see.'

It was, Alli could see, all the excuse she was going to give. And it was also a definite goodbye. She didn't blame the older woman; each sight of her niece had to be an exercise in remembered bitterness.

'It's all right,' she said swiftly. 'I do understand. Thank you for giving me this photograph—I'll treasure it.'

Marian's smile was a mere sketch, and before she could speak Slade said, 'It's time we went, Alli.'

'Caroline will be so sorry to have missed you,' Marian said.

But Caroline must have come in while they were talking, because she was in the hall when they came out. Alli felt the other woman's resentment, cloaked though it was with a gracious smile, when Caroline asked, 'Are you going to be at the Thorpes' tonight, Slade?'

'Yes,' he said, smiling at her.

'Oh, good. I'll see you there, then.' Her look at Alli held a flicker of smugness. 'Lovely to have met you, Alison. Goodbye.'

Less subtle than Marian's farewell, but no less definite. Alli nodded and said goodbye, and went out with Slade into a blue and gold and crystal day, warm as a welcome and heady as champagne.

Its beauty was almost wasted. As they drove north they spoke little. A few hours ago she'd woken up in this man's arms; by the time they reached the Lodge she felt as though he'd withdrawn to the other side of the moon.

Sadness almost closed her throat.

'Who was it,' Slade remarked as they swung off the road onto the rutted track that led to the Lodge, 'that said to be careful what you wish for because you might get it?'

'Bluebeard, probably,' Alli returned jauntily. 'Don't

worry, I'm not shattered. I was surprised to discover that my upright father was an adulterer—and with his wife's sister—but I suppose I always suspected there was something odd about the situation. Men who find refuge at the back of the trade winds usually have something to hide from.'

'Indeed,' he said dryly. 'A very philosophical attitude.'

Outside the Lodge she held out her hand for her pack and said formally, 'Thank you very much for—for everything. Goodbye.'

But her plans to get rid of him quickly were countered by Tui, who marched out through the door and said, 'Are you coming in for lunch, Slade?'

He shook his head with an appreciative smile. 'No, I have to get back to town.'

'You're missing hot scones,' Tui said, adding slyly, 'With whipped cream and home-made tamarillo jam.'

'You know how to tempt a man; unfortunately I have an appointment in Auckland. Thank you for the offer—can I take you up on it another time?'

'Any time,' Tui told him.

He looked at Alli, green eyes gleaming. 'Take care,' he said, and turned and strode lithely back to the big car.

Left to herself, Alli would have gone inside, but Tui stayed and waved, so she did too, because anything other would have produced questions.

'What we used to call a real dish,' her boss said with pleasure. 'He's got presence, that one. I'll bet the women chase him.'

'He might have made up his mind which one he'll have,' Alli said, thinking of Caroline's eminent worthiness to be Slade Hawkings's wife. He'd said she had no right to object to anything he did, but he was meeting her that night at the Thorpes', whoever they were.

And Caroline Forsythe struck Alli as being quietly determined.

'Ah, well, better get back to work,' Tui said with a last wave that was answered by a short toot as Slade's car took the cattlestop. 'You're looking a bit tired. Have a nap, and then take Lady out for a gallop along the beach.' She waited until Alli hefted her bag before asking, 'When are you going to see him again?'

'Not ever,' Alli said, the words resounding heavily inside her head.

Tui laughed. 'It's not like you to be coy.'

'I'm not!'

Her employer said cheerfully, 'Well, let me tell you something, girl—that man wants you. He'll be back, you'll see.'

Don't do this, Alli said silently. 'I didn't know you were a mind-reader.'

'Can't do minds, but I'm pretty good at body language,' Tui returned smartly. 'He's tracking, Alli. If you don't want him, you'd better start running.'

CHAPTER SEVEN

TUI BUSTLED INTO the kitchen, her expression a mixture of sly humour and surprise. 'You're a close-mouthed one,' she accused, slapping a newspaper down on the table in front of Alli. 'You haven't said a word about last weekend in town with the handsome hunk. Not even about being hounded by the paparazzi!'

Swallowing the final mouthful of delectable chicken pie, Alli turned a startled face to her. 'What?'

Tui flattened the paper out and pointed triumphantly. 'There you are—and it's easy to see it's you! Not like the other one on the beach.'

Sure enough, someone had taken a photograph of Slade's car as he'd driven out of the car park under his apartment building. Stomach roiling, Alli noticed a smile on her photographed face. She couldn't remember smiling—especially not a satisfied smirk like that, hinting at a long night of well-sated passion.

Beneath the photograph the gossip columnist had written, *Who is the woman leaving Slade Hawkings's apartment early—very early—one morning?*

'Didn't you see the photographer?' Tui asked, her curiosity palpable.

'No.'

'Can't say I blame you—if I were sitting beside Slade Hawkings I wouldn't be looking for paparazzi.' Tui pushed the newspaper closer. 'Go on, take it. That's the second time you've hit the headlines—you'd better start a scrapbook.'

'I don't want it,' Alli said defiantly, averting her eyes from the photograph.

'Well, want it or not, you'd better get ready to go out, because that's Slade Hawkings's car coming up the drive right now.'

A bewildering mixture of apprehension and awareness churned through Alli. Leaping to her feet, she muttered, 'Damn! Oh, damn!' and cast a hunted look through the window.

'Probably the first time a woman's reacted like that to his arrival,' Tui said knowledgeably. 'I'll go and meet him—you change into something that looks a bit more upmarket. Those jeans fit nicely, but your sweatshirt isn't ageing gracefully.'

'He won't notice.' Not true, she knew.

Her employer knew it too. 'That one notices everything. Go on. What about your nice mossy green jersey? It looks great with your skin. And put some lipstick on.'

Alli cast another harried glance through the window before fleeing. Once in her small bedroom she shrugged into the jersey, but rebelled at lipstick.

He'd come about the photograph, of course. No doubt he was angry. Well, so was she. Who the heck had staked out his apartment so early in the morning? And why? They wouldn't have done it for plain Alli Pierce, so they must have been tracking Slade.

Head erect and shoulders painfully squared, she walked back to the Lodge, flinching when a wood pigeon swooped across her path at eye level about two feet in front of her, its white breast gleaming in the sun.

Her pulse raced from flutter to jungle beat when she saw Slade in the office. Her first involuntary thought was that lipstick wouldn't have helped anyway. Darkly dominant, he turned to examine her, his displeasure like an icy cloud.

'Come for a drive,' he said, and forestalled her automatic refusal by saying, 'Tui says she can manage without you for half an hour.'

'Longer than that if it's necessary,' Tui said with a stern glance at Alli. 'See if you can persuade her to take her holidays, will you? She's got about ten days in lieu.'

Tui, not now! Self-preservation goaded Alli into terse speech. 'I don't need holidays, and I'd rather walk along the beach.'

No way was she going to let herself be locked in the car with him for half an hour.

Equally crisply, Slade returned, 'Fine. Show me the way.'

Once outside the Lodge she asked, 'Have you heard how the boy in a coma is?'

'Recovering well,' he said. 'No brain damage, apparently.'

'Thank God,' she breathed.

'He was lucky; if he's got any sense he'll learn from it.' Slade looked around as she indicated the boardwalk between the dunes. 'This is very different from Valanu.'

'Much colder,' she said with a half-smile, then swung into tourist mode. 'Tui and Joe and the local conservation society are doing their best to reclaim the dunes. They've got them fenced off so no one can ride through them, and, as you can see, it's working.'

Out on the beach, the sun smiled down on rows of waves sweeping onto the beach in perfect formation. Lithe black forms played amongst them—surfers. The water was warming, and very soon they'd be able to discard their wetsuits.

'Why are you here?' Alli asked.

'Partly to discuss the photograph in the paper today.'

'We can't do anything about that,' she said with a casual shrug. 'No one knows who I am, so any gossip will die. What I'd like to know is why the photographer was so conveniently there. Do you usually have paparazzi staking you out?'

'Occasionally.'

'Why that day?'

'I doubt if it was anything to do with you,' he said shortly.

She glowered at him. 'Of course it wasn't. You're the celebrity, not me.'

'I'm not a celebrity, and gossip doesn't worry me.'

'I'm afraid I don't have your lofty attitude to it. Finding myself in the newspaper made my skin crawl. What I can't work out is where the photographer was. I didn't see anyone.' Probably because she'd been too busy sending Slade sideways glances through her lashes. The thought of people all over New Zealand drawing conclusions from that smile rankled.

'It was taken with a telephoto lens from the park across the street.' Slade stooped and picked up a length of driftwood, hefting it a moment to test its weight before hurling it into the surf. Watching it sink below the waves, he said, 'Don't worry about it—you won't appear in any other photographs.'

'I'm glad to hear it.' Keeping her eyes on the distant place where the beach receded into a soft salt-haze, Alli frowned against the sun. A painful needle of hope pricked her heart, tormenting her with its persistence. To get rid of it once and for all, she said briskly, 'It's very kind of you to come and tell me this, but really I didn't expect it. A phone call would have been enough, although that wouldn't have been necessary either. After all, we've already said our goodbyes.'

Stone-faced, Slade scrutinised her. 'You surely don't believe that Marian would just hand over a photograph of your mother and send you on your way without another word?'

She'd believed just that—after all, Marian's farewell had seemed more than definite.

'I see you do.' His voice was dry. 'You're her only relative.'

'For which she's probably devoutly thankful.'

'You were certainly a shock to her,' he admitted. 'However, she doesn't want to lose sight of you.'

Alli didn't know what to say to this. In the end she contented herself with a cautious, 'That's very kind of her, but I don't want her to feel any sort of obligation to me.'

'It comes with the territory,' he said shortly. 'Families work like that. She's asked me to tell you that she'd like you to stay with her so you can get to know each other.'

His expression didn't alter, but she knew he disapproved of this latest development. Alli fought a brief, bitter battle with herself. Marian was offering what she'd always wanted—a family. Yet a deep-seated wariness held her back. 'Caroline—'

Slade cut in with abrupt authority. 'Caroline won't be there.'

Meanly relieved, she said slowly, 'How long does Marian want me to stay?'

'A couple of weeks.' He smiled briefly and without humour. 'I suggested that she and you spend time together at the bach.'

Alli knew that northern New Zealanders used that word to refer to a small, unpretentious holiday house by the beach, but she had a pretty fair idea that Slade's bach would be neither modest nor unsophisticated.

'I don't think that's a good idea,' she said quickly, before she could change her mind.

'Why?'

'I can't believe that she'd want to know me. I must bring back some pretty shattering memories.'

'That won't wash,' he returned instantly. 'She had a very happy marriage with my father—happy enough to rob the fiasco of her first marriage of its sting.'

'I suspect she feels sorry for me. Well, I don't need to be rescued—I've made a good life for myself, with friends and a job I enjoy. I'm not a charity case.'

She angled her chin up at him, the feline enticement of her face temporarily overwhelmed by a cold, still pride. The wind snatched up a handful of dry sand and hurled it at them, making her blink and turn away.

Coolly he said, 'I don't recollect either Marian or I insinuating that you were some orphan in the storm.'

She flushed at the memory that phrase brought back,

and he said something under his breath before resuming on an impatient note, 'And since Tui says you're over-due for holidays I can't see why this is such a big deal.'

That, she thought wearily, was the problem—for him it wasn't a big deal. For her it was becoming increas-ingly so. His suggestion came wrapped with such tempt-ing possibilities—a family, and a man she was starting to dream about whenever she loosened the reins on her will-power...

If only Tui had kept her mouth shut!

'Thank you very much,' she told him firmly, 'but it's not necessary. I wanted to meet my mother and find out why she abandoned me. OK, meeting her is impossible now, but I do know what happened. I have no claim on either of you, so it's probably better that we leave it at that.'

He said calmly, 'You prised the cat out of the bag, Alli; it's too late to thrust it back in again. If you turn Marian down she'll keep trying. She doesn't give up easily.' He looked around at the beach and the surf, the wild exuberance of the gulls whirling over the surf like scraps of white paper, and said dispassionately, 'It wouldn't surprise me if she turned up at the Lodge.'

Alli tightened her lips to hide an odd feeling of being driven discreetly but inevitably into a decision she wasn't ready for. 'She'd hate it. It's very casual and laid-back, and most of our clientele are surfers or fish-ermen or naturalists.'

'She's adaptable.'

Alli turned her face to the sea. While they'd been talking the wind had dropped away, and the breeze that feathered across her face now was soft with the promise of summer.

Indecision kept her silent. She longed to forge some links, however casual and fragile, with the only relative she had; it was, she thought with a touch of bitterness, ironic that if she let herself be drawn into the family she faced real danger from Slade.

Well, not from Slade—from her reckless feelings for him. Prudence counselled her to refuse; the heady thrill of being close to him weakened her resolve.

And from what Slade had said he didn't plan to be at the bach.

In the end she licked the salt from her lips and surrendered. 'All right, then. I'll go to the bach for ten days if Poppy, Tui's daughter-in-law, can take my place at the Lodge.'

Within half an hour she was staring at the road twisting away in front of them.

'Your employer still doesn't entirely trust me,' Slade observed, uncannily echoing her thoughts. 'She wasn't going to let you go unless I gave her the address and phone number of the bach.'

'I don't think Tui trusts anyone but her family.'

He nodded. 'Probably a good maxim to live by.' He didn't add, *And sometimes you can't even trust them,* but no doubt he was thinking it.

Alli certainly was.

Slade's bach turned out to be the only house on a hillside above a melon-slice of champagne-coloured sand. The building *was* far from modest; backed by the dark luxuriance of coastal forest, the double-storeyed colonial gem stood four-square and proud, surrounded by a columned verandah with balconies above.

'It looks like a doll's house!' Alli exclaimed, leaning forward as they negotiated the steep drive. 'A very large doll's house.'

'It used to be the original homestead for the area.' With the skill of familiarity Slade steered around a hairpin bend shaded by the thick, feathery canopy of kanuka trees.

Just north of Auckland they'd left the main road and driven through fertile valleys where dairy farms, vineyards and orchards mingled in harmony beneath a range of high hills sombre with a thick, tangled cloak of New Zealand bush.

'I don't see any farm,' she said, beating back a giddy mixture of foreboding and anticipation.

'We've been coming through it for the past fifteen minutes—it started at the first cattlestop. When my father decided he wasn't made for country life he put in a manager's house closer to the road and replanted this hillside in native trees.'

The drive swung around the back of the house onto a wide gravel forecourt. Slade stopped the vehicle and turned off the engine. 'Welcome to my home.'

Alli froze. 'I thought you lived in Auckland.'

'I spend about half my time there. Why? Does it make a difference?'

'No,' she denied, because what else could she say? *Nothing would have persuaded me to come if I'd known you intended to be here too.* Not likely.

He saw through her, of course. Steel edging his

words, he drawled, 'Don't worry, I'm off to Tahiti to-morrow.'

Her relief must have shown too clearly, because he smiled—not a nice smile. 'You could come with me,' he suggested, in a tone that was a subtle insult.

Alli scrambled out of the car, her nerves twanging. 'No, thanks.'

He climbed out and reached in the boot for her pack, straightening up with a strap over one shoulder. 'Scared, Alli?'

The direct challenge made her seethe. 'I came to see Marian.'

Tall and dark and compelling, he slung her pack onto his shoulder and walked across the forecourt to a door. It opened as he got there, and Marian beamed at him.

Feeling awkward, Alli followed him and was greeted with a more restrained smile. 'Come in,' the older woman said. 'How are you, Alli?'

'Fine, thank you,' Alli replied automatically.

'I'm so glad you could come. Slade, I've put Alli in the middle bedroom.' Chatting lightly about the journey, she led Alli up the stairs to the top storey and into a room decorated in shades of ivory and soft cream.

Acutely aware of Slade following them with the pack, Alli said, 'Oh, this is lovely. So restful.'

'It has a pretty view out over the bay.' Her hostess gestured towards the glass doors that led out onto the balcony, then indicated another door. 'Your bathroom is through there. We'll leave you to refresh yourself, and when you come on down we'll have afternoon tea. Turn left at the bottom of the stairs and follow the voices!'

The room had been decorated with a deft hand—an

old-fashioned iron-framed bed looked as though it had always been there, and long curtains puffed gently in the breeze. Instead of unpacking, Alli went out onto the balcony and discovered with delight that it was a private one.

She took a deep breath, inhaling the delicious spicy scent of kanuka trees and the ever-present tang of salt.

Time enough to admire the view later, she thought, turning reluctantly away. Swiftly she sorted her clothes into the wardrobe, then picked up her sponge bag and walked into the bathroom.

After washing her face and combing her hair, she tracked the other two to a room that opened out onto the same magnificent view of the sea.

'Slade tells me you drink tea,' Marian said cheerfully. She patted the white sofa beside her and said, 'Come and tell me how you like it. So many young things don't drink tea or coffee nowadays, I find. It's almost a relief to find someone who does!'

After ten minutes Alli decided her hostess's exquisite manners were a mask. But then, she thought with a fleeting glance at Slade's angular face, they were all wearing masks. The time she'd agreed to spend in this lovely house stretched before her like a small taste of eternity.

After she'd drunk her tea Marian commanded, 'Slade, why don't you show Alli around? I'm sure she'd like to see the beach.'

With his trademark lithe grace Slade rose from the chair. 'Come along, Alli,' he said, with a smile as burnished and bland as sheet metal. 'Let me introduce you to Kawau Bay.'

He took her out onto a wide deck, overlooking the beach, and led her down a couple of steps and across a lawn.

'I love pohutukawas,' Alli said, stopping by one huge tree. 'They symbolise Northland's summers, with their crimson and scarlet flowers like millions of tiny tassels, but they don't grow by the Lodge.'

'They like it rocky,' Slade told her as they went down another two steps to the beach, 'but they can't stand the cold west and southerly winds that sweep over the west coast. Give them a cliff overlooking an island-sheltered bay and they're happy.'

'This is charming.' Smiling, she took in the small curve of sand, the smooth waters of the wide inlet and the shapes of islands to the east. Loyally she added, 'But I do love the west coast. It's so wild and free and dangerous.'

'This can be dangerous too,' he said. 'Don't swim on your own. It's not like the lagoon at Valanu, where you might as well be in a bath.'

'That had its dangers too,' she said quietly, thinking of a friend who had been taken by a shark.

'Life's full of danger.' Slade sounded sardonic. 'The Maori say that the west coast is like a man, strong and virile and warlike, whereas the east coast resembles a woman, beautiful and soft. I'm sure they'd be the first to admit that women can be just as dangerous as men in their own way.'

The sand crunched beneath Alli's feet when they reached the tideline. She stopped there and looked around, her expression grave and considering. To one side, under the low headland that separated this bay from the next, a wharf ran out into deep water. Two boats were tied up to it: a large cruiser, with swept-up bow and all the flashy mod cons, and an elegant dowager from the thirties, solid, dignified and restrained.

'I used to jump off the end of the wharf,' Slade told her. He looked down at her. 'I suppose like me you learned to swim before you could walk?'

'Literally,' she agreed. 'The lagoon was an ideal place to learn, of course.'

'Do you miss Valanu?'

She said thoughtfully, 'Yes, but I always knew I'd have to leave one day. Living there was like living in a fairy story.'

'How long was your father ill before he died?'

'I'm surprised you don't know,' she said, the acid in her voice tempered by irony. 'A year.'

'He didn't think to come back to New Zealand for medical care?'

She looked at the pink-gold sand and said desolately, 'He wouldn't go anywhere, not even to the clinic until it was far too late. I think he wanted to die.'

It was the first time she'd admitted it to herself.

To her astonishment Slade's warm hand enclosed hers. Sensation ran up her arm, quick and shocking as electricity, and somehow transmuted into ripples of slow, wondrous sensuality that gave her a tantalising glimpse of what it might be like to be loved by Slade Hawkings...

Except that it wouldn't be love. So, although the comfort he offered was powerfully seductive, she pulled her hand from his. 'I think he really loved Marian all the time.'

'I won't say forget it, because the past casts long shadows, but mulling it over and wondering what really happened is a waste of time and mental energy,' Slade said in a voice that lacked any emotion. 'Not only are you never going to know, but I'm sure your father would have wanted you to make your own life without dwelling on his mistakes. Let your parents sleep in peace, Alli.'

She was touched by his understanding, and surprised at the slight abrasiveness of his tone in the latter part of it. 'Yes, sir,' she said meekly.

He laughed, a deep sound that twisted her heart. 'Did I sound like a grandfather? I can pontificate with the best of them.'

'I don't think you were pontificating,' she said, trying hard to be objective. 'It's just that—well, my father was difficult to love because he never unbent, but he was always *there*, and he was reliable. And he was a man of honour. He was respected. When he died they buried him with the chiefs.' She looked up and said simply, 'And he made sure I didn't lie, or steal. He had very strong moral principles, so I suppose I want to know how a man like that could betray someone as comprehensively as he did Marian.'

'He may never have had a grand passion before he met your mother, and been totally unable to deal with it. The thing you have to remember is that he didn't betray you,' Slade said austerely.

She nodded, thinking that this was a strangely intimate conversation to be having with him—one she should not have embarked on. It would, she thought warily, be dangerous to reveal too much of herself to Slade.

She stopped beneath a pohutukawa branch over-spreading the beach. A large tyre had been tied to it. 'Your swing?' she said brightly.

'I believe my father was the original user, but this is not the original tyre, or even the original chain. We often have visitors here, and their children love swinging as much as I did.'

The thought of him as a child did something odd to her heart. He'd have been a handful—bold and deter-mined and intelligent...

Banishing such subversive thoughts, she said even more brightly, 'This is a wonderful place for children.'

And almost winced at the banality of her words.

'Indeed,' he said gravely. 'But I hope you will enjoy it too. As soon as I'm gone you'll be able to relax.'

'You don't make me nervous!'

The moment she said it she knew she should have kept her lips firmly buttoned. He looked at her with a gleam of something very like amusement in his green eyes, but as she glared at him it died, to be replaced by a piercing intensity. Alli's mouth went dry. She heard some bird calling, the clear notes dropping into a spreading silence.

He said quietly, 'Then why do your eyes go dark on the rare occasions when you look at me—?'

'I look at you quite often!' Too much—but usually when he couldn't see.

'Mostly you concentrate on an ear, or my hair, or the pocket of my shirt,' he said blandly. 'And did you know that tiny pulse in the base of your throat speeds up whenever I come near?'

Mesmerised, she shook her head. 'I—no.'

By then her mouth was so arid she almost croaked the words. He lifted a lean, tanned hand and touched the hollow in her throat, and any further attempt at speaking was doomed.

How could a fingertip do so much damage? It drained her of will-power until all she could do was stare into his narrowed eyes as though they were her one hope of salvation.

He laughed softly, and then his face came nearer. Alli closed her eyes against the fires in his, but by the time he kissed her mute, imploring mouth she could no longer think. Lost in a rush of heat, she swayed, and he pulled her against his strong body.

It was so familiar, as though she'd done this thousands of times, and she relaxed into him and let his kiss wreak devastation on her already shaken defences.

Her skin tightened deliciously. She shivered as his hand slid down her back to find the curve of her hips, but she didn't pull away.

Whenever she'd kissed other men their arousal had always faintly repelled her, but now, with Slade, she relished the evidence of his desire. Response, white-hot and elemental, scorched through her, washing away inhibitions and fear.

He lifted his mouth, but before disappointment struck he pressed a series of kisses along the line of her jaw. Delight leapt from nerve-end to nerve-end in a tornado of sensation, a delight that turned fierce and wild when his mouth found the soft lobe of her ear and he nipped it, using his teeth with exquisite precision.

That tender nip made her acutely, deliciously aware of the weight of her breasts, of over-sensitive tips against his hard chest. From her breasts, that wildfire sensation homed in on the place deep inside her, a place that ached with desperate hunger.

His hand swept from her hip to cup the side of her breast; while she dived further into the wilder seas of sensation his thumb played with tormenting slowness over the pleading tip.

Alli's groan was torn from her innermost feelings—a sound, she dimly realised far too late, of surrender.

And then his mouth left hers and he said in a voice entirely empty of any emotion, 'Still positive you don't want to come to Tahiti with me, Alli?'

Stunned, she met coldly calculating eyes, green and cold as crystals. Shame flooded her as she understood that he'd been testing her.

She wanted to slap his arrogant face, and then, humiliatingly, she wanted to burst into tears!

CHAPTER EIGHT

PRIDE GAVE ALLI the strength to pull herself together. She stepped back and said, in a voice she prayed was composed enough to fool him, 'I came here at Marian's invitation, so going to Tahiti would be rude.'

Slade smiled cynically. 'More entertaining, though.'

She shrugged. 'What's fun got to do with it?' She hoped she'd managed to prick his pride with her scorn.

If she had he didn't show it. Instead he stood back courteously to let her walk ahead of him up the steps to the lawn. 'You are, of course, entirely correct,' he said evenly. 'Security is always important.'

She stopped. 'What exactly do you mean by that?'

The gold rays in his eyes glinted. 'What do you think I meant by it?'

'Listen to me,' she said fiercely. 'I don't want money from Marian.'

If she'd thought her directness might throw him she had misjudged the man. He said, 'I'm glad to hear that.'

But she could tell he didn't believe her.

Clenching her jaw to hold back a bitter disillusionment, she said, 'I'm not going to try and justify myself—people with prejudices are rarely able to change them even when confronted by the truth. And this *is* the truth. I've managed my life so far without asking for money from anyone; I don't intend to start now. Besides, if you think I'm here to feather my nest why did you bring me?'

'So you didn't *ask* Barry Simcox on Valanu to pay you three times the rate everyone else was paid?' he observed, taking her elbow and turning her towards the house.

Even that brief touch shortened her breath. 'He said that because I was a New Zealander that's what I should be paid...'

Her voice faded under Slade's sardonic glance. How stupid she'd been! Of course she hadn't been entitled to the extra money; Barry had made the decision after her father died, no doubt thinking she needed extra income.

'It seemed logical at the time. I just didn't think,' she said lamely. She dragged air into her lungs and spoke into the disbelieving silence. 'I'll pay back every cent I owe you, and you can stop testing me. It's harassment and it's demeaning.'

He said on note of mockery, 'Indeed? I don't want your money—you've more than repaid it with your excellent ideas about getting Sea Winds back on its feet. As for harassment—while it was happening I could have sworn you enjoyed it just as much as I enjoy kissing you.'

Stunned, she risked a glance at him, and met a coolly watchful scrutiny. Pleasure it might have been, but he'd been in complete control of the situation—unlike her, weakly melting in a puddle at his feet!

He added, 'And making love to you would be pleasure also.'

Colour stained her skin. 'Lovemaking as a test of integrity? The thought makes my flesh crawl.'

'If we made love,' he said silkily, 'I suspect that by the second kiss everything but carnal appetite would fly out of the window.' He watched more colour roil up through her skin, and went on, 'I had reason to distrust you. You must admit that your first letter to Marian was aggressive enough to make her very wary.'

Alli flushed. 'I was—angry, I suppose,' she said reluctantly. 'I wanted to know why she—why my mother had abandoned me.'

She still didn't know that, and now she never would. But it no longer overshadowed her life. Somehow Slade had redirected her energies.

I am not in love with him, she thought, sudden panic kicking her stomach.

Slade said, 'It's the primal fear of children, isn't it—abandonment by the mother? I was barely four when my mother died. I remember the shock and the bewilderment and the terror.'

Heart-wrung for the small, heartbroken boy whose mother had left him in the most final of ways, she said quietly, 'At least I didn't know what I was missing.'

At the bottom of the steps leading onto the deck, he said, 'Just to set the record straight, if it *is* money you're interested in you should know that Marian's income is derived from a trust fund. She can't touch the principal.'

Alli went white. 'I find you utterly disgusting,' she retorted, and ran ahead, across the deck and into the house.

Once in her room she paced the floor until she regained control over her seething emotions. That final cut from Slade had been calculated to wound.

Why did he dislike her so much?

Because their kiss had affected him as much as it had her?

She dismissed the thought immediately. Slade had probably been born with an innate knowledge of how to please a woman, a skill honed by practice.

So kissing her hadn't been a big deal for him. Oh, he'd wanted her—but lust came easily and meant very little.

After all, she wanted him...

She walked out onto the balcony. While she'd been pacing the sun had dipped low in the west, its long rays gilding the bush behind the house and edging the clouds with gold. Slade was strolling towards the beach, tall and confident, his gait as smooth as the silent, killing lope of a predator.

A knock at the door made her jump.

It was Marian, smiling and pleasant. 'I thought you might like to come down and have a drink with us. A fax has just come through for poor Slade—he has to leave tonight instead of tomorrow morning, so we'll have dinner early.'

Alli glanced down at her clothes. 'Should I change?'

'Oh, no—you look lovely.'

Something in Marian's tone made her look up sharply, but the other woman had already turned away. 'See you in a few minutes,' she said brightly, and disappeared down the stairs.

Slowly Alli tidied up before following her hostess.

It was an odd evening, with hidden tensions prowling beneath the relaxed, sophisticated surface. As always, Marian was the epitome of a gracious hostess, and Slade was amiable enough—in the fashion of a well-fed tiger.

Apart from the lazy appreciation in his tone when he spoke to her, Alli thought savagely, you'd never know that he'd kissed her senseless.

At last she could bear it no longer. 'Do you mind if I go up now? I'm a little tired.'

Slade's gaze rested thoughtfully on her face as Marian said, 'Not at all. Do let me know if there's anything you need, won't you?'

'Thank you.' Pinning a smile onto her mouth, she turned to Slade. 'Have a safe journey,' she said quietly.

'Thank you.' His eyes were more golden than green, and unease brushed like a feather across her skin.

Back in her room, she sat down in the darkness and tried to work out what had set her intuition jangling.

Something about this situation didn't ring true. Slade warning her off was logical. She suspected he trusted very few people, and only after they'd earned it. And he was hugely protective of his stepmother.

Frowning, she struggled to make sense of a jumble of hunches and faint impressions.

Marian had asked her to come here, supposedly so that they could get to know each other, but beneath the older woman's superb manners lay something else, something so tenuous it was only visible in swiftly concealed flashes.

Not dislike, she thought carefully, not even caution. If she had to pin it down to one thing, she'd say that Marian was in the grip of tightly controlled fear.

'No,' she said aloud, shaking her head.

She had to be over-dramatising, because why should Marian be afraid of her? And if she was, or if that emotion she sensed wasn't fear but something else—say, repugnance—why had the older woman asked her to stay?

It simply didn't make sense. 'So you're wrong,' she said slowly.

The hands in her lap suddenly clenched. She didn't know what Slade thought or felt or wanted, but he'd made no secret of the fact that he didn't trust her.

Perhaps he'd seconded his stepmother's invitation in the hope that Alli would reveal herself in her true colours, whatever they were?

That made sense. Marian might not be able to spend more than the interest from her trust fund, but in comparison to most people she was rich. And Slade was well on the way to becoming a billionaire, if he wasn't already. So when a relation showed up out of the blue naturally they'd want to know what sort of person she was.

Especially as her parents seemed to have had very low moral standards!

'In other words,' she murmured to the distant sound of an outboard motor puttering quietly around a nearby headland, 'you're on trial because they think you might be like Alison.'

As a child, when she'd imagined finding her family she'd always assumed they'd accept her freely and lovingly. Maturity had tempered that first innocent belief, of course, but it still hurt to know that any hope of acceptance lay in convincing Slade she hadn't come to prey on Marian.

* * *

She woke to a silent house and a breathless dawn shimmering across the bay; the trees on the hillside were cloaked in mist that streamed upwards in transparent tendrils.

It was an exquisite beginning to a time that was an odd mixture of laughter and tension. Marian had a keen sense of humour that often bubbled over into wit. She never asked personal questions, but she wanted to know about Alli's life in Valanu, and Alli was happy to tell her.

But gradually, while they walked along the beach and beneath the canopy of the forest Slade's father had planted, while they ate meals at charming vineyard cafés and explored the lovely countryside around, visiting a marine reserve to watch fish that approached them without fear, Alli realised two things.

One was that whenever someone approached Marian she introduced Alli as a friend, chatted briefly, and then moved on within a few minutes.

The other was that Marian revealed very little of herself. She didn't speak of her family, and she never talked about the sister who had borne her husband's child—she didn't even mention Slade often.

While the sunny days passed in golden serenity, Alli's resolve hardened. Once this was over she'd go back to the Lodge and pick up her own life. She might even, she thought, go to Australia. And although that felt like running away, it also seemed eminently sensible, because she didn't want her presence to upset this woman she was learning to like.

Once she asked, 'Did my father have any relatives?'

Marian looked at her with quick sympathy. 'He was an only child, and his parents died young. He never spoke of cousins or any family.'

'And you?' Alli ventured.

Marian's face closed down. 'A few distant cousins in England—I've long lost touch with them.' Smoothly she moved onto another subject, cutting off any further questions.

Not that Alli would have asked them.

Almost a week after Slade had left, she was walking down the stairs when she heard what sounded like a soft groan from behind her. Every sense alert, she swung around. The housekeeper usually spent the couple of hours after lunch at her cottage in the next bay, so Marian was the only other person in the house.

The silence suddenly turned oppressive, weighing Alli down. It had to be Marian, who always rested for a short time after lunch. But it hadn't been a snore…

Oh, well, she could only make a fool of herself. Biting her lip, she turned and ran lightly up the staircase. Outside the door to Marian's room she stopped and listened, but heard nothing else.

Her swift, tentative knock seemed to echo, but she heard a faint noise from inside the room. She drew in a deep breath and said, 'Marian? Are you all right?'

No answer. By now worried, she said, 'I'm going to open the door.'

Carefully she turned the handle and peeked in. The curtains were drawn, but through the dimness she could see the older woman in an armchair; she seemed to be asleep, but something about her stillness alarmed Alli.

'I'll just check that you're all right,' she said quietly, and approached the chair.

Halfway across the room she realised that Marian's eyes were open and fixed on her. Was she enduring some sort of waking dream?

Tensely, Alli said, 'Are you not well?'

No answer, although the muscles in the older woman's throat moved as if she tried to speak. Panic punched Alli in the stomach; she took Marian's hand and said steadily, trying to fill her voice with reassurance, 'Marian, wake up. It's all right, you're at home and in your bedroom...'

Silently Marian continued to stare at her—no, Alli thought with a shiver, *through* her. Something was seriously wrong. She said, 'I'll ring Mrs Hopkins and get her to call an ambulance and your doctor. Don't worry—you'll be fine.'

She lifted the telephone by the bed and punched the housekeeper's number through, only to get no answer. Mrs Hopkins had been going out to lunch, she suddenly remembered.

For the second time in too few weeks she dialled 111 and, when an impersonal voice answered, explained exactly what had happened.

'Just talk gently to her,' the voice at the other end said, before the connection was cut.

Alli picked up the older woman's flaccid hand and said quietly, 'An ambulance is coming. It won't take long—you'll soon be in hospital, where they can find out what the problem is.'

The housekeeper arrived back from lunch just before the ambulance, and packed her employer's bag while the medics stabilised her. Feeling like an extra leg, Alli hung around, desperately concerned. Gone was Marian's smiling charm; she'd suddenly become old and desperately fragile.

'Should we ring Slade?' Mrs Hopkins worried as the stretcher carried Marian down the stairs. 'It looks like a stroke to me.'

'He's in Tahiti, but I don't have an address.'

'Neither do I.'

They looked at each other, the housekeeper clearly seeking guidance.

Alli said, 'I'm going to the hospital with Marian— I'll drive her car down. Can you ring Slade's office and tell his PA or secretary or whatever he has what's happened, and where Marian is?' She hesitated, then said, 'I'll ring you as soon as I can and tell you what's happening.'

Clearly relieved to have something to do, the housekeeper nodded. 'All right.'

Torn by fear and compassion for the woman in the ambulance ahead, Alli drove Marian's powder-blue Mercedes down, wondering if this attack had been her doing.

And things got worse at the hospital. She didn't know the simplest things about Marian beyond her name; she had no idea what other illnesses she'd had, what the address of her Auckland residence was, or even how old she was.

But at last a very small, pale Marian was in bed, hooked up to an array of instruments. She still hadn't moved. Her helplessness shocked Alli. For the first time she felt some sort of kinship with the older woman.

'I'll stay with you,' she told her, touching her hand. 'But first I need to ring Mrs Hopkins and reassure her that you're in good hands.'

Marian looked gravely at her, not a flicker of comprehension in the blue eyes. Sick with worry, Alli took herself off to the payphone.

The housekeeper asked urgently, 'How is she?'

'She hasn't changed, and no one's told me anything, but she's comfortable. Have you heard from Slade?'

'Yes, he's on his way home and expects to be here later tonight. He's going straight to the hospital as soon as he gets in.' Mrs Hopkins sighed. 'It must be a stroke. It doesn't seem possible—she's not a day over fifty-five!'

'If it is a stroke, it's not a death sentence,' Alli said crisply, hoping she was right.

'Of course it's not, and they can do such wonderful things now, can't they?' She sounded too emphatic, as though trying to convince herself.

On the way back, Alli discovered she was trying to convince herself too. Refusing to accept any possibility but a full recovery, she sat down by the bed, taking Marian's lax hand in hers. It seemed ridiculous to feel as though her touch helped, but in this world of beeping, gurgling machines it was at least human. Some distance away a baby cried—thin, exhausted wails that made her ache.

She never had any idea how long she sat there, holding her aunt's hand and talking quietly to her; as night closed down outside she dozed, and was more than half asleep when a subtle scent brought her to full alertness. Twisting in the chair, she looked up at Slade's face, its strong framework sharply prominent. Her heart leapt and she scrambled up awkwardly, so relieved to see him that she almost burst into tears.

He said quietly, 'How is she?'

Marian's eyelids flickered. 'Better now you're here,' Alli said, her voice wavering. 'Look, she knows you've come.'

He leaned over the bed, kissing his stepmother's forehead. 'It's all right,' he said in a deep voice. 'It's all right, Marian, I'm here.'

And, to Alli's astonishment, Marian's mouth moved a little and she sighed.

Slade straightened. 'Alli, there's no need for you to stay now. Sally Hopkins says you've got Marian's car?'

'Yes.'

He tossed her a swipe card. 'It's the key to my apartment. I've ordered a driver to take you back there.'

She caught the card and said, 'But how will you get in?'

'I have a spare.' He looked keenly at her. 'And, Alli—thank you.'

CHAPTER NINE

ALLI WOKE WITH heart thudding and ears on full alert. Darkness pressed heavily on her until a subdued noise from the kitchen indicated that someone had just closed the fridge door.

She drew a sharp breath and swung her long legs over the side of the bed, hooked her thin cotton dressing gown over her shoulders and padded warily out into the hall. More homely sounds reassured her—the clink of a glass on the granite bench, the sound of a tap being turned off—but it was a muttered swear-word that told her who was there.

Slade couldn't have heard her, but before the door was more than a few centimetres open he'd swivelled around to face her. She froze, because in his face she saw a cold anger that stopped her mind.

Something had gone very wrong.

'It's all right,' she said quickly.

He put his glass of water down on the bench and said politely, 'I'm sorry—I thought I was being quiet.'

'How—how is Marian?' she asked, aching for him.

'She's recovering. It wasn't a stroke.'

So what was wrong? Alli said tentatively, 'That's wonderful—isn't it?'

He drained the glass and set it back on the bench with controlled care. 'Indeed it is.'

The discipline of his expression and tone sent shivers scudding down her spine. 'Do they know what the problem is?'

He shrugged and leaned back against the bench. Hooded eyes dispassionate yet intent, he said, 'So far they don't know, but the general conclusion seems to be that she's exhausted and needs to conserve her strength, so her body just shut down. They expect her to revive when her unconscious decides it's safe to do so.'

She asked quietly, 'Was it me?'

Unreadable eyes searched her face with icy detachment. 'I don't know.'

The words came without conscious thought. 'Why is she afraid of me?'

'She's not afraid of you,' he said with sharp emphasis.

'I'll leave tomorrow.' Her voice was flat and completely determined.

'It's too late for that.'

Her skin tightened. She thought she could feel the tension like an electrical force around them, a dark turbulence shot by lightning.

Desperate to get away, she turned and fumbled for the door handle, her heart blocking her throat when he said something explosive beneath his breath and reached past her to wrench open the door as though he'd like to tear it off its hinges.

Startled by the silent ferocity of his arrival, she flinched.

For several seconds they stood facing each other.

Alli's breath came faster as her heart sped up; she saw the colour in his eyes swallowed up by darkness, and knew that her own were widening endlessly…

Afterwards she could never remember who broke first—whether the hand she held out to ward him off found his muscled forearm, or whether his hand lifted to touch her face.

Whatever, when he cupped her cheek and said her name in a low, raw tone excited anticipation prickled through her in a response as elemental as it was dangerous.

Some hidden part of her brain warned that she'd be sorry, but it was swamped by an intense, entirely carnal desire. 'Yes,' she said simply, knowing exactly what she was agreeing to and unable to think of any good reason why she should deny herself this.

For her own protection she wouldn't dare stay in contact with Slade, but before she disappeared from his life she'd know what it was like to make love with him.

Freed at last from fear, she opened her mouth beneath his hard demand to give him what he wanted— what they both wanted. His arms tightened around her, and she gasped when he picked her up and shouldered his way through the door, carried her down the hall and into a bedroom. Once inside, he set her down on her feet, supporting her by the shoulders. His scrutiny was so intense she could feel the gold and green flames licking around her.

'I've wanted this since I first saw you in Valanu,' he said harshly.

Passionate anticipation bubbled up through her. Eyes enormous, she nodded.

As his lips found the spot where her neck joined her shoulders he pushed her dressing gown from her shoulders, his hands sliding on down her back to the hem of her T-shirt. They were warm and strong, and instead of whipping the shirt over her head they slid up beneath it.

Alli shivered, and he said, 'Are you cold?'

'No,' she whispered, on fire from her skin to the aching centre of her being.

This time he kissed her lips, tormenting her with the teasing lightness. A hungry little noise escaped from her throat and she looped her arms around his neck, trying to bring his mouth closer to hers.

One lean hand cupped her breast. Alli shuddered, and dragged an impeded breath into famished lungs. Electricity arced from her breast to the pit of her stomach, relaying the torrid effect of his touch through every cell in her body. Her breasts felt heavy, so responsive to his caresses that she was sure they throbbed.

'You can touch me if you want to,' he murmured, and gently bit the lobe of her ear.

Excitement whipped up higher through her body. Swiftly she unbuttoned his shirt. The heat from his taut skin seared her fingertips, and when she looked up the gold lights in his eyes scorched through the ragged remnants of her self-control.

The soft material of her T-shirt became an unbearable barrier; she fumbled for it, hungering for the feel of his skin against hers.

'What is it?' His voice was a sexy rumble. 'What do you want?'

'I want—I want—' Unable to formulate the words,

she pushed the sides of his shirt further apart. Finally, she muttered angrily, 'I want you.'

Black lashes almost shaded the green and gold glitter of his eyes. 'Good, because I want you too,' he said, the words such a blatant act of possession that they stopped the breath in her throat.

She stared at him, meeting his narrowed eyes with a hot shiver of urgency that exploded like a fireburst inside her. 'Then take off your shirt,' she said raggedly, unable to dissemble.

Her whole body longed for him, craved him, demanded him—if she didn't get what she wanted she thought she might die of need.

He dropped his hands, stepping back in silent invitation.

Dry-mouthed, she pushed his shirt from his shoulders and down over the corded muscles of his arms, letting it fall to the floor.

The impact of his bare torso hit her like a shockwave. Lamplight burnished the powerful shoulders and chest to bronze, sheened the sleek skin of his flat abdomen.

Any more, she thought feverishly, and I'm going to swoon at his feet!

Slowly, her heart beating a tattoo in her ears, Alli pressed the flat of her hand over his heart, reassured when she felt its uneven beat driving into her palm. Against his formidable masculinity her hand looked pale and fragile, but at her touch his chest rose sharply.

Acute, gratified pleasure pierced her. She wasn't the only one lost to this overwhelming desire. Although she couldn't make herself look into his face, his silence and his stillness reassured her; with tentative strokes she examined the texture of hair and skin until her questing fingers reached a small dark nub.

Again that sudden rise of his chest startled her, and she whipped back her fingers, only to have them clamped beneath his. He said, 'Surely you know that men and women aren't very different? We like to be pleasured, and your touch pleasures me.'

At last Alli gathered enough courage to look into his face.

What she saw there shocked her; raw need hardened his features and gleamed in his eyes, so concentrated she could feel it blasting into her. A rising tide of passion almost blocked her thoughts.

'Take off your T-shirt,' he said, the words soft and rough.

For a second she hesitated, tempted to demand that he do it, but something about removing her own clothes appealed to her pride. Head held high, she met his eyes as she slid the material over her head, lowering it to stand before him in nothing but narrow cotton briefs.

Silently he reached for her, and some part of herself was comforted because his hand shook slightly when it mimicked hers, his thumb lightly stroking the pink centre of her breast.

Sensation arrowed through her, white-hot and elemental. Slade pulled her into the heat and strength of his body, and she sighed and linked her arms around his neck and mutely offered herself to him.

He kissed the hollow at the base of her throat, and then his mouth slid slower, tasting, teasing, exploring each gentle curve with slow, erotic finesse.

And when he reached one pouting, pleading centre he drew it inside his mouth. Her knees buckled and she cried his name in a voice that betrayed every molten, reckless sensation bursting through her.

Slade lifted his head and surveyed her with narrowed, glittering eyes. Wonderingly, she touched his mouth, so uncompromising, yet capable of delivering such intense delight. He kissed the tip of her finger, and when she slid it into the moisture inside he bit the skin tenderly, his sharp teeth sending a thrill of desire through her.

'I can think of a better place for us to be,' he said, and he picked her up.

The coolness of the sheet beneath her back and legs provided an intriguing contrast to the urgency that sizzled through her; she relaxed onto the pillows, only noticing then that he had taken her into his bedroom.

When he'd finished undressing she forgot everything in the wonder of watching him with complete absorption, every cell in her body throbbing in desperate anticipation.

On Valanu she'd seen male tourists in bathing suits so minuscule they might as well have been naked. Now she realised that the scrap of material swathed around hips had made a huge difference; without it, Slade was magnificent.

She swallowed, wondering feverishly if this was going to work…and if she should perhaps tell him that she'd never made love before.

He came to the edge of the bed with the silent, powerful grace that marked him out from other men. Alli held herself still while he eased down beside her, and for the first time she felt the shock of nakedness—skin flexing against heated skin, the slow play of muscles, the feeling of being overwhelmed by sheer masculinity.

Utterly exposed, her skin colouring under his gaze, she buried her shy face in his shoulder and nuzzled him, and his faint, tantalising scent filled her nostrils, replacing the nervousness and fear with a quiet, lovely certainty. She kissed his shoulder, and then sank her teeth delicately into the skin before licking it.

Big body shuddering, he said harshly, 'For this once, let me do the work, all right?'

Surely he didn't expect his lovers to lie there and do nothing? Puzzled, she glanced up and met his eyes, almost flinching back at their heat.

He finished, 'Otherwise it might well be over before we start.'

Perhaps it had been a while since he'd made love.

That thought excited and pleased her, as did the suggestion that he wasn't in full control when he was with her.

She touched the taut skin over his solar plexus. 'I can do this, though?'

'Only if I say the times tables aloud while you do,' he said, and kissed the throbbing little hollow in her throat, and then the curve of her breast.

This time when he took the tight little bud into his mouth and began to suckle she thought she knew what was coming, but the exquisite sensation wrested what was left of her control from her and sent it whistling down the wind. Alli groaned, her hips rising instinctively against him.

'Not yet,' he said softly, moving to the other breast

while one hand discovered the small hollow of her navel and the curve of her hip.

Ravished by delight, she made an incoherent little noise in her throat and ran her hands up his back, relishing the way the muscles bunched beneath her palms.

His hand moved further down. She wanted him to continue more than life itself, yet she stiffened in instinctive fear.

'It's all right,' he said softly. 'I just want to see if you're ready.'

Ready? Oh, she thought longingly, she was so ready—couldn't he sense it? But, although she arched upwards again in silent plea, he sat up and reached for something on the bedside table.

She watched as he donned the condom, and wondered at her pang of sadness.

Slade looked at her. 'The first time I saw you I thought of the golden pearls of the Pacific, because your skin glows like them. You seem to radiate light and heat and passion.'

And he kissed her again, and this time when his hand reached the cleft between her legs she relaxed, most of her apprehension vanishing like mist in sunlight, and groaned harshly when he stroked her there before easing a finger inside.

Torn by unbearable anticipation, she didn't know whether to obey the urge to pull him over and into her, or the equally strong one that insisted she lie there and let this voluptuous lethargy carry her wherever it wanted her to go.

Slade took the decision from her. He moved over her

and pressed against the slick entrance. Slowly, carefully, he eased a little way into her.

Her breath locking in her throat, Alli stared up into his face, a savagely carved mask of primal appetite.

'Am I too heavy?' he asked.

'No.' She swallowed and tried again. 'I like it.'

And, indeed, lying like this beneath him was probably the closest to heaven she was ever likely to get.

He frowned, but pushed a little further, focusing entirely on her, his face clamped in severe lines as he controlled the hunger she sensed in him.

And control it he did, tormenting her with his restraint until pleasure burned through her and she whimpered with the need for more than this slow, cautious progress. Driven by wild desire, she gripped his hips, holding him against her. He thrust deeper, and again even deeper, releasing a hunger that smashed through her final barriers.

Alli twisted recklessly against him, clasping him with inner muscles she'd never used before until he gasped, 'No!'

Too late. Slade's mouth came down on hers and somewhere in the fire and passion of that kiss, his control shattered.

Joined with him in ecstatic union, Alli closed her eyes and welcomed each movement of his powerful body, her every sense so acute it was almost painful to feel his heat and the coiled steel of his body as he took her with him into unknown regions of the heart.

No wonder desire brought down kingdoms!

Nothing could be more wonderful—but then a cresting wave of sensation flung her up, up, up into a storm of sensuality, holding her on a knife-edge of intolerable rapture.

Slade, she thought with what was left of her mind. Slade…

Somehow she forced her eyes open, filling her vision with his darkly drawn face, the fire in his half-closed eyes and the gleam of sweat on his body. Her lips formed his name as, overwhelmed by unbearable ecstasy, she cried out and convulsed beneath him.

Slade went with her on that incredible journey into the heart of the storm, eventually collapsing on the distant shores of satiation, his chest heaving as she cradled him in her arms and let ebbing passion lull her into dreamy bliss.

When he moved, her arms tightened around him in the instinctive need to keep him so close that nothing could ever come between them. But he used his great strength against her, rolling so that he lay beneath her.

He lay there for long moments, her slim, lax body light on him, her flushed, languid face half turned on his chest and her eyes already closing, and swore silently and at length.

How the hell had it got to this? You blew it, he told himself grimly. You knew it was dangerous, but you couldn't bloody well control yourself.

When he was seven Marian had come like sunlight into his life. Slowly, suspiciously, he had trusted her enough to let himself love her.

And now, only a few miles from here, she lay in a fugue of exhaustion caused by the girl who slept on him in sensual exhaustion. He tensed as Alli yawned and rubbed her cheek against his chest in a gesture as artless as it was seductive. His body stirred beneath her, and mentally he cursed his total lack of will-power where she was concerned, each cold, biting word reeking of disgusted derision.

Yet he watched her while she slept, storing up every moment, every second, with the eager greed of a miner hoarding gems.

Alli woke to silence. Dazed by unremembered satisfaction, she stretched and yawned, wondering sleepily why her body felt different—and then she remembered and shot upwards, searching the room for a man who wasn't there.

She was alone, and in her own bed. Well, Slade's spare bed, she thought, feverish colour scorching her cheekbones. He must have carried her there after they'd made love and she'd gone to sleep in his arms.

Jumbled images of the previous night circled her brain. She might have been a virgin but she could recognise expertise when she came across it. Making love was no novelty to him.

So, while it had been a slow, incandescent trip to heaven for her, for him it had just been fun as usual.

She listened, but the apartment was silent. Biting her lip, she got out of bed, flushing again when she realised that she was still naked. A neat pile on a chair indicated that Slade had returned her discarded clothes too. Hastily she made for the bathroom.

After a shower she dried herself down and examined her gleaming, naked body for sombre moments in the mirror. Apart from lips that were fuller than usual—and more tender—she looked the same. Several marks, too slight to be called bruises, startled her. His beard, she thought confusedly, must have been just long enough to abrade the delicate skin of her breasts. At the time she hadn't noticed.

'But then you probably wouldn't have noticed a fire-work display on the end of the bed,' she muttered, and hid her face by towelling her hair dry.

He had left a note outside her door. Stupid dread constricting her heart, she stared at it for a second be-fore stooping to pick it up. Without salutation, his bold writing informed her that he had gone to the hospi-tal, where he would see her when she was ready. He'd signed it with a formal signature, *S T Hawkings*, and added a postscript. Marian had been transferred to a private hospital; he'd sketched a map showing her how to get there.

'I wonder what the T stands for,' she said, folding the paper and putting it in her pocket. 'Thunderbolt, perhaps?'

But although her tone was wry, silly tears stung her eyes, and she found she couldn't manage anything for breakfast beyond a cup of coffee.

That downed, she left the apartment and drove se-dately across town, stifling her nervousness at the traffic with the hope that Marian had recovered con-sciousness.

The new hospital was considerably more upmarket than the public one Marian had been taken to the pre-vious day. She was shown into a kind of ante-chamber to Marian's room, and while the nurse went in to check that the patient could see her Alli absently noted bowls

of flowers and a couple of pretty, unassuming landscapes on the walls.

When the door clicked open again she looked up,
startled when she met Caroline Forsythe's eyes.

'She's not up to seeing you just now,' Caroline said
calmly. 'Slade is with her, so I'll wait with you.' She
glanced out of the window. 'In fact, I'd like to go for
a walk, and they have lovely gardens here. Would you
like to come with me?'

'I think I'll wait here, thanks,' Alli said. The other
woman, she saw, wore an engagement ring.

Caroline shrugged. 'It'll be a while.' She surveyed
Alli. 'You look as though you've spent a sleepless night
too. Come on, some fresh air will do you good.'

'How is she?'

'Conscious,' Caroline said readily, holding open the
door to the hallway. 'Which is wonderful. But she says
she feels very tired. What on earth happened?'

Caroline's voice had softened when she spoke of her
godmother, so Alli got to her feet, feeling mean for refusing to accompany her when the other woman was
so clearly worried. Together they went down in the lift,
and, while they walked in gardens sweet with the first
roses, she told Caroline what had happened.

'It must have been terrifying,' Caroline said sym-
pathetically. 'Oh, look! That glorious Graham Thomas
rose is out in the arbour. Let's sit down here for a moment, shall we?'

She waited until they were both seated, then asked,
'What happened to give Marian a heart attack?'

Alli stopped abruptly. 'A heart attack! But Slade said
it was something else!'

'Did he?' Unsmiling, Caroline examined her. 'Why did you agree to stay with her when you must have known that the mere sight of you brought back the most hideous memories?'

Her words shocked Alli into rising, but Caroline's hand shot out swiftly as a snake and fastened around her wrist.

'Listen to me,' she said flatly. 'I don't know whether you've been told what happened with your parents, but if you haven't, it's time you were.'

CHAPTER TEN

DISCONNECTED THOUGHTS TUMBLED in jerky confusion around Alli's mind. She said, 'I don't think—'

'Normally I wouldn't intrude,' Caroline interrupted with pleasant firmness, 'and I owe you an apology for what I said to you the first time you came to see Marian, but I was awfully worried about that meeting.'

Alli couldn't hide her shock, but Caroline went on smoothly, 'Yes, I know all about it. I did mention that Marian and I were very close, which is why I'm telling you that your presence is so utterly traumatic for her. It's not personal, believe me. Your mother—'

Interrupting her in turn, Alli said shortly, 'I know what my mother did.'

'It must have been a terrible thing to hear.' Caroline glanced at her engagement ring. 'When we were in Tahiti Slade thought that perhaps the best thing to do was get Marian to go to counselling.'

She paused and turned the ring so that it caught the light. Alli's fragile composure fractured into splinters.

Frowning, Caroline looked up. 'Now he's worried she might have a complete nervous breakdown, and he feels responsible because he agreed to let you meet her.'

Nausea roiled in Alli's stomach; so he had taken Caroline to Tahiti—and did that ring mean an engagement?

Caroline explained, 'He is very protective of Marian. But then, strong men usually are protective of their women.'

Fortunately she didn't seem to need an answer, because Alli couldn't think of a word to say.

'She was so good to him as a child. His father was away so much that he'd sent Slade to boarding school when he was only six, but Marian insisted that Slade come home. She was a real mother to him, so you can see why he's so worried about her now.'

Ungracefully Alli stood up. 'I've always seen that. Neither of them need worry about my presence any more.' The words felt thick, clumsy on her tongue.

'I'm so sorry.' Caroline scrambled to her feet. 'It's an impossible situation for you all.'

'So impossible that the simplest and quickest way to resolve it is for me to leave,' Alli said with a twisted smile.

'Yes, that would probably be the best thing. Only— Marian will feel obliged to keep in touch.'

Alli shrugged. 'If she doesn't know where I am I won't be able to,' she said briskly. 'Give her my love, won't you? And tell her I never meant to hurt her.'

'Of course I'll do that.' She asked, 'Do you have money?'

'Enough.' The thought of borrowing money from this woman, however kind she was trying to be, stung.

Caroline nodded. 'Good luck, then.'

Three months later Alli slung her bag onto the Valanu wharf and turned to wave to the Californian couple who'd let her work her passage from Sant'Rosa. 'I'll be back in a couple of days,' she called.

They waved, and she walked into the port.

Heat settled onto her like a steamy blanket, in spite of the soft caress of the trade wind. She looked about, wondering how she could feel so little for the place she'd called home. Now, home was wherever Slade was.

Because she didn't dare think about him, she pushed the memories into the furthest recesses of her mind. Tui at the Lodge had overcome her fear of computers and emailed that Marian was fine, and that Slade had come looking for her in a towering rage the day after she'd grabbed her clothes, offered a garbled explanation for her departure, and run.

Her instinct to take refuge in Valanu like a wounded animal, hadn't been the most sensible decision, but then she hadn't been thinking sensibly when she'd left New Zealand.

Staying at the resort was out. Not, she knew, that Slade would come looking for her now; no doubt he and Marian were only too glad to see the back of her. If he was engaged to the lovely, oh-so-helpful Caroline, the last thing he'd want was a one-night stand hanging around!

Grimly she headed for a small, somewhat sleazy motel close to the port. This was only a respite, anyway. During the long, lovely nights when she'd kept her lonely watch on the vast Pacific, she'd worked out a plan of campaign.

First a pilgrimage to her father's grave and a visit to Sisilu.

Then she'd sail with her nice Californians to Austra-

lia, find a job there, and make a life for herself without
Slade, without Marian, without emotional complica-
tions.

Just like her father.

Of course, she thought with wintry resignation, you
could call a broken heart an emotional complication.
Hers didn't seem to want to heal; so far time hadn't
eased the intense ache of loneliness and longing at all.
Instead of outrunning her pain, she'd carried it with her.

At the motel the receptionist took an impression of
her credit card, showed her a small room overlooking the swimming pool, and with mechanical courtesy
wished her a good stay on Valanu. Alli didn't know her,
which was a relief.

A weary lethargy imprisoned her in the room for the
rest of the afternoon; she lay on the surprisingly comfortable bed and watched the ceiling fan whirr around,
only stirring at sundown to shower and change into a
pareu. Tomorrow she'd contact Sisilu, but right now
she needed air.

The decision made, she was locking the door when
a prickle of danger lifted the hairs on the nape of her
neck; she froze, then glanced over her shoulder. Slade
was striding towards her through the purple dusk like a
silent, lethal force of nature. Heart jolting into a pounding, uneven rhythm, she fumbled the key into the lock
again. But before she could take refuge inside a hand
closed over hers and pulled the key out of her fingers.

'You took your damned time getting here,' Slade
said icily.

She was shaking, her vision dim and her mouth dry,
the faint, essential scent of him swamping her senses.

'What—is it Marian?' she finally managed to ask huskily, refusing to look any higher than his throat.

'She's fine,' he bit out. 'She is, however, worried sick about you.'

Possessed by fragile joy, she didn't move, couldn't speak.

'Aren't you going to ask what I'm doing here?'

'So tell me,' she said thinly.

His fingers on her elbow brooked no resistance. 'We'll go back to the resort. This place is about as unsavoury as Valanu gets.' He opened the door of a waiting cab and ushered her in.

She should have resisted, but running away hadn't helped; this meeting might provide some sort of closure, free her from the intolerable weight of lost expectations and forlorn hope. They sat for the short trip in silence; Alli knew she should be shoring up her defences, but it was too late for that.

Was this, she'd wondered on those long night watches while she'd gazed at the familiar impersonal stars wheeling in their grand patterns, how Alison had felt about her father —so in love that anything, even betraying a sister, had meant little?

In that case, why had she abandoned him and their child? Why had she told Marian that she'd aborted the baby? Nothing made sense—but then, loving Slade didn't make sense either.

He took her to the private entrance of the honeymoon suite; once inside she stared around, avoiding the part of the room where Slade stood watching her. 'It's been redecorated,' she commented jerkily, trying to impose some sort of normality onto this meeting.

'The whole resort's been refurbished.' He sounded completely fed up. 'Alli, look at me.'

His will forced her to obey. 'Is Marian fully recovered?' she asked.

'Once she got over the shock of your flight,' he said caustically. 'What the hell drove you away? Caroline said you were fine when you two walked in the garden together.'

Presumably Caroline had done her best to save Marian worry. 'I left because my presence stressed Marian so much she couldn't cope. I know she tries to think of me as an ordinary human being, but every time she looks at me she must see my mother.'

'Possibly,' he said bluntly, 'although she certainly doesn't blame you for your mother's behaviour. I thought I'd convinced you of that.'

'She suspects I might be like Alison, amoral and greedy.' When he frowned, she persisted, 'So do you. That's why you assumed I was sleeping with every man who came near me, wasn't it?'

'Is that what you believe?' He came across the room to her, and when she took a step back he stopped. In a voice she didn't recognise he said, 'I have never lifted my hand to a woman, and I will never hurt you, Alli. But I need to know something.'

Her lips formed the word. 'What?'

His hard, beautiful mouth tightened. 'Whether you were a virgin when we made love.'

Astonished, she blinked. 'Why does it matter?'

'It does. I had you targeted as a thoroughly relaxed young woman, taking sex lightly and without angst.'

'Promiscuous, in other words.'

He hesitated, then said, 'No. You grew up here, where sex is considered a recreation.'

'Only,' she said tartly, 'for those who aren't married, or promised in marriage. My father didn't seem to worry about the islanders' attitude to sex, but he certainly didn't approve of liaisons when it came to his daughter.' She smiled bitterly. 'Amusing, isn't it? I just thought he was old-fashioned.'

'He knew—none better, I imagine—what damage it can do,' Slade said. 'You haven't answered me.'

Admitting that she'd been a virgin would be giving too much away; only a woman in love would risk so much for a man who wasn't in love with her. 'I don't think it's any of your business. I haven't asked you how many women you've made love to. Where did you get the idea that I was Barry Simcox's girlfriend?'

He shrugged. 'His attitude, which backed up what I was told—that you had broken up his marriage.'

'Who told you that?'

'It doesn't matter,' he said briefly. 'Is it true?'

'No. His wife hated Valanu, but she wouldn't admit it because she'd pushed him to take the position. I think she'd imagined living some sort of colonial life, sipping gin slings and flirting with the unmarried men while servants did all the work.'

At his snort, she said with a bleak smile, 'She was a romantic, I suppose. The reality—a failing resort with precious little social life of the sort she'd expected—was a huge shock, and she didn't try to hide how miserable she was. So she looked around for something to give her a reason to leave.'

'You don't think finding you naked with her husband

was reason enough?' He spoke neutrally, but she saw the flicker of a muscle in the angular line of his jaw.

She said curtly, 'I'll bet whoever told you that didn't say that I was screaming at the top of my lungs at the time.'

'What the hell was he doing?' An intimidating, ice-cold combination of steel and fire, Slade's voice sliced through her words.

'He was rescuing me from a cockroach,' she told him with acid precision. 'I was changing in the staff bathroom for the evening show when it jumped me.' She shuddered. 'Have you ever seen one? They're huge and black, and this one dropped from the ceiling and ran down my back. I freaked. Barry was on his way to the men's room, and when he heard me yelling he thought I was being attacked. He came tearing in and saved me. I was hauling my pareu on when his wife came racing in and called us every foul word under the sun. She left on the next plane with their little boy.'

'He wanted you,' Slade said harshly. 'Everyone knew it.'

'Possibly, but I didn't want him.' She stared at him with flat defiance. 'Why is this important—or even interesting—to you? I might be my mother's daughter, but I don't sleep with married men. Or engaged ones.'

He said abruptly, 'Are you insinuating that I'm engaged?'

Her conversation with the other woman suddenly took a new twist. Caroline hadn't said she and Slade were engaged, though she'd certainly implied it. Had she set Alli up?

'Are you?'

'No.' His mouth closed like a clamp. 'I have never been engaged. And you still haven't answered my question.'

He might not be engaged, but that didn't mean he was interested in Alli as anything more than a convenient outlet for his sexual needs.

Pain burning like fire through her, she walked across to the window and looked into the garden, barely noticing the lush greenery starred with flamboyant hibiscuses and the pure, sculpted blooms of frangipani.

'Yes, I was a virgin,' she said quietly, uneasily aware of anticipation running through her like an underground river.

'I thought as much,' he said remotely. 'I'll take you back to the motel and you can pack; we're leaving in half an hour.'

Anticipation died a swift, brutal death. She reached out and clutched a curtain. 'Why?'

'I don't seduce virgins,' he said savagely.

'So if I hadn't been a virgin you'd leave me here?'

He stared at her as though she'd suddenly gone mad. 'Don't be an idiot.'

Outraged, she snapped, 'And you didn't seduce me—I wanted to make love to you! So don't go thinking that because you had your wicked way with me you owe me something! You don't. As an introduction to making love it was pretty damned good, but women nowadays don't feel any obligation to marry the first man they sleep with.'

She could have bitten her tongue out once she realised what that final sentence indicated. Sickly she waited for a put-down.

He said levelly, 'Marian asked me to bring you back.'

Bewildered, Alli shook her head. 'Why? My presence brought about her collapse—'

'It didn't.' He spoke with such assurance she turned to search his hard face for some indication of what was going on. Without any success. The mask was back in place, hard and unreadable and totally ruthless. He finished, 'She has something to tell you.'

'More secrets?' she asked wearily, shoulders slumping. 'I've had enough of them. In fact, I've had enough of this whole situation.'

'Tough. You don't have the choice. You've tried running away, but wherever you go I'll be one step behind until you've heard what Marian has to say. After that no one will follow you if you want to go. But she's not going to rest until she's told you what she has to say. And I'm not going to leave you until you've heard it.'

Alli dithered, but in the end she said with grim resignation, 'All right, then. I'll come back—but after that I'm going.'

At Auckland airport, the luxurious private jet was met by a car that dropped them off at Marian's apartment.

Outside her aunt's door Alli took a deep, jagged breath, astounded when Slade's hand covered hers, its warmth and strength offering support.

She didn't dare look at him, and before the door opened he let her go, but she carried his touch inside her like a fire in the depths of winter.

Marian stood there, the anxiety in her blue eyes fading to relief. 'My dear,' she said, putting out a hand to draw Alli inside. 'Oh, my dear, I've been so *worried* about you!'

'I've been worrying about you too,' Alli said on a half-laugh, 'but you look great!'

'Such a silly thing to have happened! Exhaustion, the doctor said, and the aftermath of the flu, and I seem to have developed a propensity for fainting now and then—as you know only too well, poor girl. But it won't happen again; I've promised Slade and my doctor that I'll eat regularly and sleep eight hours a night, and take iron pills every day! Come through and tell me what you've been doing.'

Slade allowed them ten minutes of catching up before saying, 'Marian, you're procrastinating. Tell Alli what you told me.'

Marian sighed. 'You were such a dear little boy— what happened to turn you into a despot? Very well, then.' She sipped water from a glass, but instead of returning it to the table beside her she clutched the tumbler. In a level, almost conversational tone she said, 'First of all, Alli, your mother and I were half-sisters.'

'Half-sisters?'

'Yes. We had different mothers. I think my father loved Alison's mother, but he was a snob, and she wasn't the sort of person who satisfied his rigid ideas of suitability, so after Alison was born he married my mother, who came from a good family.'

She looked past them both, seeing other faces, other events. Stunned, Alli said, 'He abandoned his first family?'

Marian looked tired. 'Oh, no.'

But she didn't continue straight away. Instead she

took another sip of water, replaced the tumbler on the table and gazed down at the large diamonds winking in her engagement ring and gold wedding ring as though seeking strength from them.

Alli almost screamed with the tension, starting slightly when Marian began again in a tightly controlled tone.

'He kept them in a nice house in the nearest city. We lived in the country. I knew nothing about it, of course, and neither did my mother. My first intimation of the situation came when I was seventeen and had newly left school. Alison tracked me down and told me everything.'

She stopped again, her expression blank. Swallowing to ease a dry throat, Alli thought desperately, *Please, finish it quickly!*

'Keep going.' Slade's voice was calm and steady.

Marian took a deep breath. 'She wanted to tell me that she resented being supplanted by me. Even more, she resented the fact that she was a bastard. She called herself my father's dirty little secret, and it was obvious that she despised both her parents—but especially her mother. She told me that everything I had, everything I'd been given—a good school, social standing, legitimacy—had been stolen from her.'

She hesitated before adding, 'She told me she wanted it back.'

When Alli shivered the older woman nodded sadly. 'She meant it. I didn't know what to say to her—to be truthful she frightened me—but after that she stalked me. I didn't realise that's what it was, of course—in those days we had no word for such a thing. But wherever I went, there she was too. Sometimes it would be several weeks before I'd see her, but she always came back. She sent me birthday cards and Christmas cards.'

'Why didn't you tell your father?' Alli asked, horrified.

'I couldn't bring myself to.' Marian seemed to have retreated into herself. 'My mother might have found out, and I knew how dreadful that would be for her. Marrying Hugo was such a relief. I loved him very much, and he lived on the opposite side of the world. But Alison was in the crowd outside the church when we were married.'

She swallowed and sipped more water.

Slade frowned, hard gaze fixed onto his stepmother's beautiful face. 'Go on,' he said gently.

'So we came to New Zealand, and it was as though a weight fell off my shoulders. For a year I was happy. When I discovered I was pregnant Hugo and I were so delighted and life was wonderful—and then she knocked on my door.'

Alli sat frozen, her hands clasped so tightly in her lap that her knuckles shone white.

'To cut a long story short,' Marian said tiredly, 'she was obviously pregnant.'

Any remaining colour drained from Alli's skin, taking all warmth, all joy with it. It was like standing on the brink of a precipice, unable to stop herself from taking the fatal next step.

Marian said, 'She boasted that she'd seduced Hugo and that the baby was his. Her next step, she said, was to stake a claim to my inheritance. My mother had died shortly after my wedding, and Alison was certain she could persuade our father to change his will so that she was the only beneficiary of the trust fund he'd planned to set up for us both. It was the first I'd heard of that, and it meant, of course, that he acknowledged her legally as his daughter.'

With the blood drumming in her ears, Alli heard Marian say, 'Of course I asked Hugo if it was true. He was desperately ashamed, but he admitted it. She had sought him out and dazzled him—he said that he loved me, but he hadn't known what passion was like until he met her.'

Alli swallowed.

Remorselessly Marian's soft voice went on, 'I sent him away, and then I lost my baby—it was born premature and died within minutes. Then I had a telephone call from Alison—as soon as she'd heard that my child was dead she'd aborted hers. She said—she said—' She shuddered.

'I don't want to hear anything more.' Alli's voice grated on the words.

Marian looked at her with eyes filled with tears. 'I know. But—it's almost over.' She waited until Alli gave an almost imperceptible nod. 'She said I could have Hugo back if I was desperate, but that whenever we made love he'd be holding her in his arms.'

Alli said numbly, 'I'm so sorry.'

Slade's hands closed over her shoulders, holding her in place, his strength pouring through them into her body.

Tonelessly Marian finished, 'Some months later I was contacted because Alison had been killed in Thailand. Apparently she was on her way back to England

and our father when she stepped into the path of a truck. I never heard from Hugo again; when we divorced it was all done through our solicitors.' She closed her eyes.

'She must have been mad,' Alli breathed.

Marian opened her eyes and said simply, 'She was seriously disturbed. But I married Slade's father and we were very happy together. I don't think even my half-sister could have stolen him from me.'

'I wish I'd never contacted you,' Alli said fiercely. 'I had no idea of the pain I'd cause.'

'My dear, it's better to know the truth,' the older woman said. 'Although when I realised who you were I was afraid.'

'That I'd be like my mother?' Alli produced a twisted parody of a smile. 'I don't blame you.'

'You're not like your mother,' Slade said calmly. 'You are a warm, responsible, loyal woman.'

His words warmed some part of her that had been frozen since the first time she'd met Marian, in this very room, and heard her talk about her sister's betrayal.

'Exactly,' Marian agreed. 'I couldn't have said it better myself.' She looked at Alli and seemed to be readying herself to say something, but Slade cut in.

'That's enough for the present. Both of you are exhausted, and anything more can wait until later. Come on, Alli, I'll take you home.'

For the first time since they'd met at the door Marian smiled. 'What a good idea.'

Alli said, 'We can't leave you alone.'

'Don't worry about me. I feel as though I've just shed a huge load from my shoulders. I'm sorry you had to hear that, but knowledge truly is power.'

Alli got to her feet. 'I think he—my father—realised that he had always loved you,' she said slowly. 'He cut out the newspaper article about your marriage to Slade's father and kept it with his marriage certificate. That's how I discovered who you were and where you lived.'

The older woman looked bleak. 'Between us, Alison and I made a wasteland of his life.'

Slade said with ruthless logic, 'You had nothing to do with it—it was his decision to be unfaithful. And he spent years working hard and extremely well for the people of Valanu. I don't think his life was wasted.'

On the way home Alli said, 'Thank you for what you said about my father.'

'It's the truth,' he said negligently. 'You can be proud of him because he did an enormous amount of good in the islands. Possibly he tried to atone for his mistakes that way.'

'I hope so,' she said quietly. She didn't want to think about her mother. Fixing her eyes on the harbour, smiling beneath a late summer sun, she asked, 'Where are we going?'

He'd told Marian he was taking her home, but she had no home now.

'I think we've had this conversation before,' Slade said coolly. 'I'm taking you back to the homestead.'

She sneaked a glance at him; he turned his head and smiled at her, and she knew that she would go with him wherever he asked her to.

If he wanted her she would expect nothing from him but fidelity. As long as she had that, she thought dreamily, she'd be happy.

They drove silently through the blue and gold evening, arriving at the bay with a glory of scarlet and crimson and apricot streaked across the western sky.

'It's going to be a fine day tomorrow,' Slade remarked, lifting her bag from the car.

Alli stood a moment, inhaling. 'I missed the scent of the kanuka trees,' she said, smiling at him without reserve.

'I always do too.'

He put her in the room she'd occupied before. When she'd showered and changed into a pareu, a restrained length of cotton the colour of the red highlights in her hair, she came shyly down the stairs to join Slade on the deck as the first stars trembled into life in the indigo sky.

He handed her a glass of champagne. 'Here's to the future.'

'I'll definitely drink to that.' But she'd barely tasted the delicious wine before she set the glass down, saying, 'You knew about my mother, didn't you?'

'Yes. When the researchers I employed finally tracked down the details of your birth I told Marian. She was shattered, and it all came spilling out.'

Keeping her eyes on a pair of fantails fluttering around just beyond arm's reach, their black eyes bright as small beaks snapped up night-flying insects, she asked, 'Is that why you distrusted me so much?'

Accurately divining her secret fear, he said bluntly, 'You were right when you accused me of testing you. I did wonder if you were like her, damaged in some basic way. I bought the resort so that I could use it as a lever if I had to.'

'You paid a lot of money for a lever that might not have worked if I'd been like my mother,' she said quietly.

He shrugged. 'It had good prospects. The area was already settling down, and I had plans for it. I didn't expect to lose anything on it. Then I got there and realised that Barry couldn't look at you without salivating.'

'No!' she said indignantly.

His brows rose. 'Trust me. I know,' he said dryly. 'And, although I was as suspicious of you as hell, I hated that.' Irony and something like self-derision curled his mouth. 'Of course I wouldn't allow myself to realise it, but I was jealous—black, deep, dog-in-the-manger jealous. So I offered you the chance of staying on Valanu and saving your friends' jobs.'

Alli said, 'I should hate you.'

His eyes gleamed. 'But you don't, do you?'

She bit her lip.

The fantails' high-pitched squeaks faded as they flew into a bush. Slade put his glass down and walked across the deck to join her in the gathering dusk.

'You stayed on Valanu. Even when you left, you made no effort to contact Marian. And when you thought that your presence was causing Marian real problems you left. As far as I can work out Alison would have pulled the world down around her in flames to get her way. She didn't care a bit about hurting other people.'

'No.' It hurt so much to say that single word.

Very deliberately he said, 'You are entirely normal.' And he turned her into the circle of his arms. When she stared at him, her face coloured by the dying glow of the sun, he asked, 'You've had a hell of a shock. Do you want to stay in your own bedroom tonight?'

'No,' she said on a sigh.

If this was all she could have she'd take it. And as he pulled her into his arms she lifted her face to his kiss and felt happiness flood through her, fierce and elemental.

CHAPTER ELEVEN

ALLI LAY IN sleepy bliss, so replete with pleasure that when Slade came into the room she could barely summon the energy to smile at him.

'Poor you,' she said dreamily. 'Work…and with boring old politicians too.'

He finished knotting his tie and bent to kiss her. Lazily, gracefully, she looped her arms around his neck and matched his kiss with enthusiasm.

'Stop that, baggage.' Slade pulled her hands away and tucked them under the sheet. 'This is a very important meeting, and politicians hate it if you're late. It makes them feel less powerful.'

She loved the way the gold glints in his eyes lit up whenever he looked at her. In fact, she loved everything about him.

'And I'll bet they're not all boring and old and male.' She sat up against the tumbled pillows while he shrugged into the jacket of his superb suit. 'I noticed a couple of very glamorous creatures in the caucus.'

'Not today,' he said.

A tiny arrow pierced her happiness and lodged in her heart. Looking like that, in clothes superbly tailored to fit his wide shoulders and lean hips, Slade was no longer of her world. They had spent the last three days in isolation, cooking for themselves, seeing no one, hearing no one, making love…

In his arms she had learnt so much about herself—so much about him. Sometimes he gentled her sweetly into an ecstasy that brought her to tears. Other times they loved like tigers, fiercely, without inhibition, losing themselves in rapture so intense she had to muffle her cries in the hard strength of his shoulder.

In bed, she thought, watching him check the contents of a slim leather briefcase, they were equals.

But outside it? She suspected that while she had given him her heart completely, for him this fierce flashfire of desire was enough.

Slade came across and dropped a swift, stinging kiss on her mouth. 'Go back to sleep,' he commanded, surveying her flushed face. 'You're looking very slumbrous around the eyes.'

'That isn't tiredness.'

He laughed beneath his breath. 'I'll be back late this afternoon.'

When he'd gone Alli turned over in the huge bed, holding back stupid tears. This, she thought wearily, was what love did to you—stripped you of independence and common sense.

The low snarl of an engine brought her upright. She snatched a T-shirt and a pair of shorts and hauled them on, just making it to the balcony in time to wave at the helicopter.

Not that she could pick out Slade. He'd be sitting up at the front with the pilot—possibly even piloting it himself. It was stupid to let such a simple thing make her feel desolated, but as she showered she felt as though she'd never see him again.

'Besotted,' she informed her reflection severely. 'You're utterly besotted! You should be working out what you'll do next—at the very least considering some job!—but, no, all you can think of is that you're not going to spend the day in bed with him!'

She pattered downstairs and emptied the dishwasher, then sat out on the deck with a cup of coffee and the newspaper and tried to concentrate on the job market.

Nothing attracted her. Gloomily she put the paper down and watched a tui plunder nectar from the spidery pink blooms of a shrub. The bird's white throat-knot bobbled as it drained the sweetness, and the sun glimmered in blue and green iridescence on its black plumage.

The trouble was she didn't know what Slade wanted from her. She didn't even know what he felt for her. He hadn't told her he loved her—well, she hadn't admitted her love for him either! But he seemed perfectly content to make love to her without any promises or commitment.

This sensuous idyll couldn't last much longer. She certainly wasn't going to let him keep her, even if he wanted to. And she doubted very much whether she'd fit into the life of an extremely rich man anyway; the prospect of spending days like this waiting for him to come home and make love to her did not appeal.

'Certainly not the waiting about part,' she muttered.

What Slade seemed to want from her was mistress duty—no intimacy beyond wild sex and heady passion.

Exactly what her grandfather had wanted from the woman he didn't marry. Did she love Slade enough to stay faithful to him if he married another woman and had children with her?

Never, she thought, pushing the newspaper away with revulsion. She loved jealously and possessively. If he even suggested such a thing she'd—well, she wouldn't submit to such an unequal relationship.

Women nowadays had more options; she had more pride. She'd rather live alone for the rest of her life than be the other woman in a triangle.

Utterly depressed, she watched the tui for a few more minutes, then rang its namesake at the Lodge and asked how things were going there.

'Very well,' Tui said cheerfully. 'Poppy's loving the job, and with Sim going off to school once the holidays are over she'll be able to give me longer hours. What are you doing?'

'Lazing about in the sun,' Alli said brightly.

The tui chose that moment to burst into song. She held the receiver out to the bird, and waited until the clear paean of bell notes had faded to say, 'Your namesake said hi.'

'And lovely it was to hear it,' Tui said. 'Hang on a minute, will you? Something's come up.'

Muffled voices indicated she was holding her hand over the receiver; when she came back on she said, 'I have to go. Great to hear from you, Alli. Come up and see us some time soon.'

You can never go back. Her father used to say that, and, God knew, he'd had enough reason to believe it. There was nothing in Valanu for her now, and nothing at the Lodge either. Her whole life was bound up in one man—whereas she suspected that the big bed upstairs marked the limits of his interest in her.

Certainly there had been no trips to local cafés or vineyards. Did he have friends? Presumably. But he hadn't introduced her to any.

Perhaps he was ashamed of her?

The thought stung so much she spent the rest of the morning scouring bathrooms, changing the sheets on the bed and cleaning the kitchen. She cut a bunch of roses that someone had coaxed into growing behind the house and put them beside the bed, lingering a moment to touch the soft, cool coppery-apricot petals.

After a snack lunch she went down to the beach and sat in the old tyre, missing Slade with an intensity that scared her.

She had no idea how long she'd sat there swinging quietly, when the noise from an engine whipped her head around. Slade, she knew, was coming back by helicopter, so who was this driving down the road in a blue car?

Marian.

Heart lifting, she jumped down and jogged back to the house. Over the past few days she'd spoken to her aunt a couple of times on the phone, and she felt that they were cautiously approaching some sort of understanding of each other.

But it wasn't Marian who stepped out of the car. And Caroline's smile—smug as any cat's, yet oddly set— jolted Alli into wariness.

'Hello,' she said, despising herself for the uncertain note in her voice.

Caroline's smile tightened as she surveyed her. 'Hello, Alli. You're looking well. Can I beg a glass of water from you?'

'Of course!' She led the way into the house, trying to emulate Marian's unforced charm—and failing. Something was wrong. 'Is Marian all right?'

'She's fine.' Caroline's tone was clipped.

The cold patch beneath Alli's ribs expanded. 'Let's go out onto the deck,' she suggested.

Caroline followed her and sat down in one of the chairs. She sipped the water, that faint smile still on her lips, and when Alli's fund of small-talk had dried up she put the glass down with decision.

'You're going to hate me for this,' she said rapidly, 'but I think you should know. Has Slade said anything to you about a trust fund?'

Alli's eyes narrowed. 'No,' she said, before remembering that he'd mentioned Marian's fund when warning her off.

Before she could qualify her answer Caroline said, 'No, I didn't think he had.' She looked around the deck, then back at Alli. 'Your English grandfather left everything in trust to his two daughters,' she said. 'And their descendants. It was quite a substantial amount, although not a fortune.' Her mouth widened into a smile. 'Running two households must have eaten up his capital.'

'How do you know this?'

'Marian told me,' she said, sounding surprised. 'After your mother's death no one knew you existed, so Marian became the sole beneficiary. By then she knew she wasn't going to have any children; after she miscarried things went so wrong she was told there would be no more pregnancies. When Marian married Slade's father she backed his expansion plans with money from the trust fund.'

'What has this to do with anything?' Alli said, worried by the implacable note in the other woman's voice.

Caroline gave an impatient shake of her head. 'I'm sure you know that Bryn Hawkings was a business genius—and Slade is even better than his father was. Hawkings Tourism is now a huge, extremely profitable concern.'

'Why are you telling me this?'

Her companion leaned forward and fixed her with an intent look. 'When you wrote to Marian claiming to be her daughter she knew there was no way you could be that. So she did what she always does—she told Slade and he organised a search for information about you. You know what the result of that was—you are Alison's daughter.'

A chill scudded down Alli's spine. 'Caroline, I know all this. What—?'

'As Alison's daughter, her interest in the trust fund devolves to you.' Caroline sat back, an enigmatic little smile playing around her perfectly painted mouth. 'Any court would grant it to you once you proved who you are—and if the information Slade found convinced him it would convince a court. But even if it didn't Marian is determined to give shares to you. You now effectively own part of his business.'

Alli stared at her. 'Nonsense.'

'It happens to be the truth,' Caroline said calmly. 'You've got power, and if you wanted to you could cause Slade a lot of grief. Being Slade, of course, he's realised this, so he was set himself to neutralise any threat to his business.'

The cold stone beneath Alli's ribs expanded to press on her heart. 'Tell me exactly what you came to say.'

'I told you you'd hate me.' When Caroline looked at her, Alli saw dislike in her eyes. 'And, yes, I do have an interest in this—I love Slade, and for a while I thought he loved me.' A trace of chagrin marred her smooth voice. 'I'll get over it. But he's going to marry you so that he can control your inheritance, and, quite frankly, I think that's appalling.'

She got to her feet and looked down at Alli, her face devoid of every emotion. 'Beneath his sophisticated surface there's complete ruthlessness. His business is his life. As soon as he realised that you were Alison's daughter he dumped me.' Her glance flicked like a whip across Alli's white face. 'I can see you're in love with him. I pity you. But you should at least know what you're getting into and what sort of man you're in love with.'

And she walked away. Alli got to her feet, but she didn't follow; instead she watched in numb silence as the car sped up the hill into the shadowy darkness beneath the kanuka trees.

Walking like an old woman, she turned and went back to the tyre swing.

She was still sitting in it, keeping the motion going with an occasional kick of her bare foot in the sand, when the helicopter flew over the house and landed— and she was still there when Slade came striding down to the beach.

During those long, bitter hours she'd worked out

exactly what she was going to say. But although she watched him until he stopped a few steps away, her aching heart blocked her throat and she couldn't speak.

He said her name, then said it again, this time urgently as he cancelled the gap between them. 'What's the matter?' he demanded, pulling her out of the swing and into his arms.

Steeling her will against the shaming desire to forget everything she'd been told and let herself be seduced into going along with his scheme, she said distantly, 'Caroline called in today.'

'So?' But he let her go, and she felt the concentrated impact of his gaze on her face.

Concisely, without letting her eyes stray above the open neck of his shirt, she told him what Caroline had said.

When she'd finished she heard the small hush of the wavelets on the sand for long seconds before he said, slowly and deliberately, 'She's clever. She's also an eavesdropper, because Marian would never have discussed this with her.'

'That's not an answer,' Alli said tonelessly, hope dying.

'Would you believe any answer I gave you?'

Oh, she wanted to—she craved reassurance like a thirsty man in the desert craved water—but she knew she wouldn't be getting it.

His expression hardened. 'No, you wouldn't,' he said levelly. 'As I said, she's clever. Before you damn me entirely, however, you should know that she sold that photograph of us driving out of the car park to the newspaper.'

'Why?'

'For spite.'

'Because you dumped her?' she said, white-faced.

'Is that what she told you?'

She nodded.

'I've underestimated her,' he said, his tone so evenly judicial it sounded like a death sentence.

'Is it the truth? Were you lovers?' The moment she asked the question Alli knew she'd betrayed herself.

'No,' he said calmly. 'I'm not a sadist, and making love to a woman suffering unrequited love for me would be cruel.'

Alli digested this, knowing she couldn't afford to let the tiny flare of hope grow to anything more. 'How do you know that she took the photo?'

'I have contacts in the press, people who owe me favours. She did it.' His voice was grim.

'Did she lie at all?'

'Not in the facts,' he said with brutal, intimidating honesty. 'It's her reading of my motivation that's way off. And that, I'm certain, was done with malice.'

Alli desperately wanted him to convince her, but she didn't dare trust her own emotions. During that interminable afternoon while she waited for him she'd made up her mind; she couldn't allow hope to weaken her.

A white line emphasising the ruthless cut of his lips, Slade said harshly, 'You'll need to apply through the courts for those shares, but morally, and ultimately legally, you do own them. Marian is determined to give them to you. You could certainly use that to damage me financially.'

'Why didn't you tell me?' she asked, at last voicing the question he had to answer—an answer she dreaded.

He had never looked more arrogant, never more ruthless. 'I didn't intend to make love to you the night of Marian's collapse. I couldn't help myself. And I didn't mean to bring you here—but I couldn't stop myself then, either. In fact, Caroline was right; I brought you here to make you fall in love with me.'

Slade saw the colour abruptly leave her skin, then roll back in a silken wave, but her lion-coloured eyes met his steadily. 'So that you could control me?'

'When have I ever been able to control you? I made love to you because I was completely incapable of resisting you.'

'I don't believe that.' Alli fought for control, because if she gave him what he wanted she'd be asking for a lifetime of regret.

A muscle flicked in his angular jaw. 'Then believe this,' he snarled. 'Why should I seduce you into marriage? That's a lifetime sentence. And if you divorced me I'd have to pay you out more than the worth of those shares.'

'No,' she said angrily.

'Oh, yes—New Zealand's law is fairly tough. Assets are split down the middle. The sensible way to deal with the situation would have been to tell you about the shares, offer you their worth—' with savage precision he named a sum of money that drove the last remnants of colour from her face '—and buy them from you. That way I'd have had control of them without having to pretend that I want you enough to enter into some fake marriage.'

'Then why didn't you do that?' she cried furiously. 'Not that I want them. I'll sign them over to you for a cent, or whatever it takes to make a deal. As far as I'm concerned the money's tainted.'

Holding herself together with fierce will-power, Alli began to walk up to the house. 'Say goodbye to Marian for me,' she said, each word an exercise in determination.

From behind, he said uncompromisingly, 'Just like that? Goodbye and thanks for the memories?'

'What do you expect me to do?' Fists clenched at her sides, she turned on him, allowing anger to give her the strength to say what must be said. 'Let this whole farce go on?'

Hooded green eyes burning in his dark face, he said stonily, 'It's no farce. These past few days have been— magical.'

She made a swift, dismissive gesture. 'Oh, yes, a magical time. You're a superb lover, but it was going to end anyway. We can't stay in bed all our lives. And once it was over—when real life intruded—what then? A practical marriage to safeguard those miserable shares?'

'Practical?' He astonished her with a furious, humourless smile. 'Do you have any idea what you've done to me? Right from the first? Whenever I look at you I can't even think. My brain seizes up so all I can do is want you. Practical? If you leave me I'll spend the rest of my life looking for you, loving you, aching for you—and you call that *practical*? Damn it, Alli, I love you.' He flung out his arm in a gesture. 'Do what you like with the shares. Sell them on the share market if you want to, put them in trust for our children, scatter

them to the winds—I don't bloody care! Just tell me you'll marry me.'

Incredulously she scanned his face, its tanned skin stretched starkly over the bold bone structure. He had to know he could make her say anything if he only touched her—yet he stood scrupulously apart, although every muscle in his big, lean body was taut with the effort.

'Oh, Slade,' she whispered. 'Why didn't you tell me you loved me?'

'Why didn't *you* tell me?'

'You must have known,' she muttered. 'For heaven's sake—I was a virgin. Of course I fell fathoms deep in love with you—'

He said with raw intensity, 'Sex isn't love, Alli. I've discovered that these past days. I thought I could bind you to me with sex, make you so addicted to it that you'd never know the difference between that and love. But while I flew home today I accepted something that's been gnawing at my conscience ever since I realised that I love you. I have no right to keep secrets from you, not even the secret of my love. I have to give you your freedom if you want it.'

Her half-laugh, half-sob silenced him. He groaned and reached for her, and then he kissed her and muttered, 'Don't cry. Please don't cry. Of course I love you, my darling, my precious girl. I am utterly besotted with you. Women are supposed to be much better at this sort of thing than men—how could you not know it?'

'I didn't dare even think it,' she wept, clutching him. 'I love you so much, and it hurt so much… My mother… I look like her…and—'

He kissed the stumbling words away. 'I love the way

you look. I dream about the way you look. I don't want to hear anything more about your mother. You're you, not her.'

'But Marian—'

He kissed the frown between her brows, and then her eyelids, and then the corners of her mouth. 'Darling, leave those sad old ghosts where they belong, in the past. The future belongs to us and to our children. Do you trust me?'

She nodded. 'This afternoon I didn't think I could ever trust anyone again, but love is trust,' she said. 'Lots of other things too, but trust is the basis for it, isn't it?'

It was a statement, not a question.

'Yes,' he said simply, and this time their kiss sealed their commitment to a future free of the bitter shadow of the past.

* * * * *

COMING NEXT MONTH from Harlequin Presents®
AVAILABLE MARCH 19, 2013

#3129 MASTER OF HER VIRTUE
Miranda Lee

Shy, cautious Violet has had enough of living life in the shadows. She resolves to experience all that life has to offer, starting with internationally renowned film director Leo Wolfe. But is Violet ready for where he wants to take her?

#3130 A TASTE OF THE FORBIDDEN
Buenos Aires Nights
Carole Mortimer

Argentinian tycoon Cesar Navarro has his sexy little chef, Grace Blake, right where he wants her—in his penthouse, at his command! She should be off-limits, but Grace has tantalized his jaded palette, and Cesar finds himself ordering something new from the menu!

#3131 THE MERCILESS TRAVIS WILDE
The Wilde Brothers
Sandra Marton

Travis Wilde would never turn down a willing woman in a king-size bed! Normally innocence like Jennie Cooper's would have the same effect as a cold shower, yet her determination and mouth-watering curves have him burning up all over!

#3132 A GAME WITH ONE WINNER
Scandal in the Spotlight
Lynn Raye Harris

Paparazzi darling Caroline Sullivan hides a secret behind her dazzling smile. Her ex-flame, Russian businessman Roman Kazarov, is back on the scene—is he seeking revenge for her humiliating rejection or wanting to take possession of her troubled business?

HPCNM0313RA

#3133 HEIR TO A DESERT LEGACY
Secret Heirs of Powerful Men
Maisey Yates

When recently and reluctantly crowned Sheikh Sayid discovers his country's true heir, he'll do anything to protect him—even marry the child's aunt. It may appease his kingdom, but will it release the blistering chemistry between them...?

#3134 THE COST OF HER INNOCENCE
Jacqueline Baird

Newly free Beth Lazenby has closed the door on her past, until she encounters lawyer Dante Cannavaro who is still convinced of her guilt. But when anger boils over into passion, will the consequences forever bind her to her enemy?

#3135 COUNT VALIERI'S PRISONER
Sara Craven

Kidnapped and held for ransom... His price? Her innocence! Things like this just don't happen to Maddie Lang, but held under lock and key, the only deal Count Valieri will strike is one with an *unconventional* method of payment!

#3136 THE SINFUL ART OF REVENGE
Maya Blake

Reiko has two things art dealer Damion Fortier wants; a priceless Fortier heirloom and her seriously off-limits body! And she has no intention of giving him access to either. So Damion turns up lethal charm to ensure he gets *exactly* he wants....

HPCNM0313RB

REQUEST YOUR FREE BOOKS!

2 FREE NOVELS PLUS
2 FREE GIFTS!

YES! Please send me 2 FREE Harlequin Presents® novels and my 2 FREE gifts (gifts are worth about $10). After receiving them, if I don't wish to receive any more books, I can return the shipping statement marked "cancel." If I don't cancel, I will receive 6 brand-new novels every month and be billed just $4.30 per book in the U.S. or $4.99 per book in Canada. That's a saving of at least 14% off the cover price! It's quite a bargain! Shipping and handling is just 50¢ per book in the U.S. and 75¢ per book in Canada.* I understand that accepting the 2 free books and gifts places me under no obligation to buy anything. I can always return a shipment and cancel at any time. Even if I never buy another book, the two free books and gifts are mine to keep forever.

106/306 HDN FVRK

Name _____ (PLEASE PRINT) _____

Address _____ Apt. # _____

City _____ State/Prov. _____ Zip/Postal Code _____

Signature (if under 18, a parent or guardian must sign) _____

Mail to the **Harlequin® Reader Service:**
IN U.S.A.: P.O. Box 1867, Buffalo, NY 14240-1867
IN CANADA: P.O. Box 609, Fort Erie, Ontario L2A 5X3

**Are you a current subscriber to Harlequin Presents books and want to receive the larger-print edition?
Call 1-800-873-8635 or visit www.ReaderService.com.**

* Terms and prices subject to change without notice. Prices do not include applicable taxes. Sales tax applicable in N.Y. Canadian residents will be charged applicable taxes. Offer not valid in Quebec. This offer is limited to one order per household. Not valid for current subscribers to Harlequin Presents books. All orders subject to credit approval. Credit or debit balances in a customer's account(s) may be offset by any other outstanding balance owed by or to the customer. Please allow 4 to 6 weeks for delivery. Offer available while quantities last.

Your Privacy—The Harlequin® Reader Service is committed to protecting your privacy. Our Privacy Policy is available online at www.ReaderService.com or upon request from the Harlequin Reader Service.

We make a portion of our mailing list available to reputable third parties that offer products we believe may interest you. If you prefer that we not exchange your name with third parties, or if you wish to clarify or modify your communication preferences, please visit us at www.ReaderService.com/consumerschoice or write to us at Harlequin Reader Service Preference Service, P.O. Box 9062, Buffalo, NY 14269. Include your complete name and address.

SPECIAL EXCERPT FROM

H HARLEQUIN®
TM

Presents~

*These two men have fought battles, waged wars and won.
But when their command—their legacy—is challenged by
the very women they desire the most...who will win?*

*Enjoy a sneak peek from HEIR TO A DESERT LEGACY,
the first tale in the potent new duet,*
SECRET HEIRS OF POWERFUL MEN,
by USA TODAY bestselling author Maisey Yates.

* * *

CHLOE stood up quickly, her chair tilting and knocking into
the chair next to it, the sound loud in the cavernous room.
"Sorry, sorry." She tried to straighten them, her cheeks
burning, her heart pounding. "I have to go."

Sayid was faster than she was, his movements smoother.
He crossed to her side of the table and caught her arm, drawing her to him, his expression dark. "Why are you running
from me?" he asked, dipping his face lower, his expression
fierce. "It's because you know, isn't it? You feel it?"

"Feel what?" she asked.

"This...need between us. How everything in me is demanding that I reach out and pull you hard against me. And
how everything in you is begging me to."

"I don't know what you're talking about," she said.

"I think you do." He lowered his hand and traced her
collarbone with his fingertip, sliding it slowly up the side of
her neck, along her jawbone.

She shook her head, pulling away from him, from his touch. "No," she lied, "I don't."

She didn't understand what was happening with her body, why it was betraying her like this. She'd never felt this kind of wild, overpowering attraction for anyone in her life. But if she was going to, it would have been for a nice scientist who had a large collection of dry-erase pens and looked good in a lab coat.

It would not be for this rough, uncivilized man who believed he could move people around at his whim. This man who sought to control everything and everyone around him.

Unfortunately, her body hadn't asked her opinion on who she should find attractive. Because that was most definitely what this was. Scientific, irrefutable evidence of arousal.

* * *

Will Chloe give in to temptation? And will she ever be able to tame the wild warrior?

Find out in HEIR TO A DESERT LEGACY, available March 19, 2013.